FIT
for the
THRONE
III

THE SEASON FINALE

S. MCPHERSON

This book contains varying degrees of the following:
Dub/non con, violence, torture and open-door scenes
intended for an audience of 18+ Please read safely and
responsibly.

FIT FOR THE THRONE 3: THE SEASON FINALE

Book 3 in the Fit for the Throne series
Published by S. McPherson
ISBN: 978-1-9163026-7-9
Copyright © 2024 (eBook)
Copyright © 2024 (Paperback)
All rights reserved.

To learn more about the author visit:
Instagram:
https://www.instagram.com/smcphersonbooks/
Tiktok: https://www.tiktok.com/@s_mcpherson_books
Bookbub: https://www.bookbub.com/profile/s-
mcpherson
Facebook:
https://www.facebook.com/Smcphersonbooks

For those who see the red flags and think,
"That's a pretty color."

Unleash
the
Dragon

1

VARIALLA:
UNCHAIN ME

My blood was fire. All I saw was red. A manic roar broke from my cracking throat. Not a human's cry, but a beast's. A dragon's.

Somewhere, I vaguely registered Loch's blue eyes widen. I heard distant shouts of guards as they rushed into the cell where I was chained. I inhaled the reek of piss that spilled from the tin can I'd kicked over.

What day was it? What time was it? How long had I been down here, a prisoner of the Coral Court?

The guards reached for me, then whipped their hands back. Their fingertips were singed; burnt by my inner fire. The chains around my wrists glowed red with heat. Scales covered my skin. Horns curved from my skull. I was going to burn this place down. I was going to make them bleed.

Loch wrenched on our bind and pulled my magic from inside me. A spasm of pain shot through my chest. I bared my teeth that felt more like fangs. He pulled again until my knees buckled and my breaths were ragged. Until the world spun around me.

Endless days passed like this. Loch and his guards entered my cell. They tried to hold me down and temper my rage. He tried to break me and force me to kneel.

The fucker didn't realize that a dragon couldn't be tamed. I would not break. I would not bow.

But one day, through my haze of rage and despair, a voice murmured through the grate in my door. Five simple words: "You cannot fight in chains."

I vaguely recognized the voice. It was the siren who I'd found beside my bed when I'd woken up in the Coral Court ward. Exekiel's friend; Aquarius de L'eau.

Before he'd died, Exekiel had sent Aquarius a letter asking him to fight with us. To be our eyes beneath the sea and search for *Sonu di Carghel*—the weapon designed to brainwash the realm.

That letter was the reason I was still here. I could have run. Aquarius and his allies had had systems in place to get me out, but running wouldn't have stopped what was coming. I needed—wanted—to fight. In order to do that, I had to break the chains that bound me; both physically and mentally.

2

VARIALLA:
UNRAVEL ME

I was surrounded. One siren styled my hair into an afro puff on top of my head. Another rouged my lips. Another plucked my brows. Others yanked me out of my large t-shirt and forced me into a white clamshell bra and a seaweed skirt that swayed with the current of the sea.

It was his favorite outfit for me. They always did what he liked. They groomed me for Loch. Dressed me in the outfits he chose. Did my hair in the styles he preferred.

Rage rose in my chest. I choked it down. This was what I'd wanted. I'd chosen to remain in the Coral Court to exploit our enemy's weaknesses. I'd decided to endure whatever I had to, to bring this Court to its knees.

Behind me, more sirens flitted about the small room I'd been given. They made the bed, folded my few items of clothes, and set up seashell bouquets on my pearl encrusted bedside table. They did their best to erase the fact that Loch had kept me here for almost three months. His prisoner; his pet. Although this room was a considerable upgrade from my cell.

Finally, the sirens who dressed me stepped back to survey their work. Bay and Marlin, guards of the Siren Army, stepped forward. They'd once laughed with me at the dinner table and told me stories of my mother. Now they didn't look me in the eye as they clamped cold steel manacles around my wrists and ankles.

I let them walk me backward and didn't struggle like I used to. With each step, the chains that were fastened to some contraption inside the sand-packed wall tightened. My arms and legs were splayed and I could barely move. Again, exactly how the bastard liked me.

"Is this necessary?" My throat was dry and voice raspy.

They only gave me enough water to not die of thirst except on the days they took me out for training.

"A few weeks of good behavior doesn't erase all the times you tried to kill our king," Bay hissed.

Her rage was palpable. It tremored in every syllable she spoke.

I grinned. "I can't argue with that."

If Aquarius hadn't talked me down all those weeks ago, when I'd been chained up in that cell, Loch would be dead. I would have killed him. However, the Royal Court would still be in power. The Outer Isles would still be abandoned and left to rot. And any loyalty the sirens might have for me would have been destroyed.

For that reason, I swallowed the bile that climbed up my throat and pretended my skin didn't crawl when Loch entered the room.

He was shirtless as was custom for males in the Coral Court. His golden-brown skin and tightly-packed muscles on show. His lower half was reserved for the thrum of his powerful tail. Its deep red was the same shade as the stain on my lips.

Loch trailed his ice-blue eyes over my exposed flesh. His gaze lingered on every curve and drank in the swell of my breasts. I hated the effect that look had on me. The way heat climbed up my body and something tugged low in my gut.

"Princess." His voice was deep and endless. "Are you hungry?"

I glared at the bastard. I was always hungry. Partly because of the dragon that rumbled beneath my flesh. Partly because the assholes constantly kept me on the edge of hunger. It was like they were afraid of what I'd do if I had my full strength.

Two sirens wheeled over a table stacked with covered platters, a fruit basket and pitchers of fresh juice. Ever since, the barrier had fallen, food was no longer an issue in the Coral Court thanks to Loch's alliances. The people praised him for it. They didn't know it had cost him our souls.

He gave the girls a curt nod. They instantly left the room. The door clicked shut behind them. The fine hairs on the nape of my neck rose.

"I went to the Inlands today. The mourning period is over. The final five have been announced."

I did my best to keep my expression blank. Phase Two of the Games had ended a few weeks after my alleged death, and the realm had gone into a month of mourning to honor the last dragonborn queen and the infamous Shadow Saint. The story was that we'd died in a building collapse. It was the only way the Court had been able to explain the countless dead bodies they'd had to burn that week who had really been the soldiers Exekiel's shadows had killed. Now the month of mourning was over and Phase Three had begun.

"Do you want to know who they are?"

Loch lifted the silver lid from the largest platter on the table to reveal a plate of roasted wing-bird, mashed potato, and Five Isles vegetables I'd started to recognize. Ardovar jewels that looked like pink corn, burnt bitter berries, and salted-lemon lettuce.

Like all food in this place, the meal was enchanted to stop it from turning into soggy mush. This was the only thing I truly enjoyed about Loch's visits. I was given more than crumbs of bread and watery soup.

He raised a questioning brow. I sucked on my cheeks. Of course, I wanted to know who had made it into the final five. I was deliberately kept in the dark down here. I found out everything eventually through Aquarius's sources but it took longer for news to reach us.

"Who?" I finally ground out.

Loch grinned. In his mind, that one question confirmed that I was weakening. Once, I'd vowed to never speak to him again. Now I answered his questions more often than not. In order to play this right, I had to find the balance between resistance and surrender. Loch had to believe he was breaking me but if I succumbed too easily, he'd see through the ruse.

"Camal Silverhound is one of them."

That was no surprise. The wolf shifter was a willing puppet in the Council's game. Loch sank two fingers into the bowl of mashed potato. His movements were slow and deliberate. He growled low in his throat. My core tightened. The toxic power of the bind tugged on my insides.

When I said nothing, Loch curled his fingers then scooped out a dollop of white fluffy potato. He brought it to my lips.

"Open your mouth."

My nostrils flared. The urge to say no was on the tip of my tongue. I'd lost count of how many times he'd fed me over the last few weeks. Of how often he'd had his hands on my body; his mouth on my breasts. We hadn't done more than that but it was only a matter of time. Eventually, I'd have to give him more.

According to the laws of the bind, Loch couldn't force himself on me. He'd always said he wanted me to go to him; to beg for it, but I hadn't realized until recently, that that wasn't his choice. When the bind was officially consummated, it had to be consensual.

However, Loch could do things to me. He could manipulate my mind and play with my body until I willingly gave in.

"Open. Your. Mouth."

For the Nine Isles. I chanted in my mind. *For Exekiel.*

I opened my mouth. Loch slid the salty potato between my lips. His fingers dragged along my tongue. His other hand grasped my hip and squeezed. Desire pulsed through my body like it did every time he touched me.

"Clean me off."

My nipples involuntarily peaked at the command. It felt like I was walking a tightrope. I had to give into the lust the bind provoked enough for Loch to feel it. At the same time, I couldn't let it consume me and convince me I wanted something I didn't.

I clamped my mouth around his fingers and sucked every salty, buttery speck of potato down my throat. Loch groaned and pressed closer. His ocean scent, like salted seaweed mixed with coconut surrounded me.

"Good girl."

My heart pounded. His proximity made me dizzy—heedless. *Shit.* I battled through the bullshit of the bind. I reminded myself who I was and what this asshole had done to me. Taken from me.

Flashes of Exekiel's slanted smile and burning pink eyes filled my mind. Once the thought of him would have broken me. Now it fueled my fury and gave me the strength to push through. For him, I would stomach whatever I had to, to see his killers burn.

"Would you like to know who else?"

My jaw clenched. So, this was the bastard's game today. To make me beg and barter for information. If I was good, if I pleased him, he would reward me with a name and a bite of food. Maybe he would say the two names I cared about most. The two contestants he intentionally never mentioned—Lucinda and Maximus.

He waited. I sucked on my cheeks and glared at the bastard. I wouldn't break so easily, even if the whole thing was an act and I wasn't breaking at all.

Loch chuckled then pushed more potato into my mouth. "You'll be pleased to know that we were given a fragment of the Conduit to use on those in the ward today."

My eyes met his. Apparently, we'd moved on from the contestants unless I admitted I wanted to know.

"Sienna's showing signs of improvement already."

My heart skipped. Loch knew how much Cherise's mother mattered to me. He knew I felt responsible for taking care of her. Not only because I'd killed her daughter but because I'd promised Cherise that I would.

I almost sagged with relief.

"See?" He fed me a bite of the warm wing-bird drizzled in gravy. "I'm not all bad."

I savored every morsel of the bite and licked the remains off my lips. I was rewarded with another mouthful of meat.

"If you would just accept what we have, we could move forward."

Loch withdrew his fingers from my mouth and ran them over my lips.

My skin prickled. "We have nothing."

He stepped closer. My chains clanked as I instinctively tried to move back.

"You can't lie to me, Princess. I'm as tortured by the bind as you are." Loch lowered his head and breathed me in. The sound he made was explicit. "I crave you. In every breath I take." He ran his hand down the side of my body. My stomach flipped. "You haunt my every thought and consume every nightmare."

He fisted the tendrils of my seaweed skirt and hitched them up. Water sloshed around my legs.

"Be mine, princess. Be mine."

His hand pushed between my thighs. My head tipped back as pleasure scorched through me.

"This desire between us is written in our blood. Etched onto the very marrow of our bones." Loch stroked his fingers up and down. Only the thinnest layer of cotton divided us. "The longer you deny it, the stronger it grows—the tighter it pulls." His fingers pushed down the front of my panties and brushed my clit.

"Fuck." I couldn't hold back the cry; a burst of lust and rage.

"This is our destiny."

Loch's pale blue eyes were pinned on me. He waited to see if I would stop him like I usually did. However, approximately every ten days, I gave Loch a little more of me. I gave him a reason to believe he was wearing me down, that he could lower his guard. Today was a tenth day.

When I didn't pull back, his eyes lit up.

"We want the same things."

My body tightened as he worked his fingers lower.

"We can save our people and free the Outer Isles. We could be happy if you gave us a chance." Loch hissed when his middle finger reached my dripping entrance. His thumb continued to stroke my clit. Once. Twice.

I gritted my teeth. I was perched on the edge of oblivion. Caught between somehow giving in but not giving up.

"Let me make you happy." Loch sank his finger inside me.

My hips bucked. My fists clenched. The chains around my wrists and ankles rattled.

"Say yes to my proposal." He brought his mouth to my neck. His tongue slid out and tasted me. My entire body trembled.

"To become your pawn in the Games?" I panted.

"To win." Loch watched me as I fought the urge to move on his hand. "I have the ear of the Council. I can find out what your trials will be and prepare you beforehand."

Loch flicked my clit. I jumped and clenched around his finger. Need thundered between my thighs. I wanted to hate this, but, fuck, I didn't. I wanted it. Wanted *him*.

That thought turned my stomach, but not enough to restrain the moan I released when Loch slid another finger inside me. It was so much deeper and more forceful than the first.

"Join me and the Throne will be ours."

His thumb rubbed my clit with more intent. My breaths were ragged. I clung to my fraying control.

"Every time you ask, my answer is the same."

"Yes." His fingers pumped deeper. "But your reaction to me isn't."

I wanted to deny it but my treacherous body gave me away. I was so fucking wet for him.

Loch's grip on my waist tightened. His thrusts were more powerful.

"You're insane."

His fingers curled the same way they had inside the potatoes. Pleasure ricocheted through my body and pulsed where his hand pushed.

"All geniuses are." He grinned as he watched me unravel.

The beat of his fingers intensified. I was trapped between delight and despair as an orgasm built inside me. Until now he hadn't had more than my breasts. This was a test for both of us. I'd never pushed the bind this far.

"That's it, Princess," Loch's serrated teeth flashed.

I gritted my own.

"Pretend to hate me if you must." Loch twisted his fingers.

My hips jerked and my back hit the hard-packed wall of sand. Shells dug into my spine.

"We both know you love the feel of me inside you."

I couldn't breathe. My nerves sparked. My heart raced. I hadn't expected it to feel this good. He was right. The longer I resisted, the tighter the bind pulled.

Ecstasy consumed me. Sweat dappled my brow. I rode Loch's fingers like I didn't hate him. Like I didn't want to carve him open and let maggots feast on his flesh. My hips moved until all I was aware of was the rhythm of his fingers, and his bruising grip on my waist.

The chains clanked and shook. A deep guttural sound came from my throat.

"Loch," I cried. My orgasm tore free.

The bastard chuckled darkly and continued to pump his fingers inside me until the only thing holding me up were the chains.

3

VARIALLA:
THE RAVEN COMES

It figured the man I hated more than anything would give me one of the best orgasms of my life. Chest heaving, I hung from the chains and replayed every twisted moment in my mind. I expected to feel sick, anger or regret. All I felt was hollow. Seducing Loch was a means to an end and the ends were all that mattered.

My head snapped up when the door swung open. If we weren't underwater, it would have smacked into the wall. Aquarius studied me from the doorway. His wavy golden locks were pulled into a bun on top of his head, and he wore his new bronze and blue Royal Guard's uniform. It was a role he'd recently been appointed since Exekiel's shadows had wiped out almost half the Siren Army that night on the beach. However, Aquarius had worked in the palace for centuries. Back then he'd been a forager. I'd even worked alongside him a few times but he'd mostly kept to himself.

I could tell from the furious blaze in his blue eyes that he'd heard. Heard the chains clanking. Heard me moaning Loch's name. He said nothing. We never talked about the things I let Loch do to me; what I sacrificed for access to the Rebel King's resources and insight into his plans.

The siren swam towards me. His warm brown skin glittered in places as he moved. This was a result of his mother having *glittari*—a type of glitter-fish—in her bloodline.

"If the information you got for us wasn't so valuable, I would have dragged you out of here kicking and screaming a long time ago," he grumbled.

Sometimes I thought Aquarius hated what I put myself through with Loch more than I did. Like he had somehow let Exekiel down. But Exekiel wasn't here.

"Then I guess I should consider myself lucky that the information is valuable."

"Lucky." Aquarius grunted in disgust but he couldn't argue.

Loch's arrogance made him sloppy around me. Over the last few weeks, I'd overheard countless conversations and read letters over his shoulder. The biggest news was that the Court had started to spread the poison throughout the realm. However, the antidote was the true threat. Something in it reacted with the venom and infected the people's minds. It made them more vulnerable to a sirens command; to the weapon. They apparently planned to launch *Sonu di Carghel* at the season finale. There, almost everyone in the Isles would be gathered in one place—an easy target.

Aquarius went to my ankles and unhooked the clasp then he moved onto my wrists.

"Besides, it won't be for much longer." I gave him a pointed look. "Please tell me you have good news today."

My arms dropped when the chains fell away. I swam over to the bed and pulled on my weighted boots that kept me from drifting off or having to constantly doggy paddle.

Aquarius glanced over his shoulder at the partially open door. It was forbidden for anyone but Loch to be alone with me in a closed room.

Apparently satisfied that no one was nearby, he pulled a piece of enchanted parchment and quill from beneath his scales.

Finally. Since anyone who entered my room was usually searched, it had been almost impossible for Aquarius to get these to me. Not to mention, his shifts rarely put him on my duty and another guard was always on watch.

"You'll be going up for training again in a couple of days. That's when the Messenger Raven will arrive. Loch will send out his responses the following day." His words came out in a rush.

Weeks ago, I'd come up with the idea for me to contact Lucinda. Aquarius had connections in the Outer Isles but none in the Inlands. If I could reach Lucinda then her and her coven could find a way to smuggle me across the border and get me back into the Games.

Once the public knew I was alive, the Court would have to let me compete. Not even they could defy the laws of the Conduit. I hadn't lost the jousting tournament, or died like they claimed which meant that I was still an active contestant in the Games. I still had a claim to the Throne.

I swiped the parchment and quill from Aquarius. "Make the arrangements."

He hesitated. "Are you sure about this? When Loch comes here without invitation, you have every right to refuse him. But if you go hinting that you want to dine in his rooms…" His voice trailed off and he shook his head.

He was right. Loch might get the wrong idea. However, in this case it was exactly the idea I wanted him to get. I needed to write this letter to Lucinda and put it in the stack of scrolls that were going to be sent out with the Messenger Raven. Loch wouldn't handle the letters himself which meant there was no chance of him noticing the extra missive. However, the scrolls were kept in his rooms so that was where I needed to go. Aquarius and his allies didn't have that level of clearance.

"I'm sure."

It was time to set the plan in motion. Loch would never believe me if I asked to dine in his rooms but we were going to plant the seed for him to invite me.

Aquarius and his allies would drop subtle hints to Loch and the other guards that chaining me up and treating me like a prisoner wasn't going to get him anywhere. They'd mention how my room was dingy, and how my tiny bed was no space to shag a future queen, or some other alpha bullshit.

Aquarius opened and closed his mouth. His shoulders sagged.

"You shouldn't have to do this."

The despair in his eyes almost broke me. I looked away. I couldn't take the concern—the caring, in those blue irises. All that look had ever gotten me was pain. Families that fled. Friendships that were snatched away. Lovers that were…taken. I cared about Aquarius but I didn't want to. More attachments invited more pain and I'd had my fill.

"I want to do this."

His eyes widened.

"To save the people of the Nine Isles," I went on. "To build the world Exekiel and I dreamed of. I want to do this to claim the Eternal Throne."

Aquarius straightened; as if my words had reminded him of his purpose; his goals. "We have two maybe three days to secure you an invite."

"Then we better work fast."

4

LOCH:
TAKE A BITE

Infinity city. No matter how many times I visited, I couldn't stomach the place. The extravagance that these people had lived in for centuries whilst mine had suffered and starved beneath the sea.

My foot tapped on the velvet floor of the carriage as one picturesque scene after another rolled past the open window. Beings danced in the streets and fucked behind taverns. Tables were left with plates that were half-full. Abandoned drinks spilled onto the cobbled stone. Always so much waste and nobody cared.

These fateless shits had drunk, danced and fucked their nights away for the last six hundred years, whilst the Outer Isles had been left to slowly rot.

"I have to admit, you have proven yourself a worthy accomplice, Loch."

My stare slid to Alexov. The senior councilman leaned back in his seat; his ankle propped on his knee. His graying beard was slick with oil and he had that smug expression that made me want to pry his eyes out and feed them to the tentracores. One day I would. I'd tear him apart with my bare hands and let the sea monster's feast on his remains.

"After your misstep with Varialla's heritage, I'd started to question your loyalties."

I curled my tongue behind my teeth and cricked my neck. Across from me, Pre-Primary Knox; my one true ally, nudged me with his boot. When I glanced his way, the shifter levelled me with those pitch-black eyes of his and subtly shook his head. His curtain of blonde hair barely moved with the motion. The message was clear: *Don't rise to the bait.*

I exhaled through my nose and resisted the urge to lunge across the carriage and slit Alexov's throat.

"As I've said, I had no idea Varialla was part dragon." The lie slipped off my tongue easily. It was one I'd told since the day my Mate-Sworn had decided to reveal her true self to the entire fucking realm.

I looked from the Councilman to Adir who lounged in the opposite seat. The eye-patch he'd worn over his left eye since Varialla had almost gouged it out, was marked in gold with the four-petaled flower emblem of the Five Isles.

"I'd known her mother was seducing the Dragon Prince as a way to infiltrate their court, but I didn't know Varialla was his daughter."

Alexov narrowed his eyes. My fingers twitched; itching to plunge into those cold depths. Instead, I adjusted the sleeve of my tunic.

Finally, the councilman nodded. "Let's just thank the Fates she died in that attack. Imagine the threat she would have become if she'd turned out to be like her father."

"Quite the threat indeed," Knox agreed.

I smirked. These poor bastards had no idea Varialla was still alive. That the Shadow Saint had given his life for hers. He'd tried to be some fucking hero. Instead, he'd handed me the key to the realm. He might as well have strapped the chains around her too.

"Speaking of threats," I cocked my head. "Has there been any news on the council members you lost?"

Knox groaned. The air in the carriage became thick with tension.

Alexov puffed out his chest and curled his fingers into a fist. I grinned. *Punch me, old man. I dare you.*

"Watch your tone, siren."

"Consider it watched." My teeth flashed.

The bastard had the sense to sit back a little further in his seat.

"A warlock reported seeing a man who matched Vladimir's description in Wiccan's Wharf," Adir cut in. "The Royal Guard are looking into it."

"Good." I didn't look away from Alexov. "When it comes to fuck ups, that one was colossal."

Vladimir and Nyla were the only two Council members who hadn't known about *Sonu di Carghel* or our plans to warp the minds of the people. Recently, they'd found out. Now they were on the run.

An orb had recorded them in the Council's supposedly secret lab setting the place on fire. But not before Nyla had swiped a file; evidence that could ruin us. They were loose ends that needed to be cut.

Alexov nodded, trying to take back some control. "Follow up on that. And have the alchemists increase their production of the antidote. We need to make sure enough people are under our control in case those two are plotting something."

Scents of wildflowers wafted through the carriages open windows as we rolled past the wrought iron gates of Perennial Park and towards Park Square. Flames flickered in the street lamps. Voices and laughter filled the night. Eventually our Pegasus-pulled carriage came to a stop at the steps of Eons Art Gallery. It was a large white marble building with grooved pillars and a statue of the Fates at its entrance. A crowd was already gathered to meet us.

I pushed open the door and stepped out into the unnaturally cool night's air. A light frost coated the ground which was unheard of this close to spring. I shared a glance with Knox. The shifter grinned. Everyone knew that the Conduit was responsible for the strange shift in weather, but no one besides us understood why.

A player was out of the Games. Not dead nor in service to the Crown. Varialla had simply left which was a violation of the rules and the laws that had been set when the games were created. Now the kingdom would crumble unless the princess agreed to rule at my side.

I drew up the collar of my coat and ascended the steps. The Council members followed. I probably should have let them lead, but I didn't give a shit.

The gathered crowd quieted when they saw me. I'd visited the Inlands frequently in the last few months, but this would be the first time I stood before the people as an equal.

A female shouted, "Fateless sea slug!"

Something bright and pink flashed in the corner of my eye. I turned and caught the velvety druador fruit that had been intended for my head in one hand. I inspected the fruit then took a bite. The sweet juice dribbled down my chin before I licked it clean.

My eyes scanned the crowd. I could have compelled the coward who'd flung the fruit to show themself. I could have told them to jump and had them ask how high. I could have rammed this fucking druador down their throat. Instead, I took another bite then let the fruit roll down the steps, staining them red as the pulp burst across the concrete.

I smiled with all my teeth. Those closest to the front shuffled back. With the stench of their fear in the air, I continued my assent. One day these fateless shits would pay. When they dropped to their knees and begged, I'd be sure to show them the same kindness they'd shown me and my people.

At the top of the steps, Adir and I made our way to the podiums that had been set up.

The Primary stood tall; his brown wings folded at his back. "People of Five Isles. Today marks the dawn of a new day."

Overhead Pegasus-pulled chariots flew in. Each one carried at least fifty vials of the antidote. As Adir addressed the crowd, the chariots descended and lined up at the foot of the stairs.

"I do not have to remind you all how severe this plague has become."

As if in answer, several hacking coughs rippled through the crowd. A few bubbles of water bounced around people's noses and mouths to protect them from contagions in the air. The poor shits didn't know that the poison wasn't in the air. It was in the food they ate and the wine they drank. It was the Royal Court's duty to distribute produce and other goods to the Isles. They controlled what was laced and what was not. Only our allies were being spared.

"Over the last few months, we have realized that no siren has contracted the virus," Adir went on. "For that reason, the ruler of the Coral Court has agreed to work with us and allow us to test siren blood to see if they hold the key to immunity."

Now the eyes in the audience regarded me with something other than disdain. Some were curious or envious. Others were wide eyed with shock.

"As a result, you will be seeing a lot more of Sir Loch and his kind in the Inlands."

Sir Loch. Still unworthy of the title Count. Still not one of them despite all I'd done.

"I expect them to be shown respect. Not insulted or abused." He glared at the crowd; at the woman we both suspected had thrown that fruit.

Some of the audience had the decency to hang their heads. Not because they were ashamed but because they regretted not treating us better when they'd had the chance. Now their lives were at stake and they had to turn to the very people they'd condemned, to save them.

"Tonight," Adir gestured to the chariots. "We have brought with us three hundred vials of the antidote and will be offering them to anyone showing symptoms of the illness for a fraction of the price."

I almost laughed. Not only were the people going to take the very remedy that would hand over their minds and their lives to us but we were charging them for the pleasure.

Adir gestured to the healers at the foot of the steps.
"Everyone form a line and we'll begin."

5

VARIALLA:
INTO THE SERPENT'S NEST

I studied the conch communication shell Aquarius had slipped into my hand earlier. It was identical to the com-shell Loch had once given me to reach him. However, it was a fraction of the size and linked to our own personal sea current. This meant its messages couldn't be intercepted. The only drawback was that to use it, the com-shell had to be submerged in water and a ripple needed to flow directly into it as I spoke.

I fastened the enchanted device onto a pearl bracelet with other seashell charms and clasped it around my wrist. If anything went wrong tonight, I was supposed to use it, and the Alliance—Aquarius' allies—would get me out.

It wasn't long after, that three sirens swam into my room, not with a tray but with a dress.

"The Rebel King wishes to dine with you tonight," said a fair skinned siren with golden ringlets. "In his rooms."

She smiled sharply with the final words as if she expected me to flinch. I merely suppressed my own smile. I'd already expected the summons. The Alliance's hard work had paid off. Loch had taken the bait.

*

It took three guards to push open Loch's heavy stone door. All others in the palace were made out of rotted wood or curtains of shells and weed, but not his. Loch had a lot to hide inside his haven.

My jaw nearly dropped when I stepped inside. Floor to ceiling windows rose up higher than I could see. Daylight streamed in from somewhere overhead. Not the watery wisps of light that I could sometimes make out in the palace but actual blazing sunlight. My heart spasmed with longing. Over the last few months, I could count the times I'd seen the sun and each time had involved having to fight on the training field.

There was a large concave window across from where I stood. It gave the feeling of being in a submarine and magnified the fish that swam passed.

The floor was velvet-soft sand. The furniture crafted from stone, seashells and pearls. Sand-packed cushions covered in warm red and orange fabrics were piled on top of a brown sofa for two. The armchairs beside it were the same. Between them was a coral coffee table with a glass bowl of smooth stones in its center along with a decanter and a set of tumblers. I shook my head. This place was a palace in itself.

On my left, an alcove led down a narrow tunnel to what I guessed was the bathing chamber. To my right, three limestone steps led up to the largest clamshell I'd ever seen. It was easily big enough to hold three people comfortably. A mattress lay inside it covered with a deep red quilt and soft yellow pillows. It was stunning. Like the inside of most shells, the headboard was smooth and shimmery. It reflected the light that filtered down. Streaks of color stretched across the space.

Behind the bed was an archway that led into Loch's study. There was a desk off to one side and on it, the Messenger Raven sat on a perch. Beneath it was a stack of scrolls inside a basket. I pulled my stare away like someone might notice me looking and figure out what I planned to do. Somehow, I'd have to sneak the letter I'd hidden inside my updo hairstyle, onto that stack before the end of the night.

Something pinged. I looked up. At first, I saw nothing but swathes of blue and white fabric draped from coral beams. Then something caught my eye. A glass elevator was moving down towards the seabed. There were two figures inside. One was a female siren who'd often brought food to my room. The other was Loch.

They'd both shifted their tails to legs which meant they'd been on the surface. This elevator was another way out of the Court. The fact that Loch was letting me see this meant he truly believed he had me.

I licked my lips. My mouth was suddenly bone-dry. I'd faced Loch a thousand times but Aquarius was right; tonight, would be different. Tonight, he would expect more from me—all of me.

The closer the elevator came, the more my heart pounded.

Eventually, the lift doors slid open. A large bubble stretched across the entrance to stop the water from rushing in. As soon as the female stepped through the bubble's membrane, her legs morphed into a tail and gills appeared on her neck. The transformation was as seamless as blinking.

She swam towards us and announced in a sing-song voice, "He's ready for her."

Without a word, the guards marched me over to the lift. My gaze shot to the desk where the raven slept—where I needed to be.

Before I could think, I was pushed through the lift's protective membrane. I just managed to steady myself so I didn't slam straight into Loch.

His mouth quirked. "Princess."

When I stepped back, my flustered response wasn't entirely fake. The lift was large but under the Rebel King's penetrating stare, it felt small. His depthless eyes burned as he admired the dress, he'd put me in. It was made entirely of strings of pearls that clasped in a halter around my neck. Enticing glimpses of flesh showed between the threads. My back and the underside of my breasts were entirely exposed.

My breath hitched. There was no denying that Loch was attractive, but tonight he was devastating.

His square jaw seemed more pronounced. His smooth hazel-brown skin glistened in the daylight that streamed in from above. He wore a white tunic that loosely clung to his frame in a way that highlighted the hardpacked muscle beneath. He had the sleeves rolled up to his elbows which served to emphasize the veins in his forearms.

He stepped forward and wrapped a thick fluffy towel around my shoulders. I hadn't even acknowledged the cold or the warm air that blew from drying vents in the ceiling.

"Thanks."

The glass doors slid closed and the lift began to rise. I dried myself off, thankful that my updo hairstyle had held. I smoothed my hand over it in a casual gesture, and subtly made sure the scroll for Lucinda was securely tucked out of sight. Then I kicked off my weighted boots and wandered over to the glass. The ocean spanned around us. All types of fish, eels and other creatures swam past the windows. In the distance larger animals moved.

"This is incredible."

Loch stepped up behind me. "Isn't it?"

His fingertips skimmed the gaps between the pearls as he snaked his arm around my waist and grazed the underside of my breast. Every cell in my body perked up.

The elevator climbed higher. It was only a matter of minutes but it felt like days. Loch's breath fanned across the tip of my ear. My eyelids fluttered closed. *Shit.* The pressure of the bind was so potent I could taste it. Salty and sweet, as if Loch's magic and mine had merged. His ocean and coconut scent enveloped me. My knees fucking trembled.

"I'm glad you agreed to do this."

I blinked to clear the haze that had settled over me. I needed to get a grip. I hadn't just agreed to this, I'd orchestrated it. I was here for a reason; to get a letter to the Inlands.

"What is this?" I gestured to the lift. "Where are we going?"

Loch chuckled and planted a soft kiss on my head.

"You'll see."

6

VARIALLA:
Tempt Me

A path of dark, slick rocks led from the elevator to a familiar cave. For the first time in a long time, I was gripped by an emotion outside of indifference or rage. This was Cherise's cave. The one she'd brought me to and shown me the dragon's egg I was born in. Little had she known how close she'd been to Loch's rooms.

At the entrance of the cave, a table and two chairs had been set up and covered in white linen. Candles flickered in the setting sun and a bottle of wine chilled in a bucket of ice. Loch led me over the rocks and we settled into the seats.

I pasted a smile on my lips as he uncorked the bottle and filled my goblet, then his own.

He lifted it in a toast. "To us."

I rolled my eyes but tapped my goblet to his. "To keeping an open mind."

After taking a sip, Loch set his goblet down on the table where wicker-mats inlaid with shells and silver-plated cutlery had been set out.

"I have a surprise for you."

"Oh?"

"When you first arrived here, I asked what you missed most about your home in England. You said your local fish and chips from Lace Market Fish Bar."

I winced at the memory. Right after I'd said it, I'd apologized and asked if that was an act of cannibalism. Loch had laughed harder than I'd thought possible. It had been a beautiful sound. We'd laughed a lot on my visits to the Coral Court, back when I'd believed he was good. That he could've been a better fit for me than Exekiel.

He nodded to someone in the cave. My mouth dropped open when two sirens stepped out carrying armfuls of brown paper bags with a deliciously familiar scent of cod and vinegar.

"No way." My stare bounced from the food to Loch. His smile was bright and his blue eyes shone like sapphires.

"I went across the veil to bring us a very special meal."

If I didn't hate the bastard, I would have lunged across the table and smothered his face in kisses. The sirens set the food down. I peeled open the greasy newspaper and tucked in. He'd even got the mushy peas.

Whilst we ate, Loch told me about how he was now an official advisor to the Royal Court. Despite everything, he was about to give the sirens exactly what he'd promised. Freedom, riches; a better life. On the surface, it almost sounded admirable.

Throughout our conversation, he asked for my opinion. Genuine compliments replaced his usual threats. There was no sinister smirk or forced touches, only us and a fragment of the friendship we'd once shared. I was…enjoying myself.

I downed a large mouthful of wine and focused on its sweet berry and citrus tang. I counted down the seconds until dinner ended. I wouldn't let one nice meal cloud my judgment. The bind was waiting for a moment of weakness to override my common sense.

Eventually we stepped back into the elevator. I refastened my weighted boots then turned to take in the view. Once again Loch stood behind me only much closer. My body was trapped between his and the wall. My breasts crushed to the cold glass.

"Are you ready for dessert?" His hand gripped my waist as he pressed himself against me.

My heart slammed into my chest. My breath fogged up the glass. I closed my eyes and tried to center my thoughts. I could do this. I could conquer my mind. My will could override the bind—the curse. All I had to do was remember why I was here; what I was doing this for.

"Wasn't dinner enough?" I panted as he trailed his finger around my breast.

"Nothing will ever be enough." He spun me to face him. The hunger in his eyes was predatory. "Unless I'm inside you."

He bowed his head to claim a kiss. I almost lurched back. The last lips to touch mine had been Exekiel's and that's how it would stay. I didn't know if I would ever be ready to kiss another man but if I did, it would not be Loch Orqanz.

The lift pinged and the doors slid open. I practically ran through the membrane and back into his rooms.

As soon as he exited the lift, Loch's legs morphed into his deep red tail. I used the seconds of his transformation to put some distance between us and wandered deeper into his cavernous rooms. My gaze flicked to the still slumbering raven in the office. The scrolls beneath its feet were illuminated by a glass orb of glow fish. I had to somehow get there then get the heck out.

"How about a tour?"

Loch dragged a hand across his jaw. "I'm going to be honest with you. If you stay in this room a second longer, I'm going to bury myself between those legs and fuck you raw."

My pulse spiked at his words. My nipples peaked and the spot between my thighs grew damp. *Fuck.* He shouldn't turn me on. The thought of him inside me; fucking me, should have made me sick but all I felt was need. Not basic lust but a visceral ache like the need for air after drowning.

But I couldn't leave yet. I had to get this letter to Lucinda.

I can do this, I chanted in my mind. For my people and our freedom, I could pretend to be the monster's whore.

I forced a nervous laugh. "Maybe we start with a tour?"

He nodded slowly as if he'd decided I needed time to warm up to the idea of him and me.

He shrugged. "There's not much to see. This is the lounge."

He gestured around us then swam up the steps that led to his bedroom.

"My room."

I feigned interest in the stone walls and the Zen Garden he'd made out of a coral, sand, shells and sea moss. I hadn't missed the way his voice had lowered seductively, or how his eyes followed every step I took. I should leave. He'd told me what would happen if I stayed yet here I was indirectly consenting to it.

"What's over there?" I strode into the office and let out an impressed whistle. I just had to get my letter onto the stack and get out.

I trailed my fingers along a wall of bookshelves and skimmed the titles. My heart beat in my throat. The letters were so close. Loch's gaze followed me as I moved throughout the space. I did my best not to look at the scrolls. Instead, I focused on the ornaments and armored statues. Then, at last, I faced the desk.

"And this is the Messenger Raven."

Heart hammering in my chest, I made my way over to the bird. Every step was controlled as if the scroll I'd written to Lucinda would somehow slip free and roll across the floor. As if Loch would realize this was all a con and everything I'd sacrificed for over the last few months would be undone.

I leaned closer to the raven and lightly stroked its head. Its wings ruffled but it didn't wake. Before I could figure out my next move, Loch was behind me. His hands on my hips.

"Tour's over."

7

VARIALLA:
BREAK ME

Loch spun me to face him. My back hit the desk. His hand closed around my breast. There was unrestrained hunger in his movements, like he felt he might die if he didn't devour every inch me. The hard press of his cock dug into my thigh. His rough fingers pulled me close.

"Get on the desk."

My breath caught. I braced a hand on his chest; trying to steady him. To steady myself. Loch circled my nipple with his finger and held my gaze. My body burned.

This was it. The moment I'd always dreaded but had been preparing for. From the first day, I'd decided to stay here, I knew I'd have to use whatever weapon I had in my arsenal to take the bastard down, including my body.

I didn't look away. I suffered the slow intoxicating torture of his hands on my breasts and pushed myself up onto the desk. I'd chosen to stay and fight our enemy anyway I could. This was just another kind of battlefield.

With a grin, Loch parted my thighs and pushed between them. His swollen cock pressed into my entrance. I gasped. My toes curled. Loch kept his eyes on mine as he hooked his arm around my waist and dragged me closer. The pearls of my dress dug into the backs of my thighs and rolled beneath my backside as they shifted upwards. I counted the beads in my head; anything to suppress my rising desire for this monster.

Loch rocked his hips. My eyes slammed shut. My fingers curled around the edge of the desk. My other hand went around the back of his neck. I moved with him.

"Fates be blessed," he breathed and pumped his hips harder.

My head tipped back. Fuck, this felt…incredible.

His smooth, and suddenly silky scales shifted. His hard, thick cock was unveiled and rubbed between my legs. I cried out; trembling.

I had to stop this; to slow things down. But as Loch's hand slid between my thighs and tugged aside my underwear, it felt like trying to stop a train on a one-way track.

Desperate, I took his cock in my hand and pulled.

His hips bucked and he hissed through his teeth. "Fuck, Princess."

I grinned and stroked him again. I dragged my thumb over his tip and watched his blue eyes blaze.

With a low groan, Loch teased my hole and pushed a finger inside me. He'd partly shifted so it was humanoid and not webbed; which let it go deeper. My mouth fell open. Pleasure sparked through my core.

He grasped my hip; his eyes hooded. "I like you wet for me, Princess. Coating my fucking fingers."

I wanted to point out that we were underwater but I knew he could tell the difference. So could I. Precum was a different consistency and so much warmer than the cool slap of the sea. I quivered as Loch's hand pushed deeper inside my underwear and molested my pussy.

"I like you hard," I panted and pumped him; once, twice.

I relinquished a little more of my resistance to the bind and rolled my hips into his pulsing motions. In order to believe I was succumbing to him, Loch had to feel it relayed through the bond, the same way I did.

I continued to tug him hard in my hand and we moved into each other. His ragged breaths and heated gaze said he wouldn't last much longer.

"Lay down." His voice had taken on a husky drawl that made me leak.

Before I could think of a reason not to, Loch hooked his arms beneath my legs. I fell backward on the desk. The orb of glow fish toppled to the sandy-ground, along with the raven's perch and a decanter of liquor.

The bird screeched and fluttered around us. I barely noticed as Loch spread my legs and pushed his fingers back inside me. He watched intently as they slid in and out. As I rolled my hips and gave him a show. I was half lost to his motions. My other half racked my brain for a way to take the scroll from my hair and get it onto the pile.

"I'm going to eat your pussy, Princess," his voice rumbled low in his chest. "I'm fucking starving."

Loch sank lower and pushed his mouth between my thighs. I gasped and gaped down at him. He moaned and fisted the hem of my pearl dress; forcing it higher. The strings snapped. Pearls bounced across the desk and skittered over the floor.

"Loch." I panted, breathless and overawed. I wasn't prepared for the sensations he elicited inside me. "Fuck!"

His only response was a sweep of his tongue.

That first lick had my eyes rolling into the back of my head. My nails dug into the desk. My heart almost beat out of my chest. I wanted to deny it but there was no ignoring the raw lust that rocketed through me as Loch explored me with his tongue.

"L-Loch," I stammered.

His fingers dug into my hips as he drew me closer. I moaned, hotly. My back arched. Yes. Yes. *Fuck.*

Loch made a guttural sound that rumbled across my clit. Then he sucked it into his mouth. My body shook.

"Beautiful," he growled before he plunged back in.

In that moment, every version of Loch I'd known melted into one. The father who'd rocked me in his arms and tucked me in at night. The man who'd cared for me and sung me lullabies. The friend who'd brought me a home and a family. The enemy who'd destroyed it all, including me. They all bled into this toxic twisted version of a lover.

"It's official." The heat of his breath shuddered across my pulsing flesh. "I'm going to keep you."

Loch sucked me into his mouth again. I gasped and lost all grip on my sanity. I willingly gave myself over to the circles of his tongue. The pump of his fingers. This was the best and worst thing he'd ever done to me.

If this was a perfect world, this wouldn't be happening. But this world was far from perfect, and I'd accepted this fate the minute I'd decided to stay here to help my people. I was the only one who could get close to Loch; who could use his tainted desire to get him to answer questions he ordinarily wouldn't. For that, I would endure. I would moan and quiver and part my thighs, as long as he was left broken in the end.

Loch shifted. My hips bucked. My inner thighs grazed the stubble on his jaw before he grasped my thighs and spread them wider. *Holy shit.* He was thorough. His tongue devoured every inch of me, then trailed up to my clit where he sucked and nipped.

I blinked through the haze and tried to focus. With one hand, I reached for the scroll tucked inside my hair. Blindly, my other hand fumbled for the message basket.

My hand slipped over something smooth—maybe one of the silver cups—and my thumb grazed the soft flesh of his decorative anemones. I arched back, reaching further for where the scrolls might be.

Loch took that as encouragement. His tongue seared deeper.

"Fuck!" I shouted.

My legs seized up. My fingers clamped around the back of his head and tugged on the soft tufts of his hair. I pressed him closer to my most intimate part. My hips undulated and I took from him the only thing I would ever want.

Loch growled as he feasted between my legs and I let him. Fuck, I let him take everything. With my knuckles leached of color, I clung to his curls and begged him to devour me.

"Loch, yes." I pushed into the wicked slashes of his tongue. "Right there. Don't stop!"

I grinded into his mouth and met each delicious lick.

"That's it, Princess," he purred when he came up for air. "Fuck your king."

He plunged his tongue inside me. My head kicked back. I swear I saw stars. My nipples ached. My walls tightened. I felt hot and cold at the same time.

Focus, I screamed inside my mind.

Face scrunched in tortured bliss, I squinted up at the strewn parchments and ledgers. Finally, I saw the skewed basket. Aquarius had managed to forge a replica of the Coral Court seal and my own scroll would blend perfectly. I stretched to drop it into the basket just as Loch sank two fingers inside me and placed his mouth over my clit.

I half screamed; half choked. The scroll rolled from my fingers and landed amongst the others.

Magic sizzled in my flesh. Need burned in my lungs. *Fuck*. Our powers tangled. A sweet and sour zest coated my throat. My eyes rolled. I was being undone—rewritten by the bind. My needs, my wants, were being altered to match those of the one I was sworn to.

Desperation rocketed through me as I moved my hips to the beat of Loch's tongue. O god. *O god*. Everything in me went tight. My breaths became ragged. With an earth-shattering cry, I erupted. Screaming in both frustration and euphoria, I came all over Loch's thirsting tongue.

8

LOCH:
A Tomb so Black

Leaned back in a rickety metal chair, I drummed my fingers on my knee as the man screamed. Unlike my companions, I didn't get excited or revel in the sound. Maybe I would have, if the one screaming was one of the Four Chosen: a Fae or an elf, a witch or shifter. But it was a werewolf; an Outlier. It was always an Outlier. These fateless shits never used one of their own for this part of the tests. The process was painful and the results could be deadly.

In the corner of the cell, Ripple and Shora sang. They were two of the few sirens who knew the truth about the weapon. They knew how far I was willing to go to make sure the Coral Court never fell again and they stood with me.

As the melody of *Sonu di Carghel* crooned from their lips, the Court and Council members had their fun barking orders at the captive. The prisoner raged inside himself. His teeth turned to elongated canines but his full shift had been effectively stopped by Alexov's command.

He let out a low whine then howled at the nonexistent moon.

Whilst the Council played, I let my thoughts drift. An image of Varialla splayed out on my desk and dripping for me, flashed across my mind. My dick twitched. I recalled the way she'd let me lick that sweet little pussy of hers. The way she'd writhed into me and clung to the desk to keep from falling off as I'd taken her over the edge. Varialla had come twice on my tongue that night. Then she'd closed herself off, as I'd expected, and asked to return to her rooms. I hadn't argued. If I'd pushed too hard, I might have undone the exceptional progress she'd made.

The werewolf bawled again. I adjusted my trousers to alleviate some of the pressure in my cock then dragged my attention back to him. His once thick, black hair was now stringy and damp with sweat. His once muscular form was withered and pale from the plague and his time spent here in Blacktomb Bay.

Gwendoline sashayed towards him. Like the others, she wore a set of silver headphones that she believed warded off the effects of a siren's song. She thought she had some level of protection against me and my kind that was further enhanced when she was connected to the weapon.

The truth was, there was no protection from me. During these sessions, my sirens didn't target the Court or Council members. We let them believe in their immunity. When they did eventually realize the lie, it would be too late.

"Don't move." Gwendoline trailed the sharp edge of her blade down the prisoner's cheek. Blood spilled in its wake.

Anger flashed in the werewolf's eyes but he didn't move. He didn't even flinch. He was paralyzed inside himself. The effects of the song were working with the antidote we'd given him, enough to override his own need for self-preservation.

Ordinarily, it took an exceptionally skilled and powerful siren to coerce someone to remain still through bodily harm. This hadn't taken more effort than a flick of the wrist. The antidote dulled his senses and ability to resist. As long as a siren sang, anyone could give an order and it would be obeyed.

That was another mistake these fateless shits hadn't realized they'd made. The antidote gave them control over their people, but it also enhanced our control over everyone, including them. Not only that but for their command to hold, they needed a sirens song. They saw us as their weapon but didn't realize we were also their armor. Without our cooperation, they were as vulnerable as the rest. I was looking forward to showing them just how much once they'd placed that crown on my head.

Gwendoline laughed and sank the blade through the man's cheek. Something innate caused tufts of fur to creep across his skin but he still didn't move. She cackled.

Between Gwendoline and Adir I didn't know which one was worse. The red-headed Fae enjoyed the sounds of suffering like one enjoyed wine. Adir was equally as depraved. He punched the prisoner hard in the gut.

Pain was etched across the werewolf's face and blazed in his eyes but he did not move. He couldn't. Again, and again the Primary of the realm struck until blood dribbled from between the were's lips.

I clicked my tongue against my teeth. "Can we get on with it?"

The purpose of these tests was to check the potency of the antidote when amplified by the Song of Change. The torture was unnecessary.

Adir sneered at me over his shoulder but dipped his head. He turned and plucked the knife from between Gwendoline's fingers, then he held it up to the werewolf.

"Take this blade and plunge it through your heart."

The were's eyes flashed but his hand reached for the weapon. Adir's grin sharpened. Alexov straightened. There was an eagerness in his eyes. Even Knox stepped forward like he believed the man would do it. Only I read the murderous gleam in the werewolf's stare and saw his intent.

Instantly, he transformed from man to beast and swung for Adir's throat.

"Stop!"

His hand froze mid-swing.

With a growl, the werewolf rounded on me. "You turned on the Outliers. You piece of—"

"Shut up!"

His lips slammed shut.

I rose from my seat. "Revert back to your human form."

Defiance flashed in his harsh yellow eyes but he couldn't defy me. No one could. There was a reason I'd been Queen Zenera's righthand and why I'd taken over after she'd been imprisoned. My power level was only matched by those of the royal bloodline. In some ways, it surpassed them.

The werewolf reluctantly shifted back into his human form. A sheen of sweat coated his pasty skin.

"Stand over there and do not move until we leave."

He stumbled to the corner of his cell and sagged against the wall. I doubted he'd survive the night.

Alexov kicked the ground. "Self-preservation wins again."

I shared his irritation. We didn't want the people of the Isles to be mindless, however, we did want them to be obedient. To go ahead with their daily lives but heed our every command when given—even if it meant the cost of their lives. It was the only way we could be sure of our complete control; no threat of a rebellion.

"We need to double the dose. It's the only way." Adir stormed towards the heavy stone door and wrenched it open.

The promise of freedom beckoned but the prisoner did not move. He was bound by my command.

I followed the others out. As soon as the door clicked shut, the prisoner launched himself at it with a thud. His bony fingers clawed at the grate.

"You Fate-stained bastard!" he hollered. "You turned your back on us! You promised we'd be free."

It was a promise I was going to keep. He just wouldn't be around to see it. He didn't understand that I'd sacrificed as many souls as I had to, to see our people freed. More obscenities left his mouth. I turned away and took in the view.

That view was a torture of its own to those locked in these cells, never to witness it other than through the narrow slitted window.

Blacktomb Bay was built into the side of the Realm's highest-known mountain which was situated on a small island of black sand. True to its name, the roughhewn walls, pillars and domed ceiling were all carved from black stone. The floor was polished black marble, run-through with streaks of silver. However, inside the cells, they slept on grained concrete and straw.

I strode over to the arched glassless windows that let in a sea-scented breeze and allowed my eyes to feast. From up here, I could practically touch the low-hanging clouds in the greying sky. The sun, a milky dot on the horizon.

"If we're done here," Adir adjusted the sleeves of his deep purple cloak and shook out his brown wings. "I'm going to go and blow off some steam."

Alexov rolled his eyes. "Which one today?"

"I'll take my pick." The Primary shrugged as he stalked down the hallway. "There isn't an inmate in this place that doesn't want to fuck a Primary."

"They also want to kill you," I pointed out.

His grin only deepened. "Which only makes the sex that much better."

9

LOCH:
KNEEL

I wasn't one for butterflies in the stomach and clammy palms. However, there was a definite surge of adrenaline as I approached the black cell door marked with a green X. She was inside.

In all the decades since she was taken from me, I'd been allowed to see her three times and only through the grate in her door. Now they'd handed me the key and let me meander through the prison unguarded. How times had changed.

The key clicked in the lock. I paused for a heartbeat then the door groaned open.

"Fancy seeing you here."

The figure spun at the sound of my voice. Her bright green eyes, so unlike her daughters, widened when she found me in the doorway.

"Loch?" The word came out half-formed seeing as they'd taken her teeth and half her fucking tongue.

Old hatred rose in my chest, but it was mildly sated by the sight of her.

I dropped to one knee and bowed my head. "My Queen."

Despite the decades of darkness and solitude, Queen Zenera pursed her lips in a crooked smile. Her body was thin but there was strength in her stride as she moved from her corner and paced towards me. Her threadbare white robe was stained and riddled with holes. They hadn't given her proper clothing, a bed, or even a blanket. This woman deserved the world.

She took the pitcher of water I carried and drained half of it in one gulp. Water droplets splashed from her jaw and dotted the concrete. She coughed but kept going.

Finally, my Queen lowered the jug and ran slender fingers down my cheek. They were as soft as I remembered. I looked up and our gazes held. My throat worked over a swallow. She had reduced me in this moment to the boy I'd been when I'd first knelt at her feet, rather than the man—the victor—I had become for her.

"I have something for you." I dug my hand into my jacket pocket and retrieved a small velvet box. Still bent on one knee, I held it out to her.

Zenera took the package; intrigue in her eyes. She opened it and a raspy laugh escaped her as she beheld a fresh set of teeth.

"How can you be sure they'll fit?" Each word was garbled as she struggled to speak.

I grinned. "I think I remember the shape of your mouth well."

My queen laughed. Blood rushed to my cock. She removed the teeth from the box and placed them inside her mouth. Her broken tongue ran over them.

"Perfect fit." I nodded.

"Your memory serves you well." Her words weren't entirely clear but easier to understand.

"It was impossible for me to forget."

The nights I'd spent with her were what had kept me going. The need to carry out her vision and see her freed were my motivation.

"You place so much on a simple interaction," she stated. "You always had such a soft heart."

"But I was always hard where it mattered," I ground out.

It annoyed me when she reduced our time together to nothing. It had been brief but, to me, it had been everything.

My queen lifted a brow and pulled her plump lips into a smirk.

"I couldn't in good conscience set you up with my daughter without sampling the goods."

I remained quiet. She claimed our time together had been nothing more than a test to make sure I could perform; that everything was as it should be. But the way she'd responded to my touch; the way she'd writhed beneath me and sucked on my cock, said otherwise.

My dick twitched against my trousers at the memory. The longing I felt for this female was nothing like the tainted and unrelenting lust I had for her daughter. This was pure, hot and visceral. But my Queen had never returned my affections only toyed with them. For five nights, she had let me do whatever I wanted to her and in turn I had let her do anything she wanted to me. Five nights to ensure I had what it took to impregnate a queen when the time came, and to rule alongside her daughter as King.

Five nights of her letting me hold her in my arms, then we'd returned to sovereign and subordinate and she'd never looked at me in that way again.

It had been the promise of those five nights that had led me to agree to the Ceremonial Bind in the first place. Now I craved her daughter. I wanted to be inside Varialla for the rest of my life. But when I stood before her mother, in moments like this, those lines blurred.

Queen Zenera jerked her chin. "Rise."

At last, I stood from where I'd knelt. Her warm golden eyes trailed over me.

"How are things progressing?"

Over the years, Knox had been able to visit the prison more than I had. He'd relayed certain information regarding the weapon and my progress to have Varialla rule at my side. His visits had been short so that no one would notice or start to ask questions but she knew enough.

"Has my daughter proved useful?

"Not willingly," I confessed. I strode to the narrow window and looked out. "You were smart to create the Ceremonial Bind between us to give me that extra control. If you hadn't, I'd be dead and she'd be ruling the kingdom with the Shadow Saint right now."

Zenera made a disgusted sound in the back of her throat.

"I can only do so much from this cell, Loch." she snarled. The disappointment in her tone affected me more than I cared to admit. "Now that she is back in this realm, my daughter will soon inherit the gifts of her father. We need to have control of it—of her—before then. Tell me I did not make a mistake in entrusting you with this."

My back straightened. I clasped my hands in front of me to keep from fidgeting with them like I used to. She'd always had a sharp tongue and that hadn't changed with half of it carved out.

"You made no mistake, my Queen." I dipped my chin. "I will conquer your daughter. Then I will conquer the realm."

10

VARIALLA:
MOTHER ME

I regret nothing. Or, at least, that was what I told myself as two surly guards led me from the palace. They gave me derisive glances like they knew what I'd let Loch do to me the other night. They probably did. Or maybe that was guilt making me see things that weren't there. What happened between Loch and I, had been a means to an end. I didn't regret it. Equally, I didn't need to enjoy it as much as I had.

I swallowed a curse. The letter to Lucinda had gone out the following morning and that was what mattered. Now all I had to do was wait until the raven returned.

We swam along winding paths of pearl that cut through the mountains of coral, and headed for the top of the Coral Court dome. Here, the seashell homes crumbled. The stone stalls that had once sold goods were abandoned. The forests of algae, now wilted. We drifted through the remains of what once must have been a vibrant court. Now centuries of neglect had left it to rot.

Eventually we reached the ward; a large circular building forged from shimmering opal shells. A guard shoved open the rusty door and I stepped inside.

The reek of week's old fish, rotten eggs and fetid sea kelp, didn't bother me like it used to. I left the guards at the door and maneuvered around the patients' sand-packed beds until I spied Sienna. Like the others, she sipped on a weak tonic that was sprinkled with flecks of power from the Conduit. It wasn't much. Just enough to keep them alive. Supposedly, Loch's alliance with the enemy would lead to more salves and tonics being sent down but no one knew when. That was how the Court kept Loch on a leash. They needed him and he needed them.

My chest tightened the closer I got to Sienna. Even aged and unwell, she looked so much like her daughter—a grown up version of Cherise that no one would ever see.

When she saw me coming, a smile curved her cracking lips and her pale eyes brightened. Some color had returned to her once umber brown skin that was now ashen like dried soil and she sat taller than usual. However, her large peach tail still lay heavy and motionless. Her silver-streaked hair was knotted and patchy.

"Daughter," she rasped.

As always, the term of endearment warmed my heart and broke it in the same breath. Sienna called me "daughter" because Cherise had called me "sister". Apparently, she'd told her mother all about me and shown her the dances I'd taught her. From Beyonce's Single Ladies routine, to the wonders of twerking.

"How are you feeling?" I scooped up the enchanted pitcher from the log by her bed, and poured her a thimble-sized cup of fresh water.

Sienna accepted it and somehow managed to savor the cool liquid, one tiny sip at a time. Until the Royal Court actually delivered on their promise of supplies, many things still had to be rationed.

"I'm awake in the middle of the afternoon," she said with a throaty laugh. "That's a miracle."

It was. When I'd first visited Sienna after what had happened—what I'd done—to Cherise, she'd been unconscious. She'd stayed that way for nearly a fortnight.

When her eyes had finally opened, Sienna looked up at me and whispered, "Is it true?"

Those three words had shattered me. All I'd managed was a nod and a broken, "yes." Cherise was dead.

We'd both fallen apart after that and cried in each other's arms. I'd repeated how sorry I was. Sienna had held me close and told me I had nothing to be sorry for. She'd said I'd given her daughter a quick death where those monsters would have made her suffer. From the second Cherise had been captured there'd been no way out for her. Her death at my hand and her command had been the kindest she could have asked for.

I was pulled back to the present when bony fingers latched around mine.

"Are you well?"

I swallowed. The feel of Cherise's blood on my hands, of Loch's tongue between my legs and the way I'd responded, echoed through my mind.

My smile was tight. "I am now."

Sienna must have seen the remnants of sorrow in my eyes. She whispered, "Don't let him break you."

Unlike most, Sienna had believed me when I told her of Loch's betrayal And everything that had gone wrong as a result of it.

She squeezed again. "We are never set a challenge we cannot conquer, so long as we have the guts to face it."

I nodded and drew strength from this withered woman. The Nine Isles would be free. A realm united. I would honor Exekiel's vision and mine. I would fulfill Cherise's and Jia's last request. No more oppression. No barriers. No bullshit.

A wave slammed into the dome. I toppled sideways—my hand ripped from Sienna's. Yelps went up through the ward then countless heads turned in my direction. Their eyes narrowed as if this was my fault. Technically it was. Earthquakes, blackouts and storms had grown more frequent over the last few weeks. All because I had defied the cardinal rule of the Games. The only way out was to win, die or serve the Crown. Yet here I was having done none of those things. Now the Conduit demanded payment.

Apparently, this had happened before when a contestant had refused to play. Back then the islands had almost sunk, until the player was eventually hung for treason. Now the sirens looked like they wanted to hang me.

According to the lies Loch had fed them, I'd refused to return to the Games. I supposedly wanted the realm to suffer because of what happened to Exekiel. My people didn't know that I would gladly return to the Games. What I refused was to do it as Loch's puppet. They didn't know that he chained me up on his visits and tried to force me into his bed so he could claim my mind, body and power. Only those in the palace knew the truth about that situation. Even then I wasn't sure if they knew everything.

"You really must put an end to this," Sienna sighed.

I met her eye, careful to mask my expression in case the guards were watching.

"It won't be much longer."

Her thin brow arched with intrigue but the sparkle in her eyes faded when she noticed something over my shoulder.

I turned and found three guards coming our way.

"It's time to go," announced the brawny female guard in the front.

"I just got here."

"And now you're leaving. You need to get ready."

"For what?"

The guard couldn't hide her smile. "Haven't you heard? Siren blood could hold the cure to the plague. Some of us are being moved to Shifter Springs and that includes you. Now get up."

11

LOCH:
Bitter Beauty

I'd waited centuries to see this. My people welcomed into the Five Isles. Hundreds of us—thousands—traipsed across the border where Knox and an army of inlanders waited to greet us. My people carried what little goods they had from the Coral Court. Some seaweed oil because we preferred its taste when cooking. A few canisters of our finest wine though it paled in comparison to what they would soon drink. And sentimental items that could never be replaced. Things that had belonged to those lost during the Brutal War and after, as a result of it.

Knox and I clasped forearms when I stepped through the wrought iron gates of the Inlands. I'd walked this path a thousand times but it felt different when I was backed by my kin. Pride swelled in my chest as I turned to watch them. Their eyes were wide with wonder. Their gasps audible, even from a distance.

"Dragon Spire is all set up for you," Knox murmured.

Dragon Spire, situated in Shifter Springs, had been home to the dragon shifters and was a kingdom unto itself. It was where we would have moved to centuries ago if it hadn't been for the Shadow Saint.

"Better late than never."

Knox scoffed then cursed when an icy wind blew across the beach.

"If you don't get her back into the Games soon, there won't be a realm to conquer," He hissed through chattering teeth.

I pulled up the collar of my cloak. It was colder than it should be for this time of year. Patches of the ground were slick with ice and the trees had started to wilt like a rot had seeped into the earth.

Knox jerked his chin to where Varialla strode across the bridge, surrounded on all sides by guards. Her back was straight, her chin held high and hands chained. Nile marched beside her in his siren's guard armor. Whatever he said had Varialla's lips pursing but she didn't lash out which was exactly why I'd placed him on her guard. The soldier and Varialla had been friends once. I'd guessed that would make her more agreeable out here. Back on the beach where she'd lost her mate, and I'd taken her as my own.

Knox blew warmth into his hands. "Do you think she'll go along with it?"

"She has no choice. She's bound by my command."

"Is that why she's heavily guarded with manacles at her wrists?"

I tucked my hands into my pockets. They were one of the few things I'd come to appreciate about Inlander clothing.

"A precaution." My gaze followed Varialla.

Her steps were lithe and powerful. Her jaw clenched. When her eyes found mine, they filled with conflicted desire. I didn't conceal my grin.

"After what she let me do to her the other night, I know she'd breaking."

Knox let out a heavy sigh. "I bet she looks great when she comes."

My mind immediately went back to how exquisite Varialla had looked sprawled on my desk and writhing on my tongue. My dick pulsed.

"Careful, Pre-primary; that's my Mate-Sworn you're talking about." There was no threat in my voice.

The truth was the thought of him—of anyone—watching me claim Varialla; watching me fuck her until she screamed my name, had me painfully hard.

Knox clasped my shoulder. "If you can pull this off, you'll be the greatest conqueror of all time."

"I already am."

The Royal Court and Council were so far up their own asses, they couldn't see that they'd invited a snake into their bed. They didn't feel me coil around them; sizing them up, ready to strike.

Half my plan had unfolded without a hitch. My people and I were moving to Dragon Spire with me in a position of power. All I needed to do now was announce Varialla's shocking return and reinstate her in the Games. That could only happen when the bind between us was consummated and that endless power that simmered beneath her skin was mine.

The guards led her to a carriage pulled by four Pegasus and climbed in behind her. I'd wanted Varialla to ride with me so I could seat her on my lap or have her between my thighs, but Knox and I had business to attend to with the Royal Court. Apparently, they'd found a possible lead on Nyla's whereabouts and the stolen files.

Still, I couldn't just let her walk away. I strode towards the carriage and hopped up on the large golden wheel.

My hips were at the perfect height of the window. This meant that when she turned, her mouth met my crotch. Varialla gasped and pulled back.

I chuckled and bent down. My face was inches from hers. "I'll be back in a couple of days."

She raised a brow. "Am I supposed to care?"

"What's the matter, Princess?" My voice whispered across her cheek. "Are you still mad I made you come on my tongue?"

Her hazel eyes widened and she swiveled to face me. The soldiers in the carriage straightened. One tried and failed to smother his snort of laughter.

I trailed a finger down her jaw. When she tried to jerk away, I clutched her chin between my forefinger and thumb and held her in place. Her gaze locked with mine. Her breaths became shallow. I leaned in and felt them beat across my lips. My dick hardened.

I wanted to kiss her. For all that was fucked up and holy, I wanted to kiss her. But every time I'd tried in the past, Varialla had shoved me away. Considering where my mouth had recently been, I didn't understand it, but I couldn't risk her outright rejection in front of my people.

They believed that Varialla was coming around. They believed she would step up and win us the realm. I needed to maintain that illusion.

I brushed my lips across hers. As usual, I felt her stiffen—though not as much.

I didn't pull back as I said, "I loved the feel of you fucking my mouth, princess."

Varialla quivered and for a brief second, her lashes fluttered closed.

"I can still taste you."

I kissed the corner of her mouth; savored the salted sweet fragrance of her skin. Then I leapt down from the wheel and returned to Knox.

He eyed me as I adjusted the waistband of my trousers. These things made it fucking difficult to walk with a hard-on.

Knox smirked. "Something tells me your eyes aren't the only thing blue right now."

I smoothed down my coat. "Not for long."

Soon I would be balls deep inside my Mate-Sworn. I'd give her a couple of days to settle in at Dragon Spire, then I would claim her in every way. Whether she liked it or not, Varialla would break.

12

VARIALLA:
JOURNEY TO DRAGON SPIRE

We rode hard and fast through the streets of Shifter Springs. I got the impression they were afraid we would be ambushed; like not everyone was happy we were here. Not that I blamed them.

The carriage I shared with three guards bounced over the pebbled roads. It was too dark to get a good look out the windows but I spied some huts, trees and a small marketplace. We didn't slow until we rolled through the wrought iron gates of Dragon Spire. A guard elbowed me in the side. Another wrenched open the door.

"Move."

I was half shoved, half dragged out of the carriage and marched towards the most stunning castle I'd ever seen. This was where the dragon shifters had lived. It had stood empty since the last of them had fallen. Since we, the sirens, had killed them or coerced them to kill each other.

It was bittersweet to walk these grounds. The same paths my father had walked. It had taken longer than Loch had wanted but finally he had claimed the dragon shifters' home.

I tipped my head back to take it all in. Dragon Spire was massive with outdoor walkways, an impressive keep and stone bridges that connected one building to another. The whole structure was easily the size of a small village. It had concrete pillars, arched glassless windows and steepled spires that resembled a crown. Statues of dragons prepared to take flight from the rooftops and turrets. Some hunkered down as if keeping watch.

A guard tugged on the chain around my wrists and I was forced to climb the steps.

"Keep up."

They marched me through enormous passageways with high ceilings and tapestries on the walls. In places there were deep grooves in the ground which suggested the shifters had roamed these halls in their dragon forms. Candle chandeliers hung down. An image filled my mind of dragons breathing fire onto them to light the flames. Wooden beams crisscrossed overhead and great stone pillars lined the halls.

I made it halfway down the corridor before a large tapestry stretched across the furthest wall caught my eye. In a trance-like state, I moved towards it. There was a crackle in the air here—a presence of something familiar and known in the core of who I was.

The tapestry was a depiction of five people backed by five fierce dragons. They each had the same almond-brown skin. The youngest was a girl with thick afro curls. Her head was thrown back in laughter as she banged on a drum. Beside her, was an older boy who looked to be in his late-teens. He leaned against his dragon and read from a scroll; a quill in hand. An older couple stood beside him. Their fingers interlaced. Their smiles warm.

It was the fifth figure that held my attention. He looked like the oldest of the three children and had deep hazel eyes. My eyes. He was the only one not posed before a dragon. Instead, he was perched on the back of one. His dark jaw-length curls were tussled like he'd just finished a flight. He had one foot propped up on the dragon's back and his other leg hung over its side. His elbow rested on his knee and flames danced from the palm of his hand.

A knot of emotion tightened in my throat. The sheer size of this tapestry marked these people as important; as royal. This was my family. My aunt, uncles, my grandparents and my father. I let out a breath and blinked back the burn of unshed tears. According to the little I knew about the man, he'd promised to be with my mother and help free the sirens but when the time came, he abandoned her and chose another. I didn't know if he'd known about me at the time. If he had, would things have been different today?

I didn't realize I'd stopped walking until the chains were yanked on again. With a sigh, I followed the guards down the corridor and into a large room.

My heart leapt when I spotted Aquarius and two other guards already inside. Our eyes locked for a second before we both looked away. I hadn't seen him in a while. A few days ago, Loch had sent a small contingent of soldiers ahead to prepare the castle and eliminate any threats. Aquarius had been one of them. Hopefully, he'd found something. A secret passageway or trapdoor we could use to get out of here before Loch returned from the Eternal City.

Now that we'd made it across the barrier, we didn't need to wait for Lucinda's reply. I could find my way to Wiccan's Wharf. The High Priestess knew me and believed I was integral in ending the war. I had to believe she would let me stay whilst we came up with a plan to get me back into the Games.

Aquarius greeted the others with handshakes and slaps on the back. They were genuinely happy to see him. He'd slotted into his role as guard seamlessly.

Finally, he turned and stalked towards me. A set of keys twirled on the end of his finger.

"Wrists."

I glared at him like I would any of the other guards and held up my manacled hands.

Aquarius gruffly gripped the chain and yanked it towards him. His fingers fumbled with the lock. I caught a flash of parchment. I didn't dare look. With my face a mask of disgust, my fingers curled around the small scroll he slid into my hand The lock clicked open.

Aquarius pulled away the cuffs.

"Misbehave tonight, I dare you." He sneered. "Just give me a reason."

They all laughed and left the room without a backwards glance.

When I was finally alone, I leaned against the door and unrolled out the scroll.

My chest tightened when I saw Lucinda's handwriting and read:

It's about bloody time.

I knew you were alive. I'd followed the scent of your blood from the sands of the beach into the sea as far as I could go. We have a lot to catch up on.

Meet me at the place I made my first friend. Come after dark on any Qhithday you can. I'll be there.

Postscriptum: Maximus says hi. He lost level nine of the Games and is currently working as a stable hand in the palace. It's not his favorite thing, however he gets to ride the Pegasus and the stable boy so it's not all bad.

I let out a splutter of laughter, surprised when teardrops smudged the ink. I'd thought I'd cried all the tears I had left. I held the parchment to my chest and inhaled the faintest whiff of my friend.

She'd said to meet on a Qhithday which I'd learnt was *Qhithalas* day. Each Fate had their own. Six Fates; six days. Today was Ule-day for the Fate *Ulius* and in two days, it would be Qhithday.

13

VARIALLA:
The Past Before Me

My feet wore grooves into the red carpet as I paced back and forth. Aquarius should have been here by now. We needed to move. Loch was on his way back from the Eternal City and tonight, he'd requested me for dinner. Not to join him, but to be his meal. The guard who'd delivered that message had thought he was hilarious.

"The King says he's going to be eating you tonight," he'd announced with a bawdy cackle. "You might want to put some whipped cream on it."

That had had the other bastards around him howling and making lewd gestures.

I glanced at the sundial that rested on the desk near the latticed windows. It still amazed me that I'd learnt to read it. According to the shadow, it was close to sunset.

Come on, Aquarius.

My door swung open. Aquarius rushed in.

"You're late."

"Then we better move fast."

When Aquarius had volunteered to come up here ahead of everyone else, he'd not only found a secret passageway, he'd also arranged for me to stay in the perfect rooms to use it. My father's rooms. Loch had loved the irony but he'd missed the fact that my father had apparently been a master at sneaking out. Out of his siblings, he'd been the rebel which would explain how he'd ended up in a relationship with my mother—a threat from across the border.

Aquarius raced across the seating area and down the gothic-arched corridor that led to the bedroom. I rushed after him. A massive bed with a wrought-iron frame took up most of the space. The headboard which was the top half of a dragon with its wings splayed and arcing over the bed as if about to lunge out, still took my breath away.

I expected him to lift up one of the tapestries on the wall or heft up one of the weighted rugs on the floor to reveal a trapdoor I'd somehow missed. Instead, he stalked towards the armoire and pulled open the doors. All I saw were moth-eaten royal robes and tunics that hung on a rail.

Aquarius pressed his hand to the mirror that was on the inside of the door. His hand went through the glass. His arm disappeared down to the elbow. My mouth dropped open.

"What the heck?"

"Your father may have been a backstabbing bastard but he was also a genius."

I didn't know what to say to that so I said nothing. Aquarius stepped inside the mirror. Fully inside it. Despite all the things I'd seen in this realm there was still something fascinating about half his body hanging outside of the mirror. I peeked around the door just to be sure his legs weren't sticking out the other side.

When his entire body vanished, I watched his silhouette turn towards me. Then it faded until I was once again staring at my reflection.

"Come on," Aquarius' muffled voice came through from the other side.

I exhaled quickly then stepped into the mirror.

The air was bitingly cold. The only warmth came from a flaming torch Aquarius must have taken from the hook on the wall.

"Stay close," he whispered, then paced ahead.

We were in a narrow passageway with low ceilings and damp stone walls. Patches were furred with moss. The ground was uneven; churned earth and craggy stones.

It wasn't long before shouts started and bells tolled. They knew I was gone. The sirens sent to dress me had found my rooms empty and sounded the alarm. I couldn't make out whatever Aquarius grumbled ahead of me, but he took my hand and we ran.

Our firelight flickered and jumped as we raced down the passage, skidded around corners and ducked under low beams. This place was enormous. A fricking maze. The fact that Aquarius had memorized the path and seemed to have some idea of where we were headed gave me a newfound respect for the siren.

"You should know, the way out is in—" Aquarius' stilled then he whirled around and slammed me against the wall. His hand crushed over my mouth. He dropped the torch on the ground and stamped it out. I'd heard it at the same time he had. The pound of footsteps. We weren't the only ones in this passage.

Aquarius leaned in; his breath brushed over the tip of my ear.

"Don't let go," he whispered.

In confirmation, I squeezed his fingers and let him lead. We turned and barreled blindly through the now pitch-black passage. The sound of soldiers' feet thundered closer. I was convinced we were headed right for them.

"She couldn't have gotten far!" Someone shouted.

"We barred the exits. Even if she makes it out of the castle, she won't make it off the grounds."

My heart ratcheted in my chest. We only had one shot at this. Of finding Lucinda and getting back into the Games. I'd learnt all I could from Loch and gone as far as I was willing to go. Now I had to run.

A swarm of soldiers were suddenly on us. We flung ourselves against the wall. Our backs pressed to it, like we could disappear inside it. We were fucking surrounded. Scents of sea salt, sweat and brine filled my nostrils. It was impossible to tell how many of them there were but it sounded like hundreds. I just hoped their scents masked our own.

A few of the guards carried torches. I'd never wanted to be invisible more. I might have been able to coerce some of them into believing they couldn't see me, but not all of them.

My pulse pounded in my throat. Beside me, Aquarius fumbled like he looking for something. I heard the faintest click. When the sounds of the guards finally thudded away, he shoved open a hidden door in the wall. We tumbled into a room. Pale moonlight shafted across the dusty space. Cobwebs clung to my hair as I stepped down onto cool concrete.

We were in a baby's room. White lace curtains hung over latticed windows. Some stained with the image of a sun setting over the sea and a dragon flying overhead. It seemed to be a theme. Tattered tapestries of dragons in flight and sprawling oceans were hung around the circular chamber. A pastel yellow dresser was off to one side with a small stuffed dragon perched on its top. In the center of the room, bathed in silver moonlight, was a white stone cot. It looked like a carriage with large spoke wheels and an adorned golden edge.

I moved towards it, vaguely registering the shift from cold concrete to a fluffy rug beneath my feet. I didn't know why I hesitated before I peered into the cot. Time froze. Commotion echoed in the hallways and footsteps pounded past the door but I couldn't bring my own to move. There was a name engraved on the soft white blanket: Varialla Zairenyth. It was the name Goather had called me during the jousting tournament. It was my father's family name.

My fingers curled around the bars of the cot, like if I let go, I might fall. I thought Aquarius said something but I didn't hear what. There was a ringing in my ears that drowned out every other sound.

A small velvet box rested on the snowy silk pillow with a piece of paper beside it. I squinted and read: *For our daughter.*

With trembling hands, I picked up the box and flipped open the lid. A stunning silver locket lay inside the box. It was cut into the shape of a clamshell and carved into its surface was a dragon. Its sapphire encrusted wings were splayed and its diamond-studded tail drooped over the edge of the shell. It was breathtaking.

I braced myself before I flicked the clasp and the locket opened. Two faces stared out at me. One I'd only seen in memories stored in the mark on my skin. The other, I'd seen in tapestries in this very palace. My mother and father. The black and white photos weren't portraits, they were pictures of them together. In one they laughed. My father's arm was slung around my mother's shoulders and their heads were thrown back. In the other, my mother smiled at the camera, but my father was looking at her. Engraved around the edge of the locket, were the words:

To our darling, draconice.

A part of me innately knew the word; little dragon.

I let out a weighted breath. Lately, there were very few things that affected me. I got by on determination, rage and pent-up hatred. Everything within me revolved around making those who'd hurt the ones I love, suffer. However, what I felt now was a mix of sorrow, confusion and things I couldn't name.

This locket was another link to a life I'd been deprived of and one I may never understand. This room was proof that my father had known about me. More than that, he'd wanted me. So, what had happened that led him to betray my mother? How had things gone so horribly wrong?

A hand lightly touched my arm. I jumped and looked to where Aquarius waited. His eyes said everything. We had to move. We had to run.

"Put it on," I whispered.

A muscle feathered in Aquarius' jaw. He wanted to tell me we didn't have time for this. Instead, he took the necklace from my hand and I lifted my braid to give him access to my neck. Once the clasp was fastened, I nodded.

"Let's go."

Aquarius ran for the window. I followed. From what I'd been told, the windows had been warded against entry and exit, but not those that were hidden for this purpose.

Aquarius flicked the lock and yanked on the handle. The window swung outwards.

"Shit," he cursed, and grabbed it before it could slam into the wall and catch a guard's attention.

We weren't high up. Most of Dragon Spire was on one-level. It was a small jump down to the ground but the number of guards that patrolled would be hard to avoid.

"Find her!" Loch's booming voice sounded across the grounds.

My stomach lurched. I swung my legs over the window ledge and leapt down, landing in a crouch.

A hand fisted in my hair and wrenched me up.

"Look who it is," a sinister voice hissed.

I tried to turn but the guard pinned my back to him and had a blade pressed to my side.

He chuckled gruffly then shouted, "Found her!"

14

VARIALLA:
POWER & PAIN

The last word had barely left the guard's mouth when I curled my hand into a fist. I didn't have a plan but I pulled on my magic. My magic pulled on him. Without direction, it latched onto the tendrils of water in his flesh and drew them out.

The guard grunted. "What have you done?"

He shoved me away and stumbled back. I swiveled. His brown eyes were wide. The corners of his lips started to peel. Thin cracks scored across his face.

What the fuck? From what I knew, a few powerful sirens could manipulate the flow of water. I'd realized I was one of them the night Loch had cornered me in my bath chamber. I'd briefly created a water dagger until he'd launched himself at me and my thoughts had scattered. However, I'd never heard of anyone who could manipulate the water inside a living thing.

Before I could stop it, some innate melody hummed between my lips. Power percolated in my veins and the water within the guard was sucked through his pores. He looked like he was sweating. A lot.

It happened fast. Seconds that felt like hours. From a crack down his face to powder puffing from between his lips. The guard collapsed in a husk to the ground. Dried skin particles plumed around him on impact.

My stomach lurched. *Holy shit.*

Aquarius gaped from the body to me. "I'm glad you're on my side."

I opened and closed my mouth. We didn't have time to process what I'd just done or how. A blur of guards hurtled after us. We ran.

Since there was no longer any need to hide, we pelted from the footpath and out into the open. It was faster than trying to scale the towering walls like we'd planned and was a straight shot to the gate.

Guards charged us. I tunneled deeper into the chasm of power inside me. It felt like something intrinsic had shifted. Like I'd widened a crack into a gaping hole that magic poured out of and flooded my system.

A song spilled from my lips. It locked around the limbs of the guards and froze them in place like I'd done during the Games. Aquarius whooped.

We skidded across the courtyard towards the large iron gates. They were bolted shut. Beyond them, the portcullis had been lowered and the drawbridge lifted. There was no way out.

More soldiers surged around the side of the castle. Sirens sang their own song to combat mine. Shifters burst into beast form. Snakes slithered across the concrete and over the fountain. Wolves howled and lunged over the dead. High ranking warlocks created portals which brought them closer to us, each time. Autumn elves tore down trees and rolled them into our path.

Fuck, fuck, fuck.

We lunged. We dove. We blocked. The entire time a song crooned from my lips and I held on to every visceral note.

Finally, I shouted, "We need a plan."

My wings itched to be free but I'd never actually used them to fly, and I wouldn't leave Aquarius down here to face this on his own.

"The carriages!" He veered to where they were parked near the gates.

I swiveled back to the castle and altered the pitch of my song. The windows tremored then shattered. Shards of glass sprayed across the grounds and slammed into soldiers' backs. They went down hard. Blood stained the concrete but it wasn't enough. More kept coming.

I glanced over my shoulder to where Aquarius was untying a Pegasus. It wouldn't do us any good unless we got through those gates.

The metal groaned. My head whipped in the gates' direction as they began to open. A handful of goblins heaved on the lever to raise the portcullis. Colette stood beside them, cranking open the gate.

My heart stopped. Colette hadn't said a word to me since she'd discovered what I'd done. How I'd killed our own kind to save our enemy. There were so many times, I'd wanted to talk to her, to explain, but Loch never let us get close. Colette never seemed to care.

Aquarius had insisted that she did. Apparently, she'd beaten Orla bloody when she'd found out that Orla had been the one who stabbed me. Apparently, she'd visited me every day whilst I'd been passed out in the ward.

Now our eyes met. Colette nodded. Loch would never forgive her for this. She'd turned her back on him, on her people, and chosen me.

Pain ripped through my shoulder as an arrow tore through the flesh. I searched the guards but couldn't tell who'd fired or if they planned to shoot again.

"Varialla!"

I spun to the right. My gaze collided with Loch. He was halfway across the grounds. Pure hatred simmered in his eyes. His body was frozen, mid-stride, but his mouth could move and his limbs shuddered as he fought to break through the hold. My power hadn't affected him like the others. Another bitter crux of the bind.

"I won't let you get away from me!" His blue eyes blazed. "You're mine."

I blew the fucker a kiss on my middle finger.

The sound of hoofbeats approached. I turned and caught Aquarius's outstretched hand as he galloped past and heaved me up onto the animal's back with him. I cradled my arm and adjusted my seat as we careered through the gate and across the still lowering drawbridge.

The soldiers pursued. I breathed through the pain in my shoulder and tried to refocus my power as more of the soldiers thawed. Another arrow punched through my back. My body bowed. I toppled sideways; headed straight for the moat. My hand scrabbled at air. I was going down.

Someone caught my wrist. Their fingers were calloused and grip unyielding.

"You're a fucking fool." Loch wrenched me up onto the bridge. He savored the sound of my shout as he flung me down.

My gaze searched for a way out. Aquarius attempted to spin the Pegasus around and return for me but the creature had already taken a flying leap off the edge of the drawbridge that wasn't fully down.

Before I could try to stand and go after him, Loch was over me. He fisted my hair in his hand and pulled. The arrow in my shoulder burrowed deeper and snapped. My vision swayed.

"Nothing will keep me from this path, Varialla. The things I have sacrificed. The things I have *done*!" His wine-soaked breath beat across my face. His nails cut into my scalp. "For this, I will destroy everything and everyone you love. I will make you watch as they die screaming. Until all you have left is me."

"The one who'll die screaming, is you."

My eyes slammed shut and I unleashed my wings. They surged from my spine; a deep red rimmed in teal. Loch jerked back. I swallowed the nausea that roiled with the pain and shoved the bastard off of me. Breathless, I pushed to my feet.

The drawbridge was fully down now. Aquarius galloped back across it. I raced for him. Half in flight and half on foot. The unfamiliar weight of my wings after so long made me unsteady. It didn't help that every beat of them aggravated the arrow wounds.

"Stop!"

Loch's shout rallied through me. My muscles tightened, eager to honor his command—his sirens song. But I was a siren too and I was stronger.

Aquarius was close. He stretched out a hand. I strained to reach him.

A burst of blood rained over me. I gaped; horrorstruck. An arrow now protruded from between the Pegasus' eyes.

My stomach lurched. The animal went down. Aquarius was thrown off its back into the moat.

Overhead, the sky rumbled. Every gaze snapped up. Then shadows descended. Shadows I recognized like the cords of my favorite song. The air shifted behind me. A familiar energy prickled up my spine.

"Hello, little bud."

The hairs on the back of my neck rose. My entire body went still.

"I've found you, at last."

The words parroted what he'd first said to me; his voice was deep and raspy. It was him...and yet...it couldn't be. Shadows surged over my head. A strong arm shoved me aside as Exekiel—*Exekiel*—charged out in front of me. He took down the countless guards surrounding us with a curl of one finger. The men barely had chance to scream before his shadows erupted and they crumpled to dust.

How was he here?

The impossible figure of the Shadow Saint moved like a lethal wraith. His body was harder than before. Muscles engorged and veins jutted from his forearms where the sleeves of his black tunic were rolled up. His piercing eyes pooled with black. And his wings. *Fuck.* His wings.

My breath caught. They were almost twice the size of what they once were. Their edges were tipped in silver, and the threads of violet that rippled through them, now crackled like bolts of lightning.

Symbols of the Fates lit up on his skin like a beacon as his shadows claimed the world.

It could have been seconds or hours later when Exekiel swiveled to face me. All air was sucked from my lungs. He was more gorgeous than I remembered.

Every step he took pulsed with power. The very air around him hummed with it. His eyes were now a searing red made brighter by his lethal shroud of shadows. Even the pronounced point of his ears seemed threatening.

Shouts raged at his back as he stalked towards me.

"You're too late, Shadow Saint!" Loch roared from the courtyard.

Around him the others tried to pick themselves up off the ground but he stood tall, cloaked in a thin veil of power that he'd siphoned from inside me.

"She's mine. Ask her how she moaned when I had my tongue inside her!"

My heart splintered. Exekiel's jaw tightened.

"Ask her how she begged me to make her come!"

Exekiel's eyes briefly closed but he said nothing as he scooped me into his arms. His scent was so familiar. So *impossible*. Woodsmoke, warm apples and the underlying musk that was purely him—fire and shadow. He held me close then, without a word, shot into the sky.

15

VARIALLA:
A LOT & NOT ENOUGH

We didn't speak. Loch's shouts faded into the distance but the echo of his words lingered between us. Wind howled through my hair. Its cold bit into my blood-soaked dress and stung my cheeks. With a stifled wince, I curled my arm around Exekiel's shoulders and burrowed closer. He was here. How was he here?

Magic spread from his fingertips and warmth seeped into the skin around my arrow wounds as it knitted itself back together. I hadn't heard Exekiel summon the power of Fate *Thesona*, but I felt her healing energy now. I'd thought I'd never feel it again.

"How are you here?" I finally shouted over the cry of the wind.

Exekiel glanced down at me. "Long story."

"Shorten it."

I needed to understand. Was he truly alive or an apparition? Did the children of Fates die differently? Had he died at all? I'd seen his body vanish with the light. I'd watched his barrier disintegrate.

"Not here."

Exekiel veered towards Infinity City.

I squeezed his arm. "We need to go to Elf Bay."

Lucinda had said to meet her at the place she'd made her first friend. She'd once told me that that had been a giant. She'd met the Outlier after a grueling argument with those who envied her in her own coven. She'd gone to sit on a rock in Elf Bay at the border of the barrier to clear her head. She'd chosen that rock because it'd looked like the hat her High Priestess wore. Apparently, the giant girl had wandered over. They'd been friends ever since.

Exekiel changed course. I couldn't relax as we soared over the isles. I was caught between joy and dread that he was here and what it might mean.

Eventually I spotted a rock that looked like a pointed witch's hat. There, sitting atop it, was Lucinda. My heart kicked. Icy tears stung my cheeks. I swatted them away.

My lungs burned with the cold as Exekiel descended. Something flickered above Lucinda's head. When I drew closer, I made out smoky letters that read: **Persistence: 10 points**. Before I could fully make sense of it, the letters vanished.

Exekiel's feet touched the rock. I leapt from his arms and rushed into hers. Lucinda pulled me close; her hand clutched around the back of my neck.

"Took you long enough," she murmured into my mass of curls that had been windswept and tussled during my escape.

A part of me expected that when I turned around, Exekiel would be gone. That I'd wanted to see him so badly, I'd imagined the whole thing. However, when I pulled away from Lucinda, Exekiel was still there. The air around him simmered with power that was emphasized by the shadows that coiled around his wrists and throat.

Lucinda dipped her head. "You found her."

"I told you I would."

I blinked between them. She'd known he was alive.

Lucinda opened her mouth to retort then stiffened. Her head tipped to one side. I heard it just as she did. Shouts and the distinct beat of wings. The clang of chariots.

"You were followed."

Exekiel's thick black wings arced from his back. Their silver tipped edges forked like blades. He was beautiful. Not a man but a god. Scarred bronze skin and corded muscle caged around raw, ruthless power. The veins in his neck were pronounced as he peered up at the sky.

"I'll handle this." He turned to leave but spun back around. His piercing pink eyes hit mine. "I'll find you."

I licked my lips. "You always do."

Lucinda gripped my hand. "Let's go."

I wanted to argue; to stay at Exekiel's side.

"If you're worried about him then you've forgotten how powerful he is." Lucinda tugged me down the side of the rock.

I reluctantly followed. She was right. Exekiel could handle this. I was the one who needed to get away. I was the one Loch wanted.

Together, we slid down the rocks and raced across the sand. We charged through Creature's Copse and down deserted alleyways of Elf Bay until we came to a glass bridge, similar to the one that connected the Outlands to the Inlands. Only it was much shorter. A golden sign hammered into the ground read:

Wiccan's Wharf

Until now, I'd spent most of my time on the Isle of the Eternals. When I wasn't there, I'd flown from one isle to another by Pegasus or chariot. This must have been how the isles connected on land. Through bridges and footpaths.

We raced across the shimmering bridge and into Wiccan's Wharf. Unlike the flashy stores of Infinity City or the laidback beach vibes of Elf Bay, Wiccans Wharf was a land carved from nature. Every home was made from roughhewn stone, enchanted straw or logs.

My feet ached by the time we'd padded down countless gravel streets and arrived at a red stone cottage with a black steepled roof. It was surrounded by tall, billowing red birch trees.

The cold press of wards zipped across my skin as Lucinda pulled open the gate and we stepped into the overgrown garden taken up mostly by red thistle and wild rose bushes.

When we reached the door, Lucinda bit into her lip. She used the blood from the cut to draw a symbol on the aged wood. Most witches of the Red Maiden Coven were bloodwitches and female, hence the name. The first time I'd seen Lucinda use her gift she'd animated a skull in the sand. This was equally as creepy and captivating. Her blood sizzled and popped until the door finally groaned open.

Mt steps faltered at the threshold. A grand staircase lay ahead of me. Beyond it, passageways led through gothic arches and stretched further than I could see. From the outside, the cottage had looked like nothing more than a three or four-bedroomed bungalow. On the inside, it was a manor house carved from twisted trees, smooth stone walls that dripped with vines, and beveled brick flooring.

To my right, in a cozy room with a swinging chair made out of branches, was the most stunning fireplace I'd ever seen. It was huge and had ornate iron rods that crisscrossed around the hearth. In its center a cauldron pot bubbled.

Lucinda grinned at me over her shoulder. "Welcome to the Red Maiden coven."

"Varialla!"

I'd barely taken a step inside when someone slammed into me. The air was knocked from my lungs and I struggled to get it back as I was enveloped in a bear hug and spun around.

"What took you so long to send a bitch a letter?" That voice held my heart in a vice.

"Maximus!"

When he finally set me on my feet, I flung my arms around his lean shoulders and buried my face in his chest. I didn't know whether to laugh, cry, or pass out. After so long of getting by on grief and rage, I was in a state of emotional overload.

I'd known I missed them—needed them. However, over the last few months, the emptiness I'd felt without them had become a companion. A shield. I didn't know how to lower it. How to relinquish that hollow feeling and let these people take up the space they'd once held.

I'd been through hell but hell had become the norm and this, I couldn't trust. It could all be taken away again.

I stumbled out of Maximus' hold and sucked in a breath just as two more figures barreled into the hallway. Calder and Kylin.

My mouth dropped open.

"We each get one night off a week. Qhithday," Maximus explained.

"There she is," Calder boomed.

He all but tackled me with Kylin on his heels. Once again, I was swept up in a flurry of limbs and laughter. By the time they set me down, my mind was spinning. A part of me wanted to cry, but the tears wouldn't come. I was…frozen. Paralyzed. My face must have said as much because Maximus shot me a sympathetic look.

His mouth bunched to one side. "It's a lot, isn't it?"

I half scoffed. "It's…something."

He took my hands in his and squeezed. "You're safe now."

I wanted to believe him but somehow being with them felt more dangerous than in the belly of the beast. Here, there was more to lose.

I mustered up what I hoped was a convincing smile and nodded. "What have I missed?"

Lucinda led me down a narrow passageway. Vines drooped down from the ceiling and odd relics hung from hooks in the walls. Some looked like ancient masks whilst others looked like pieces from a steampunk revival.

Whilst we walked Lucinda filled me in on the state of the Games. She was currently in the top five with Kraxus, Vivienne, Bennet Ridgely who was some asshole in Camal's wolf pack, and, of course, Camal

Silverhound himself. She suspected, as we all did, that the Games were being rigged in his favor.

In Phase Three of the Games, whoever was in the lead at the time of the finale, could dictate where the celebrations would be held. Meaning that if Camal Silverhound, or his buddy Bennet, were in the lead at that time, he could choose a location that would give the Court a clear shot at the people and enhance the force of the weapon.

He would give them the power to create a world where the leaders would never have to answer for their actions. Where they could compel others into corruption, torture, murder; whatever they wanted, without consequence. And the people would be aware of their actions but unable to stop it, to stop themselves. He would hand over the realm to Loch.

We stopped in the entrance of a large room similar to the infirmary in the Game's residence manor. There were at least two dozen beds lined in rows. In each one there was a gaunt figure with pale and clammy skin scored with black lines. The stench of death lingered in the air. The sounds of phlegm rattled in throats, chorused with hacking coughs and wheezing breaths.

A knot tightened in my chest. "Who are they?"

"People who learnt the truth too late."

She nodded to a group of four female elves whose beds had been pushed together. They held hands. Their eyes were puffy and closed.

"They say they know exactly when they were infected. They'd come across a group of guards who'd uncharacteristically shaken their hands and patted them on the shoulder. They'd each felt a sharp pain at the time."

An injection.

I stepped further into the room. Some of the carers wore water bubble masks over their nose and mouths. Others wore gloves. Neither were necessary. The plague wasn't contagious. It was implanted. Although inhaling the scent of sick and diarrhea probably took its toll.

"How come they didn't go to the Council for the antidote?"

"You mean the one that fucks with their minds and makes them puppets of the Court?"

So, they knew.

"The Court created a sickness only to administer an antidote. One that they recommended everyone take—infected or not." Lucinda scoffed. "It didn't take us long to realize that the antidote was the real threat."

I let out a breath of relief. These people were at death's door but if they hadn't taken the antidote, there was hope they could come back from this.

A man coughed so violently his rib snapped. He howled and fell backwards as healers rushed to him. They could slow the deterioration of the sickness but they couldn't stop it. All they could do was prolong his suffering and hope we somehow found a cure before Zorsch claimed him.

I looked at the others in the room. Most of them barely moved. Some groaned and cradled their stomach. Others puked over the edge of their bed or wept and begged for death. They each had distinct black veins running beneath their sallow skin. They wouldn't last much longer.

Anger burned in my chest. This was what the Royal Court wanted; to force their people into submission or death. They were so desperate for a world that they controlled they were willing to sacrifice the very people they were supposed to protect.

"We'll save them." I didn't know if I was speaking more to myself or to the others. "We'll save them all."

16

VARIALLA:
GOBLINS & GAMES

I used a basin of water to send a quick message through the com-shell to Aquarius, telling him where I was. I didn't know if he would receive it or if he'd even survived the fall into the moat. Or if Loch had found him. But I had to hope he was alright and that he was out there looking for me.

I followed Lucinda and Maximus into a small room. It had several eclectic armchairs. A round coffee table in the center was stacked with tea and cakes. Shelves of leatherbound books lined the walls. Between the books were lit jars of herbs and various objects from water weeds to insects, eyeballs—animals' I hoped—and other things I couldn't name.

A stunning woman with night-black skin, grey catlike eyes with long lashes and sharp features lounged in a plush purple seat. Like the first time I'd seen her during the jousting tournament, she wore a blue pointed hat that drooped at the top and had black flowers climbing up one side. She also wore a soft red cape with a collar of thorns around her shoulders. Azalea Frost, High Priestess of the Red Maiden coven.

"Varialla von Hastings. Or should I say, Zairenyth?" She rotated her finger and a golden spoon swirled in her teacup. The drink had a sweet flowery scent that filled the room. Her striking grey eyes lifted to mine. "The true queen returns."

My lips twitched. "Only time will tell."

The whole idea of being queen still baffled me. However, if that was the title that came with winning the Games then that was who I'd become.

The High Priestess waved her spoon at me. "If not you then, who?"

I strode over and sat in the armchair opposite her. Maximus slumped into the other chair and pulled Lucinda onto his lap.

"Your confidence in me, is moving," Lucinda drawled.

Azalea chuckled. "You would make a fine queen, my dear. But it is not your destiny nor do I feel it is what you want."

I eyed Lucinda who shrugged her agreement. She'd been chosen like all of us, to participate in the Games without a choice. She'd always said she aspired for change and a role where she could enforce it but that didn't mean she'd ever wanted to rule.

"Don't get me wrong, I do care about the people. I just don't want to have to take care of them." Lucinda wrinkled her nose and snatched a biscuit from the cake stand.

"That's my girl," Maximus enthused and smacked her thigh.

I snorted. "In that case you're going to have to tell me all you can about the Games and what I'll be expected to do."

I'd missed the last three levels of Phase Two but thanks to the month of mourning, I'd only missed three weeks of Phase Three. However, it was my understanding that my rank was the same as it had been before whilst the others had gone on to accumulate thousands more points.

"First thing you need to know is that Phase Three is different to the others," Lucinda said around a mouthful. "You'll need to be sworn back into the Games and linked to the Conduit. Points can be given at any time for anything."

I thought back to the smoky letters I'd seen above her head earlier. I'd meant to ask her about them later. I guessed that explained it.

I scooped up my own biscuit. "What else?"

"You'll have an orbs-director." She rolled her eyes. "They'll follow you everywhere and record everything to make sure you aren't cheating. They're tricky buggers to get away from but," she gestured around herself and grinned. "Not impossible."

I laughed. "You'll have to teach me your ways."

A fissure of energy crackled down my spine. My gaze went to the window as if drawn to it. A winged figure descended and landed in the gardens. My stomach flipped.

For the last hour, I'd almost convinced myself that I'd imagined him; that he couldn't be here. But there he was. Exekiel V'alin, the Shadow Saint and Prince of Death. He was right there. He was alive.

"Six weeks ago, I was as shocked as you are right now, to find a six-foot-plus literal god of a man waiting beyond my coven's wards. A fallen angel. An omen." The High Priestess shrugged. "A Fate."

I couldn't look away. Exekiel shook snowflakes from his dark tussled hair then tapped on his Five Isles phone. The holo-screen emerged but was angled in a way that I couldn't see who he was talking to. His immense wings trailed behind him as he walked. The silver edges glinted in the moonlight.

"I didn't understand when he died. That wasn't what the Stars had told us," Azalea continued.

The Red Maiden coven had always claimed, that the realm would be won through love and war. *Two mates divided to become two mates united.*

"But we were right. He gave up his title as a True Fate and chose to traverse the River of Resurrection to be at your side just as it was meant to be."

I dragged my stare away from the window. "River of Resurrection?"

"It's said to be an extremely grueling journey for those desperate to return to life. However, none have ever made it out." Her gaze slid back to the window. "Until now."

My tongue stuck to the roof of my mouth when I turned back to the window. Exekiel wasn't there which meant he was inside the house. The pound of my blood seemed to echo the thud of his footsteps as the door to the small tearoom creaked open. Exekiel strode in.

"News?" Maximus barked.

I felt Exekiel's gaze on me but couldn't bring myself to meet it. For three months, I thought he'd died. Now his familiar scent surrounded me. It soaked into my skin. The depths of his shadows threatened to pull me under.

"The Alchemist has found us a way into Residence Manor." Exekiel strode over and rested his hand on the back of my chair. I shivered as if he'd run that hand down my arm. "We go first thing tomorrow."

Maximus thumped the air. "Finally. The goblins have been riding my ass about those plans and not in a good way."

"Is there a good way to ri—"

"Don't finish that question," Lucinda cut her High Priestess off with a snort of laughter. Then she turned back to Exekiel. "And Manticore manor? How did that go?"

It was like they were speaking another language. For so long, my life had revolved around the Coral Court. I'd deliberately pushed this place and these people from my mind. It had been the only way to fully immerse myself in the deception—to give myself to the enemy without falling to pieces.

Now I'd resurfaced. Like coming up from drowning, my lungs ached. My mind spun and I was completely disoriented. I'd been down there believing the fate of the Realm rested squarely on me and the Alliance. However, my friends had been up here making plans of their own. They'd developed systems and strategies to take down our enemies; to get me back and save the realm.

Exekiel clicked his tongue against his teeth. "Another dead end."

Maximus stroked a hand through his dreadlocks. "I suppose that narrows our search down at least."

Lucinda must have read my confusion. She leaned forward and said, "Exekiel's spies reported seeing six large contraptions covered in tarp being delivered to six different locations. Apparently, they're going to be unveiled at the season finale celebrations." She scoffed. "If one of them isn't the weapon then I'm not a bloodwitch."

From there they went on to discuss disappearances in the Outer Isles and poorer sectors of the Inlands. Especially in Evermore—the land Exekiel had given to the outcasts.

Goblins had recently confirmed that those who went missing were being taken as test subjects for the weapon. I suspected there was a story about how they'd found out but I didn't ask. I simply listened and tried to catch up on the last few months of my life that I'd missed. This must have been how undercover agents felt when they returned to their real life; like strangers in their own skin.

I didn't know how much later it was when Exekiel tapped me on my shoulder and said, "Let's go."

17

VARIALLA:
THE RIVER OF RESURRECTION

Exekiel and I flew overhead whilst Kylin and Calder led a group on foot. Until tonight, Exekiel had come and gone as he pleased. He'd been off doing whatever he deemed needed to be done and had occasionally checked in with the coven and rebel recruits. Now that I'd returned, we'd decided to split into two groups with two strongholds in the Isles. It meant there would be more space for the sick to recover and a place for those who were marked as rebels to lay low.

The frigid night air bit into my skin. The snowstorm had picked up. Flurries of white swirled around us and settled on my lashes. I buried my head in Exekiel's chest and savored the sound of his heartbeat. The warmth of his skin.

Eventually, we landed on the steps of Fates Cathedral. Exekiel set me on my feet but didn't let me go. His hands remained on my hips. His powerful body so close to mine.

I took a breath before I stared up at him, afraid that if I blinked, he would disappear. His familiar eyes, like star-kissed cherry blossoms, stared back at me. Dark hair shuddered across his forehead. He was more stunning than I'd remembered. More than I'd built him up in my mind which I hadn't thought possible. I'd told myself that I was remembering him better than he was; that no one could be that perfect, that powerful but I was wrong. My memory hadn't done him justice.

"How are you here? Where have you been all this time?"

A muscle feathered in his sculpted jaw. "Adrift in the River of Resurrection."

I'd known that much from the High Priestess. I stepped back.

"What does that mean? How are you alive? When did you return?"

Are you here to stay? It was that unspoken question that made breathing difficult. What if this was only temporary? What if the Fates had let him return to resolve unfinished business and then he'd be gone again?

Exekiel glanced around the square. "Not here."

My mouth opened and shut. A million responses tangled on my tongue. There was so much I needed to say; needed to understand. But he was right. We were the two most wanted beings in the realm. Standing out here in the open, in the middle of the night with the Siren Army and probably half the Royal Guard out looking for us wasn't the best idea.

Exekiel interlaced our fingers. My hand tingled where our palms met. He tugged me forward and inside the cathedral. The air was deliciously warm; enhanced by the multiple lit candles perched on tall brass candlestick holders. He greeted every Mother as we strode down the grand marble passageways. Cloaked in their red robes, the hooded women dipped their heads and carried on. Like those in the coven, none seemed surprised to see him alive. Some even got on their knees and pressed their heads to the tiles as he passed.

"It must be nice to have every woman bowing at your feet."

His gaze slid to me. There was a glint in those rose depths that said there was only one woman he wanted to see on her knees and it was me. Heat flushed my skin. No matter how conflicted I felt about his return—about everything, my body was perfectly clear.

We rounded a corner into an empty hallway. Exekiel's strides slowed.

"The River of Resurrection exists in the land between life and death. There was no concept of time there but when I returned, I discovered it had been close to two months." His voice was low, rough; each word sounded like an effort.

"I don't know how much of that time I spent fighting off souls that wanted to devour mine. How many days I faced my greatest fears and was forced to relive them on an endless loop."

His wings twitched. Shadows swirled around his fingers. I brushed his arm with mine. There was a haunted look in his eyes that suggested he'd gone somewhere far away. That he was reliving every moment he'd spent in that river.

"Come back to me," I whispered.

Exekiel blinked and stroked his hand across his jaw. "Some days I had to deny the River's Mistress my body when she fueled me with her lust and tried to drag me under. But the Fires of the Fjord were the worst. My wings had shredded. My skin had burned. My lungs had filled with smoke. Only my desperation to return had kept me going so I didn't burn in the Fjord forever."

My chest tightened. The River of Resurrection was so much more than just a river.

"Every minute I spent in that water drained me of my power and my soul. It became a race to save my life or face my true death."

I swallowed thickly. Exekiel had endured weeks of physical, mental and emotional torture. He'd survived what no one else had. He'd chosen to put himself through hell. I hadn't wanted him to die but I hated the fact that he'd suffered to return.

"Why?" The word stuck in my throat. I cleared it and tried again. "Why did you put yourself through that?"

Exekiel threw me a sidelong glance. "I think we both know the answer to that."

He released my hand and headed up a set of stone steps that led to a narrow walkway. It was lined with iron doors carved with symbols of the Fates on one side, and a sheer drop off the other. The path was barely wide enough for Exekiel and I to walk side by side so I walked behind him. His dark wings tipped in silver moved with every step he took. The corded muscles in his back shifted to accommodate their weight, and were visible through the thin fabric of his tunic.

Eventually we reached a door engraved with the hourglass emblem of Zorsch. It was a gothic-style hourglass with a sun on one end and a crescent moon on the other. Inside, instead of sand, it plumed with shadows.

Exekiel rested his hand on the insignia and pushed open the door. Light flooded the narrow walkway. I followed him inside and almost toppled backwards off the ledge when a small figure bounded towards us. She wore a red robe like the other Mothers but her hood was down to reveal brown hair pulled into a messy bun. Her pale skin was flushed pink.

She flung her arms and legs around Exekiel. My brows shot up.

"You return!" the Mother squealed. Her laugh was high-pitched. "You stayed away too long. Too long."

She pulled back and cupped his cheeks. Exekiel laughed. My eyes narrowed. Mothers weren't supposed to touch another or be seen with their hood down. Clearly this one didn't give a crap about the rules.

I didn't know if she felt my glare but her dark eyes drifted to me then instantly widened.

"It's you. You."

Exekiel finally put her down then took her hand in his. My own curled into fists.

"I know who I am." I couldn't keep the bite out of my voice. "Who are you?"

Exekiel's brow lifted. He looked like he was holding back a smile. I turned my glare on him.

"It's her," the woman whispered to no one in particular, then she spun back to Exekiel with that same childlike wonder. "Your love."

My gaze swung from her to him. Exekiel's chuckle was low and slid through me like warm butter.

"Yes," he glanced at me. "It's my love."

"Now my brother smiles." The woman snorted when she laughed.

My brows knitted together. *Brother?*

Exekiel turned to me. "This is Satrialla. My sister."

Vaguely, I recalled what Orla had once told me.

"There's a rumor that one member of his extended family survived. She was the mate of his brother. However, after she witnessed the murder of her child and mate, she apparently lost her mind."

Exekiel watched me closely, like he was waiting to see if I would put the dots together. He'd never told me about Satrialla. However, he had told me about how he'd grown up and about his family. He'd never mentioned what happened to his brother's mate and I hadn't wanted to prod at painful wounds by asking. Now, here she was.

I schooled my expression and swallowed my condolences.

"Nice to meet you," I finally said.

Satrialla blinked at me liked she'd forgotten I was here.

"Nice." She seemed to test the word. "Some things are nice."

Her eyes saddened. Exekiel took an imperceptible step forward like he was anticipating something. Satrialla repeatedly bobbed her head up and down, then settled on the soft red carpet by the fireplace.

"Nice. Nice. Nice." She leaned back against a large silver vase and closed her eyes. A single tear rolled down her cheek.

My heart went out to her.

Exekiel flicked his head. "This way."

I followed him beneath an archway and down a rich marble-stoned corridor. Torches that hung in wall sconces bathed the area in warm amber light.

We turned into a small candlelit room with plush red carpeting and a candle chandelier overhead. Hymns were etched into the two marble pillars at either side of the room. Against the back wall was a stone table covered in white silk and lace. It was lined with red tea candles and held a stunning stone carving of the Fates gathered in prayer. It was a shrine.

Exekiel strode towards it and lit a candle at the ivory feet of *Othio*, Fate of wisdom and clarity.

"I have a question." He blew out the taper and set it down.

"Okay."

He turned to face me and leaned back against a pillar. His arms folded across his chest.

"How did you moan when the Rebel King had his tongue inside you?"

18

VARIALLA:
EXCUSE ME, FAE-BOY?

My stomach pitched. I knew this conversation was coming but not now. Not like this. What could I say? Where could I begin?

"What?" I floundered, desperately trying to buy myself some time.

Exekiel arched a single brow. "What part would you like me to repeat?"

His shadows gathered around him like a hooded cloak. They billowed at his back and occasionally veiled his features. My gut tightened. He was the living embodiment of the Grim Reaper. He was death incarnate.

I almost stepped back; a tendril of fear in my chest. There was something otherworldly about this version of Exekiel. Something deadlier, more terrifying and definitely more powerful. It was like he'd gone to Fatevale and though he'd rejected the title of True Fate, he'd kept everything else that went with it.

Exekiel continued to lean casually against the pilar. As if the very ground didn't quake in his presence. As if his question hadn't emptied my mind.

I'd always planned to tell him the truth. I'd let fear and wanting to have the perfect time to tell him hold me back. Then I'd lost my chance.

"It happened before I hatched." My voice came out steadier than I felt. Exekiel deserved to know. "My mother and Loch performed a Mate-Sworn ceremony that created a bind between us."

"That doesn't answer my question."

Exekiel pushed off from the pillar and prowled towards me. There was something predatory in the way he moved and how intensely he held my gaze.

"How did you moan when the Rebel King had his tongue inside you?"

I physically recoiled from the words and the flash of hurt in his eyes.

"How long did you wait before you climbed into his bed?"

"Excuse me?"

Exekiel let out a humorless puff of laughter. "Again, what part would you like me to repeat?"

His eyes flashed red. Exekiel was more than hurt, he was angry. But with each scathing word, my own anger rose. The bastard glared down at me like he thought I'd be intimidated by his towering height. I glared right back.

"I did what I had to, to get information and save my people."

His jaw clenched. I hated the pain that flashed across his face. I wanted to take the words back but that wouldn't change the truth. We'd been given a second chance. This time we'd start off by being honest with each other.

"Things only went as far as they did because I thought you were gone." My eyes begged him to understand. "All that mattered was getting Loch to trust me."

Exekiel's upper lip curled. "I leave you for three months and—"

"You shouldn't have left me at all!" My voice rose and cracked on the last word. "I was the one who got stabbed and you went in my place. You left me! I thought you'd died!"

"I did!" he barked.

The air crackled between us. I stood taller and met his burning stare. Anger and pain shone in his eyes. His shadows roiled at his back and plumed around his wings like acrid smoke. If I was smarter, I might have tried to defuse the tension. Being in the same room with him felt like being caught in the eye of a storm. Like if I stepped one toe out of line, I would be swept away.

"And I spent every day after fighting my way back to you," he growled. "Maybe I shouldn't have. Maybe you would've preferred to keep playing the Rebel King's whore."

I slapped him. Before I could think, my hand shot out and struck him hard across the face. Exekiel grabbed my wrist. He stepped forward, crowding me until my back hit the cool stone pilar. His searing vermillion eyes glowered down at me. There was so much to say but too much aggression, passion and sorrow blazed between us. I didn't know how to navigate this unforgiving territory.

"Since that day on the beach, my every thought has belonged to you. Every breath consumed with the need to be with you." Exekiel spoke through clenched teeth. "When I closed my eyes, I saw your face. When I strained to listen, I heard your voice. It was you who kept me going, who fueled my determination to survive the Flames of the Fallen, and the Depths of Despair. I crawled through hell to be by your side."

My heart stammered. A part of me wanted to lean in; to close the gap between us. It was like he had his own gravitational pull and I was being sucked into it. Another part of me wanted to stay mad at him. Anger I could trust. Anger staved off the tears, the doubt, the dread, the desire. Anger had helped build the shields around my heart. The thought of taking them down terrified me. Especially when it came to him. I'd suffered the pain of losing him once. I doubted I would survive it a second time.

"But whilst I was clawing through the gorge and bleeding my soul in the River of Resurrection you were parting your thighs for the Fate-stained fucker that murdered my entire family." Exekiel pushed his hand between my legs.

My body tensed. I didn't know how to react; what to think.

"You gave him your body. You gave him this cunt like you forgot it belonged to me."

His words were half-growled like he caged a beast inside him, and it took everything he had, not to let it loose. His finger stroked over my clit. I shivered and clutched his wrist, but I didn't push him off.

"I was in my own hell." My chest heaved as pleasure scored through me. I braced my other hand on his bicep and squeezed. Was I urging him to keep going or begging him to stop? I didn't know. All I knew was that I was mad at him and that I loved him.

"I did what I had to, to protect this realm and you have no right to judge me for it."

His hand pressed harder. Exekiel groaned when he felt the damp spot that had soaked through my panties.

I gritted my teeth. He couldn't just touch me and end our fight. "You have n—"

His mouth crashed into mine and effectively shut me up. Any argument I had was eviscerated. His lips were hungry, demanding. As angry as I was, I gave myself over to them. My heart galloped in my chest. A chorus sang in my soul. Exekiel had kissed me more than a thousand times before but this kiss rewrote the very essence of who I was. It ripped me apart only to piece me back together; whole, renewed and entirely changed.

My fingers curled into the leather of his trench coat. It felt like he was the only thing keeping me upright. His tongue swept over mine. His fingers worked my core. I pressed closer. My legs shook.

Hot pinpricks of pleasure coated my skin as Exekiel teased beneath my underwear. I gasped into his mouth. My grip on his bicep tightened. The smooth bastard slid two fingers inside me. Every cell in my body zeroed in on that point.

Fuck! The sound I made would have been embarrassing if I could've cared about anything other than how good he felt. The way his fingers twisted and flicked and knew exactly what I needed. He worked me into a frenzy with just a few focused thrusts. I flung my arm around his shoulders. Our movements turned jerky and wild.

Exekiel groaned. He grasped the back of my thigh and yanked my leg up around his waist. His hips slammed into mine and rammed me against the pillar.

My vision swam. "Shit."

My nails dug into his shoulders. My knuckles brushed the smooth ridge of his wings. I took each one of his bruising thrusts and gave back just as fiercely. My face scrunched in agonized bliss.

With every thrust of his hips, Exekiel forced his fingers deeper and assaulted my clit.

"I'm coming," I panted; half desperate to stave off my orgasm just to stay suspended in this moment of ecstasy. "I'm coming!" It was a cross between a whimper and a shout.

Holy shit! Nothing had ever felt this good. Exekiel's mouth devoured mine again. We were a collision of tongues and teeth. His fingers pushed deeper. I quaked and screamed into his mouth then erupted all over his hand.

19

VARIALLA:
WORSHIP ME

The world that had been fractured by my orgasm slowly came back into focus. With a shuddering breath, I sagged against Exekiel; my head rested on his chest. This was right. This was home. Despite everything that had been stacked against us, I'd chosen him. He'd chosen me. Whatever our argument was, in the end, we'd always choose each other.

"Oh no, little bud." Exekiel gripped my hair and yanked my head back. He forced me to meet those deep pink eyes. "I'm not finished with you yet."

His tongue plundered my mouth. I responded just as keenly. As if my body wasn't still shaken from the last orgasm, he'd wrung me through.

Exekiel drew me closer. I leaned in. It was like we each feared the other one would disappear. He pawed at my breasts and tugged at the soft fabric of my dress. I fumbled with the ties of his breeches. Our lips never parted. We tore at each other's clothes and stumbled through the small space until we struck the altar. The lit candles flickered and nearly toppled sideways.

When nothing caught fire, I dragged Exekiel against me. We moved into each other. His hard cock pressed into my stomach. I pushed up onto my tiptoes, desperate for our hips to align. Desperate to feel him where I needed him most.

"Get on the dais." The low baritone of his voice rumbled through my skin.

I hesitated. "I can't. Not there."

Exekiel's hand closed around my neck and he dragged his thumb along my bottom lip; curling it down. "Get on the fucking shrine."

Shivers of desire rippled through me. I glanced at the candles, sacred oils and hallowed statues. My heart punched. I should say no. I'd never been particularly religious and this wasn't a church altar or anything, but there were some things you just didn't do.

Exekiel tightened his grip on my throat. He lowered his head until his lips brushed my ear, "Do as you're told."

Heat throbbed between my legs.

"I'm going to fuck you hard. I'm going to restrain you on my cock until every drop of me is inside you. I'm going to worship your beautiful body the way it should be; laid out on a fucking altar." He forced me backwards. The backs of my thighs pressed into the stone. "I won't tell you again."

Before I could remember my morals, I turned and climbed up on the slab of hewn granite. I was careful to avoid crushing the offered flowers and scrawled prayers.

Exekiel patted my backside. "Good girl."

Shit. The way he whispered those two words had me shaking with need. On all fours, I looked at him over my shoulder. "Like this?"

Exekiel grinned. It was a pearly slash of pure sin. "Just like that, little bud. Don't fucking move."

He grasped my hips and yanked me against his rock-hard erection. I choked on a gasp. Even tucked inside his trousers, his cock felt incredible.

"M-maybe we shouldn't," I argued weakly. At least I could tell the Fates I tried. "We're in a place of worship."

Exekiel stroked a hand over my ass. "And I'm about to make you see god."

He moved into me. My toes curled.

"Look what you do to me, little bud. Look how hard I am for you."

My arms shook. The taste of lust lingered in the air and coated my tongue. Exekiel trailed a hand up my spine. His large hand curled around the back of my head. He pushed it down until the side of my face was crushed to the white silk and lace that covered the dais and my ass was up in offering. The earthy scent of flowers and herbs wafted up my nostrils from the now crushed petals and bronze bowls filled with fresh herbs.

"Fuck," Exekiel breathed. "You look so good bent over for me like this. So, fucking sexy." His hands came to my ass and squeezed. "So soft. So, fucking delicious."

As he spoke, Exekiel trailed kisses over my ass cheeks then he drove his tongue between them. I cried out, stunned by the sensation. My eyes slammed closed. It felt incredible. Liquid heat seeped out of me and trickled down my thighs as his tongue prodded my anus. Fuck. I didn't think I'd like this so much.

"Beautiful," Exekiel rasped.

He dragged his tongue down my ass crack and around to my dripping cunt.

I bucked and pushed back into him. "Yes. Please," I begged. I needed him to bring me the ecstasy that only he could. "Please."

Exekiel sucked me into his mouth. Spots burst across my vision. I couldn't catch my breath.

"Please what?" he purred against me.

When I glanced back at him, all I saw was the top of his head and the peaks of his shuddering wings as he continued to taste me.

Words choked in my throat. "P-please," I stammered. "Fuck me. Please fuck me, Exekiel. Fuck me."

He tipped his head to the side and his punishing pink eyes met mine.

"You want me inside you, little bud?"

"Y-yes."

Exekiel straightened. His dark hair mussed and slanted across his brow. His folded wings shuddered at his back. He was so hot. My heart skipped.

He didn't look away as he finished undoing the ties of his trousers and slid them down. His thick cock sprang free. The head was swollen and purpling. He wrapped his large hand around it but most of it still stood exposed and erect.

My core tightened. My mouth watered.

Exekiel stroked his hand up and down his length. "Spread your cheeks for me."

It was an awkward angle, but with my weight distributed on my knees and upper body, I reached back and parted my ass for him. My teeth curled over my bottom lip as I sucked it into my mouth. The promise of what was coming left me breathless.

Exekiel moved closer. I gasped when his cock nudged my anus. He was huge. Terror trickled through me but I didn't argue. I wanted to take whatever he wanted to give.

"Please," I whispered. My voice shook with need.

Exekiel braced one hand on my hip. The other he slid over my ass and circled his thumb around my ass hole. *Holy shit!* I moaned deeply.

"P-please."

Exekiel's solid cock slid down and nudged the slick entrance between my thighs. My inner walls spasmed; seeking him, needing him.

"Anything for my girl, since you asked so nicely." Exekiel drove his thumb into my ass at the same time he thrust his cock between my thighs.

I screamed. Overwhelmed by a visceral bite of pleasure. A heady rush swept over me.

Exekiel impaled me on his powerful cock. His motions were relentless. His hips a piston as they repeatedly struck my ass with a sharp slap that I felt in every cell of my being.

I savored every wild, intoxicating thrust as he ploughed into me like a machine. My arms dropped to my sides and my fingers curled around the edge of the rough stone. I gasped when Exekiel tightly clutched my thighs and dragged me up and down the length of his engorged cock. I couldn't breathe. I was losing my fucking mind.

"That's a good girl," he groaned. "That's it. Fuck."

My breasts rubbed the rough stone beneath the silk. My nipples caught on the latticework of the lace. It slipped beneath me; smooth and cool on my fevered skin.

More than one candle fell. Somewhere, parchments and fabrics went up in flames.

"Don't stop," Exekiel grunted. "Keep fucking me, little bud."

Darkness consumed us as his shadows devoured the fire. They snuffed out the rising flames and left only the candles alight.

Exekiel fucked me harder. His shadows slid over my skin and teased my breasts. A soft caress like the stroke of a feather. My heart ricocheted in my chest and I pushed back into him. A bronze prayer bowl clattered to the ground. Something warm and greasy seeped into my skin and soaked my dress. Perhaps it was the sacred oils. The porcelain bottles fell and rolled from the dais. The sticky remnants coated my hot, sweaty skin.

Shit. Exekiel was fucking me on a shrine with the eyes of the Fates staring down at us. It was wrong and yet I couldn't stop. The thought only turned me on.

"You feel so fucking good," he panted. "The way you move—fuck, beautiful. Yes."

The candle chandelier swung overhead. I heard the groan of its chains and the clink of Exekiel's wings as they rhythmically tapped into its metal. I heard the breathless grunts of my mate behind me. The clap of his skin slapping mine.

My walls clenched around him. "Exekiel! Ah…Exekiel!"

"That's it," he grunted. His nails dug into me. "You're doing so well."

My vision swayed. My hands scrabbled for something, anything to hang onto.

"Exekiel!" I came undone on his pulsating cock.

Exekiel doubled his thrusts. Within seconds, he followed my release with a guttural groan. But he didn't stop. He barely slowed.

As I struggled to bring the world back into focus, my mate flipped me—not onto my back but onto my side. He took hold of one of my legs and rested my ankle on his shoulder. My other leg dangled off the edge of the altar, leaving me splayed for him.

My body sparked when he brought one knee up to rest on the dais.

He whispered, "Brace yourself."

Then his perfect cock rammed back inside me.

20

EXEKIEL:
OVER BRAMBLES AND BUSH

Three months ago, I died. Seven weeks ago, I returned. This was the first time I truly felt alive. The sounds Varialla made breathed air into my lungs. The way her hips undulated prompted my heart to beat. I hunched over and pushed her leg almost up to her ear as I drove my cock deeper. I was so hard, it hurt.

My little bud seemed to choke on her tongue. It hung from her mouth and she panted like an animal. The new angle had turned her cross-eyed. She emitted soft breathy moans and deep soulful cries that pounded through my aching cock.

"Atta girl," I groaned. "That's it. Just like that."

She was a goddess. A fucking goddess. I bowed my head and watched as my cock disappeared inside her.

My balls tightened. "Fuck. Look how well you take me."

With gritted teeth, I slammed into her tight, dripping cunt. Once, twice, three times, until I sent us both soaring over the fucking edge.

I bent and fused my lips to hers. I needed to taste her. Consume her. I only broke the kiss when she seemed to strain for air. Slowly, I drew her up with me.

With a sleepy grin, Varialla rested her head on my chest. I stroked my fingers down her arms. I wanted to stay like this, but in the absence of her screams there was nothing to drown out the chatter of my thoughts.

"Why didn't you tell me?"

Varialla blinked up at me. Her brow slightly creased. She was clearly disoriented from the hours I'd just spent fucking her on the altar of the Fates. I took some measure of satisfaction from that.

"Why didn't you tell me you were bound to Loch Orqanz?"

She sucked in her cheeks. The air in the room that reeked of sex, sweat and sweet oils, immediately shifted.

Varialla had the decency to at least look me in the eye when she said, "I was afraid of how you'd react."

I nodded and pulled back. She cupped my cheeks; holding me still.

"I was going to tell you."

"When?" I bit out. "After I saw the fucker fingering you on the sands where I died?"

Anger quickly chased away the last vestiges of my desire. Images of that night flashed through my mind. I'd seen the conflicted hunger that had shone in Varialla's eyes. Her hands had been cuffed behind her back, as the one male I hated more than anything, had shoved his hand down her pants and felt what was mine. The one male who had taken everything from me and now held a part of her.

"Ask her how she begged me to make her come!"

"Not like that." Varialla gaze burned into mine. "I didn't want you to find out like that."

I pulled my face from her grasp and tucked my cock back inside my trousers.

"The thought of him touching you. Tasting you." I didn't trust the shadows that rippled from my skin. "I don't think you realize what that does to me. What I see every time I close my fucking eyes!"

Varialla licked her lips. Minutes ago, that gesture would have made me hard. Now, all I could think was how that tongue had slid along my enemy's cock.

I needed to get out of here before I said or did something I'd regret.

"I need some air." I turned and strode from the room.

"Exekiel."

I didn't reply. Didn't slow down. I had to keep moving. Had to get out before I fucking exploded.

"Exekiel!" Varialla's footsteps chased after me.

I didn't look back. I pushed open the iron doors that led into the cathedral grounds, then spread my wings and shot into the sky.

*

The night was a cold companion. I wrestled with thoughts of returning to the cathedral; to Varialla, or stewing out here in my rage.

Eventually, Residence Manor came into view and the choice was taken from me. Dawn glimmered on the horizon. The others would arrive soon. I adjusted the angle of my wings and tucked them in slightly then I descended. I'd make things right with Varialla once this was done.

Gravel crunched beneath my boots when I made my way through the trees at the edge of the grounds. It was the point where Creature's Copse connected to the isle. A familiar figure leaned against a tree.

"You're early."

Vivienne turned at the sound of my voice and smiled. "I had the perfect opportunity to sneak out, so. I took it." She stepped over brambles and bush to reach me. "Why do you look like you haven't slept?"

"Maybe because I haven't." I sagged against the nearest tree and crossed one ankle over the other.

Vivienne's blue eyes narrowed. "I heard there was some commotion at Dragon Spire last night. Does that have anything to do with it?"

"Some."

135

She scoffed. "Always so cryptic. Out with it, Bravinore. Tell me you didn't have anything to do with the attack on Dragon Spire."

I dragged a hand along my chin. "I would but I promised I'd never lie to you."

A flicker of emotion passed across her face.

Maybe I shouldn't have said that. It was the same thing I'd said the day I'd ended it between us. Vivienne had told me how she felt about me and how she'd wanted more than just sex. I'd told her it would never happen. When she'd called me harsh for not even trying to soften the blow or give her some scrap of hope, my response had been that I would never lie to her. After, I'd ended it to keep from breaking her heart though we'd both known it had been too late for that.

Vivienne recovered and said, "You found her then?"

I didn't have to ask who she meant. There'd been one thing, one person on my mind since I returned to the Isles. I'd spent weeks searching for her. When it had become clear that Varialla wasn't on land, I'd known exactly where she was; in the one place I couldn't go. Aside from the fact that swimming to the depths of the ocean floor for a prolonged period of time took more air than I had in my lungs, no one truly knew where the Coral Court was after it'd sunk during the land shift.

That hadn't stopped me from trying. I'd scoured every inch I could of that seabed using whatever enchantments the witches could give. Then finally we'd received word that the Coral Court was coming to us. The sirens were moving to Dragon Spire.

I nodded. "I found her."

Vivienne cocked her head. Her dark hair slid across her shoulder. "Is she the reason you haven't slept?" Her nose wrinkled in disgust. Vivienne had accepted my relationship with Varialla but she didn't like it. "Although, if she was the reason, then you wouldn't be here this early."

I sighed. Vivienne had an infuriating way of reading me and dissecting situations.

"Exekiel?" she prodded when I said nothing.

I rolled up the sleeves of my tunic then told her everything. From the bind between Varialla and my greatest enemy to the fact that she hadn't told me. I told her what Varialla had spent the last three months doing, to how my shadows had taken out every soldier in the gardens but hadn't touched him because he'd cloaked himself in her power.

Vivienne listened in rapt awe. Dusk gave way to dawn.

When the story ended, Vivienne shook her head and clicked her tongue against her teeth. It was clear from her expression that her low opinion of Varialla had reached a new depth.

Eventually, she made a frustrated sound in the back of her throat. "She loves you; you know. No one and nothing could stop that siren from loving you." Vivienne scoffed. "I wish she didn't but…She thought you were dead and she made a choice to sacrifice her body to help save her people." Vivienne raised her eyes to the sky. "I can't believe I'm saying this but if Varialla had you, Exekiel. Truly had you. Nothing would tear her away. No ancient magic. No toxic bond. Not even the Fates themselves."

My chest tightened. I'd already known this. But the fact that it was coming from Vivienne meant more than I thought it would.

I sighed when I sensed the presence of someone else. "We've got company."

21

EXEKIEL:
Already Dead

Kraxus stalked towards us. His long, dark hair was pulled into a bun on top of his head and his beard had grown thick since I'd last seem him.

"Who invited the rabbit?"

The shifter bristled. "Bite me, little shadow."

"Don't tempt me." I grinned in a way that was all teeth. "I do like smoked rabbit."

Before he could get in a retort, Vivienne spun to face him. One hand rested on her hip.

"What are you doing here?"

"You didn't think I'd let you come out here on your own, did you?"

I smothered a snort as Vivienne's voice went up an octave like I knew it would.

"Let me?" She stalked towards him and jabbed her finger into his chest. "Let's get something straight. You don't *let* me do anything."

Kraxus held up his hands and took a step back but Vivienne continued to advance. I liked her when she was like this, especially when her rage wasn't aimed at me.

"You know what I mean."

"Do I?" she snapped. "You seem to think I'm some helpless vapid little female who couldn't possibly go into the woods on her own. Besides." She waved a hand in my direction. "I'm not on my own."

Kraxus snickered. "What good is the little shadow?"

"Would you like a demonstration?" Shadows slid from my hands and rolled across the ground. The shifter's muscles flexed. The veins in his neck jumped.

"Put those things away," Vivienne hissed.

"I second that," Ilbryen's voice cut in as the alchemist strode towards us. "We need to get moving. Now."

Like the rest of us, he was dressed in all black. He'd replaced the usual silver stud in his lip with a dark hoop. His close-cropped hair was a deep shade of green. He used his potions to change it so often, I'd almost forgotten what color his natural hair was.

He beckoned us with his head and we followed, staying hidden beneath the cover of the trees. We made our way to the servers' entrance of Residence

Manor. There was a line of chariots parked outside the building. Two were marked with the four-petalled emblem of *De Cinque Istrovos*. In the center they were embossed with an R to mark them as property of the Royal Court. Another held the encircled tree sigil that represented Elf Bay.

Since the Games had entered the final stage, the top five contestants had been moved into the palace and Residence Manor had been closed. No one was supposed to be here. However, according to Ilbryen's source, the Court members kept showing up. They'd lock themselves inside a room and the sounds that followed were never pleasant. I'd wager the place was being used as another testing facility. Today we were going to get a closer look and recover the weapon plans from my old room.

Ilbryen signaled for us to wait as he approached the door. We stayed a few feet behind, mildly concealed behind an iron skip. His dark wings unfurled from the seam of his back. Then he slid a pair of horn-rimmed glasses that he didn't need over his near black eyes.

He grinned when he noticed my raised eyebrow.

"I have to give the ladies what they want." He shrugged.

I shook my head. If that Fae wasn't thinking about chemicals and potions, he was thinking about females.

Lantern light flickered above the door and reflected on Ilbryen's oak-brown skin as he reached up and tapped out an intricate rhythm using only the tips of his fingers. When he was done, he crouched in the bushes near the door.

Within seconds, the wood creaked open. A slim redheaded nymph with bright green eyes, and a large rose growing from both sides of her head stood in the doorway. I immediately recognized her as one of the nymphs who had been put on Varialla's team of stylists.

Ilbryen rose from his crouch. His eyes bright.

The nymph's lips tilted to the side. "Alchemist."

Ilbryen ran his gaze over her.

"Flowers," he purred.

With her codename confirmed, Vivienne, Kraxus and I joined them.

Flowers swallowed when she saw me. "Prince of Death." She seemed to say it more to herself than to any of us. "I knew you were here but…" Her tone was filled with a reverence I'd grown used to. She hurriedly dropped into a low bow.

"That's not necessary."

"But it is."

Because I was the Prince of Death. Now that my father had claimed me as his own and welcomed me into Fatevale, I was officially recognized as his son. Those who knew I'd survived didn't care that I'd turned down his offer and returned to the Realm. In all ways but one, I was a True Fate. My increased power level and silver-edged wings reflected that.

Flowers—though if I remembered correctly her real name was Cyrus—ushered us inside. We entered the manor's kitchen. There was a large stone breakfast bar in the center and pots hung on the walls. Cauldrons boiled on stovetops and the scent of fresh herbs and spices blended with curried meat.

"Your room was warded to alert the Council if anyone tried to breach it. However, I have someone who can get us through." Flowers nodded to the satyr seated on a stool at the breakfast bar nursing a pint of ale.

Shadows coiled around my fists. "Goather."

The satyr smiled but there was no light behind it. He was slimmer than when I'd last seen him, and heavy bags hung beneath his eyes.

"I always knew you were too stubborn to die," he grunted.

I looked from him to Flowers. This didn't feel like a trap but the last time I'd checked the satyr had been firmly in the Rebel Leader's pocket.

He met my murderous stare and shrugged.

"There's only so much one can overlook for the greater good." The satyr drained the last of his drink and wiped the spilled droplets from his orange goatee. "I reached my limit when I was ordered to send a little girl to be hunted in the Games." He slid off the stool and trotted towards the door. "This way."

Goather led us down the familiar corridors of our old Games home until the sound of screams had us ducking into the nearest servant's passage. Female. High-pitched and ringed with terror.

The rest of us exchanged glances but Goather and Cyrus took it all in stride.

The satyr glanced back at us. "If you want to see that poison in action; if you want to know what the poor will become to the rich if Camal or one of his cronies win the Games, now's your chance."

He trotted ahead. The passage was dark except for a single torchlight we passed near the entrance. I tapped into my heightened sight and vaguely made out Goather's silhouette. He stopped and ran his fingers along the stone wall like he was looking for something. There was a faint click and the satyr pulled open a latch. A small brick came away in his hand. Light streaked through the narrow gap. I stepped forward and peered out.

The Dining Hall looked the same as I remembered from the steepled ceiling and towering pillars to the long rectangular tables covered with purple cloth and silver lace. Only now blood stained the fabric. At least three figures lay dead; their bodies broken. A nymph's torso hung awkwardly off a table. Her eyes wide and brown hair matted with blood. Her lower half was nowhere to be seen.

Behind me, Kraxus pressed a hand to his mouth like he was going to be sick. Poor little bunny wasn't made for such gruesome scenes. I turned back to the carnage. The only thing I felt was rage.

Four other beings stood between two tables. Tears streaked their faces. They held hands and whispered words of comfort. Useless, given the circumstance. They were all infected with poison. Visible black lines writhed beneath their skin. Their eyes were sallow and hacking coughs wracked their bodies.

Instead of elves in uniform manning the cooking station, there was a choir of sirens in song. Beside them were four figures of the Court. Council member Gwendoline, Pre-Primary Knox, Count Victus and High-Priestess Delora. I swallowed a curse. Delora was a pinch-faced witch who'd never hid her disdain for the other covens of Wiccan's Wharf. She believed they should each fall under her reign given her superior power rank. She disregarded the fact that there were others of equal or greater power who simply didn't seek to rule. It was no surprise to find her here, aligned with our enemies.

Like the others, she wore silver headphones that were joined by threads of shimmering gold power and linked to a siren.

"Look how they buckle beneath the song." The witch's eyes danced; her smile sharp. "Tore each other apart with a single word."

"Imagine how susceptible they'll be once they face the weapon." Count Victus sneered. "Imagine the fortune we could make in the ring."

Vivienne's hair tickled my cheek as she peered out of the small opening. Her body stiffened. I suspected this was harder on her than all of us. She'd been the only one who'd believed in the unfailing honor of the Court only to discover that they'd created the monsters she despised. For centuries Vivienne had blamed the sirens for the devastation of the realm. Now she knew it was a Court who'd let them in.

Knox lowered his headphones, and stood. "Who next?" His grin was serpentine as his cold stare swept over the prisoners now huddled together. "How about you?" He pointed to a centaur. "Versus you." His bony finger landed on a goblin.

Shadows gathered around my fists. The urge to go out there and drain the life from the Fate-stained fucker's eyes was more than a little tempting.

In a matter of seconds, the centaur had the goblin in headlock. The sound of snapping bone was like the crack of thunder. Vivienne gasped and looked ready to tear down the wall.

My fingers brushed hers. "They're already dead."

I gestured to their wilting forms and broken coughs. The goblin screamed, the centaur roared and the Court members clapped. The centaur ripped the head from the goblin's body. My shadow's rose in response but there was nothing I could do for them now. This demonstration or the poison would kill them within the day.

I nodded to Goather. I'd seen enough. We had to keep moving.

*

With the weapon plans tucked under my arm, I reached for the door to my rooms in the cathedral. My hand froze. *Fates, fuck me.* I knew the voice that came from the other side.

Behind me, Cyrus shifted to peer over my shoulder. "Are we going in?"

Shadows curled around the hand I rested on the stone. The low drone of the voice and the rhythm of the words were unmistakable. It was like the echo of a forgotten dream. I hesitated then finally pressed on the emblem of my father and pushed the door open.

Varialla sat by the fireplace wearing nothing but one of my knitted sweaters as she brushed Satrialla's hair. She hummed a soft tune and there was a faint pulse of her power in the air. It suggested that my sister had had an episode and Varialla had used her song to soothe it.

The second thing I noticed was what had probably caused Satrialla's breakdown. The owner of that familiar voice. His skin was the same shade of golden brown. His eyes were as blue as I remembered. His sandy-brown locks which were longer than when I'd last seen him were tied back from his face. A face I hadn't seen in centuries.

Aquarius smiled. It was so familiar, it hurt. "Hey Ex. Sorry." He held up a placating hand. "I forgot you hate that name."

I did. I had. But now it was one of the greatest things I'd ever heard.

I dragged my hand across my chin as I took another step into the room. "From now on, you don't call me anything else."

The corner of his mouth lifted. "Long time no see."

"Too fucking long brother."

I lunged across the coffee table in the same second, he dove at me. We collided in mid-air; our arms locked around each other as we hit the ground. We rolled and I got him in a headlock just like I used to. Aquarius shoved at my chest.

"Get off," he grunted.

His siren magic slammed into me with the command. My grip slackened. He'd gotten stronger over the decades but not strong enough. My shadows latched around his legs and lassoed him to the ground.

"Males. No matter the cast, they're all the same," snickered a girl with white braids who lounged on the sofa with her legs up on the coffee table. Varialla had brought her to the Inlands once during Phase Two of the Games. Colette; a siren of the Coral Court.

Aquarius squirmed. "Get off you Fate-fucker!" His magic struck like tiny knives that prickled at my skin.

I chuckled. "Just like old times."

Aquarius snorted and finally sagged into the ground; admitting defeat. "Fucking shadows."

22

VARIALLA:
ASSHOLES & APOLOGIES

Time passed in a blur of tears, laughter and warm bowls of stew sent up from the Mothers. Colette, Cyrus and Aquarius were here. It felt like a dream. We sat around the burning fireplace. The unnatural frost outside had turned into yet another snowstorm. This meant the temperature inside the cathedral had dropped to a new low. Hail pelted the stained-glass windows with a steady clink and wind howled through the halls.

Seated on the floor, I leaned back against the sofa with my legs crossed and a hot mug of koko milk clutched in my hands. It was like hot chocolate, only better.

I'd changed out of Exekiel's large knitted sweater. Now I wore black leather leggings with khaki green laces up the side, and a thin green top with three-quarter sleeves. I'd slicked my hair up into a bun but left some of my teal curls to tumble free at the top. The outfit fit surprisingly well considering it was Kylin's and my ass looked great. A fact I'd savored when I'd caught Exekiel staring earlier.

We hadn't spoken much since he'd returned. The arrival of Cyrus and the others had trumped our fight.

My eyes drifted to him now. He sat by the large bay window with a steaming bronze mug in his hand. His elbow rested casually on his propped-up knee. The pale afternoon light that streamed in behind him highlighted the hewn angles of his face, the strong cut of his jaw, the depth of his shadows.

Since he'd returned from Fatevale, Exekiel's dark tussled hair seemed to absorb all light. The points of his ears were more pronounced. His eyes were rose kissed flecks of starlight. Today, he hadn't sealed his wings away. They draped behind him; a weapon and a shield.

His eyes lifted to mine over the rim of his cup. I quickly looked away and returned to the others. Kylin and Calder had joined us. We each shared stories of what had happened during the time we were apart. Aquarius sat beside Exekiel probably sharing stories of his own.

For what felt like the hundredth time, I glanced down at my phone and tapped the translucent surface. When the holo-screen emerged, I swiped my finger over it.

Nothing. No unanswered chat bubbles. No message on Enchnat-a-Gram. No missed communication or Face log.

"I'll be back in a sec."

I got to my feet and pressed the Face-bubble of Lucinda. I resisted the urge to pace as the communication went through. It was at least the fifth time I'd called her today. Once again, the bubble bounced across the screen, unanswered.

I chewed on my bottom lip.

Tonight, a ceremony was being held at the Gamer's Dome. It was a weekly check-in to inform the public of the contestant's progress. Since points could be awarded at any time during Phase Three, it was impossible to know who was in the lead until the Weekly Review. It was also an opportunity for the contestants to answer questions, strengthen alliances and show why they were the best candidate.

The plan was for me to hide behind the tallest oak tree on Pixies Path. There, Lucinda would pick me up on her way from the palace to the Dome. Each contestant had their own royal carriage. These were immediately cleared to bypass security and went straight to the grand purple carpet lined with orbs and journalists. When Lucinda stepped out of her carriage tonight, I would be right behind her. Or, at least that was the plan. If she ever picked up.

I tried Maximus next which also went unanswered. Unease squirmed in my gut. I tried to convince myself that everything was alright but a voice inside screamed that something was wrong. In need of distraction, I headed to the dining table and took in the spread the Mothers had set out for lunch. I scooped up a pastry that looked like a donut-shaped croissant and took a large crumbly bite.

"I don't think I like you being mad at me." The low rumble of Exekiel's voice rippled through me.

My breath caught. He moved like a frigging wraith.

I turned to find him inches away. My heart beat against my rib cage. "Then you should try being less of an asshole."

"I'm not sure I can do that."

I rolled my eyes and stepped around him. I didn't want to fight but, at the same time, what he'd said last night stung. The Rebel King's whore, he'd called me. In those three words Exekiel had diminished every sacrifice I'd made over the last few months. He'd judged me, hurt me then to add insult to injury, he'd left.

Exekiel caught my wrist and pulled me back. He spun me around so we were toe-to-toe.

"But I can say, I'm sorry." The sincerity in his voice stole my breath.

He ran his thumb along my bottom lip and wiped away the sugar from the pastry. I watched, mesmerized, as he sucked it into his mouth. His lashes fanned across his cheeks when his eyes closed. When they reopened, their pink was brighter and cut right through me.

"Can we talk?" Exekiel jerked his head towards the door.

"Okay."

We left the room, headed down the narrow corridor and descended the wide stone steps. At the bottom, we turned to face each other. I said nothing. Last night, I'd wanted to talk and he hadn't wanted to listen. Now it was up to him.

Exekiel raked a hand down his face. "I don't know a better way to say it so I'll start off with, I love you. Maybe you'll never understand how much." A muscle flexed in his jaw. "How the thought of another male touching you, kissing you drove me fucking insane." Shadows slid across his shoulders and outlined the prominence of his wings. "I didn't like it and I didn't handle it well."

Considering how I'd felt when Satrialla had just hugged him, I supposed I could understand. How would I have reacted if the tables were turned? If he'd spent the last three months seducing Vivienne to save the realm?

"I was angry, insensitive and I left." Exekiel took my hand. His thumb trailed over my knuckles. "I'm sorry."

I licked my lips. My mouth was suddenly dry. "I didn't sleep with him." The words were almost a whisper. "And I never let him kiss me."

A medley of emotion flared in Exekiel's eyes. Relief, shock and something astoundingly more profound. The pink gave way to red. His mouth opened but he struggled to find the words. It was possibly the first glimmer of vulnerability I'd ever seen him show. I rested my hand on his chest and felt the pound of his heart beneath my fingers.

"These lips, Exekiel V'alin, are yours," I vowed. "The last lips to touch mine then, now and forever are, were and will be yours."

His Adam's Apple worked over a swallow. Before I could make sense of the sheen in his eyes, his hand came up around the back of my neck. Exekiel's lips found mine. The ground beneath my feet titled. My heart hammered in my chest and heat pooled low in my stomach. Kissing him would never get old. The taste of his tongue merged with the earthy herbs of the tea he'd drunk and the sweetness of my pastry. I lightly sucked his bottom lip into my mouth and he unleashed a low moan that I felt deep in my core.

I forgot where we were. I forgot about battles and games and overthrowing regimes. All I was, all I wanted, was this kiss.

Someone cleared their throat. Exekiel drew me closer. His fingers tangled in my curls. His other arm wrapped around my waist as he lifted me onto my tiptoes. My own arms coiled around his shoulders and my fingers curled in the softness of his dark locks. My pastry was now forgotten and on the floor.

"Do I need to remind you that this is a house of worship?" The brisk tone of Mother Margareet had Exekiel and I leaping apart like children caught sneaking a cookie before dinner.

My cheeks flushed. If she thought this was bad, what would she think if she knew what Exekiel had done to me on the shrine of the Fates?

Before I dropped to my knees and confessed my sins, the Shadow Saint took my hand. He murmured a quick apology to the Mother and led me out into the gardens.

"It's freezing," I squealed.

Thankfully, the hail had stopped but clumps of snow continued to gather on the ground.

Exekiel pulled me towards him. My soft breasts bounced against his chest.

"I'll warm you up." His wings folded around us then his mouth claimed mine again.

23

VARIALLA:
New Player Activated

The carriage bumped along the cobbled streets of Infinity City. I peered out the window and spied the imposing silhouette of the Gamers Dome in the distance. The first night I'd been there, my image and countless other contestants' images had been projected on its black glass surface. Tonight, was no different.

Amidst the floodlights, faces of the Top five remaining players panned across the dome. Vivienne Foraglade. Kraxus V'alin. Camal Silverhound. Bennet Ridgely. Lucinda Ironclaw; but a red circle had been drawn around Lucinda's face. The word: *Disqualified*, flashed in white across her chest.

What the fuck? I'd tried to contact Lucinda and Maximus all day. Neither of them had answered. Now this. Disqualified.

The knot in my gut tightened. My skin grew hot and the threat of fire simmered in my throat. Ever since I'd fled Dragon Spire and felt the shift in my power, the prickle of magic within me had grown more intense. It was like the slightest spark would set it off. I grabbed the handrail and let out a breath.

"Are you alright?" Goather asked from where he sat across from me.

"Fine," I bit out.

When the sensation of rampant power finally settled, I jerked my chin at the dome. "Why was Lucinda disqualified?"

Goather's bushy brow furrowed. "Your guess is as good as mine."

That wasn't encouraging. Goather was the host of the Games. It was his job to know everything. If he didn't it meant we were all intentionally being kept in the dark.

The carriages ahead of us slowed so they could be searched and let passengers out. I slid down in my seat to avoid being seen through the window. My heart beat so hard, I was sure the satyr could hear it. This wasn't how tonight was supposed to go. I was supposed to be in Lucinda's carriage headed straight for the main entrance.

Our carriage didn't slow. It continued to where others were parked around the side of the building. Goather's level of clearance wouldn't get us to the main entrance but it would get us inside the building without being searched.

He glanced down at me. Of all the people I'd imagined helping me with this, it hadn't been him. For centuries Goather had been Loch's faithful spy fighting against the Royal Court. However, like the rest of us, he'd been forced to face the truth. Loch was the worst of them.

"Thanks for doing this."

Since I hadn't been able to find Lucinda, Cyrus had suggested we contact the satyr. I'd been stunned when the others had agreed and more so when Goather had been on board.

"For decades I believed the Rebel King was working to free the Outer Isles and break the barrier. But he'd only been concerned with strengthening his alliances with the enemy. He'd agreed to genocide to secure his reign and turned the people he was supposed to protect, into murderers and collateral damage." A sharp bite filled his tone. "He'd made me an accomplice to that and more. This is the least I can do."

Goather nodded to the large wooden chest placed on the floor between the seats. "It's time."

Staying below the lip of the window, I lifted the heavy lid. The velvet lined chest was supposed to be filled with props and costumes for the nymphs that had been ordered to perform at the ceremony. Instead, only a few dresses and masks covered the bottom. The rest of the space was left empty for me. I pulled the things out as the carriage rolled to a stop.

Goather hissed. "Quickly."

Footsteps approached. I inhaled a large gulp of air then climbed into the chest. Goather rushed to cover me with the few items then clicked the lid shut.

I tempered my breathing. As a siren I could go long stretches of time without much air but I'd never put that length of time to the test.

There was a murmur of voices as the carriage doors squeaked open.

"Someone get the costumes," Goather called.

My stomach dipped when the chest was lifted.

"Fate's gorge," a man bellowed. "What the heck are these nymphs wearing tonight?"

I couldn't make out Goather's reply but I heard his showman's laugh.

My body rocked from side to side as the chest was carried inside the building. I curled my fingers into the velvet and did my best to hold still.

It wasn't long before I was unceremoniously dumped on the ground. My elbow whacked the side. I stifled a yelp as painful tingles shot up my arm. *Fuck.*

Rubbing at the abused flesh, I snuggled into the dresses and made myself comfortable. All I could do now, was wait.

It was over an hour later when the chest finally moved again. The air was starting to thin and I didn't think I had much longer.

The latch clicked open. I went rigid. My hand folded around the hilt of the blade I'd tucked into my boot. When light didn't rush in and the lid remained closed, I let out a breath of relief. This meant I'd been moved into position. Goather said the chest would be placed in the wings, so the nymphs would have easy access to it during their show. If I was here and the latch unlocked, it was almost time for me to make my entrance.

I braced my feet on the base of the lid and pushed until it opened just a crack. The audience were applauding. Vivienne's voice came moments later. She said something about the rise in crime since the barrier fell. She claimed that if she were Primary, she would double the guard and build a border wall.

She wouldn't implement an entrance or exit fee but there would be a record of anyone who crossed the border. It would be noted where they were going and how long they planned to stay.

In some ways, it was no different to being at an airport or the border of any country but for some reason it made my stomach turn. There was no need for a divide of any kind. We were all the same. The sooner we stopped placing imaginary barriers between us, the sooner we could accept that and truly live as one.

Camal Silverhound spoke next. Just the sound of his voice had my hackles rising. He touted some bullshit about the people of Evermore being prisoners of the Five Isles and how he had started to return them to their rightful homes in the Outlands. He spoke as if he was some saint caring for the displaced souls of the Outliers. However, he completely disregarded the fact that they'd spent the last two hundred years building lives here. This was their home now but he didn't care. He wanted them out. He wanted to burn their businesses and leave them destitute again.

The audience didn't see it. They saw a kind heart where there wasn't a heart at all.

Goather bellowed over their applause, "It's going to be hard for anyone to top that."

I didn't know if he'd intentionally given me the perfect cue but I leapt out of the chest and stalked onto the stage.

"I think I can top it."

Camera-orbs swiveled to face me. In seconds, I was surrounded. Their flashes went off like fireworks. People in the audience shrieked. Some cheered. Others simply stared in shock.

I pushed through the orbs and faced the audience. As I did, I let my scarlet wings unfurl from my spine, let my horns crest from the crown of my head. I felt the shift as my eyes slitted to the golden eyes of a dragon. Magic buzzed beneath my skin.

"I am Varialla Zairenyth; heir to Shifter Springs and the Coral Court. I am the last dragonborn and I am here to fight for my claim to the Eternal Throne. As a link between both worlds, it is my dream to unite us as one. To mend what was broken and build a truly free world."

Camera-orbs panned around me.

"Some of you were told that I was dead but the Fates spared me so that I could see this done."

There was a deafening silence; nothing heard beyond the whir of the orbs swirling lenses and their incessant clicks. Then the auditorium filled with applause and riotous booming cheers.

Goather must have left the stage because he now returned. The Conduit was being carried in behind him by four elves. Its pool rippled inside a large bronze basin rested on top of a stone plinth. Its shimmering beam of blue and green flecks of power blazed from the center; bright enough to rival the stage lights.

Beyond its glow I caught sight of four familiar faces; the remaining members of the Gaming Council and the Primary of the Court. Their looks morphed from shock to fury. As suspected, Loch hadn't told them I survived; that he'd been keeping me locked up beneath the sea. They shared hushed whispers. Alexov's fingers curled around the arm of his seat; his knuckles leeched of color. If looks could tear someone to pieces, I'd be a pile of severed limbs.

I smiled sweetly at the bastards and barely resisted the urge to bring up my middle finger.

"I think I speak for everyone when I say, we are happy to have you back," Goather's voice boomed over the auditorium.

The audience cheered. My eyes skimmed over the other contestants. Kraxus' expression was blank but his eyes took in everything. Camal Silverhound and his lackey Bennet Ridgely looked like they wanted to slit my throat. Vivienne's expression was harder to read. Possibly for the first time, she regarded me with something other than contempt. There was the smallest hint of a smile on her lips.

However, when our eyes met, she pointed a perfectly manicured finger at my wings.

"*Overkill*," she mouthed.

I shook my head. Some things never changed. The seat beside her was empty. Lucinda should have been here. Where was she?

Each elf held a long handle of the platform. Once they positioned the Conduit in the center of the stage, Goather gestured for me to step forward. I did. The power of the Conduit hummed in my veins. Its essence was a cool stroke over my skin.

Goather raised a dagger with sapphires along its golden hilt. "It is time for you to be officially sworn in to Phase Three of the Games." He gestured to my hand. "With a single drop of your blood, it begins."

I gave him my hand. Goather used the blade to pierce the tip of my finger. Blood dripped from the wound and into the Conduit. I felt the connection like a current of electricity crackling through my skin.

The words: **New Player**, flashed above my head in smoky black letters. The auditorium erupted with applause.

24

VARIALLA:
GARDEN PARTIES & GORE

The lavish quarters I was given in the palace, made my rooms in Residence Manor seem basic. Beyond a bedroom with a beautiful four-poster bed, and a red stone bath chamber, I had a dressing room, a small study, and a seating area where a fire burned low.

Overhead, a grand candle chandelier hung from a concave ceiling that was adorned with a painting of the Fates. Arched windows framed in oakwood took up one wall and looked out at the expanse of the realm. The sea and Outer Isles shimmered in the distance.

The little I took in was breathtaking but I couldn't appreciate it. My mind bounced back and forth between Lucinda and Maximus's sudden disappearance and the fact that Lucinda was disqualified. Nothing had been mentioned about it during the ceremony earlier but it was safe to say that the Court were involved. Although, how did that include Maximus as well? Maybe something had happened. Maybe they'd been forced to run.

My boot heels tapped across the hardwood floors and smooth rugs as I paced back and forth.

"What did they say the last time you saw them?" asked Kylin, who was done with her palace gardening duties for the day. "Did they give any indication that they might be in trouble?"

I racked my brain and picked apart the conversation I'd had with them in Red Maiden Coven.

I shook my head. "None."

Nothing. There was no clue or hint of where they'd gone. Or why.

A low whistle came from the dressing room. I turned and through the archway entrance, saw Cyrus with her head inside the hand carved armoire. It was packed with clothes. I didn't have to look to know they'd fit perfectly. They'd been tailored by the same seamstress that weaved shifter clothing and enchanted it to morph into their bodies when they transformed.

"Dressing you for this Phase is going to be fun." Cyrus sighed wistfully. "Eudora would have loved this."

My stomach dropped. Eudora would have loved this. According to Cyrus, after I'd supposedly died,

Eudora hadn't been allowed to return to work. She was no longer needed as my stylist and the Council had claimed that her missing leg meant she couldn't help around Residence Manor either.

Cyrus had been kept on as a cook and cleaner but the last she'd heard from Eudora she'd been washing Pegasus-pulled-carriages in the streets. Nymphs weren't permitted to own Five Isles phones, so they'd arranged to have weekly meetings. However, at the last three meetings, Eudora hadn't shown up.

A knock at the door pulled me from the edge of my spiraling thoughts. Before either of us could respond, the door swung open. A centaur trotted into the sitting room with what looked like a game's remote in his hand.

A female satyr walked at his side. She wore a frilly yellow dress and her hooves had been painted bright pink. "Varialla von Hastings." Her black curls bounced around her horns as she dipped her head. "I'm Trixie Mangrove. Allow me to introduce Godric Tor, your orbs-director."

"My what?"

"The one who'll be in charge of following you around," Kylin explained from where she sharpened her swords by the fire.

A cameraman; right. I vaguely remembered Lucinda saying something about that.

"As you know, Phase Three of the Games is about forming political alliances, connecting with the people and revealing your true nature through trials.

This means that a lot of the Games will take place outside of a set location." Trixie gestured to the centaur. "It will be Godric's job to trail you and record the journey."

It was also his job to make sure that I didn't cheat or tamper with the recordings.

"I'll be as inconspicuous as possible," he said with a nod.

For the first time I truly looked at him. He had thick brows, a pointed nose and dark hair pulled into a braid half way down his back. Recognition lingered at the edge of my mind. I'd seen him somewhere before.

"A centaur at my side and a camera constantly in my face. Why would I notice?"

His lips quirked. Then it hit me. I'd seen Godric what felt like a lifetime ago being bullied in Residence Manor. It had been my first morning of the Trials. I'd found members of a wolf pack trying to lasso him and had decided to intervene. Of course, I'd ended up turning their wrath on me, instead, but then Phoebus had shown up. My chest ached at the memory of my friend who'd lost his life during the Blood Battles.

If Godric remembered me from that day, he didn't show it.

"Well, if it makes you feel better, these orbs are smaller and have the ability to become camouflaged."

Godric pressed a button on his remote. A camera-orb about the size of a golf ball floated from the satchel slung over his flank. He turned a knob and the silver casing of the orb slowly began to blend into its surroundings. Eventually it was barely visible and would only be seen by those who knew it was there.

"Phase Three of the Games will require many discrete moments and conversations. Though they'll have to be documented for the journey, we can't constantly have visible camera-orbs announcing where a player is at all times." He puffed out his chest and seemed particularly proud of the orb's ability. "That's where I come in. I make sure everything's above board and record evidence if needed."

"Since you're a late start to Phase Three we'll have to fill you in as you go. Tomorrow will be your first Test." Trixie pointed her finger at me. "However, trust me when I say they'll be assessing for more than what the test claims."

I opened my mouth to ask exactly what else they'd be testing for but she went on.

"We'll let you get settled tonight and Godric will officially start filming first thing tomorrow."

I forced a tight-lipped smile. "Can't wait."

Although there was some truth to that. The sooner I got back into the Games, the sooner I took out the competition and gave the people of the Isles a fighting chance at survival.

Godric and Trixie headed for the door.

"I look forward to working with you," the centaur called over his shoulder. "As the slogan says, real scenarios. Real reactions. Are you fit for the Throne?"

"Yes," I called as the door clicked shut behind him.

*

My first test, the Trial of Combat, wasn't held in the arena like I'd expected. Instead, we were led to the palace grounds where a garden party was being held. Fae, elves, witches, warlocks and shifters sipped on fruity wines and nibbled on tiny pastries. A band of goblins played upbeat music off-to-one side whilst a female centaur sang of sweet sorcery and broken spells. There were picnic blankets and parasols, and satyrs doing ribbon dances.

It was all very civilized except for the battles of blood that took place in the center of the grassy lawn. Those gathered around occasionally clapped. Some cheered and placed bets. I was further surprised when a glass of wine was handed to me. Like I was supposed to drink it and then dive into the fray. Today contestants weren't competing against each other but some of the strongest warriors known in the realm. I couldn't stomach anything right now especially not booze.

A pair of piercing blue eyes burrowed into me from across the lawn. My spine stiffened as I met the gaze of Loch Orqanz, the Rebel fucking King. He sat at the head of a white wooden table, laden with food. Beside him were members of the Court and Council. They laughed and shared stories like old friends, but Loch didn't take his eyes off me. Cold prickled up the back of my neck.

The bastard dipped his head. There was a cruel quirk of his lips that made my stomach turn. It was the type of smirk that practically announced that he knew something I didn't. The kind that made me more convinced than before that he had something to do with Lucinda and Maximus' sudden disappearance.

A part of me wanted to march over there and demand to know what he'd done. Another part of me, the game player, knew that I needed to do this the right way to gain the peoples trust and support. I couldn't lose control and lash out in an emotional tirade. I had to appear to be level headed and in control; like I had my shit together. In this fight for the throne, more battles would be won behind the scenes than in the public eye. Even the Council abided by those rules.

"It is time for the next contestant to demonstrate not only their combat skills but their ingenuity and ability to think on their feet." Goather called from where Kraxus limped out of the center of the audience that encircled him. He seemed pretty banged up but by the looks of it, he'd gained enough points and respect to advance his progress in the Games. In Phase Three, the people's votes were almost as important as rank.

"Varialla von Hastings."

I blinked at the sound of my name. Suddenly I wished I'd taken that wine. With a steadying breath, I pushed back my shoulders and strode towards the ring of spectators.

25

EXEKIEL:
SMELLS LIKE REVOLUTION

If anyone had told me that one day, I'd be in my room at Fates Cathedral, watching orb-vision and gazing at the hologram of some girl, I would have told them they'd lost their fucking mind. I didn't do romance. I didn't get tongue-tied or lose myself in someone's smile. I didn't dream of their eyes and I sure as shit, didn't pine. Until now.

Varialla moved across the holo-screen. I couldn't look away. She was perfect. She dominated her opponent with intelligence as well as skill. She outwitted him, sensed his maneuvers and blocked his attacks. She did it all with a smile that made my dick hard.

My fingers curled around my tumbler of *Volgiskey* and I took a deep swig. Fates, I missed her. The way her nose crinkled when she laughed. The way her eyes

172

shone when she told a joke that wasn't always funny. I missed the way she curled in my arms when she slept; the way her mind challenged mine.

Right now, more than anything, I missed the feel of her body pressed against me; riding me.

Varialla dropped low to kick a Fae's leg out from under him. Her short dress climbed up her thigh and gave me a flash of that sweet cunt scantily covered in white lace. I got to my feet and let out a breath. My cock throbbed. Varialla continued to grapple with her opponent. Her breathy grunts had my mind drifting somewhere else.

I leaned against the wall like that could put some distance between me and her life-size hologram. Fates, fuck me. It had only been three days since I'd seen her. Four nights since I'd ravaged her tight little body on that altar, but my cock ached with the need to be buried inside her. I felt like a starved man being deprived the greatest meal.

She continued to glide across the screen. Her ferocity was captivating. Her lips inviting. The bounce of her breasts, the tilt of her head; all of it had blood rushing to my cock. My hand followed.

An opponent tackled Varialla to the ground. Her skirt ended up around her waist; her legs splayed. My pulse jumped. My fingers fumbled with the ties of my breeches as she sprang to her feet and punched the fucker in the jaw. *Beautiful.*

My hand slid inside my trousers, closed around my cock and squeezed. *Fuck.* My eyes crossed.

Varialla fought hard. I drank in each flash of her leg, every close up on her pulse that fluttered in her neck. Every smile that lit up her eyes in a way that made everything around her cease to exist.

I stroked my cock as I watched her. It hardened in my grip. I didn't look away. I watched her full breasts bounce and her pouty lips pucker. I was reminded of how they felt wrapped around my cock. Lipstick smeared down my length. *Fuck.*

I turned and pressed my forehead to the cool stone. My teeth bit into my bottom lip. Stifling a groan, I pumped my cock hard and fast and thought of my mate.

I saw her on her knees; panting on all fours. Her dark skin dripping with sweat. Her legs open for me. Her cunt glistening. My hips bucked and moved in the opposite direction of my hand.

"Fates," I rasped; on the verge of coming.

My chest heaved with each rough pull of my hand. My cock hardened and fucking throbbed. It needed release.

My mouth fell open; eyes half closed. I couldn't breathe. Head braced on the cold wall; I shoved my fist into my mouth to stifle my rising groans. Pain lanced through my knuckles; but I didn't let up as I fucked my fist and thought of her.

I imagined her scent. The way her pussy had wept and milked my cock. I thought of her begging me to fuck her and parting those pretty ass cheeks for me. I remembered her moans. The way she hiccupped over her breaths and whimpered for my dick. It was the sound of sin and sweet fucking salvation.

"Fuck!" My head kicked back and I came so fucking hard, my shadows rose then shattered across the room.

I didn't know how long passed. Minutes. Seconds. Someone pounded on the door.

"We've received the signal," Calder's voice came from the other side. "We're ready to leave when you are."

I hissed out a breath and uncurled my fingers from around my cock.

Tonight, we would continue to sow seeds of dissent amongst the people and fan the flames of our revolution.

I closed my eyes and blinked away visions of Varialla.

At last, I found my fucking voice enough to rasp, "I'll be right out."

*

My boots crunched across the graveled ground that led to Sable Tree tavern. Through its latticed windows I spied the flicker of candlelight and the silhouettes of the gathered crowd. At this hour most businesses were closed, but Pyrah, the owner, had left the tavern open at my request. There was very little the witch wouldn't do for me.

As far as she was concerned, I was an omen; a symbol of things to come. The son of a Fate who had died and been resurrected. Pyrah was a member of the Red Maiden Coven and believed that I was going to right the wrongs of the Realm one day, with Varialla at my side. She would to do whatever she could to be a part of that.

I slipped through the backdoor to avoid being spotted and sidled over to the bar. Pyrah seemed to appear out of nowhere.

"What'll you be drinking, Prince of Death?" The golden-haired witch bowed low as always.

"How many times do I have to tell you not to do that?" I shrugged off my cloak.

The tavern was warm. Partly due to the candle chandelier that swung from iron chains in the dark wood ceiling. And partly due to the fire that burned in a small fireplace.

"At least a dozen more times." Pyrah waved her finger and a flare of magic plucked the cloak from my hands.

I raised a brow. "Fates forbid I should hang it up myself."

She tutted and pulled out a pint glass that she topped with Faeries-ale. I accepted the drink and made my way to the back wall furthest from the crowd.

There were twice the number of potential recruits here than there was the last time. They whispered to one another and shot fervent glances at Ilbryen and Ryul who stood on the small stage backed by an amber spotlight.

"You're being lied to," Ryul bellowed. "Deep down you know it or you wouldn't be here.

Those who had attended previous meetings nodded their agreement.

"There's so much that hasn't added up over the decades. The anomalies continue to pile up but no one thinks to question it," Ryul went on.

The warlock had become an unofficial spokesman for the revolution. He had a way with words, a command of the people, and the type of smile that invited them to trust him. Ilbryen had the facts and figures. He spoke of formulas and remedies and inconsistent timelines that further proved our point. This war had begun long before any of us had realized. It was time to fight back.

I was that fight. I didn't have facts or invite others to trust me. I was the flame that ignited the torch. I showed the rebels the power that stood with them and reminded them of their own. I was the promise of blood and victory.

"We all saw what that poison did to those beings at the banquet. Supposedly it was the work of Loch Orqanz; the leader of the sea folk." Ryul dragged a hand across his stubbled chin. "But has anyone noticed how similar those symptoms are to the alleged plague that now sweeps through the isles?"

"The main ingredient of the antidote is not to stave off fever, nausea, or any other ailment. It is Travorgal root. Its sole purpose is to stop the spread of poison," Aquarius added. "It's no secret. Anyone who has taken the antidote has confirmed the taste."

"I can confirm it." A pale-skinned elf with dark blue eyes raised her hand. She'd attended our meetings before. Elladire Allard. "I can also confirm that I started feeling sick a week after I bought some fruits and vegetables from the Regal market."

Giants were responsible for most of the fresh goods and grains supplied to the capital. From there, they were distributed to the rest of the Isles. Based on recent reports, it seemed the produce was being contaminated before it was passed on.

"I was in the worst pain I'd ever been in," Elladire continued. "I didn't know what else to do so eventually, I volunteered for the Court's testing program. The antidote worked fast and I was grateful. But my partner is Fae and he finds it funny to use compulsion on me sometimes. He says it's for my own good and a way to strengthen my Mind-Shield. But since the antidote my Mind-Shield is weak at best."

People in the crowd exchanged glances that said they'd experienced something similar.

"Did you go to the Court about it?" A warlock asked.

Elladire nodded. "I did. They said it was a possible side effect but nothing to worry about. I found it strange that it hadn't been one of the side effects they'd listed before the test, however, I didn't worry. Not until I heard their theory." She gestured to Ilbryen and Ryul. "The Court have built a weapon and are working with the sirens to control our minds."

Someone laughed. I searched the crowd and found the elf leaned against the window with his arms folded.

"Don't you think that's a little farfetched?"

"We all did," a witch snapped. "Until the sirens were invited to stay at the home of those they'd killed. The very leader of the sea folk now sits at the Court's table."

"It's no more farfetched than a building that has stood for millennia suddenly collapsing," Ryul added.

"And supposedly killing the Shadow Saint and his mate who are miraculously both alive." Elladire snickered. "The Court said that they'd honored the dead with a proper balm and burning ritual. You'd think they would have noticed that two of the most important beings weren't there."

"We all know what it really was," snarled Parker, the goblin who'd handed me the weapon plans after Reek's death. He'd quickly become my new source and friend. "A cover up. The Court didn't honor the dead. They burned the evidence."

Someone else snapped, "You say the Shadow Saint isn't dead but where is he?"

It looked like that was my cue. Usually, Ilbryen and Ryul made the introductions and started these things off. We liked to give the people a chance to adjust to the idea before I made my appearance. Tonight, I'd be a little early.

I stepped away from the wall and pulled out of the shadows I'd cloaked myself in. Several people leapt back. Some wept and trembled. Others got on their knees and prayed.

"I actually go by the Prince of Death now."

Shadows trailed in my wake as I stalked through the crowd. My wings were tucked behind me. Numerous stares were drawn to their silver peaks and the symbols of the Fates that lit up along my skin.

"Everything you've been told here tonight is true. But don't just take my word for it."

I nodded to Pyrah who opened the kitchen door. Aquarius stepped out.

The air in the tavern shifted. Everyone wasn't against sirens but out of all the Outliers, the stigma that surrounded them was the worst. Where the room had filled with awe and fear at my arrival. It now bristled with something sharp and cold.

Aquarius pretended not to notice as he joined me on stage.

"There are many of you here who have taken the Courts antidote." I glanced at the elf who'd been against our theory. "I'd wager you are one of them."

His jaw ticked but he nodded curtly.

I indicated Aquarius. "This is a good friend of mine. We're going to do a little demonstration. He's going to sing you all a song."

Aquarius shrugged out of his jacket and tossed it to Ilbryen. He stood tall; his stare severe. I admired that my friend didn't try to appear likable or smile to appease the crowd. He'd always been himself no matter what.

"Everyone, activate your Mind-Shield and we'll see how you do."

Aquarius barely got past the first word before a quarter of the room burst into a song of their own. They waved their hands and stamped their feet. The others watched them in wide-eyed horror. Aquarius stopped singing.

"Out of those of you who joined in, how many have taken the Court's antidote?"

Every hand went up. The silence that settled was heavy as they each looked around the room.

I planted a hand on Aquarius' shoulder. "This is just one siren. What the Court have planned is an entire fleet of sirens with a weapon that will amplify their song and sustain the effects. Let this be your warning. Do not take the antidote and do not trust any produce that does not come directly from Giant's Keep. Spread the word."

26

VARIALLA:
STRENGTH OF HEART

Day four. Colette and Cyrus arrived at dawn. They wore almost identical purple petticoat dress's which were a standard uniform for a stylist to the Final Five. I couldn't stop laughing as I sipped on a sherry-leaf tea. With a scowl in my direction, Cyrus took charge.

Colette was put on makeup and hair duty. Cyrus gave herself the task of finding fragrances tailored to complement my natural scent, and of narrowing down the outfit I would wear. Eventually, she chose black leather leggings with white lace up the side, and a white off-the-shoulder blouse that exposed my midriff and was paired with a black leather bustier. Then she tackled the shoes.

Today I would schmooze with visiting nobles and get acquainted with the palace staff—those I would be living with if—*when*—I won the Games. These people could become my confidants. They would know who was in the Court's pocket. They may also know if there'd been any unusual deliveries lately. Items that could be ingredients for the poison or better yet, the antidote.

It was bittersweet to be back in the chair gossiping about the Games and potential Court allies. I'd managed to survive my Trial of Combat the other day, with a cracked jaw, black eye and fractured rib. All things considered it had been a good afternoon. After my fight, there'd been a few noblemen and women who had eyed me with newfound respect. They'd seen a glimmer of the leader I could be and not just a clueless foreigner from across the veil. Loch thankfully hadn't approached me. Probably because he didn't want me to lash out and say something I shouldn't. Like how he'd kept me prisoner for the last few months; how he'd known I was alive and was plotting against the Court.

I leaned closer to the bronze-framed mirror on my dressing table and prodded the sensitive flesh around my eye. The bruise was finally starting to fade. In Phase Three of the Games healing magic was only allowed on the most severe injuries. Everything else had to be suffered. Scars to remind us of our victories and losses in our quest for the throne.

Godric hovered in the background. His orb recorded everything. For that reason, we spoke in code. We never named anyone directly and didn't discuss anything related to the weapon or antidote. Instead, they told me about how they'd spent their days. They put emphasis on the palace staff they'd met who may be on our side. Servers and cleaners were our best source of information. They saw everything but no one saw them. If anyone had information on the happenings within the Court; on potential threats and allies, it was them. Today, I intended to find out, if I could just find a way to evade Godric.

A sharp knock sounded on the door.

Colette set down her powder brush. "I'll get it."

"No." Godric gestured to me. "She will."

As orbs-director, his main priority was to satisfy the viewers. Every so often, he could make suggestions and minor tweaks to my reality if he felt it would enhance the shows entertainment value and potentially boost ratings.

With a sigh, I slipped out of my chair and padded towards the front door. Goather waited on the other side. His smile was unnaturally wide; his eyes void of all hope. The hairs rose on the back of my neck.

"Varialla von Hastings, it is time to test your Strength of Heart."

"What?" I cocked my head to one side and hoped the gesture blocked the orb that bobbed behind my back.

It must have because Goather's placid smile dropped. It was just for a second, then Godric repositioned the camera.

Goather straightened. "Can I come in?"

Before I could respond, he trotted inside. The severity I'd seen on his face only seconds ago vanished and he slipped back into presenter mode.

"Real scenarios. Real reactions. Are you Fit for the Throne?"

With a flourish, Goather held up a translucent Five Isles phone. He swiped his finger across the base and a large holographic screen emerged. On it, was live footage from the arena where a crowd had started to gather. I looked from Goather to the screen. I hadn't been told about anything happening in the arena today.

"Is that a guillotine?"

My mouth went dry. A stage had been set up in the center of the sand. On it was unmistakably a guillotine. The sharp edge of its silver blade glinted in the sun.

"According to the newscaster, it is intended to be used on the disqualified player; Lucinda Ironclaw."

I wasn't sure I heard him. My gaze snapped from the screen to Goather.

"What do you mean?"

"Apparently, the young witch has betrayed the Court. She and an accomplice will be beheaded today in a public execution."

The ground tilted. An accomplice…Maximus. Loch had done this. He'd captured them to punish me. Now he'd kill them.

I shook my head. "This doesn't make sense."

There were no laws on how brutal a trial could be but surely the bastard couldn't go around beheading people on a whim for the sake of the Games.

"Lucinda Ironclaw is a known traitor." The words clanged around in my head louder than cathedral bells.

"What?"

"All will be revealed in due time." Gother grinned.

I recognized the flatness in it and the dimness in his eyes.

"This is to test your strength of heart. Prove yourself and you will receive an extra one hundred and fifty points, plus however many points you accumulate throughout the challenge."

"What is the challenge?" I cried.

To save them? Say goodbye?

"That depends on you and whatever lies in your heart." Goather tapped on the screen and cut off the broadcast. Then he trotted towards the door. "By the way, the execution begins in exactly twelve minutes."

My stomach lurched. We'd never make it across the island in that time.

The door slammed shut.

Cyrus cursed. "This is griffin-shit! I saw the earlier tests. Vivienne had to choose between saving herself or risking her life to save a Pegasus from a room with the walls closing in. Kraxus had to play a board game and decide whether to let his opponent win the prize of a thousand gold pieces or take it for himself. And they all had more than twelve minutes notice."

"It doesn't matter." My voice was hollow.

None of that mattered. It wouldn't change that my trial was this. Loch didn't want me to win the Games unless I was playing by his rules and controlled by the bind. This was my punishment for going against him.

"During the Games certain warlocks had the ability to teleport." They'd used it to their advantage in the maze round.

Cyrus nodded. "It depends on their power rank."

My mind pieced together a shoddy plan. A way to get me to that arena fast.

"Who were they and where can I find them?"

*

Hood drawn and head down, Colette, Cyrus, Kylin and I maneuvered through the crowded arena and searched for servers near the wings. Thanks to the unnatural frost in the air no one batted an eyelid at four cloaked figures.

According to the clock counting down on the holo-screen that hovered over the arena, there were six minutes until execution. I sent up a silent prayer of thanks to the warlock Cyrus had managed to find with Goather's help. Without him, we wouldn't have reached the arena in time.

Godric was somewhere nearby. For a centaur, he had done a great job at blending in with the crowd.

He must have activated the camouflage setting on the orb because I couldn't see that either.

Whilst most people ascended the steps, the four of us moved closer to the battlefield. We paused when a hulking satyr wearing a black leather waistcoat trotted out onto the sand. He was taller than other satyrs I'd seen. From here, he looked like he'd reach my shoulder. He had washboard abs and long black hair that billowed in the breeze. There was a cruel slant to his lips and a sinister gleam in his eyes as he stalked towards the stage where the guillotine stood. He was the executioner.

Kylin who had abandoned her gardening duties to help us, tapped my hand. I followed her gaze and spotted three servers—a centaur and two nymphs—dressed in hooded, dark green robes and red silk scarves. They stood at the edge of the field. Each of them carried a tray of silver chalices and waited for someone to beckon them over.

I scanned the arena. There were no signs of the prisoners or the bastard who had brought them here. However, members of the Court and Council stood at the foot of the stands in their purple robes marked with the four-petalled crest of the Five Isles. They stared out at the audience; their heads held high. However, their usual smug expressions were cold and angry. Adir's most of all.

I traded a glance with Kylin but neither of us said a word. As if we both thought someone might recognize our voices over the din of the crowd.

We slowly made our way to the servers. Their eyes widened when they caught sight of our faces beneath the hoods. Colette and Cyrus could blend in, but there was no chance they hadn't recognized Kylin and I.

One of the nymph's cried, "You're—"

"Don't speak." My command rang over her. Her lips snapped shut.

Beside me, Colette began to hum. She wrapped her melody around the servers and used her power to amplify the force of my words.

"We work here," I told them. "You know us." My voice carried a lilting echo. The servers' eyes glazed over. "You trust us."

I hated using my ability like this. It felt dirty like oil had replaced my blood. It was shocking how easy it was to slip into the mind of another and bend them to my will. I wondered if Loch had felt like this way at first, but then over the years he'd developed a taste for it.

Behind us, Kylin kept watch. My plan was in no way foolproof. I just had to hope that with everyone focused on getting good seats, they wouldn't notice us.

"We need to get into the wings of the arena," I imbued my voice with more power. Colette enhanced it. Her song was sweet and soft. Low enough to not attract attention but powerful enough to leave these servers at our mercy.

"Take us."

Magic hummed in my veins and I prayed Loch wouldn't sense it. I wanted him to know I was here. The whole damn realm would know soon enough. But not yet.

I held the centaur's stare. "Get us beneath the arena and make sure we don't get caught."

The servers nodded in unison like creepy puppets pulled by the same string. With frozen smiles, they turned and led us towards the gate on the side of the arena that led into the labyrinth of rooms beneath. This was where prisoners were held whilst they waited for their judgement.

We walked fast. Our robes were dark but they didn't match the moldy-green shade of the servers'. If anyone looked over, they'd know we didn't belong.

We approached the open gates. Two guards waited at each side. One Fae. One shifter. We kept our heads down which was custom of servers. Eye contact with a superior was completely forbidden. Usually, that notion made me sick. In this case, it worked in our favor.

"We need more trays," the centaur announced as we passed.

The sand changed to stone beneath our feet.

A gruff voice snapped, "Wait."

My stomach flipped as the shifter grabbed Colette's arm. He yanked down her hood and bared his teeth. My pulse pounded. I pulled magic into my palms just in case.

"This is not the uniform of a slave." His teeth morphed to deadly points.

"Apologies. The execution was arranged quickly and we left in a hurry."

The shifter couldn't argue with that. No one had known about my Strength of Heart trial until this morning. No more than an hour ago. Though that was at least better than my measly twelve minutes.

Colette tried to tug her arm free. "We're going to change right now."

The guard tightened his grip. His hard stare raked over her. His eyes lingered on her breasts. "I'll be sure to find you later to deliver the appropriate punishment for your insolence."

The Fae beside him chuckled.

The shifter lowered his head. I stiffened when he ran his tongue from Colette's cleavage up to her collarbone. She tensed. Her eyes flared with hate. My stomach turned. I wanted to maul the bastard. This was how Outliers were treated every day. Like they were less than because they were on the wrong side when the land shifted. Punished for simply existing. I clenched my jaw and breathed through my rage. Maximus and Lucinda would be brought out any minute. We had to keep moving.

"As you were," the shifter growled. His eyes had turned gold and resembled a lion.

Finally, he unhooked his fingers from Colette. She visibly swallowed her retort and we rushed inside. As soon as we crossed the threshold and rounded the corner, the servers stopped abruptly and blinked. I'd only compelled them to get us this far. Now, they came out of the trance and frowned at each other.

Before they could realize what had happened, Cyrus knocked them out with three quick blows to the back of the head. I blinked at her. She'd once told me that she'd had to learn to defend herself growing up in a world where she was seen as nothing more than an object of judgment or unwanted affections, but still her speed and skill in combat stunned me. The centaur weighed at least three of her.

"Nice job," Kylin whispered as one of the nymphs fell into her arms. Colette caught the other.

"Thanks," Cyrus grunted as she and I caught the centaur before she went down.

We dragged the unconscious servers into the poky storage room beside us. Here the ground was sand again. Softer than in the arena. Sacks of grain and herbs covered were stacked against the wall.

"Now what?" Colette whispered.

I grimaced. I'd thrown together two hasty plans but was basically making this up as I went along. In a perfect world, we would stumble across the prisoner cells and break them out but that was unlikely, especially not in the next three minutes. We'd have to go with Plan B, and wait until they were brought out to us.

I crouched beside the centaur and tugged on the ties of her robe. "Help me get them undressed."

In a matter of minutes, we had the servers out of their clothes and we had stepped into them. Seeing as Cyrus was the shortest and had a notable rose growing out of her head, she'd agreed to go in the back of the centaur's dress and act as the rear. Colette who had a similar build to the centaur acted as the upper body. We pulled up the hoods of the robes and as an extra precaution, tied the scarves around our nose and mouths to hide our faces. They were supposed to be around our necks. However, I'd take my chances at being scolded for not wearing my uniform properly over being recognized.

Colette and I started singing before we left the room. By the time we reached the guards at the gate, their eyes were glazed over. A dopey smile stretched across their lips. Colette glared at the one who'd put his hands on her—licked her.

"If you want to stab him, I'd be okay with that," I whispered.

Colette grinned.

I shrugged, adjusted my hood then stepped out onto the sands with a tray of drinks in hand.

27

VARIALLA:
YOU SHOULDN'T HAVE

I t wasn't long before Goather trotted out of a warlock's portal and onto the sand. He paused when he reached the center and turned to face the audience. He'd changed since he'd shown up at my door. He now wore a deep green-striped shirt with puffy sleeves and a large ruff collar like something from the sixteenth century.

"Viewers." His voice echoed through the microphone clipped to his shirt. "Welcome to another level of the fascinating, fierce and fantastic, Phase Three of the Royal Games."

A camera-orb circled him and his holographic image was projected over the arena.

"It is time for our foreign temptress from beyond the veil; our Queen of Shifter Springs and the Coral

194

Court, to face her second challenge. Strength of Heart."

The audience whooped and drummed their feet on the ground. Some waved banners and others broke into song. My breath caught. The symbol on the banners that represented me had changed. It was still a clamshell but instead of a mermaid's tail in its center, there was a dragon. Its wings were splayed and its tail drooped over the edge of the shell.

"The question is, will Varialla make it to the arena in time?" Goather strutted before the crowd. "If she does, does she have the heart to see justice served and say goodbye to those who have defied the Crown? Or does she have the heart to look past the crime and see the being beneath? Which way does her heart sway? What will our foreign temptress do about this?"

Goather gestured to the guillotine with a dramatic wave of his hand. More shouts went up in the crowd.

"Come forward, Varialla. Show us what's in your heart," he bellowed. "Real scenarios. Real reactions. Are you Fit for the Throne?"

The audience shouted the last part with him. A band of goblins on the edge of the arena started to play. People leapt up and danced. They gave each other high-fives and whipped out their phones to snap photos and continue the trend of #StrengthofHeart on Enchant-a-gram. It was all a show to them; a game. They didn't realize the Court were playing with their lives as well.

Goather took a bow then trotted off the sand as three battered people in scraps of clothing were marched out. Their wrists and ankles were bound in manacles and they were linked to one another by a chain around their neck.

Lucinda was at the front. Maximus was in the middle. Pulling up the rear was a slender elf with mocha-brown skin and high cheekbones. My stomach dropped. A stunned silence preceded the shouts and jeers that swept through the crowd.

Fuck.

There was only one reason why she, Evangeline Degalos, Second Primary of the Realm, would be here. Only one that explained her chains and the furious glimmer in Adir's eyes. His mate's affair with Lucinda had been discovered. Now both would pay the price.

It was no coincidence that the Court had found out about the affair just in time for my Strength of Heart challenge. Loch must have known about them for a while. He'd simply stored the information for when he could use it to best serve him.

Lucinda stumbled when a guard struck a whip across her back. Her blood sprayed over the sand. For a second, my heart leapt. Lucinda was a bloodwitch. Then I noticed the collar fastened around her neck. An enchanted collar that was designed by the Fae bastard I called my mate.

Exekiel had meant for the collars to strip away a siren's ability. He'd seen them as a way to stop the

Court from using sirens as the weapon's ammunition. However, the collars worked the same on every cast. Now an elf, a witch and a warlock were bound by them.

Leading the prisoners like dogs on a leash was Loch. He yanked on the chain that connected their necks and sneered when they tripped and earned another lashing from a guard.

Rage reared up with the force of my inner dragon. That pounding thrum of power inside me that each day felt more like caging thunder. I wrestled it down.

Not yet.

Eventually, Loch handed over the chain. Whilst Lucinda, Maximus and Evangeline were led to the guillotine, he pulled up the collar of his deep green cloak and turned to address the crowd. The Council had let him lead this. They'd placed him as a figure of prominence and justice. They seriously didn't see how much power they'd given to the monster they believed was their pet.

Like Goather, Loch's giant holographic image was projected over the arena. Beneath his cloak he wore a long white shirt, fitted breeches and black boots. His tight curls were pinned back, highlighting the square cut of his jaw and fullness of his lips. I practically heard the collective sigh of the audience as they admired him. Other than the faint lines of gills that were visible on his neck, Loch could have fit in perfectly with a group of Fae and their unnatural beauty. My hand balled into fists. His attractiveness was cyanide disguised as sugar.

"The rumors are true." The sound of his voice made my skin crawl. "Evangeline Degalos has betrayed our Primary and his people."

Our Primary? Adir was nothing to the Outliers except a tyrant.

"And the one being who knew about it," he gestured to Maximus, "chose to keep their vile secret."

My nostrils flared. Loch was a showman. He commanded the audience and claimed their attention. Ordinarily his overbearing presence pissed me off. Now, I used it to my advantage. As the prick rambled on about right and wrong, and partners chosen by the Fates, I edged closer to the stage. The girls moved with me.

"Until now, our traitors show no remorse. They violated the rules of the Games and claim they would do it again."

There was a thunk as chains fell from around Lucinda. She was roughly grabbed by two guards who forced her to lay on the wooden slab. Her head was positioned beneath the guillotine's blade. Lucinda tried to pull away and was met with a fist to the gut. I glared at the guard who'd struck her, although this wasn't his fault.

My friends were beaten, broken and bloody, and it was all because of one man. The Rebel King and his toxic obsession with me. If Loch wasn't such a power-hungry bastard hellbent on revenge things would be different right now. If he was the male he'd pretended to be when we'd met. The siren who'd wanted me to claim the Eternal Throne so I could free the Outlands and unite the Isles. Then we'd all be working together against common enemy. I'd believed in the dreams of that siren. I still did even if they'd all been a lie.

Loch's footsteps echoed in the near silent arena as he climbed the worn wooden steps and strolled towards Lucinda. From what I knew from history class, prisoners were supposed to face away from the blade so that it came down on the back of their neck. However, the guards had forced Lucinda onto her back before they'd strapped her down. Loch wanted her to see her end coming and know that she couldn't do anything about it.

I glanced at the others. Cyrus, Colette and I carried trays of drinks. Kylin carried a basket. At some point, she would be expected to place the basket on stage to catch the severed heads. This was supposedly a symbolic moment in an execution like this. It marked the beginning of the end and filled the prisoners with fear.

Loch stood over Lucinda. His eyes cold. "Any last words?"

His voice was amplified through the giant hologram as camera-orbs panned around the scene.

Lucinda narrowed her one good eye. The other was swollen shut. Her braids were half chopped off and caked in grime. The collar had been removed to allow for a clean slice and highlighted a distinct ring of bruises around her neck. Rage and bile climbed up my throat.

I silently willed my friend to cast a spell and take the fuckers out but all traces of blood had been cleaned from her skin. Even if she somehow did manage to conjure magic, with her body bound and the guards around her, Lucinda wouldn't get far.

"You will fall." Lucinda sneered. It was cruel and sharp. "Two mates divided are finally united. You cannot win."

Wind picked up beside me as Kylin pulled on the particles of frost in the air and conjured a blade of ice in her hand. There were wards around the arena that prevented the audience from bringing in weapons. However, there was nothing to stop a winter elf from using her ability.

Loch snickered and leaned over. He tightly gripped Lucinda's jaw. "These are the ramblings of a condemned hag."

He looked to the executioner who waited by the lever and practically rocked on his hooves in anticipation. Then his stare slid to us. My heart flipped; afraid he might somehow recognize me from this distance with my hood drawn and nose and mouth covered.

"Bring the basket."

Kylin stiffened. Her eyes went wide and she looked from us to the stage. The basket trembled in her hands.

Loch barked, "Now!"

Kylin jumped and started to whimper. Her feet shuffled back. The audience jeered. I grinned behind my scarf. Slowly, I walked towards the elf masquerading as a nymph and offered her my tray, just like we'd planned. Kylin continued to sob as she handed me the basket.

"Move!" Loch bellowed. "Unless you want to be up here with them."

My heart pounded in my throat as I took the basket and the ice blades Kylin had stuck beneath it and headed over to the stage. I kept my gaze lowered as I ascended the steps and set the basket down.

I didn't move from my crouch. Silence stretched through the arena. Tension thick enough to chew.

"Get out of the way," Loch growled. "You're in the splash zone."

I remained crouched and slowly edged back, like I was afraid to move too quickly. My muscles taut and ready to pounce. Loch nodded to the executioner.

"Kill the witch."

The satyr's beefy hands closed around the lever. I sprang to my feet and drove the blade of ice through his neck. Warm splatters of blood sprayed over my face. The satyr's eyes widened. His body crumpled.

I spun to face Loch. My hood fell to reveal my black and teal curls pulled back in a half-braid. "You did all this for me?"

The audience erupted. Guards rushed out onto the sand. Colette used her siren song to hold them back, whilst Kylin continued to forge and fling her blades of ice. She impaled three guards in quick succession. Cyrus used her fists and the skill she'd gained from decades of defending herself.

In the same breath, horns curved from the crown of my head and scarlet wings unfurled from my spine. That pulsing power drummed harder inside me.

"You shouldn't have." I bared my teeth that were now deadly fangs and angled the ice dagger at Loch.

He was so busy looking at my hand, he didn't notice my foot as I brought it up and kicked him in the chest. The air whooshed from his lungs and his rib cracked beneath my boot. The bastard careened off the edge of the stage.

More applause rang in response.

Through the projected holo-screen, Goather bellowed, "Our foreign temptress has made her choice. She has the heart to see beyond the crime, now will she succeed in her mission to save them?"

I swiveled to where Lucinda struggled against her restraints. Blood trickled from her lip. She must have bitten it. Now she chanted a spell to break the clasps. It was working but slowly.

"Are you okay?" I shouted over the chaos.

"Better than dead." She yanked one wrist free then got to work on the other.

I glanced at Maximus who had his chains wrapped around a guard's neck as they wrestled for the keys. Beside him, Evangeline fought a pair of guards without breaking a sweat.

"What's the plan?"

I blinked at Lucinda. "Plan? They'd given me twelve minutes notice."

She narrowed her eyes. "Tell me you didn't charge in here with no way to get us out."

I pushed my loose curls from my face. "Alright, I won't tell you."

She snorted.

My plan had begun and ended with getting into the arena and stopping their execution. Now we had to find some way to escape. As powerful as we were, I didn't believe the seven of us could take down the Court on our own.

Lucinda freed her other wrist and dabbed blood on the cuffs around her ankles.

"I have a mild plan. Meet me with the others." I leapt off the stage and landed in a crouch.

Loch wasn't there. My stomach pitched. Where the fuck had he gone? This was my chance to take him down without question or severe consequence. The bastard would attack me and I would defend myself until his blood filled my hands. Not a petty little girl seeking revenge or a usurper taking out the

Court's greatest allies, but a queen in battle protecting the prisoners—her people.

Swallowing a curse, I ran to where Colette used her siren song to command a handful of guards to fight for us. I skidded to a stop beside her and whistled a tune that enhanced her song and sent some of the approaching guards stumbling back.

"We have to find Nadir!" The warlock had said he'd be watching the trial. If we found him, he could portal us away.

"In a sea of a thousand faces?" Kylin shouted.

The guards pressed forwards. Colette and I sang as one and created a shield around us. It tremored under the force of their attack.

My muscles shook. "Do you have a better idea?"

"I do."

I spun at the sound of Loch's voice. A chill snaked down my spine. He had Lucinda. He held her back against his front. His hand was around her throat and a dagger pressed to her side. Beside her, Maximus and Evangeline were at the edge of the stage. Guards held the ends of the chains that coiled around their necks in their brawny hands.

"How about we kill you all," Loch shouted. "One," Evangeline was shoved off the stage. Her feet kicked as the chains tightened around her neck. "By," Maximus was pushed next. His body jerked. "One."

The blade punched through Lucinda's gut.

I staggered back. My stomach heaved. It had happened too fast to react, to process. Ringing sounded in my ears. A current of power crackled down my spine. It was sharper and more potent than anything I'd felt. Like the rolling thunder of magic within me had finally crested into a storm.

Lucinda hit the ground. My body spasmed. *No.* I was supposed to save her. She was supposed to live. Fire burned in my bones. Magic sparked in my lungs. The arena quaked.

I was vaguely aware as heads swiveled in my direction and the audience gasped. The sand shuddered and swirled around me. I couldn't move. I was paralyzed by power that sank into my skin.

Overhead, something deadly roared. My gaze swung upward. My breath stuck in my chest. Was that a dragon?

28

VARIALLA:
DRAGONS, DRAMA & DESTINY

Fire streaked across the sky in a blaze of red and teal flames. The same color as my own. Two massive dragons silhouetted by the sun descended. One had deep blue scales and jagged spikes like a lion's mane around its massive head. The other was a beautiful reddish-brown shade with a barbed tail. Their mammoth wings stirred the air and swept up the sand around us the closer they got. I shielded my eyes and stumbled back.

The blue dragon opened her mouth and belched out a blaze of sapphire flames. They incinerated the guards around us. Heat licked at my skin. My heart ratcheted in my chest.

The ground shook when she landed and unleashed a deafening roar. I didn't know how I knew she was female but an intrinsic part of me knew. Her teardrop shaped scales glistened like sapphire daggers as they lifted and amplified her size. She was easily the height of a two-story building. I swallowed thickly and took a step back. Though something innate said that she wouldn't hurt me.

The guards that didn't burn, fled, only to be pursued by the russet-scaled dragon.

Everywhere I looked, guards stumbled and choked in clouds of smoke. The audience screamed. Some had leapt up and raced towards the exits. Others, astonishingly whipped out their phones and began snapping selfies.

My body thrummed in the aftermath of the dragons' flames. Power pulsed through my veins and streaked down my spine. Every jolt of power and wayward spark of magic I'd felt over the last few months finally made sense. It had all been gathering inside me for this; a song to siren these creatures to me. These *dragons*.

My head whipped in Loch's direction. He was the only one who didn't gawp or run. He grinned at the beasts like he'd expected their arrival. He'd known that my power was somehow connected to them. That was why he'd been desperate to claim me. That was why he would kill anyone who got in his way.

My gaze dropped to Lucinda who bled out at his feet. My heart cracked. I took a step towards her and almost screamed when the blue dragon nudged me with her rough snout. Her head was bigger than my entire body. Her eyes were a fierce yellow that seemed to stare straight through to my soul.

I blinked; part terrified and part in awe. The dragon growled. My heart slammed into my ribs.

"Hi," I breathed.

Her eyes narrowed and trailed over me In a way that said she found me lacking. She crouched on her haunches and lowered herself even more. The jagged spikes around her head were larger and sharper than any sword. I leaned back to avoid being impaled. She huffed. Her breath was hot and damp.

Understanding dawned. She wanted to me to climb on. That's why they were here; for me. Her yellow eyes blinked when I looked back at her as if answer to my unspoken question.

I stepped further back. "Not without them."

I jerked my head to Lucinda and the others. The words: **Loyalty: 60 Points** and **Selflessness: 30 Points** flashed above me in smoky grey letters

I swiveled back towards my friends. Lucinda lay crumpled on the floor by the guillotine. Blood seeped from her torso. Her eyelids fluttered. She was alive but barely. She needed a healer now. Beside her, Evangeline and Maximus twitched on the end of the chains the guards still held; choking the life out of them. Behind me, Kylin and the others battled guards that managed to slip past the shield of Colette's song.

We needed to get out of here. Needed to run before Loch brought down the wrath of the entire Royal Army on us. Now that my dragons had arrived, if he caught me, he would never let me go. I could order my dragons to kill. They could incinerate everything in our path but that would include the civilians, the innocent onlookers and those forced into service in the arena.

Our best chance was to round everybody up and somehow escape on dragon's back. The deranged thought would have been laughable if everything wasn't hinged on it. If my friends weren't hanging by their necks and bleeding on the ground.

I merged my own song with Colette's. Together, we backed nearer to the stage where our friends battled death.

The guards were heedless. They slammed into our barrier and blindly charged into the flames that surrounded us. It was like they were possessed. Like they were being controlled. My stomach turned. Was that it? Was the weapon here? Was that where Loch had gone?

I searched for him now within the mass of bodies but couldn't see him. I knew he was out there though; watching. He always was.

I pulled on my power and my tongue turned sugar sweet. I suckled on the flavor and let a song burst from my lips.

One word, a thousand notes, "Die."

The command landed on a handful of the nearest guards. My magic latched onto the water in their skin and pulled. They went down—at least five of them. One after the other. In seconds their bodies were nothing more than dried husks that sank into the puddles that formed around them.

My mind reeled as I spun towards another group of guards.

"Die."

They staggered and fell clutching at crumbling necks. My voice had become a weapon. Each word was a killing blow. I aimed and fired.

The guards who held the chains fell next. Maximus and Evangeline hit the ground.

"Get them," I shouted.

Beside me, my dragons roared and added to the flames that already surrounded us. Cyrus and Colette raced towards the stage and bounded up the steps. One took Lucinda's legs, the other her arms. I tried to shield them with my power as they hurtled back. They were barely able to dodge the soldiers' attacks.

When they reached the blue dragon, she growled. They screeched to a halt.

"I can't believe I'm this close to a Crowned Sapphire," Colette gasped.

I guessed she meant the dragon.

"Let them on," I shouted.

The blue dragon narrowed her eyes.

"Let them on!"

She snorted. Steam puffed from her snout. The force almost knocked me sideways. Was she kidding? Guards pounded on my shield and tried to charge through the flames. They wouldn't stop.

I glared at the blue beast. She glared right back. Her yellow eyes narrowed. There was something I was missing; some way to command her. I felt the link between us like invisible threads that connected her heart to mine. I coiled my magic around them.

She bared her terrifying teeth.

I sank deeper; submerged myself in the essence that was her. Magic lit up around me in tendrils of red and teal that only I could see. I stroked my finger along the shimmers of turquoise—of her.

"Revynath of the Zairenyth name, obey me." My voice was mine but it carried an echo. Her name was plucked from somewhere deep within.

The Crowned Sapphire dragon—Revynath— puffed up her chest. She looked like she wanted to step on me. I swallowed and clung to the intrinsic knowing that she wouldn't hurt me. Finally, her extensive wing dropped to the ground with a thud that stirred the sand.

"*Tilassiss.*" The word meant thank you. I wasn't sure in which language or how I knew it.

Colette and Cyrus hesitated for only a second before they used Revynath's lowered wing to hobble up and position Lucinda on her back. They slid down; their expressions one of horror and awe, then sprinted back for Evangeline. Maximus had staggered to his feet and leaned heavily into Kylin. I kept my palms raised and occasionally sang, holding the barrier in place, as dragons' fire encircled us.

I glanced to where I heard Loch commanding the army to hammer at my shield and try to defy the flames. His eyes were wild. His skin glazed in sweat and his chest heaving. He wasn't going to let me get away. He would sacrifice every soul, tear this arena down, brick by brick, to have me.

When my friends were finally positioned precariously on the bumps along Revynath's back, I lowered my arms. The shield fell away. The soldiers surged forwards.

I spun and ran towards the red dragon who swung his barbed tail at the advancing army. I leapt off the ground and splayed my wings to fly onto its back. My spine protested. It was harder than I expected to stay aloft. I wasn't prepared for the sheer effort it took just to beat the wings. Their weight yanked me down and threw me off balance. *Fuck.* My stomach pitched. My right wing locked and I spiraled downwards.

The red dragon shot out a wing. I landed on the tip of the leathery surface. My heart ricocheted in my chest. The beat of my blood pounded in my ears. I clung on for dear life as both dragons spread their wings and prepared to launch.

Knowing I couldn't be perched here when it did, I crawled up the smooth, veiny surface to reach the grooves of its ridged back.

Once I was more or less seated between the spikes, I patted the dragon's rough, red scales. The magnificent creature roared. I clung to one of the grooved spines along its back and we launched into the sky.

29

VARIALLA:
Start Talking

Wind buffeted my face and tugged on my braid. The dragon beneath me dipped and turned. This was surreal. I was riding a dragon. A real life, fire-breathing beast. If everything wasn't so monumentally fucked up, I might have laughed. I might have howled at the fricking sky. Instead, dread and doubt choked my vocal cords. My mind was a mess. There were so many unknowns and no frigging answers.

The world blurred past. I clutched tighter to the sharp spines of the dragon's back and hunkered down low. Blood trickled from the gashes they carved into my palms. However, if I let go, I'd be thrown backwards. I didn't trust my own wings to be any help if that happened. Flight was something I needed to work on.

Steam puffed from the dragon's snout. His slitted nostrils flared. The sight was captivating. There was a deep rumble in my thighs. I tensed as his large head turned towards me. Bright silver eyes stared into mine. There was a question in those piercing depths. Somehow, I understood. *Where to?*

Where could we go? Technically I should be returning to the palace; back to Godric and the public eye. But I couldn't take Lucinda and the others there. If I was being honest, it was the last place I wanted to be.

I hesitated for only a second before I said, "Fates Cathedral."

The dragon's large head swung back to face the front. His low answering growl vibrated through my body once more. We banked to the right. I yelped and held on tighter.

Revynath followed with a booming roar and blaze of blue fire. I scowled down at her. Clearly, she'd missed the part where we were supposed to be getting away from our would-be killers, not announcing our location.

My friends were huddled together on her back. Their fingers dug into the grooves between her scales. Judging by the lines of concentration on Kylin's brow, and the way she moved her hands, she was manipulating the wind to keep everyone seated. A feat that was made harder because Revynath bucked and dipped more than necessary. It was like she was trying to throw them off. Apparently, the Crowned Sapphire would follow my orders but not willingly.

Lucinda's eyes were closed now. Maximus' arms were locked around her.

Please still be breathing.

Over the wind there was a faint toll of bells. I looked down, and made out the distant spires of the cathedral. We weren't far.

The red dragon flicked his tail. My stomach lurched and I choked back a scream as we spiraled downwards at a dizzying speed. My eyes slammed shut but that made it worse. *Shit.* I gripped tighter and ignored the smart of pain and the warm blood that ran down my wrists. My heart was about to beat out of my throat.

I tried to suck in air. To clear the sense of impending doom. A second heart beat inside me. This one was slower, steadier. Its rhythm took over until my own heart was forced to match it. It was the heart of my dragons. These giant creatures that were somehow linked to me through my father's blood— my blood. The hum of their power was alive in my veins. I sank into the soothing sensation.

Once again, I saw the threads of blue and scarlet entwined around me. This time I touched the red. A jolt of electricity passed between us.

Urdith of the Zairenyth name let out a low rumble. Just like with Revynath I knew his name. It was like his life was being downloaded and integrated with mine. The dragon swooped lower. His mammoth wings skated over treetops and sent leaves flying. I gripped the magnificent creature with the squeeze of my thighs and one hand. I splayed my other arm out to the side and flung my head back; eyes closed. Urdith roared.

I didn't realize how huge my dragons were until they attempted to land in the courtyard outside the cathedral. Being slightly smaller, Urdith might have just fit but Revynath had no chance.

We rose up and soared over the cathedral towards the back and its sprawling gardens. Here, there were prayer paths, shrines and figures of the Fates carved out of the shrubbery. My favorite area was the field of grass beside a burbling stream. There were a few benches dotted along its edge. My dragons landed with a thud that shook the earth.

I'd barely dismounted; shakily using my wings to help lower me down, when Mothers raced out in their red robes. Only a handful bothered to hold their hoods in place. The rest were so astonished by dragons that they didn't care when their hair whipped around their faces. Some dropped to their knees in prayer when they reached us. Others wept and wrapped their arms around themselves.

"We need healers," I shouted. "Quickly."

Mother Maria—one of the eldest, which was saying something in this immortal world—turned to a few girls behind her. She barked out orders. The young Mothers raced inside. They couldn't help glancing back at Revynath and Urdith. Their expressions eager. I didn't blame them. I was doing the same thing. It was only the invigorating buzz of power I'd felt since my dragons arrived that told me they were real.

I tipped my head back to take in Revynath's full imposing height. I only just past the lower half of her leg.

The Crowned Sapphire dragon narrowed her eyes at the Mothers but thankfully didn't swat them aside. Although she looked like she wanted to. Urdith— who I knew from tracing another thread between us, was a Scarlet Ridgeback—took a step towards them and lowered his head. It almost looked like an invitation but for what, I didn't know.

The young Mothers returned with healers at their backs. Mother Maria braved a step towards Revynath then froze. She threw me a cautious glance. I wished I could tell her she'd be fine but I had no idea how my dragons would react at this point. We definitely needed more time to get acquainted but not before Lucinda and the others were taken care of.

I glanced up at Revynath. "Put them down."

She bared her teeth and bucked as if she meant to throw them off.

Cyrus shrieked.

"Carefully!" I snapped.

Revynath made a sound that was shockingly similar to a chuckle then she lowered her wing. Spreading my own, I half flew, half scrambled up the dragon's side to help them. It was humiliating. I almost plummeted to my death more times than I could count. By the time I made it to her back, everyone had already climbed onto her wing. They slid down. As if that was what I'd meant to do, I did the same.

We helped Maximus and Evangeline hobble to the healers. The Mothers carried Lucinda. Behind the healers, beds, not stretchers but actual beds floated. They were being held aloft by the witches in the convent who murmured incantations.

The healers settled my friends on the beds then headed inside.

I moved to follow but hesitated and glanced back at my dragons. "You'll still be here when I get back, right?"

Urdith bowed his head, then flopped down. The ground shook. The water in the stream behind him splashed onto the grass. He closed his eyes as if he had no intention of moving.

Revynath merely looked down at me.

"Is that a, yes?"

She huffed and looked to the sky. I wondered if she was rolling her eyes. Could dragons roll their eyes?

My hands clenched and unclenched. "Revynath?"

Her yellow eyes narrowed as she returned my stare. Steam coiled from her snout.

"Please stay."

She blinked.

"Please."

The mammoth dragon cocked her large head to one side. She grunted then stamped the earth a few times, as if she was kneading it like an extremely large cat. Eventually satisfied, she folded herself beside Urdith. However, her eyes didn't close. She watched me and I watched her.

Something pulled in my chest. I had the overwhelming urge to run to her and curl up beneath her wing. However, there was somewhere else I needed to be.

*

"Stop pacing. You're making me dizzy," Maximus croaked. His voice was hoarse from whatever damage the chain had done. The healer elves said he would make a full recovery but it would take time.

I turned to face him. My arms folded across my chest. It had been close to an hour since they'd been brought to the small sick bay of the cathedral. Max was the only one awake but he was far from the only one here. Countless infected civilians slept in the other beds. Their skin was pale, clammy and lined with veins of black. Some groaned in their sleep, clearly fighting off a fever.

All this suffering and death to satisfy the depraved desires of a few powerful fuckers in Court. They'd poisoned their own people; sentenced them to die or live a life serving their whims. All so they could manipulate the Games and keep their tarnished seats of power.

"Just be thankful you aren't dead," I grumbled.

Maximus half chuckled but it turned into a pained cough. He struggled to push himself up to sitting. I rushed over to help him and adjusted the pillows behind his back.

"Tell me Exekiel and the others had a better day than us."

"They aren't back yet." The words felt like sawdust on my tongue.

Exekiel, Calder and whoever else had apparently gone to Goblin's Gorge today to check in on the weapon plans and strategize our next move. Exekiel had made this trip countless times before. However, security had recently doubled at the border and Loch would be looking for him. For anyone he could use against me.

"Is your missing mate the reason you keep pacing?"

I stopped. I hadn't realized I'd started again. I scowled and forced myself to sit on the stool beside Max's bed.

"Amongst other things," I grumbled. "A million things."

"Like?"

I waved a hand at him. "Like you, Lucinda! The fact that I now have *dragons*."

I was on my feet again; too agitated to sit still.

"There's a lot I can't answer." Maximus grimaced and tipped his head back to lean on the pillow. "But I may be able to give some insight on your dragons."

"You can?"

He half smiled. "Only if you sit down, woman."

I returned his weak smile and once again settled in the seat beside him.

"Dragon shifters weren't the only dragons in Shifter Springs," he began. "There were certain families within the clans that were bonded to the creatures. Which leads to why dragon shifters refused to conform to the ruling system of Primary, and continued to call themselves Kings and Queens."

He leaned over and picked up the chalice of water on the bedside table. He took a slow sip. "Among dragons, royalty was not won through games and battles of blood. It was chosen through fate. Those blessed with the power to awaken dragons and strengthen their kingdom were immediately chosen to rule. Queen or King of the dragon clans."

"If multiple families had the gift, how did they decide which one would rule?"

"The title was given to those who developed the gift first. If any manifested the ability at the same time, the crown was given to those who were bonded to the more powerful dragon. In both cases, the others became important members of the ruling body."

"Okay. So, where did they all go? How are they back?" I glanced towards the window and made out the hulking silhouette of my sleeping dragons by the shimmering stream. The sun was going down. The amber rays glinted off their scales.

"There's a lot beyond our borders that we don't know for sure. But before the barrier an explorer claimed to have found a distant cave where dragons slumbered waiting to be woken by their bonded.

"When the dragon shifters fell during the Brutal War, many of the surviving dragons scorched their homes then flew across the seas. They haven't been seen since. The belief was that they'd returned to that cave to await the birth of their newly bonded."

Max's green eyes met mine. "Those two were waiting for you."

My stomach clenched. "Does the ability stay in a bloodline?"

"Sometimes. Your great-grandfather had it but then it wasn't seen in the Zairenyth family for centuries. Then your father developed it when he matured."

"Is there any way to know who will have the gift?"

Maximus nodded. "Apparently there are distinct markings on the eggshell. The dragon shifters never gave much detail about it. They were afraid outside enemies would try to steal the egg if they knew what to look for."

But Loch had known. My father would have told my mother and she would have told Loch. That was why he'd become my Mate-Sworn. Not just to siphon my magic but to command my dragons. Through the bind, that bastard had a pull on my body; a connection to my blood and the very thoughts in my head but he would not touch my fucking dragons.

Shouts and racing footsteps in the corridor had me on my feet. I'd barely taken a step when shadows spilled into the room. Exekiel appeared in the doorway. His shoulders sagged when he saw me. My heart leapt. I ran to him as his shadows slid beneath my feet and dragged me the rest of the way.

Our bodies collided. Exekiel grinned. It was a beautiful slash of pearly white teeth that almost stopped my heart. It had been one week since I'd seen him but I missed him like the night would miss the stars. His pink eyes gleamed and his arms tightened around my waist before he lowered his lips to mine.

I sagged into him. All the stress and worry of the day was temporarily overwritten. A few seconds of sweet serenity. Heat flushed my cheeks as he deepened the kiss and rocked the foundation of the earth. His tongue teased mine. Hot and probing. Expert strokes that made my knees shake. Fuck, this Fae could kiss.

Too soon, Exekiel pulled back but he kept his brow rested on mine.

"There are two dragons in the courtyard," he murmured. His breath was warm on my cheek. "I'm guessing you have something to do with that."

"What makes you say that?"

"Aside from their scent." Exekiel dragged his fingers down my spine. I shuddered. "That blue one was undressing me with her eyes."

I burst out laughing. "Was she, now?"

He tugged me closer. "She was."

His lips met mine again.

30

EXEKIEL:
RIDDLE ME THIS

We had to move. Now that two large dragons had announced our location to half the Isle, we couldn't stay at the cathedral. Fortunately, I had another place in mind. It was where I'd originally planned to stay when I'd made it out of the River of Resurrection. I'd stopped by Fates Cathedral to check on Satrialla and the Mothers had insisted I stay with them, instead. As far as they'd been concerned, I was a Fate in the flesh. There was nowhere else I should be.

Once the sick and wounded were sorted into carriages, they went one way, whilst the rest of us, on foot, went another. Varialla's dragons followed overhead, high enough to not be noticed unless someone was looking.

With the hood of my cloak drawn to stave off the night's cold, I led the way. We traversed through the outskirts of the isle passed a few aristocratic houses, and over empty moors and rolling hills.

Varialla shook her head. "Land in the Outer Isles is crumbling into the sea and they have all this space."

"Supposedly, this land is reserved for future winners of the Games." Not that there wasn't plenty of it to go around.

"Of course." Varialla scoffed. "Why help those who are currently in need when centuries from now, someone may need this space to build a swimming pool?"

I grunted my agreement. The Isle of the Eternals was the second largest of the five after Shifter Springs. More than three quarters of it stood empty.

It had been close to impossible for me to get approval for Evermore. None of the four Chosen casts had wanted the Outliers in their territory and the Fate-stained Primary at the time, had been happy for them to sleep on the streets. That was until I'd appealed to his supposed honor and pointed out that homeless drifters weren't an appropriate image for the prosperous land that homed the Conduit. The agreements had been signed the next day. Evermore was cramped and needed to be expanded, but it had been better than nothing.

"How pissed do you think they'll be when you don't return to the palace tonight?" Maximus rasped.

His vocal cords were still damaged despite the tonics and my gifted powers of *Thesona*.

Varialla looked at the warlock who limped up beside her. He was bruised, swollen and occasionally had to stop to catch his breath. However, he'd argued that he wasn't an invalid and had refused to ride in the carriage with the wounded.

Lucinda, who had been conscious by the time we left, had begrudgingly taken a carriage with Evangeline. I suspected if the witch had been able to move, she would have argued the same.

"I'll cross that bridge when I get to it. Right now, the only thing that matters is making sure you guys are safe."

"I think it's us who should be worried about you."

Varialla grimaced. "I'll be fine. It's not like I'd expected Phase Three to be three-legged races and riddles."

"Don't scoff at riddles," Calder called from behind us. The shifter had covered half his body in his inner-wolf's fur, leaving only his face visible. "They're harder than they seem."

"I'm pretty good at riddles." Maximus shrugged. "I've even made up a few of my own."

We slowed to trek across a particularly slick patch of ice on the ground. Mist curled around our feet.

The wolf shifter laughed. "Is that so? Let's hear it."

Maximus smirked. "I'm wet and hard."

Varialla and I exchanged a look. My brow lifted.

"If you hold me in your hand, I'll drip all over your fingers. What am I?"

"A penis," I drawled. "That's hardly a riddle."

"What?" Maximus shrieked; his voice cracked with the effort. "It's always about sex with you."

"I can't argue with that."

Varialla laughed. "I think we're all thinking the same thing, Maximus."

He tutted. "Bunch of perverts."

"All right. You're wet, hard and will leak all over my fingers if I hold you in my hand." Varialla could barely say it with a straight face. "What are you?"

"Ice," Maximus huffed. "Obviously."

A chorus of groans and laughter rang through the group.

Eventually, we crossed the wooden bridge that led from the Isle of the Eternals into the mountainous isle of Fae Reef. The familiar scents of freshwater, night flowers and mint filled my nostrils. My gaze swept up and down the smooth paved streets and the towering peaks beyond. There were seventy mountains in Fae Reef. Each one held a different city. Their homes, shops and cafés were built into the mountainsides.

The snow-capped peaks of the mountains were where the rich resided. Noblemen and women who kept things in order and liaised with the Royal Court. From their lip, waterfalls spilled over the edge and plummeted into the rivers below that ultimately led into the sea.

Tonight, those falls were frozen. A jagged cascade of water bent over the mountains edge and left suspended. It was another anomaly that should correct itself now that Varialla had returned to the Games.

Aquarius blew warmth into his hands. "Where to?"

It still felt strange to have the siren here after all this time. Like one day I'd wake up and he'd be back beneath the sea; an ocean of uncertainty between us. Over the last few days, we'd started to bridge that gap. In some ways, we felt like strangers. In other ways it felt like no time had passed at all.

"Peaked City." I led them through the narrow mountain pass towards Sea Street.

The ocean shimmered ahead of us. Its waves lapped at the shore. The closer we came to the reef, the more I made out the vibrant shades of coral that peaked above the water.

"This place is stunning." Varialla gazed from the ocean to the mountain peaks. Some which were too high up to see.

"There's so much I want to show you when this is over."

She squeezed my fingers that were interlaced with hers. "I can't wait."

When we reached the base of Peaked City mountain, we left the others and took the skies. Until I knew it was safe, it didn't make sense for them to make the trek up there. At her insistence, Varialla was in my arms.

It wasn't long before we were joined by her Crowned Sapphire and Scarlet Ridgeback. The sight brought me back to a time before the realm went to gorge. To when my family and their bonded had roamed the earth. It was nice to see that, perhaps for the first time, the memory didn't come with the usual sting of guilt and despair. In fact, something more like hope sparked in my chest.

These dragons were a symbol that what had been could be again. Only this time there'd be a queen we could trust on the throne.

Revynath's yellow eyes zeroed in on me. She was a magnificent and deadly beast. Her wings sliced through the air like blades. I gave her a nod and continued up the mountain face. I didn't slow until the scent of spiced lilies grew stronger.

Cut deep into the mountainside was an expansive white structure with an oasis on its roof and walls made almost entirely of glass. A long flightpath lined with pine trees led to the front door. It was exactly how he'd described it. A shimmering waterfall spilled over the mountains edge. Like the others, tonight the fall was frozen.

We landed and made our way up the path.

"What is this place?" Varialla's breath fogged around her mouth.

"It belonged to an old…friend."

I reached for the door handle. My fingers had barely brushed it when a blinding current of power knocked me off my feet. A figure hunched over me with a dagger at my throat. My shadows locked around their wrist and held the weapon millimeters from piercing the skin. Behind them, Varialla fisted a handful of silvery-white hair that she used to wrench my attackers head back.

He snarled, "I should have known it was you two."

I grinned up at the bastard. "Vladimir. Did you miss me?"

*

We followed the estranged councilman through the corridors of his grand estate. Built into a U-shape that cut through the mountains peak, most of the building had a clear view of the ocean through floor-to-ceiling windows. The space was extravagant but cold. Everything from the shimmering black tiles, to the coffee table, the chaise-longue, even the couch, was crafted from glass.

The rooms were mildly warmed with homey touches like ornaments of Fates, flowers and books. There were a few padded cushions and soft throws flung over the furniture but nothing could hide that this house was not a home.

"I hadn't expected to find you here considering the entire army is looking for you," I admitted as we turned into the main room where a fire crackled in the hearth.

A candle chandelier that resembled antlers hung overhead. For a sickening moment, I wondered if they were real. If they'd been taken from the head of some nameless nymph as punishment for an imagined slight. Vladimir wasn't as bad as the others in the Council, but that in no way made him good.

The elf grinned. "People underestimate the power of hiding in plain sight. It's the last place anyone thinks to look. Not to mention, they don't expect an elf to own prime land in Fae territory." He strode over to the mantle, picked up the poker, and prodded the fire. "You're the only one who knew about this place and you were dead."

Which was exactly why I'd thought the house would have been a good place to lay low.

After stoking a few more coals, he set the poker back into its stand. He didn't turn away from the fire.

"The day I planned to surprise Gwendoline with this place, I discovered their betrayal. They're behind the plague, the murders of the dragon clans, the attack at the banquet; all of it." He spoke through gritted teeth.

"Did you know I was supposed to die that night, not Demetrius? If I hadn't changed my fucking seat." His unbound hair shifted around his shoulders, stirred by the wind his power conjured.

Vladimir wasn't just a winter elf with the ability to create tempered storms. He was also a spring elf who could turn plant life into weapons. It was his affinity for two seasons where most held only one, that had led to him being voted in by the people of the Realm. The Fates had clearly chosen him for greater things and the people had been willing to find out what that was.

"I was focused on building a new life. She'd been focused on destroying what life there was left." He turned. Pain was evident in his clouded eyes.

Gwendoline was not the elf's mate. He'd lost her during the Brutal War. But he had cared about the councilwoman. He'd believed in a future that was all a lie. Gwendoline had seduced him to keep him busy; to keep him from noticing what they'd been up to.

"I'd wanted to protect our Court and destroy the scourge of the Realm." His cold stare slid to Varialla. "Little did I know, they were one and the same."

An orb floated into the room. From its silvery glass surface, it projected a hologram. Inside a satyr in a white blouse and feathered hat spoke into a microphone.

"News of the Royal Court mentioned," the orb announced before the volume automatically increased. Vladimir must have programmed the device to alert him.

"Hundreds more have succumbed to the plague in recent weeks, taking the number of infected well up into the thousands," the satyr reported. "Like the others, these latest individuals will be taken to the Court's research facility to see if they can determine the cause and if siren blood can cure them."

Footage of writhing centaurs and heaving Fae panned across the holo-screen. Each one was being tended to by a member of the Royal Court. They brushed stringy hair back from damp foreheads and offered the patients water from their hands. Baseless propaganda griffin-shit.

"Our Primaries and Council are doing what they can," the reporter went on. "But your donations to fund the research could save lives. If you can't afford to provide financial aid at this time, you can volunteer to be test subjects of the latest antidote." The reporter shook out her dark curls. "Let's stand together and save the Isles."

Vladimir waved a hand. The volume lowered though the holo-screen continued to play.

With a sigh, he turned to face me. "Why are you here, Prince of Death?"

"We needed a place to lay low."

"We?"

"There are more of us at the foot of the mountain and on their way in carriages."

The elf's thin lips pursed. "Let me guess; guileless rebels who believe they can make a difference."

"Among others."

"We have an alchemist who has created an antidote," Varialla said. "It's not an exact cure but it helps. He's working on perfecting it."

Vladimir didn't acknowledge her. He didn't even glance in her direction. My jaw ticked but I curbed my rage. There were several people counting on us. This space was the best hope they had. It wouldn't help to maul the host.

"Your invalids can stay." Vladimir looked at me when he spoke. "The sea-witch goes."

"Excuse me, asshole?"

Vladimir quirked a brow. Finally, he turned to Varialla. He moved towards her with slow, sure steps. "Did I stutter?"

I fought the urge to grab the bastard's cloak and choke him with it. This wasn't my fight. The animosity between him and Varialla was something they needed to work through on their own if we hoped to get through this.

"After everything you've learned how can you still be so prejudice?"

Vladimir scoffed. "Because I know what kind of creature you are and the scum from which you came. I know the depravity of your kind and how low you will sink for your own gain." Vladimir leaned in. His nose was inches from hers. "Get the fuck out of my house."

"You're a hypocritical bastard." Varialla took a step closer which forced him to ease back. "You act like your kind are so innocent but you said it yourself; they were behind it all." She continued to advance. The elf continued to step back. His upper lip curled. "My people may have been the blade but yours were the one to wield it. So, what makes my kind so much worse than yours?"

"I was there." The veins in Vladimir's neck jumped. His pale face flushed. "I was there when your mother nodded to a group of sirens barely out of swaddles. They sang a song that compelled my mate's sister to run her through, with the very weapon I'd given to protect her."

Varialla jerked back like she'd been physically struck.

"You ask me why I hate you; your whole cursed kind," the elf spat. "Tell me how you felt about the Rebel King when he tried to take your precious shadow that night at the ball. Now imagine how you'd feel if he'd been successful."

Varialla opened her mouth to respond but Vladimir had already left the room.

31

VARIALLA:
I'll Never Look at a Window the Same Way Again

One night. That was all Vladimir would give me in his home. I suspected he wouldn't have agreed to that if Revynath and Urdith hadn't crouched to peer in through the windows. The elf hadn't shown any sign of fear or surprise when he'd seen my dragons, but his asshole level had dropped a few notches and he'd conceded to one night.

It was all I needed. I should have been back at the palace already but I hadn't wanted to leave before Lucinda woke up. Then I hadn't wanted to go until I knew where Exekiel and the others would be staying. Now it was too late to return. Or maybe, I was just making excuses.

Today had been harder than expected. The last thing I wanted to do now was return to the palace; to the public's eye and scrutiny. There'd probably be some kind of penalty for evading Godric but if it meant I got to spend the evening with those I loved and exploring my new power, it would be worth it. First thing tomorrow, I would leave and return to the palace.

I ran my tongue over my freshly brushed teeth and exited the estate's sleek black bathroom. It was the most modern thing I'd seen in the Isles so far. There was no shower but it did have a clawfoot bathtub rather than one carved out of stone in the ground. Once I claimed the throne, I was going to install a shower in every room in that palace.

I padded barefoot down the corridor and made my way to the room I'd be sharing with the girls; Lucinda, Cyrus, Colette and whoever else could fit. When I rounded the corner, I stopped. There was someone outside the door.

His pink irises gleamed amidst the inky black shadows that curled around the silvered edge of his wings. His dark hair was tussled like he'd just run his fingers through it. My own fingers itched to do the same.

"Where have you been?" Exekiel murmured when I approached.

My heart flipped. His voice was low and dangerously alluring. My nipples puckered at the sound. It'd been a few hours since I'd last kissed him. It felt like a lifetime ago.

Moonlight shafted through the wall of windows. His shirt was unbuttoned and the pale glow spilled over the harsh contours of his sculpted abs. His black bottoms hung low on his hips in a way that highlighted the deep V-cut of his muscles. My eyes helplessly followed the path downwards to the prominent bulge in his pants. Even from a distance and half-bathed in shadow, it was huge. Exekiel was magnificent. Carved to make a girl lower her defenses and get on her back.

"I went to clean up." My voice shook.

All my spiel of being the last dragonborn and heir to a million thrones yet one look at this Fae and I was powerless. One touch and I would be his to use in any way he wanted.

His pearly white teeth flashed when he grinned. I had to press my legs together to keep from dripping down my thighs.

"You shouldn't have." The low rumble of his voice slid over me like warm honey gliding down my throat. He stroked his thumb across his bottom lip. "The things I'm about to do to you are filthy."

My stomach clenched. I stopped in front of him and his hands immediately found my waist. He drew my body against his. My pillowy breasts bounced into his hard chest. My skin sparked at the contact.

"We can't. It's not allowed."

I swallowed a moan when Exekiel's hands stroked up my sides. His thumb brushed over my nipples and his hands kneaded the soft flesh of my tits.

"We can."

My eyelids fluttered. Fuck; he was good at that.

"Girls in one room. Boys in another. Remember? Vladimir's orders."

Exekiel's hand climbed higher until it wrapped around my neck and pulled a gasp from my lips.

"Fuck Vladimir."

His tongue stroked across the seam of my lips. I opened for him and willingly accepted the sweep of his tongue. I tasted the hint of cider and mint on his breath. My hands gripped his shoulders and I pulled him closer. The hard swell of his erection dug into my abdomen. My eyes rolled.

"Fuck. You're destroying me," I panted when our lips parted. How was I supposed to resist this man?

Exekiel chuckled and dragged his thumb along my jawline. "Not yet."

God, I wanted him. But even without Vladimir's ridiculous rule there was nowhere to go. The manor had twelve rooms. Each one was occupied with friends and allies. The biggest suite Vladimir had, of course, kept for himself.

"Not tonight." I pulled back before I let Exekiel fuck me in this glass house where Vladimir's floating security orbs recorded everything.

With my hands balled into fists to keep from touching him, I stepped around the Shadow Saint, and pushed open the room door.

Exekiel grabbed the handle and slammed it shut before I stepped across the threshold. I spun to face him.

He planted his hands at either side of my head and leaned in. "Maybe I wasn't clear." His lips brushed my cheek. "Tonight, little bud, I am fucking you."

His hand travelled between the valley of my breasts. I trembled. The way this Fae effortlessly awakened my need for him was embarrassing.

"Today, I almost lost you more times than I can count." His thumb dragged over my nipple then slid lower; down my stomach to the waistband of my leggings.

"Tomorrow, you will be back in the palace." He undid the ties. "Tonight, you are mine."

Exekiel worked his fingers into my bottoms. I froze; paralyzed by his touch. My back pressed to the grooved wood of the door as he stroked me into submission.

"We c-can't." I bit down on my bottom lip to stifle a moan. "Not here."

Exekiel pressed closer. The warmth of his breath caressed my ear. "Are you going to stop me, little bud?"

Before I could respond, he tugged my leggings down to just below my ass. They were tight around my thighs and restricted his hand which made his movements jerky. Each jarring bump of his fingers struck my clit and spasmed through my core.

"Vladimir c-could be w-watching." Even as I argued, I rocked into his motions.

Exekiel grinned. "Then let's give him a fucking show."

His mouth descended on mine. My heart lurched and my fingers curled into his shirt. Every argument scattered. Every thought was obliterated by the feel of his tongue. I lightly sucked before pulling back to drag my teeth over his lower lip.

Exekiel groaned. It was a sound that should have been illegal. A sound that made me rake my fingers down his bare chest, desperate to hear it again.

He rubbed me harder. I gasped into his mouth. I tried to catch my breath. I tried to remember why doing this right now, against the door of the room where my friends slept in the open hallway of this house made of glass, was a bad idea.

Exekiel pushed a finger inside me and deepened our kiss. My mind short-circuited. He tasted like mint and ale. Like seduction and sin. Like everything I'd ever wanted but shouldn't have.

"Get these fucking things off." He dropped to his knees.

I instantly missed the warmth of his body but then he yanked my leggings down and pushed his mouth between my thighs. Heat blazed through my skin. My head kicked back with a thump that someone inside must have heard.

I tangled my fingers in the soft strands of his hair and brushed his wings as Exekiel pressed his tongue into the thin lace of my black thong. He made that sound again. Wet trickled from inside me. My heart raced.

"I'm going to destroy this cunt." His nose pressed into me and inhaled deeply.

My body quivered.

Exekiel rolled down my thong. I obediently kicked them off along with my leggings. I couldn't hold back my cry when his mouth fastened between my legs. He sucked on me greedily. His tongue lapped at my juices; tasted everything I had to give. My body tightened with need. It craved the release only he could give.

"Open your legs."

I did without question; without thought.

My mate used his fingers to spread me, then dragged his tongue up my core.

"Fuck!" I cried before I could stop myself.

My hips undulated, meeting each thrust of his skillful tongue. I was consumed. Overwhelmed and underprepared for the visceral way his touch ignited me.

I braced one hand on the doorframe; the other on the back of his head as my mate devoured me. Sent me to fucking Nirvana.

My ass smacked into the door. *Thud. Thud. Thud.* The wood juddered at my back. If anyone was asleep, they were about to wake up.

"Shit." We should stop but I couldn't find the strength or the will.

Exekiel scissored my clit with his fingers whilst his tongue flicked the tip. My eyes crossed. My knees buckled. Only his painful grip on my waist kept me upright.

"Mmmm," he growled. "I could get drunk off the taste of you. Intoxicated on your smell."

His hand slid up my abdomen and roughly grasped my breast as he tunneled back in. He peeled me open on his tongue; fucked me with its rough thrusts.

My fingers tightened around the back of his head. Soft whimpers escaped me.

"Oh fuck. Exekiel."

A camera-orb drifted into the hallway. I knew they were programmed to sweep the house, but this one stopped; suspended in midair. Its red light blinked right at me. It was being controlled. I didn't struggle to guess by who.

Vladimir was watching.

I opened my mouth to tell Exekiel but his tongue plunged deeper. My eyes slammed shut. My lips parted in a silent scream.

"You undo me." His hot breath wafted between my thighs. His teeth grazed my clit.

Fuck. Through half closed eyes, I watched the orb move closer. It panned over Exekiel's hand on my breast as he pinched my nipple between two fingers, then lowered to where he sucked on my clit.

"Ex-E-Exekiel…" I wanted to tell him his perverted friend was watching us but couldn't get the words out.

Ecstasy consumed me as thoroughly as he did. My hips rolled with his ministrations. My head whipped from side to side. I didn't want Vladimir seeing me like this; watching me writhe like this but the camera stayed put.

"You look so good fucking my tongue, beautiful." Exekiel breathed then plunged back in. His thumb stroked my clit. Over and over. I blinked as my vision spotted and my breaths became shallow.

"Oh god," I panted.

Everything inside me drew tight. The camera-orb swooped closer like it wanted to soak up every second of my orgasm that threatened to break free. I moaned.

Vladimir was a sick fuck. I knew he was touching himself the same way he had when he'd caught Exekiel and I in my room the night of the werewolf attack. The councilman had always had a twisted fascination with me and he'd never hid it. Not how badly he wanted to fuck me, or how much he wanted me dead.

My nails dug into Exekiel's shoulder and the wood of the doorframe.

Holy shit. The sensations he evoked had me choking; screaming through clenched teeth. Exekiel peered up at me. His pink eyes gleamed a lethal red. His grin was a flash of wicked intent.

"Come," he commanded and drove two fingers inside me. My back slammed into the door. "Come for me."

My body obeyed. I spasmed around his fingers as he sucked on my clit. My release welled up then broke free.

Exekiel was on his feet. He swallowed my moans with a toe-curling kiss. I tasted myself on his tongue.

Before I could get my bearings, he grabbed the backs of my thighs and lifted me up. My legs wrapped around him. He spun our bodies until I was pressed against the windows. The cold bit into my skin and I gasped. My nipples hard.

"There is nothing more addictive than watching you come." Exekiel lowered his hand to my neck and squeezed. His grin was wicked as he ground into me and forced me to feel the hard indent of his cock through his trousers.

"Do you want me to fuck you, little bud? Do you want me to stretch you over my cock and turn this pussy into a puddle?"

I almost lost my mind. How was this man so sexy? Why did I crave him like the last drop of water in a drought?

My head bobbed up and down. "Y-yes."

"As you wish."

Exekiel slid down his joggers. There was no build up; no preamble. His ass clenched and he thrust deep; impaling me on his pulsing, perfect cock. My head smacked into the glass. I'd never felt so full. So stretched, almost to the point of painful.

He didn't need to give me chance to adjust to his swollen girth. I was so wet, so ready to take him. I braced the soles of my feet behind me on the cold glass as his hands fitted around my ass and slid me up and down his length.

"You feel so good," he rasped. "Fuck." Exekiel bowed his head and sucked my tongue into his mouth. I clung to him; savored his taste, the feel of him hard and pumping inside me.

"So hot and tight around my cock," he groaned and shifted his hips.

My breath caught. My world spun.

Exekiel was a warrior. I was his battlefield. He pounded into me hard and claimed my entire being. His nails bit into the soft flesh of my ass as he forced me to take it all. Down to the fucking root. He showed no mercy. He held nothing back as he impaled me over and over again.

"Shit," I gasped.

My skin was clammy and stuck to the glass in places. In others, sweat pooled and I slipped, but Exekiel held me firm; imprisoned on the powerful strokes of his relentless cock. I moaned deeply.

If anyone in the houses below looked up, they would see my ass pressed into the window. They would see it bouncing on the glass as Exekiel pushed me to the brink. I was riding the edge of my release. Of my sanity.

The camera-orb recorded it all. The red light blinked in time with my raging pulse. The lens adjusted and zoomed in on my face that was creased in pleasure. It slid down to the beads of sweat that trickled between my breasts and to the vein that jumped in my throat. Vladimir watched it all; he watched me.

Exekiel bowed his head. His breath fogged up the glass as he panted, "That's my girl."

My walls tightened and rippled around his cock. My body shook.

Exekiel's wings splayed out behind him, wreathed in shadows. He'd never looked more glorious; more avenging and powerful. He was an angel of death and he was fucking me.

I dragged my fingers down the inner side of his wings and stroked the ridges of their shimmering violet veins. Exekiel groaned. His thrusts intensified.

My heart stammered. It felt like I was drowning and flying all at once.

"Ah—" I cut off my choked cry and bit my lip.

"Don't you dare," he snarled. "Scream for me."

I hissed; fighting the burn of bliss that begged for release.

"Scream. For. Me." His hips punctuated each word.

I was defenseless; strung up and left reeling in the aftermath of each powerful thrust. No matter how much I tried to resist, I flung my head back and screamed as my orgasm tore free.

"Fuck." Exekiel repeatedly rammed into me so hard I thought the window would shatter.

His body stiffened. His thighs shifted. Then with a roar, he came. The sight had my body reacting and I fell off the peak again. My walls convulsed around him.

"Fuck!" Exekiel shouted and slammed his palm down on the glass.

"For Fates sake, shut up, you two!" Lucinda's shout came from the other side of the door.

Exekiel's warm breath shuddered through my curls as he let out a breathless chuckle.

I was too riddled with the aftershocks of my third explosive orgasm to fully grasp that the entire manor house had just heard me come and that Vladimir had watched the whole thing. However, distantly, a part of me smiled at the familiar strength that had returned to Lucinda's voice.

32

LOCH:
WHO'S PLAYING WHO?

The double doors to the council chamber slammed into the wall. Five furious figures stormed in. I shared a glance with Queen Zenera who sat in the stone seat beside me. Then I returned my attention to those who believed I owed them something.

"Care to explain what the fuck is going on?" Alexov stalked to the head of the table. His purple robe billowed behind him.

I looked to Adir—the Primary. The position at the head was reserved for him but he merely sat in the high-backed chair to the right of Alexov. He was the obedient little pet doing his duty after all. The fateless shit hadn't earned his title. It had been handed to him by these puppet masters of the Court. Knox took the chair on Alexov's left. Belland and Gwendoline settled into the other vacant seats.

None of them acknowledged Zenera. She was only here because I'd told them of Evangeline's affair and solidified my worth. She was a token; a gift to keep me compliant.

"First you launch an attack at Dragon Spire claiming that someone reported seeing Varialla alive and hiding out there," Alexov thumped his fist on the stone table. "Now she shows up here with dragons?"

His eyes swung wildly around the room, like he expected any of them to have the answers. It was laughable how little they all knew.

Knox's gaze flickered to mine before he quickly looked away. Out of everyone on the Council, he was the only one who hadn't been surprised by the arrival of Varialla's dragons. On the contrary, he was ecstatic. This was the moment we'd been waiting for.

In Phase Three the people's votes counted for forty percent of a contestant's rank. Not only did Varialla's dragons increase her power level; they also enhanced her pull with the people. With our grooming and guidance, she could lead us to victory. She could seat me on the throne and Knox would serve as my righthand man. He'd be in the position of power he'd been promised before Exekiel's barrier had affected his reign and the Court were forced to choose Adir as their new Primary and pawn.

I had wanted to consummate my bond with Varialla before her dragons emerged but what mattered was that they had. Two terrifying creatures not seen in centuries. Two formidable weapons, wielded by the true heir of Shifter Springs and the Coral Court. Varialla was an instrument of beauty and destruction, and she would be mine.

"Did you plan this?" Alexov's murderous stare went to Zenera.

Beneath the table, my nails drummed impatiently on my thigh.

My queen straightened. Despite her frail frame she carried all the strength I remembered.

"You knew her father possessed the gift to awaken the sleeping beasts," she spat. "Wouldn't it make sense that she might be able to do the same?"

"Which is exactly why I'd thanked the Fates that she was dead, you Fate-Stained Sea slug!" Spit sprayed from Alexov's mouth. "Yet here she is, alive."

His face was flushed. Power rippled in the air around him.

"Careful, Senior." I tilted my head to meet his venomous stare. "You need the sirens more than we need you at this point. I won't take kindly to you talking down to my queen."

His eyes widened. I bared my teeth. I'd had about enough of his posturing. The fateless shit thought I was nothing more than his trained pet. He didn't realize I'd bitten through my leash long ago. I'd simply been waiting for him to lower his guard and put me in a position to strike.

"Yes, Varialla is somehow alive."

Adir scoffed. "Somehow."

He'd been the one to throw her unconscious body on the pile to burn with the others. I'd been the one to drag it off when everyone's back had been turned. The look he gave me now suggested he'd figured that much out.

"Yes, she now has dragons. The question isn't who's to blame, it's what the fuck are we going to do about it?" I stood and relished the small bob of Alexov's throat. He subtly edged back. "Your hope to have her killed during today's challenge, failed. As we speak, she rises in the polls. The people are calling her the true queen blessed by the Fates and destined to rule." It was a title I encouraged. "So, again, I ask, what are you going to do about it?"

I swept my stare over each of them. They looked from me to Alexov but none spoke. Not even the senior councilman himself. The truth was they had no idea what to do about Varialla and her dragons.

The Court wanted her dead. They'd claimed she'd died once; that she was killed in a freak building collapse. Since her return, the people had started to speculate about the lie. They questioned why the Court had been so quick to name her among the dead and the Shadow Saint with her.

One rumor claimed that a member of the Royal Court hadn't wanted either of them to win so they'd locked them away. Romantics claimed they'd run off together but had returned to honor their duty to the realm. Some said they were gravely injured in the building collapse and had spent the last few months in recovery. This rumor worked best to serve the Court.

I didn't care. Either way I had them all where I wanted them. The Court and Council were floundering. Varialla had come into her full potential. All that was left was to solidify her bind to me.

"In the meantime, find out where they're based. We can bet coin that they have something planned against us. Our main priority now is to find out what that is. Have the guards question the people. There have been several reports of dragons spotted near the cathedral. Start there."

No one moved. I braced my knuckles on the table.

"Why are you still here?"

Alexov pursed his lips. The fucker looked like he wanted to argue.

Knox stood. "I'll prepare the guards."

Gwendoline ran her hungry gaze over me. She'd always loved a man in charge. "Varialla's Trial of Endurance is coming up. I'll speak to the prep team. Maybe we can orchestrate her death then."

One by one they filed out of the room.

Alexov paused in the doorway. "You better hope we stop her, Orqanz. Or else I might be forced to think you were behind this."

My stare conveyed nothing as it slid to his. "And what if I was?"

What could he possibly do to stop me now? He'd given me my title, welcomed me into his nest. All he could do was trust me like the sirens had been forced to trust them all those years ago. It hadn't worked out well for us. To save themselves and their position, they'd imprisoned my queen, cut out her tongue and tore her teeth from her mouth one by one. She'd endured endless torture whilst her people were left to rot and starve beyond the barrier of their Protector. The councilman would have to hope we didn't return the kindness.

His grey eyes narrowed. He didn't know what to make of that. He couldn't decide if I was simply lashing out in anger or if I actually despised him.

"Let's hope not, for your sake." Alexov smoothed down his robe and left the room.

"You need to do something about your temper," Queen Zenera drawled when the door clicked shut.

I wanted to argue that I didn't need to do anything. One siren song and I could have those fools eating Pegasus shit out of the palm of my hand. But it wasn't as simple as that. A siren song only affected those within range. The more powerful the siren, the greater the distance, but everything had its limits. Which meant that if I coerced the Council to do exactly what I wanted, the moment they travelled far enough, they could band together and turn against me. This was why I had to keep them believing I was on their side—had to keep smiling at their pathetic jokes and following their senseless orders—until my reign was absolute.

"What we need is to talk some sense into your daughter before she hands the realm over to the fateless shits who oppressed us." I paced the chamber. "Before she puts a crown on the fucking Shadow Saints head."

"That will never happen," Zenera snapped. "I didn't do all I did, sacrifice all I had for her to part her thighs for the enemy and damn everything we've worked for." She sucked down a sharp breath.

The salty bite of her power touched my lips. I couldn't help thinking of how Varialla's magic always tasted sweet; delicious. I groaned with need.

"We vowed our revenge. That we would one day sit upon their precious throne and watch them beg for scraps as we did." Her piercing green eyes met mine. "We will see it done."

33

VARIALLA:
HYPOCRITES & HOPE

The carriage rolled closer to the Fae Reef border. I shifted in my seat. I didn't want to say goodbye. The night I'd spent with Exekiel had been perfect—better than perfect. After he'd thoroughly fucked my brains out, we'd gone into the gardens. Exekiel had commented that it was a good sign my dragons didn't try to incinerate him. Apparently, in the past, if a dragon found their bonded's partner unworthy, it often led to them chasing the potential mate away with fire. If they were fast, they lived and were accepted by the dragon. If they were too slow, they became nothing more than a memory and a scorch mark.

After that lovely anecdote we'd curled up on a blanket in the snow. Exekiel had told me about how he'd felt seeing his father and giving up his seat in

Fatevale. I'd told him about what it had felt like to lose him. How I'd channeled my grief towards revenge all those weeks I'd spent in the Coral Court.

We'd talked until we'd fallen asleep under the stars. At some point during the night, I'd woken up and found Revynath's wing slung over us. I wanted a lifetime of nights like that but fate had other plans. Tonight, I wouldn't be sleeping on the cold hard grounds of Vladimir's manor with my mate. I'd be sleeping in the palace with my enemy.

Exekiel sat beside me with his legs spread and his hand in mine. If it was just the two of us in here, I would have got on my knees, and given him a proper farewell. However, we weren't alone.

Across from us were Lucinda and Evangeline. They shared soft kisses and Evangeline constantly checked the bandages on Lucinda's side.

"Will you stop fussing, elf?" my friend grumbled but she couldn't hide her sad smile.

She probably felt like I did; like she was about to leave half their heart behind.

The carriage came to a stop. My chest tightened and I turned to look at Exekiel. A muscle feathered in his jaw then he turned his pale pink eyes on me.

"You ready?"

I grimaced. "I guess so."

He squeezed my fingers and brushed his lips across my knuckles. "Why are you doing this?"

He didn't ask for him but for me.

"To free the Outlands and unite the Isles," I said, firmly. "To put an end to the Ruling Court's tyranny and to destroy Loch Orqanz."

Exekiel bobbed his head. "So, do it."

He leaned in and kissed me; deeply, soundly. My heart rabbited in my chest. I clung to the laced-up neck of his tunic and drew him closer. The carriage driver, a goblin, rapped on the door. We'd reached the border. After a few more lingering pecks, Exekiel and Evangeline jumped out and traded places with Cyrus, Colette and Maximus, who had ridden in the carriage behind us. That carriage returned to Peaked City. Ours continued on to the Isle of the Eternals.

We eventually reached the palace gates. Footsteps thudded towards us. I sat straighter. Maximus adjusted the rings on his fingers. Two Fae guards wrenched open our carriage doors and stuck their heads in.

Their eyes searched the small space, then turned to assess me and my entourage. Their expressions darkened when they settled on Lucinda. I pulled magic into my hands and waited for them to lash out. After a lengthy pause, the Fae nodded and shut the doors before ushering us through.

"That was unexpected," Cyrus murmured beneath her breath.

I had to agree. Maybe it had something to do with the crowd gathered outside the palace gates. Everyone wanted a glimpse of the contestants—a possible future ruler of the Realm. Or, maybe it had something to do with the two large dragons that I knew circled overhead. Or maybe it was something more sinister.

The iron gates groaned open. Our carriage rolled through. The crowd cheered and waved banners for the remaining casts. I noted the clamshell with the dragon in support of me and met the eyes of a woman who waved it. She smiled and bowed her head low.

Now that my dragon side had been revealed, I'd become more of a beacon to the people. Not only to the Outer Isles but to the Inlands too. I was a symbol that both sides could exist. That they could fall in love.

Despite everything my mother had done, no one denied that she had loved my father. It was his betrayal that had ultimately broke her and revealed the monster she could be. If he hadn't turned his back on her, the landscape of the Nine Isles could have looked very different right now. I wasn't the only one who wanted that.

There were also a handful of banners being waved for Wiccan's Wharf and the disqualified witch; Lucinda Ironclaw. I looked to where she sat across from me. Her jaw, tense.

"The Royal Court may have branded you a traitor to the realm, but clearly not everyone agrees."

Lucinda's smile was tight. I wanted to reach for her hand but the carriage doors swung open again. I straightened, then together we stepped out into the stunning courtyard of the palace.

Head tipped high, Lucinda grinned and nodded to those who chanted her name. I did the same. Colette and Cyrus came up beside us; abandoning their expected position at our backs. Abandoning all customs of what nymphs and sirens could and could not do.

We made it as far as the red paved palace steps before a quadrant of guards flung open the double doors and marched down to meet us. The Council strode behind them with Adir in the lead. Like the first day we'd met, he wore a tall-hat, the same plum-purple shade as his hooded cape. A gold Five Isles medal was pinned to his breast and a purple sash hung across his chest.

At the sight of the Primary, the people cheered. They saw a hero; a leader who had kept them safe and helped their land prosper for the last century. I saw a murderer. A male who'd signed off on the deaths of thousands to secure his seat on the throne. A male who had tortured me and left me for dead. A male who had poisoned my mate and used my people for their power.

The Council stopped at the top of the steps so they could look down at us. There was a low whir as camera-orbs swooped in closer. The din of the crowd quieted. Adir forced a smile onto his thin lips. It was strained. His nose wrinkled and cheeks pinched. But he easily slipped into his role of devoted Primary; a Fae for the people.

"Varialla von Hastings. Nice to see you aren't dead." The 'yet' was implied but the people didn't notice as they applauded.

"Right back at you, Primary."

I made my meaning just as obvious as he had. I was coming for him; for his throne and this whole kingdom.

The slight twitch of his brow was the only indication that he'd understood. His brown wings ruffled behind him. Yet when his stare went from me to Lucinda, not even he could hide the malice that shone in his dark gaze. Here was the woman his mate had chosen to be with over him.

Due to cast rivalries both Adir and Evangeline had been encouraged to take consorts of their own cast; handpicked by the Court. Adir had been all too willing. However, he maintained that he loved Evangeline and had only agreed to appease the Fae and elf nobles. No one had believed him based on the way he pawed at females. However, now, I wondered if it was true. Did he truly love his mate despite their growing differences and obvious disdain?

His nostrils flared. Perhaps he could smell Evangeline on Lucinda now. I almost felt sorry for the bastard but he'd made his choice. He'd let himself be manipulated by power and greed and he'd become something other than the man Evangeline had fallen in love with.

Finally, he looked back at me. His mask firmly in place.

"However."

Guards closed in around Lucinda. One grabbed her arm. Lucinda shoved him away only for another two to pounce and force her to her knees. This was what I'd expected from the second they'd seen her in the carriage. Clearly, Adir had wanted the honor himself.

He sneered. "The witch is not welcome. She is a wanted enemy of the realm who is to be beheaded for her crimes. The boy," he jerked his head at Maximus, "can be spared. We all make mistakes trying to protect the ones we love. But her crimes are unforgivable."

I stepped towards him. "What crime is that?"

"Lucinda Ironclaw betrayed the Crown. She climbed into bed with a member of the Royal Court when she was a contestant in the Games. A clear violation of the laws and punishable by death."

I ascended a step. A guard reached for me but the look I shot him had him pulling his hand back.

"Isn't that what you wanted to do with me?"

The audience gasped and ooo'd.

Here it was. The argument we'd prepared and that I'd practiced in the mirror this morning. If it were up to me, Lucinda and Maximus would have stayed far from this fucking place but as contestants of the Games they were bound to the same laws of the Conduit. If they didn't win, then they had to die or serve the Crown. Since Maximus had been removed from his position as stable hand, they would both now serve on my team of stylists.

The Primary fell silent just as I'd expected. Camera-orbs panned closer.

"Tell me, Primary, how does what they did differ to your intentions for me?"

Someone in the crowd shouted, "Yeah!"

"Wasn't it you who offered me protection and power in exchange for my body?"

He couldn't deny it. Everyone had seen the way he'd gone after me. His attention had been the talk of the realm. Would the foreign temptress from beyond the veil choose the Primary or the Shadow Saint?

"Wasn't it you who'd hoped to control me with a few swings of your flaccid cock?"

Low laughter rippled through the people. Forgetting himself, Adir glanced behind him, at the man who was truly running this realm; Alexov.

The councilman didn't miss a beat. His gaze swept over the crowd. Most seemed to be on the side of love—of Evangeline and Lucinda.

"If this is law then the Primary should be beheaded too," a woman bravely called out.

My stomach flipped. I prayed she wasn't punished after this. But she was right. The Primary would have had me in his bed if I'd agreed.

Alexov took a step forward and rested a consoling hand on Adir's shoulder. "Perhaps the Primary is speaking from heartbreak. Our sovereign is clearly mourning the loss of a love he thought he had. A love that was cruelly taken from him."

He levelled a glare at Lucinda. He tried to villainize her as if love was something one could physically steal or demand. Of all the things in life, love was the one thing no one could control.

"The rule of no relations between contestants and court members was created by the Council to protect the integrity of the Games. However, perhaps death is too severe a punishment. It is something we will evaluate." Alexov stood taller. "As a senior member of the Council, I decree that this once, we will settle for disqualification and not death, to honor your return to the Games, Varialla." His eyes slid upwards to where my dragons circled. "And what a return it is."

The crowd went wild.

Cries of, "We love you, Varialla" and "Queen of the dragons" rang through the courtyard.

Alexov's jaw ticked and he glared down at me. I smiled sweetly. I had the people. Not all of them but enough, and he knew it. I'd always been a fan favorite but once I'd revealed myself as the last dragonborn and heir to Shifter Springs, the scales had tipped even further in my favor. The faithful now believed I was born as a queen of both sides to end the endless war. And that was what I would do.

I looked over my shoulder to where the guards released Lucinda. Though onlookers wouldn't notice it, I saw the relief in her steely gaze as she strutted up the steps beside me.

Without another word, the five of us made our way into the belly of the beast.

34

VARIALLA:
HOW TO BURN A BASTARD

That was terrifying." Lucinda flopped face down on the lush bed of my palace rooms. She let out a blissful sigh.

Maximus snickered. "I can't believe that worked."

"Me neither." I snorted a laugh.

I'd hoped it would but I hadn't been sure. If the people hadn't supported my claim that the Primary was just as guilty, I didn't know what we would have done.

I kicked off my boots and massaged my feet. "I need a bath."

I was in the same blood-spattered outfit from yesterday. I padded into the bath chamber where steam curled from a soap scented rockpool. I tore off my clothes and sank into its warm depths. Salt touched my lips. Seawater. My siren gifts buzzed in response. I hummed gratefully.

Today, there was no trial or test. It was a chance to officially get to know the palace staff. I could also go into the city; meet the people, kiss babies, and do whatever else it was politicians did in these situations. It was an opportunity to rack up some miscellaneous points and try to catch up with the others. According to Calder, my dragons would give me an edge, but until the Weekly Review, I didn't know how much or if it would be enough to put me in the lead.

Voices rose outside seconds before the door flew open. A glass sphere camera-orb swooped into the chamber. Godric trotted in after. I screeched and flung my arm over my tits. The centaur used his remote-control device to direct the orb around the chamber and over me.

"What the heck are you doing?" I tried to duck lower but the waters almost clear depths didn't hide much.

"Great job yesterday." Godric acted like I hadn't spoken. He didn't seem at all put off by the fact that I was naked.

"The footage from the arena was spectacular. You soaring off with your dragons." He shook his head and kissed the tips of his fingers. "Orb-vision gold." He continued to direct the orb around the bath chamber taking in the concave mirror cut into the wall and the oval stained-glass window.

"But you can't just run off. In situations like that, you always have to return to the palace." He threw me an admonishing look. "Since you're newly back in the Games, I won't say anything but I'll have to report you if it happens again."

My lips pursed. Lucinda had evaded her orbs-director on several occasions. A few times she'd managed to give him the slip in the town square. He hadn't been the fastest and had apparently been easy to lose in a crowd. Once, she'd had to knock him out and had stolen his coin pouch so he'd think he was robbed. Another time she'd managed to douse his food in a laxative that had kept him busy for a few hours. By that point, he'd guessed it was her but hadn't figured out a way to stop or prove it. The poor bugger was probably glad to be free of her.

Apparently, the trick was to never openly run away. Lucinda always made it look like it was his fault and so he'd never reported her. However, he'd been a satyr. My orbs-director was much larger and I wasn't entirely sure I could knock him out, especially without someone noticing. I also suspected he wasn't easy to lose in a crowd. But I'd have to try.

The plan was to get away once a week and meet with Exekiel and the others. I couldn't have a centaur trailing my every step.

Godric guided the orb across the water and around my head.

I swatted it away. "Do you want me to hit you? Is that it?"

Once again, he acted like I hadn't spoken.

"Tell me, how do you feel after yesterday? Finding your dragons. Saving your friends. Diving deeper into the Games." The orb panned closer. "If you're excited, give me a smile, maybe cover your face and kick your feet. If you're nervous bite your lip. Look off into the distance. Let me see that emotion play out on your face."

I rolled my eyes. It was going to be a long day.

When I was finally dressed in brown leather leggings with a ruffled red skirt and a white blouse with a brown leather waistcoat laced up at the front, Godric ordered me outside into the gardens. He wanted to show me adjusting to my life in the palace. More importantly the red flowers would apparently look great with my complexion in the afternoon light. I didn't love the idea of the centaur following me around dictating my every step, but I did like the sound of getting some fresh air. Plus, it gave me an excuse to check in on my dragons.

*

The palace grounds were as stunning as I'd expected. We walked along paved footpaths with low hedge walls. Fountains burbled as we passed. Polished statues of Fates and previous royals were dotted across a perfectly manicured lawn. There were occasional white stone benches beneath arches of orchids and the air was perfumed with scents of flowers and sweet berries that grew from towering trees.

The thrum of wingbeats stirred the air. My head snapped upwards. Urdith and Revynath flew down towards us. My heart soared but dropped when I noticed the violent gleam in their eyes. I caught the sharp flash of their teeth as their lips pulled back into a snarl. The ferocious sound reverberated through the gardens.

"You've got to be kidding."

I glanced at Maximus and followed his gaze. Loch and a woman I barely registered sauntered towards us. Red filled my vision. My skin stung at the sudden crackle of power that percolated in the palms of my hands. Dragon's fire burned in my throat.

I expected Loch to veer down a different path or at least hesitate but the fucker just kept coming. He wasn't going to run and neither would I. Lucinda stepped forward. I didn't know how she felt or what she wanted to do, but I wouldn't stop her. Fuck, I'd help her. Forget playing by the rules. This bastard had plunged a blade through her fucking gut only a day ago. It was only thanks to Exekiel's power of *Thesona* that she was still here amongst the living.

Revynath's huge frame skirted over us, low enough for me to stroke her underbelly if I reached up. The gust of wind almost sent us flying. The earth shuddered when she landed. Her body was low to the ground and her head angled towards Loch.

Finally, the bastard stumbled to a stop. I bucked when I felt the familiar draining sensation of my power as he siphoned it through the bind. Like I had with my dragons, I sought out the tendrils of my magic and yanked it right back. *It worked.* I looked down at my hands as if I could physically see the power returning.

Loch's head snapped towards me. I was as surprised as he was. Somehow, I'd latched onto the filaments of my magic that he'd so easily pulled into himself and I'd stopped him. He kept hold of most of it but I'd managed to cling to some. Now we were in a power struggle—a tug of war as he tried to shield himself with what was mine.

"Varialla!" He had the nerve to sound indignant as if I owed him something.

Loch took a step then jumped when Urdith landed behind him. The ground split beneath the red dragon's talons. He gnashed his teeth; a warning. I was willing to bet it was the only warning he'd get.

Revynath, however, didn't waste time on warnings. She opened her mouth. Steam curled from her snout and fire surged up the back of her throat.

35

VARIALLA:
SAVING SHITHEADS

S top!"

Revynath's mouth snapped shut. Her large head swung towards me; her golden eyes narrowed. She must have read the hatred in my heart; the desire to purge this bastard from the world but not like this. The repercussions wouldn't be worth it. It would have been one thing to let Lucinda beat Loch bloody and carve her name across his chest with a rusty blade but it was another to incinerate him on the spot. Loch had to die. I would make sure he did. However, in this fight for the throne, timing was everything.

If I killed him now, the Royal Court would spin it in a way that turned the realm against me. They'd call it an act of war or claim that my dragons couldn't be controlled; that I was dangerous. They'd sew fear and dissent through the people and solidify their right to rule. It was better to trust the devil you knew, after all.

"Don't hurt him." The words tasted bitter on my tongue.

My dragons kept their murderous glares on Loch. I didn't know if they knew all he'd done to me or if they just felt the same bone-deep disgust I felt.

Revynath prowled towards him. Loch had the good sense to step back but that only brought him closer to Urdith who growled. It was a low rumble from the base of his barreled chest.

"Revynath."

She didn't listen to me. She never bloody listened.

"Revynath!"

At last, the large Crowned Sapphire peeled her menacing yellow eyes away from Loch and pinned them on me. She cocked her head. We didn't need to speak for me to know she was asking if I'd lost my fucking mind. I almost laughed. I probably would have if there wasn't a chance my two dragons were about to eliminate the realm's greatest threat but at the same time ruin everything.

For now, Loch had to live. We'd all agreed that when I returned to the Games, I would be a team player. I would garner the support of the people on my own merits, not by discrediting the current Court. As much as I wanted to drag the Council through the dirt. As much as I wanted to use my platform to scream at the people that they were being lied to and have them gunning for the Council's heads—that was not how this war would be won.

To have lasting change, I didn't need supporters who chose me because they were against the Court. They'd only turn on me when the dust settled. I needed those who would choose to join me either way, because they wanted the same things. Change and unity between the Isles. I needed to know who I could trust in the days that followed the inevitable war.

I held up a placating hand when Revynath looked like she might take a bite out of me instead. Urdith swished his barbed tail and pawed at the ground.

"I will kill him," I vowed. "Just not today."

Loch narrowed his eyes but had the sense to keep his mouth shut. Revynath waited a heartbeat before she turned back to the blue-eyed bastard. She gnashed her teeth so violently she would have carved right through his bones if he hadn't lurched back at the last second. My heart leapt into my throat.

Fucking dragon.

Seeming satisfied that she'd sufficiently scared the shit out of him, Revynath looked skyward, splayed her wings and took off.

Urdith hunched over Loch who was now sprawled on his back. He raised his clawed foot and rested it on Loch's torso. Time froze. Loch wasn't the only one who held his breath.

My knees buckled as again the bastard siphoned magic from inside me. This time I couldn't hang onto it.

At last, Urdith pulled back and shot into the sky.

I exhaled heavily. Colette rested a hand on my shoulder. I couldn't tell if she was trying to hold me up or support herself.

Her fingers squeezed and she whispered, "It's her."

Loch pushed to his feet and dusted himself off. For the first time, I took in the woman beside him. Her sharp green eyes stared back at me. Faint lines that crinkled the corners were the only things to mark her age. She was a few inches taller than me. Her frame thin and almost swallowed by her royal blue robe. However, there was strength in her stance and in the set of her angular jaw. Her thick dark hair was piled on top of her head and braided over one shoulder. A chain of gold held the top in place.

"Finally," she breathed.

I blinked. I knew this woman and yet I didn't. Through the mark on my side, I knew the sound of her voice. I'd heard her singing to me and telling me stories through the womb and the casing of my shell. I had memories that an ordinary child would have forgotten but that I carried in my flesh. I saw her through the eyes of others. I shared their laughs and the love they'd felt. I saw her with my sister.

Now she was here. If I hadn't been certain I would have been when Colette dropped to one knee.

My tongue ran over my lips. "Queen Zenera."

My mother.

She smiled, though it didn't hold the warmth I would have expected. "Walk with me."

Almost every part of me wanted to say yes except one small fraction hesitated. My stare slid to Loch.

This woman had joined forces with our enemies once. Her name had been among the signatures on the weapon plans and she'd agreed to go ahead with the slaughter of the dragon shifters. She was the Siren Savage. She was my mother. She had bound my life to his.

"He leaves."

Loch sneered. "He stays."

"He has to," Queen Zenera added.

My eyes narrowed. "Why?"

Her shoulders tensed.

"Because I am still a prisoner." My mother's jaw tightened. Either she didn't like being questioned or hated that the answer made her look weak.

She roughly tugged up the wide-rimmed sleeve of her embroidered dress and revealed a brand on her arm. It was a raised scar of burned flesh that circled her wrist like a cuff. In its center was what looked like an abstract eye.

"The only reason I'm not in Blacktomb Bay, is because he vouched for me." She gestured to Loch. "As a result, we cannot be more than a few feet away from each other. That's not because something catastrophic will happen to us if we try but because it's physically impossible."

My stare went to the mark on her wrist. Now we were both bound to the bastard. At least hers had been a choice.

"That must make bathing interesting."

She scoffed. "After what I've endured for the last two hundred years bathing of any kind is a luxury." Her stare was sharp enough to cut glass. "And relieving myself in anything other than a tin can is a blessing."

I sucked on my cheeks. I wanted to swallow my words; to apologize. Yet every time I looked at Loch, I couldn't find it in me.

I stepped back. "I'm not going anywhere with him."

I turned to leave with the others. Godric lingered back; the camera-orb tracked every second.

"Please, Varialla."

I flinched. It was the first time I'd heard my mother say my name. I looked from her; this woman I'd dreamed about getting to know my entire life, to the monster at her side.

"I'm sure you have questions and I'd like to give you the answers."

The truth about everything. About what happened before I was born. About the alliance, the weapon, and the shifters. She could tell me about her relationship with my father, and the room I'd found in his palace. If I wanted the answers I'd craved since

I arrived in the Isles, she was the one to get them from.

My hands balled into fists.

"He walks ahead of us as far as he can get."

"Still bitter, Princess?" Loch's voice was a low purr.

It reminded me of the way he'd called me "princess" when he'd had his tongue between my legs. A knot of twisted desire pulled low in my belly. I squashed it down. It wasn't real, just a passing tug brought on by the bind my mother had let him inflict on me at birth. I'd be getting answers about that too.

With a last look over my shoulder at Lucinda's and Maximus' guarded expressions, I turned back to Zenera.

"One lap around the courtyard."

36

VARIALLA:
THE TRUTH ABOUT EVERYTHING

Queen Zenera, my mother, wasted no time. She strode towards me and I tensed. Would she hug me? Kiss my cheeks? Hold my hand? I didn't know what to think when she did neither. Instead, she sang a single note and a bubble of water morphed around our heads.

"Sound bubble," she explained. "It will muffle our voices. If we speak low enough, the orb won't be able to pick up what we're saying."

I looked to the fountain. It hadn't moved. She'd pulled the water from the air around us and effortlessly created this shield. My finger touched the watery membrane which bounced beneath my finger. Lately, there were a lot of people who wore similar things around their nose and mouths to help ward off germs they believed caused the plague, but this was on a grander scale.

Loch stalked ahead. The distance wasn't far but it was enough that I couldn't smell his cloying coconut scent. A scent that made my stomach flip with desire and disgust.

When he'd gone as far as he could, Queen Zenera, said, "We were desperate."

I didn't have to ask what she meant.

"We had been oppressed, cast out and left to fend for ourselves for decades. The Inlanders had offered us scraps we couldn't survive on for a price we couldn't afford. Especially since those of us who had worked in the Five Isles were no longer welcome without paying a daily tariff." Each word was clipped; bit out through clenched teeth.

"They'd set up a system designed for us to fail. Over time, I witnessed my kingdom crumble. I saw children die from hunger, the strong grow weak and the healthy grow sick. I watched all we had wither and fade whilst the Inlands prospered. Blessed by the Conduit the Outer Isles were no longer permitted to touch."

We turned down a path of lowcut shrubs. She didn't look at me as she spoke. Her gaze was distant as she relived every second in her mind.

"So yes," she went on. "I offered them what we had. Power in exchange for what they had. Food. Freedom. Life. I'd used the alliance as a way to get into the Isles so I could convince the leaders of

Shifter Springs to accept us as their own. That was when I met your father and fell in love."

Her eyes briefly closed. It was the most emotion I'd seen her show and it was fleeting. Her eyes snapped back open.

"After that it had felt like everything was falling into place. We saw each other in secret. When the Royal Court eventually found out, I convinced them that it was all part of my plan. To seduce the prince, get closer to those in power and then destroy them. They'd never see it coming." She plucked a leaf from the shrub beside her and squeezed it between her fingers. White pulp stained her fingertips. She brought it to her nose and sniffed. "The only one who ended up blindsided was me."

"What happened?"

According to the story my father had announced his betrothal to another on the day he was supposed to announce his union with my mother but that didn't add up to the baby's room I'd seen in the palace. To the locket I now wore around my neck.

"We found out we were expecting you."

We entered a small flower garden with a fish pond in its center and a wrought iron bench against a wall covered in vines. My mother sat. I sat beside her. Loch wandered the footpaths not too far away

"He was so excited." She smiled; a weak wistful thing. "But when his father found out, he insisted that Thraxen marry another or live in exile. I thought he would fight for me." For the first time since we'd set off on this walk, she looked at me. "He did not. And to make sure I didn't ruin his plans, the king tried to have me and my entourage killed. So, we fought back."

*

One lap around the courtyard, turned into two around the whole garden. It wasn't enough. I'd waited a lifetime to be here. To know more about the Coral Court in its glory days; to hear stories of my sister and my father and the plans my parents had had for me.

Godric trotted over. "Sorry to interrupt, but you need to be dressed for dinner."

My shoulders drooped. Almost every night there was a mandatory dinner with Goather and the other contestants. Supposedly it was to show good faith but Goather usually steered the conversation in a way that would lead to petty arguments or hair pulling and entertain the audience immensely.

"I'll walk you to your room." My mother's tone was curt. She still hadn't fully relaxed and there seemed to be something on her mind. Something she wasn't saying. I wondered if it had anything to do with the bastard behind me.

We entered the palace and made our way to my rooms. Godric and Loch not far behind.

"There's one subject we have to discuss before you go."

As expected, her eyes flittered to Loch. I sighed. This was a conversation I wanted to have as much as I didn't. I didn't want to think of this woman as the same one that had bound my life, my power, to Loch's without my consent. But maybe that fact had eaten away at her all these years and now was her chance to explain and ask for forgiveness.

I shrugged. "Why did you do it?"

My mother pursed her lips. "Fear. You were a defenseless egg. He was a powerful warrior; my second in command. I wanted to make sure you were taken care of. That you had a strong leader at your side who you could trust."

I snorted.

"Loch is a little extreme but he's been fighting for so long, I think he doesn't know how to stop." She glanced down at me. Torchlight glimmered over her angular features. "But the bind frustrates him as much as it does you. He needs you, Varialla. He wants you the same way you want him."

She spoke with unmatched passion; as if this was the moment she'd been waiting for. This was the conversation she'd wanted to have all along. Everything else was just to humor me.

"The bind was designed to help you both feel the same way; to strengthen your union. The Shadow Saint forced him to abandon your egg beyond the veil in order to keep you safe. Now you see him as the monster, when the real monster is the one you let into your bed."

Her tone was sharp; cruel. I tensed. This wasn't an apology or an explanation. I didn't know what this was. I wouldn't apologize for loving Exekiel. He'd done some messed up stuff in his grief-stricken haze. But at the time it had been the only way to protect what was left of the realm and it had been too late when he'd realized he couldn't undo it.

"You need to give him a chance."

I almost walked into the wall. She didn't regret anything or see why her manipulation of my mind and body might upset me.

"I know he's done some terrible things but for good reason."

"Terrible?" I had to fight to keep my voice low. The bubble still surrounded us but it wasn't completely soundproof.

"Loch has done things to me, to my friends that you cannot imagine."

"Things he wouldn't have had to do if you had chosen to be loyal to your people."

My chest constricted. She was just like him. She didn't understand. She was blinded by her need for revenge and her thirst for power.

"I would never support stripping the people of their will like the Ceremonial Bind did to me."

"*Sonu di Carghel* is a temporary solution to secure our seat on the throne whilst maintaining the peace." She shook her head. "You have been here for a little over a year and you're already sickened by the divide; the injustice. Imagine suffering it for hundreds of years." She gripped my shoulder. "Imagine the lengths you would go. *Sonu di Carghel* is a desperate solution for desperate people. But it will be worth it when you rule as Loch's queen; a symbol of both sides."

I jerked out of her hold and opened my mouth to argue.

She held up a hand. "Think about it."

There was nothing to think about. I would never be his queen. Loch didn't want peace. He wanted power and to condemn those who'd wronged him to purgatory. Maybe it was the things that had been done to Loch that had warped his mind and made him cruel, but that didn't make it right.

I pushed open my room door. The bubble around us stretched. "Goodnight, Zenera."

"We cannot trust these people not to turn on us again," she whisper-shouted after me as I stepped inside. "We need to take the throne for ourselves. They feared our power and in doing so, they made us the monsters they feared."

I glanced at Loch who stood a few feet behind her. Maybe she was right about that but the choice had been theirs.

37

VARIALLA:
THE BEST LAID PLANS

The next week was a blur. If I wasn't attending Q&A's with reporters or doing refreshers on etiquette training and dances, I was schmoozing with noblemen and women who made frequent visits to the palace. They each took it upon themselves to tell me and the other contestants that I was either an abomination or a blessing. Like either of us had asked for their opinion. Although Vivienne seemed to love it when they had nothing good to say.

In spite of that, I did manage to forge three alliances with those who shared my vision for a united realm and had the means to help me achieve it. Count Mari was one of the highest ranked nobles in the Winged City of Fae Reef. He had offered me use of his soldiers, supplies and land. He'd agreed to make space for those in the Outer Isles who wished to visit and had also offered manpower and resources to help rebuild their homes.

Countess Lynn of Elf Bay and Count Fang from Shifter Springs had offered the same. As well as business ideas they hoped to introduce to the Outer Isles once they were settled. These little liaisons were referred to as our Trials of Allegiance and each of us received points based on the number of alliances we made.

Every few days, I was given a short reprieve from the media circus and public frenzy. This usually came between the hours of twilight and dawn. Godric was required to stay with me until I fell asleep. Or, at least, until I pretended to. Then the centaur retired for the night and left his orb rolling. However, every now and then, the orbs needed maintenance checks and Godric would take it with him.

In that rare pocket of peace, I caught up with Lucinda, Maximus and Colette. According to kitchen staff, the orders for crushed gilstone and raw thornnuts had increased lately but they hardly used them in cooking. This meant they were most likely being used in the antidote or poison. I took note of the ingredients to tell Ilbryen the next time I saw him. If I ever managed to escape Godric.

Stylists and palace staff usually had more flexibility moving in and out of the palace when they weren't on duty. However, my friends were being watched almost as much as me. They'd clocked the guards disguised as civilians that trailed them during their trips to the Townsquare. They'd noted the gardeners that listened a little too intently to their conversations like they were hoping they would slip or lead them right to Exekiel and the others.

Maximus also filled us in on the gossip among the palace staff. Some of it was useful like late night meetings with prominent members of the Court. Most of it was scandalous and entertaining.

I didn't remember falling asleep, but I woke to the sound of birds chirping outside my window. Sunlight streamed in. The curtains weren't closed the night before and there was a foot in my face.

My eyes popped open. Maximus' black-painted toenails were an inch from my cornea.

"What the heck?" I tried to sit up only to find Lucinda's leg slung over me.

"Keep still," Colette grumbled from where her face was buried in the mattress.

I smacked her ass. "Wake up."

Somehow, we'd talked for so long last night, we'd fallen asleep and were now sprawled over each other on my massive bed.

After a chorus of, 'Get your foot out of my face', 'Watch it!' and 'You're sitting on me', we finally detangled in fits of laughter.

"What's this, then? Is the last dragonborn queen having relations with her team of stylists?"

We swiveled to face Godric who leaned casually against the archway to the room. How long had he been standing there?

"The audience will love that." His grin was crooked as he directed the orb over each of our tussled appearances.

"Get out!" Lucinda snapped.

"Bloody centaur," Colette chimed in.

I rushed to close my dressing gown since I was naked beneath except for a pair of polka dot knickers. "Don't you knock?"

Godric straightened and strutted into the room, doing his best impersonation of Goather. "Real scenarios. Real reactions." He cocked his head. "Are you fit for the Throne?"

I rolled my eyes.

"We'll go get your stuff prepped," Maximus called as he and the others rushed from the room.

"Traitors!" I scowled at Godric who brought the orb close enough to see up my nostrils.

"So, what's on the agenda today?"

To lose you in a crowd and find a way to get to Fae Reef.

To check on the others progress in finding the weapon and perfecting the antidote. Aquarius had also said he would check in with his contacts in the Coral Court to make sure Sienna was still being cared for and not punished for my escape. The not knowing was driving me crazy.

Aloud I said, "A visit to Infinity City and lunch in the square."

*

The streets teemed with people. Wealth dripped from all corners. Males in tailored tunics and females in delicate dresses were out enjoying leisurely strolls and expensive meals. Pegasus-pulled carriages maneuvered down the beveled brick roads. Music crooned from open doorways.

Godric remained on my heels through it all. His orb off to one side. I scanned the area, seeking a way out. A crowd was gathered at the entrance to Bear's Bakery. It was a beautiful, picket-fenced patisserie owned by a bear shifter. There was no real queue or semblance of civility. It was every man for himself at those pink-painted doors.

I seized the opportunity. "I'm going to grab a grizzly bun."

Before Godric could respond, I veered left. Lucinda had aways lost her orbs-director in a crowd. Mainly because the satyr had been too small to see over the heads of the people and his strides had been too short to keep up. Godric towered above most and would easily spot me in a crowd, but maybe his immense size would make it harder for him to get through.

I ducked into the shoddy queue outside the bakery and bustled my way in. I moved fast. People who thought they saw me did a double take. I could tell from their confused expressions that they weren't entirely sure it was me. *Perfect.* I didn't look back.

Godric must have been following. The whirr of the orb spiraled closer like the buzz of a fly. I darted into the restroom. A cool breeze fluttered in from an open window on the opposite wall. It looked just about big enough for me to climb through, although it would be a tight fit.

I clicked the latch on the main bathroom door, then rushed to the window. Using the trashcan, I climbed up and heaved myself up onto the narrow ledge. I swung one leg out, then the other, and shimmied the rest of the way down.

The decorative frame snagged on the hem of my dress and scraped the skin off my thighs. The sting was worth it. My feet struck the ground in an alley behind the bakery. With a triumphant smile, I spun and found Godric standing there with his arms folded and his eyebrow raised.

"Why do I get the feeling you're trying to get away from me?"

My gut plummeted.

The centaur flicked a switch on his remote. The blinking red light of the orb winked out. As its levitation mechanism shut down, he caught it in his hand.

"Directors are allowed to switch off the orb when they go to the toilet," he said in response to my slack jawed expression. "I'd reckon you've got about two minutes or in your case, less, to tell me what's going on before someone comes to investigate why the feed is down."

I hesitated. How much could I tell him? Whose side was he on?

"I remember you, you know?" His lips quirked up in the corners. "You stopped those Fate-stained shitheads from lassoing me like some wild animal. The bastards had wanted to ride me and not in the good way."

My laugh was awkward.

Godric shrugged. "In my book, that means I owe you. Now speak fast. Are you trying to go somewhere without the orbs knowing about it?"

I chewed on my lip. "Yes."

I didn't have to give him any details, but if he was serious about helping me then it was worth a shot. Outrunning him hadn't worked and I only had about thirty seconds before he turned the feed back on.

Godric nodded. "Did you know that Fates Cathedral is a sacred space where orbs aren't allowed to enter?"

My gaze snapped to his. "I did not know that."

"Not many people do. I think it's only written in the orb-director's codex." I followed him out of the alley and back into the busy square. "There's a sermon at the cathedral today. They usually last an hour. If you factor in meeting and greeting the people, it will probably buy you two." He lifted a finger. "For this to work the orb must record you going in and coming out, and the people need to see you inside."

I licked my lips. Before I could respond, he raised the remote and clicked the switch. The orb blinked to life and once again, hovered between us.

"Sorry about that, Princess," Godric said casually. "I was bursting for a wee." He trotted towards me as if he'd just left the bakery. "Where to now?"

"Fate's Cathedral." I held back my smile. "I hear there's a sermon there today."

38

VARIALLA:
THE STENCH HITS FIRST

We arrived at the cathedral as the last of the crowd made their way inside. Some were delighted to see me. They bowed their heads, shook my hand and snapped quick selfies. Godric grinned at this. *#DragonfortheFates* trended almost immediately which, according to the centaur, was great for my image. It would also help corroborate the story that I'd been here.

Others gave me a wide berth like I might randomly decide to set them on fire. Then there were those who condemned me to Gorge and spat at my feet. The Mothers assured me that all animosity would be left at the door. I didn't have the heart to tell him that it didn't matter. I wouldn't be staying long.

I settled into a pew near the back of the prayer hall. The lights dimmed. The congregation fell quiet and the Mothers stepped out to sing a song of saintdom. Once the second verse was complete, and I was sure I'd been seen by enough people, I moved to make my escape. A figure flopped down beside me.

A female with pointed ears, sleek dark hair and pale skin.

"Vivienne?" I whispered.

"I wondered when you'd figure out the Cathedral loophole." She rolled her neck. "Do you know how many of these things I've sat through waiting for you to show up?"

I was going to point out that she could have told me, then again, we were always being watched. Cameras or not, a hushed conversation between Vivienne and I would arouse suspicion.

"Why have you been waiting for me?"

"Nobody knows where Exekiel went since he left here." She handed me a slender translucent phone that blinked with florescent wires. "It's secure— warded by goblins. Doesn't even have access to the cyber-grid. See that he gets it."

A petty part of me wanted to refuse. I knew they'd been in contact over the last few months. Vivienne had been one of the first to know Exekiel was alive. She'd helped him recover after his time in the River. She'd gone with him to the first two possible locations of the weapon and she'd been there when they'd gone to retrieve the weapon plans from Residence Manor.

Apparently, her goblin orbs-director was under the impression her family would destroy him and all his loved ones, so she didn't struggle to get away. Although she didn't do it often.

Jealousy made me want to point out that he now had me and didn't need her. Which, of course, was bullshit. The more people we had on our side, especially in the Games, the better. Vivienne and I didn't share the same views but hers were better than the alternatives.

"Fine." I tucked the phone into my pocket.

When I moved to slide past, she grabbed my arm.

"What?" I hissed. Every second I spent here was a second less in Fae Reef.

"Give him a kiss from me, won't you?" She smirked.

"Oh, I will. I may even suck his cock for you too."

Her face fell. I took a second to savor her pinched scowl then pulled free of her grip and slipped out of the hall. I stole towards the gardens and out into the chilly night air.

My eyes searched the darkening sky for my dragons. I had just under two hours before I'd be expected back here to make a public exit. The only way I could reach Peaked City and return in that time was on dragon's back. No carriage or chariot was fast enough.

"Where are you?" I whispered into the setting sun.

I didn't know how to summon them. Did I whistle? Do a dance? I closed my eyes and felt the distant hum of their power that linked to mine. In my minds-eyes I reached for it and wrapped the tendrils around my fingers. I made out the vibrant red of Urdith. The shimmering blue of Revynath. There was also the milky white of Loch. It wove around everything like skeletal hands. I jerked away from his filmy presence. There had to be a way to break the connection; to sever this hold he had on me.

The thrum of wings reached my ears. My gaze shot skywards. I held back a laugh as my dragons approached. I couldn't risk them being seen. Before they landed, I tapped into my own wings and soared off the ground. My ascent was shaky at best. My stomach dipped. My spine screamed but my wings beat rhythmically; taking me higher.

Urdith dove down. I swept onto his horned back; careful to avoid impaling myself.

"To Fae-Reef," I told him.

Then we were off.

*

Any excitement I felt at returning to Vladimir's estate, was extinguished when I walked through the doors and was struck with the stench of death. It was eerily quiet. Instinct sent me to the west wing where we'd put most of the infected.

My stomach dropped when I entered one of the larger rooms that was technically Vladimir's library. The number of contaminated beings had almost doubled. The air smelt of sick and sweat. Hacking coughs racked their frail bodies. Gasses escaped them that reeked of rotted egg. I'd vowed to save these people. Now I wasn't sure they'd survive the night.

A familiar pulse of energy tugged in my chest and my eyes immediately found Exekiel. Dressed in a black fur-collared cloak with black trousers and boots he stood beside Maximus and the others who had managed to sneak out of the palace before breakfast. They'd be punished for shirking their duties. Probably denied meals or forced to work extra hours but they'd decided it was worth it.

Once I won the Games, I would alter this life of service my friends had been forced into. Game laws stated that all losing contestants had to serve the crown but I didn't see why they had to be treated like shit whilst doing it.

They were gathered around a row of beds near the back. I rushed towards them. The stricken look Lucinda gave me when she saw me coming, told me something was horribly wrong. I reeled to a stop beside them. My heart slammed into my rib cage. My knees shook.

Eudora lay in one of the beds. Odus was in the one beside her. Their lips were pale, ashen and cracked. Veins of black writhed beneath their skin. Their eyes were swollen shut. Eudora's skin was scabbed. Odus was losing his hair. Seeping bald patches were clear beneath the dim torchlight. His tail was sparse and lacked its usual luster.

"The Council got to them. By the looks of it, they've developed a stronger strain of the virus," Maximus explained.

Which meant those infected by it would be forced to take the antidote before the finale if they wanted to survive long enough to see it. I drew in a steadying breath, but it only served to remind me of the death that lurked in this room. The air was hot and putrid.

I turned to Ilbryen who rested his palm on Eudora's forehead and scribbled notes down on his clipboard.

"What's the plan?"

"Plan?" He pulled a wet wipe from a jar beside Eudora's bed and wiped off his hands.

"To help them and anyone else infected by the new strain."

"I've done all I can."

It took a second for the words to land.

"What do you mean?"

Ilbryen removed his glasses with a heavy sigh. I hated that sound.

"I mean there's nothing more I can do for them."

"Give them more antidote," I hissed. My stare dropped back to my friends. Their bones jutted against their pasty skin.

"I can't."

"Why not?"

He took a step towards me and lowered his voice. "The antidote requires essence of the Conduit and we're down to our last reserves. I can't use it on those who are too far gone to save."

I flinched. Some part of my mind understood but I didn't want to hear it.

"If you up their dosage, they might survive."

Again, the alchemist fucking sighed. "It's not a perfect remedy, remember? It only works on those who are strong enough to fight the toxin on their own to some degree. They are not. Half these people aren't."

He raked a hand over his tight curls. For the first time, his expression reflected his weariness.

My chest ached. This couldn't be it. Not after all we'd done to get them here. Not after the future they deserved to be a part of. Their options couldn't be to die in agony or go to the Court's research facilities, where they would either give them the antidote which healed their bodies and poisoned their minds. Or they'd be used as test subjects to see just how far the poison could push them.

"There has to be something you can do."

"I don't have long enough to find out."

The words were a punch to the gut. I wanted to shake him, to scream. This couldn't be it. The Court couldn't win. But if they continued to spread this version of the poison, they would have more than half the realm cured with their antidote before the season finale. Countless minds at their mercy.

"You're not going to cry, are you?"

I spun to face Vladimir. Fire burst from my fingertips.

"If you value your life councilman, get away from me."

He looked deceptively angelic in the white robes he wore. His silver hair was unbound and flowed down his slender shoulders.

"It is not my life I'm concerned about." He studied the half dead bodies around us. "It's theirs."

The sincerity in his voice made me pause.

I met the elf's stare. He jerked his head for me to follow. I extinguished the flames in my hands. With a last look at Eudora and Odus, I let him lead the way.

Vladimir didn't speak until we were in the seating room. The night sky shimmered beyond the walls of glass. The ocean crashed below with a rhythmic slap against the shore.

"When Nyla and I discovered the Court's underground workrooms where they perfected their poison and tested their victims, I'd wanted to burn everything to the ground." He stalked over to the fireplace like he was imagining those flames devouring everything. "It was Nyla who believed we should keep something valuable. Something that we could use to bargain for our lives, if necessary."

The others sat down but I couldn't relax. Exekiel stood behind me; a wall if I needed to lean against him. Strength if my own faded.

Vladimir scratched his chin. "I know where Nyla is."

He grimaced as if he regretted the words as soon as he'd said them.

"Amongst the items she stole, she has the formulas for the poison and the antidote."

39

VARIALLA:
SINFUL SERENADES & WICKED WAVES

This was crazy. I wasn't seriously thinking about leaving during the Games. I'd always said nothing mattered more than winning…except them. The people I'd sworn to protect. One look at Eudora and Odus veined in black and skin purpling. One look at all the others who'd coughed up blood and begged for death, and I knew I couldn't stand back and let them suffer. Not when there was something I could do about it.

Nyla had the formulas. With them, Ilbryen would be able to see what ingredients in the toxin reacted with the antidote. He may be able to find an alternative. At the very least, he would know the exact measurements needed and any elements he might have missed. Thanks to Vladimir, we knew where Nyla and those documents were but she moved around a lot. If I was going to find her, I had to leave now.

The others had offered to go in my place but the journey by ship would take too long and the distance by portal was too great for even the strongest warlock. According to Vladimir, on dragon's back, the flight would take one night. One night to not only save my friends but everyone who had been infected by the Court. It was a way to render their research facilities obsolete. A way to help us fight back.

Sirens could only influence people in their immediate vicinity and were limited by their power level and the duration of their song. Without the tainted antidote to weaken people's defenses, we would strip the weapon of its power.

The only issue would be disappearing for a day without anyone noticing.

I met Godric on the steps of the cathedral just as the Mothers were closing the doors to mark the end of sermon.

"Enjoy the service?"

I nodded as I strode up to his side. "I did. It was enlightening."

We walked in silence a few streets as I gathered my thoughts and tried to figure out the best way to go about this.

"Is there a loo around here?"

Godric frowned. "Loo?"

"Toilet." I shrugged. "It's a British expression."

The centaurs frown deepened. I'd just left Fates Cathedral which had some of the finest toilets in the isle. I met his curious stare and prayed that anyone watching through the orb that hovered above our heads wouldn't notice the earnest gleam in my eyes.

"There's one near Fae's Fortune." Godric jerked his head towards the casino that was near Tavern Square.

I dutifully followed.

"I might as well use the *loo*," Godric paused as if testing out the word, "as well."

I snickered. When we reached the door to the casino, Godric held it open for me and we stepped inside. He immediately switched off the orb.

For a centaur he was extremely graceful as he spun to face me.

"What's this about?"

I glanced around us to make sure none of the patrons were looking our way. They were all too busy pawing at barmaids and trying to win a fortune.

I shrugged. "They're killing us."

Those three words were all it took to get Godric to support my decision to go after Nyla. Within seconds he'd come up with a plan for how I could pull it off. It was no surprise that the centaur who'd been shunned all his life, had no love for the Royal Court. His willingness to help and knowledge of the orb, was incredible.

Orbs-director was one of the best jobs given to Outliers. The Court claimed that Inlanders were made to be in front of the camera, not behind it. That single prejudice thought had handed me one of my greatest allies.

After dinner, I pretended I didn't feel well and went to bed early. Godric tampered with the orb and played the footage of me sleeping the previous night as live feed. Then we worked all night until breakfast. After twelve hours of filming, nine different outfits and six different hairstyles, we had close to two days of footage.

In one video, I'd laid on my couch and read a book on banquets. I changed positions at least six times, got up to make a drink, and ate some food. The entire shot took just under an hour, but Godric was confident he could slow it down and make it last twice as long, then loop it so it played again. It helped that Lucinda cast a spell which meant I moved abnormally fast. When Godric slowed it down it would at least double the length and look natural.

We did the same for me sleeping; where I'd tossed and turned in bed with and without the covers thrown over me, in different pajamas. We had footage of me walking through Eternal City, visiting my dragons, scrolling on my phone, and being dressed by my stylists.

In some, I talked to the palace workers—those who Lucinda and Colette had vouched for. Those who would claim to have seen me if asked. Any task that we could stretch out a little longer, I did. It would be an obvious loop if someone looked close enough.

However, the broadcast was continually switched between me and four other contestants. The chance of someone noticing was slim.

By sunset, I was back outside Fate's Cathedral for its evening prayers. Godric filmed me going in. After twenty minutes, when the sun had set, he filmed me coming back out as if it were hours later. Then he'd headed back to the palace to put together our masterpiece.

It had seemed like the perfect plan last night. Here, out in the open, doubt started to creep in. If anyone found out what we'd done, I'd be more than disqualified. Worse, Godric would probably hang. As would everyone else who had helped me. For the sake of saving the realm, I told myself it was worth it. That didn't stop sour chunks of nausea from rolling in my gut.

Long after the prayers ended and the congregation left, the cathedral doors creaked open. A Mother cloaked in her usual red robes stepped outside. She carried a candle in hand and whispered a prayer over the entrance. Then she looked over her shoulder; right where I was hidden down the side of the steps. That was the signal. Exekiel had arrived.

*

We were about to try and sneak across enemy lines and venture into uncharted waters. My position in the Games; our very lives were at risk. I didn't need any distractions. Across from me sat a very tall, chiseled and shirtless distraction.

Our rowboat bobbed precariously over the choppy ocean that was stirred by angry winds and there was a frigid bite to the air that seeped into my bones. Exekiel was apparently immune to it.

His wings were out. His honed chest was bare as he brought our small rowboat closer to the heavily guarded border between the isles. His abs tightened and the muscles in his forearms flexed with every pull of the oars. I was supposed to be the lookout. All I kept looking at was him. The way his dark hair shuddered across his brow. The way he let out deep hot breaths and clenched his jaw. Droplets of sweat trickled down his sculpted torso. The veins in his thick neck were prominent as he looked over his shoulder to where we were headed.

I should have been doing the same. I wrenched my stare away and refocused on the vast ocean around us. We were almost at the border.

"Get ready," Exekiel whispered.

When we were close enough, I tapped into my siren gifts. A soft song crooned from my lips. It was haunting and beautiful. A song of seduction and serenity. The melody pulled and dipped with the rock of the ocean. Pale tendrils of pink billowed from my lips and up towards the guards.

I saw the moment my magic landed. The soldiers stiffened then relaxed. Some of their eyes closed as they swayed. Others searched the seas as if seeking a long-lost love. Others dove from the rocky reef and straight into the ocean's depths.

Our boat moved closer. I pushed more power into my song. I serenaded them into each other's arms, to their lovers who waited for them at home. I sang them anywhere that wasn't looking at us. Declarations of love filled the night. Some gazed up at the sky and shouted their adoration of the stars.

My magic danced at the sight; at the control my song commanded. There was something to be said for the heady rush that came with using my siren gifts. Power hummed in my veins and demanded I take more from them. That I dragged them down to the depths of the sea. That was what sirens were most known for—singing sailors into watery graves.

Exekiel grunted. The sound pulled my attention from the guards, but I continued to weave the threads of my song around them. My breath caught. Exekiel's stare was pinned on me. It burned with a heat I felt in the far reaches of my soul. I subtly shook my head. This song was not for him. He was the most powerful being in the Realm. The Prince of Death. He could resist my magic longer than they could but that look said he didn't want to.

He moved the oars with more vigor. My eyes slid down his bare chest; to the thrust of his hips as he urged us onwards. My song wavered. My entire attention was gripped by him. He smirked like he knew the effect he was having. I shivered from both the cold and the desire he ignited.

Exekiel's eyes darkened as they slid over my pebbled nipples. "I want those in my mouth."

His words chased away the cold. My breath quickened.

"Get on my lap, little bud." He licked his bottom lip in a way that was X-rated. "Let me suck on your breasts whilst I seat you on my cock and thrust up inside you."

The visual was intense. I clung to the sides of the boat to keep from obeying his command. With great effort, I closed my eyes and continued to sing. Exekiel could resist my song if he bothered to try, but I wasn't sure I could resist him.

Eventually we sailed across the border. I let my song fade, though the echo of it lingered. We weren't in the clear yet. Out in the open, we were sitting ducks. Exekiel drew his shadows around us which gave us some cover. The dark enhanced the brightness of his piercing pink gaze. He was no longer influenced by my song, but the scent of his arousal clung to the air; to me.

I let out a shaky breath. "Stop looking at me like that."

His lips pulled into smirk. "Like what?"

Before I could respond, someone from the shore bellowed., "There you fucking Fate-stained shits!"

Bells tolled. My stomach lurched. We'd been spotted.

Someone hollered, "Classic signs of a siren attack!"

"Weren't you wearing your earmuffs?"

Angry shouts rained around us, swallowed by the din of ringing bells. The alert.

A resounding boom echoed through the night. Our boat pitched sideways as something large struck the water. I peered through the haze of Exekiel's shadows which had clearly thrown off the soldiers' aim, though not by much. I couldn't see what they'd fired, but I felt another as it landed nearby.

Exekiel rowed faster. "They've rolled out the catapults."

Now that my duties of lookout and songstress were done, I snatched up the spare set of oars and joined him. I wasn't as fast as he was. I'd never rowed a boat in my life, but I pulled like my life depended on it, because it did.

Urdith was close. He waited near the caves of the Outer Isles. I'd told him to stay out of sight. If anyone saw dragons, they would know it was me who was trying to escape. The hours of footage Godric and I had recorded would be wasted and anyone caught lying for me would be killed, after they'd been tortured for information.

Fae guards took to the sky and sought us out from above. Enchanted bows were slung over their shoulder, armed with arrows that rarely missed their mark. Siren guards who had responded to the alert, plunged into the water. Their tails whipped fiercely before they sunk below.

My gaze went to the shore where another resounding boom echoed through the night. A blazing fireball hurtled towards us. There was no way to outrun it.

I wobbled to my feet as Exekiel did the same.

"Hold your breath."

Seconds before the blow struck, I took his hand, and we dove into the waves. The current was vicious. It tugged at my legs and yanked us apart.

"Exekiel!"

The filament that stopped water from flying down my throat instantly formed, along with gills down the side of my neck.

I searched the choppy ocean as the guards above continued to take aim and the Fae shot down their arrows. I cursed as one sliced across my bicep.

Lower down, a figure sank; buffeted by the oceans rage. *Exekiel.* He reached for the surface. His hands clawed at the water. His strong, powerful legs kicked behind him.

I moved to follow. A violent wave slammed into me like a thousand tiny punches. My body was thrown. Bubbles burst across my vision. I didn't know which way was up.

I blinked and peered into the murky depths. Turning one way then the other. Where did he go?

A flash of tails cutting through the water made my stomach pitch. The siren soldiers were closing in.

I pushed into my dragon abilities and enhanced my sight. There, sinking into the black was Exekiel. The angles of his face were sporadically illuminated by the flashes of flame-tipped arrows and fireballs above. He continued to fight the current. Eventually he would lose.

I dove after him. The ocean continued to relentlessly tug me in another direction. With gritted teeth, I forced my legs to kick against it. For my muscles to cleave through the torrent of the storm-tossed sea. I had to get to him.

"There!"

Fuck. The siren soldiers had caught my trail. Their speed intensified. They were practically on top of me. Any minute now they would notice the teal strands of my hair. They would know it was me.

I pulled on my power, like it could do anything to make me faster.

Please. I begged to whatever Fate or god was listening.

My legs burned. A sharp slice of hot agony before my muscles screamed. For a horrifying moment, my vision went black. Blinding pain split down the back of my calf. I chased away the rising panic and tried to make sense of what was happening. The sudden searing heat turned to a cool tingle. My lungs expanded like I was breathing in gulps of air above the surface.

Then I was moving faster than I ever thought possible. I didn't have to fight the current or kick my legs. I didn't have legs. My mind spun as I dimly registered the whip of a shimmering gold tail beating in place of where my legs had been. I'd shifted into a siren.

I fought to keep my shit together and spearheaded through the water, straight to Exekiel. My tail enhanced my speed, directed my aim and propelled me onwards like a loosed arrow. The siren soldiers couldn't keep up.

When I was close enough, I reached out and snatched hold of Exekiel's hand. His eyelids fluttered. He was conscious, but fading. I wrenched him close and pressed my lips to his. When I exhaled, a protective air bubble morphed around his nose and mouth. I didn't know if it would work. I didn't wait to find out. With his body hooked under my arm, I swam towards the surface.

Within seconds, his body shook with coughs. We crested above the water outside the caves and I released him. The bubble around Exekiel's nose and mouth popped. He coughed a few more times then heaved himself out of the water and onto the rocks.

"You, okay?"

Exekiel lay sprawled on the rocks. "Why wouldn't I be?"

I snorted and climbed out after him. Without having to think about it my tail shifted back to legs. It was quite possibly the weirdest thing I'd ever experienced. I didn't think I'd ever get used to it.

Despite having nearly drowned, Exekiel was on his feet. As planned, Urdith waited on the rocks. He narrowed his large silver eyes at Exekiel as we approached.

"We talked about this," I hissed.

Thankfully, the Scarlet Ridgeback remained in a squat and didn't try to throw us off when we ran up his tail. Exekiel sat down first then pulled me in front of him, so we were nestled between two of the spikes that jutted along Urdith's spine.

We each braced ourselves as my dragon lowered his head, splayed his wings and launched into the sky.

40

VARIALLA:
ONLY ONE DRAGON

All we had were coordinates, a map that seriously lacked information, a wish, and a prayer. There wasn't much known about the lands beyond the Nine Isles. Supposedly explorers had sailed the seas once. Some had whispered of unknown gods and fields of power where strange things happened. Others had claimed there were no gods but demons. Bloodthirsty beasts with a penchant for cruelty. Supposedly the stories had been warped and changed over the centuries. No one knew what was true anymore, if any of it.

I glanced down at the compass in Exekiel's hand, thankful that one of us knew how to read it.

After an unknown amount of time, he pocketed the device and grumbled. "Is riding a dragon always this cold?"

I snickered. Apparently, the novelty of the flight had worn off. Then again, I think it ended ten minutes after we took off. If it were up to Exekiel, he would have flown himself. Unlike mine, his wings could sustain the high altitude and wouldn't be shredded by the wind. They weren't as powerful as a dragons, but they were stronger than most. He was a full Fates-blessed Fae of Bravinore descent. The harsher wingbeats it would take to maintain this height wouldn't affect him. Speed was the only reason the Shadow Saint had allowed himself to be carried on dragon's back.

I pushed more of my inner dragons' fire into the heat of my skin. Exekiel sighed when he felt it and tugged me close. I'd used it to dry us off earlier, but it had only worked to a certain extent. My leathers were now damp and stiff. As were his trousers and the navy-blue tunic he'd taken from the sack he somehow hadn't lost to the sea. My own satchel had been ripped from my shoulder the second we'd entered the water.

"By the way," His thumb traced idle circles on my thigh. My body thrummed at the contact. "Did I see a tail here earlier?" His warm breath shuddered across the shell of my ear.

I smiled. "You did."

I had had a tail. The thought was surreal.

"I liked it," he said into the top of my head.

I snuggled into him. "Me too."

It had been a whole new sensation to have the speed and strength of a tail; to effortlessly go against the current of the ocean. Just like with my wings and horns, I now felt the echo of the tail in my skin. The ability to summon my siren and become a creature of the sea.

Points had burst above my head during the commotion. I hadn't stopped to read what they were for or the amount, but the ability to shift into two creatures had to count for something.

"You truly are incredible, Varialla."

Exekiel curled his dark silver-edged wings around us. I swore they got more beautiful every time I looked at them.

"Right back at you, Fae boy."

I stroked my finger down the soft leathery skin of his wing and admired the way sparks of violet crackled across the surface. Exekiel shifted behind me. I grinned. Touching his wings almost elicited the same reaction as touching his cock.

"Behave," he murmured.

I giggled and let my hand fall.

Encased in the warmth of Exekiel's wings, I closed my eyes. The sound of dragon wings and my mate's beating heart were my lullaby as I drifted off to sleep.

I didn't know how much time had passed when I was woken by the feel of warm, soft lips on mine.

My eyelids fluttered open. Vermilion eyes stared back at me.

"What are you doing?"

Exekiel's hand trailed down my stomach.

"I'm cold," he murmured against my lips. My heart pounded. "Warm me up."

Before I could argue, not that any part of me wanted to, his mouth descended on mine. I sighed into the kiss; into the forceful way he seized control and worked my tongue with his. There was nothing gentle about it. It was deep and thorough like he was making up for every kiss we hadn't shared whilst we were apart.

His hand slid lower until it was pressed between my thighs. I whimpered into his mouth. My hand curled around the back of his neck. My hips rolled.

"You're so responsive." Exekiel sucked my bottom lip into his mouth.

He popped open the clasp of my leathers and deftly undid the ties. Anticipation coiled tight in my gut as he worked his hand inside my trousers. My nipples peaked. I held my breath.

"So, fucking ready for me."

He cupped between my legs. The heel of his palm crushed down on my clit. My eyes slammed shut. His other hand came up and seized my breast. I moaned. Exekiel chuckled and used my two most sensitive parts to yank me back against him.

The hard ridge in his trousers prodded my back. His hand continued to assault my clit. My body tightened. One touch and he had me aching. I couldn't sit still. I rocked my hips and silently begged him to slip his fingers beneath my panties.

His mouth claimed mine again. My body twisted awkwardly to take in more of the kiss. My neck strained but I couldn't pull back. I was suspended between being comfortable and never wanting this to end.

My ass pressed into him. Exekiel groaned.

"I want this cunt on my cock." His words were raw and rough against my mouth. "Now."

My laugh was breathless. "That might not be the best idea when we're riding the back of a dragon."

"When it comes to me being inside you, there are no bad ideas."

Exekiel lifted me up and spun me around. His strong arms were steady as he hoisted me into the air. My stomach lurched. I saw everything from up here; suspended above the world by his bruising hands for one fleeting second. Below us was a large island that looked like it had a small village in its center. A building or monument seemed to be considerably larger than the rest, but it was too dark and distant to make out.

My curiosity vanished seconds later when Exekiel pulled me down on top of him. My knees bracketed his hips. My whole body went hot.

Shit. Were we seriously about to do this? My stare darted from his to our surroundings. Keeping our balance on a dragon was difficult enough without adding in death-defying sex stunts. At the same time,

I didn't want anything more. I wanted—needed—him.

As if he read my mind, Exekiel unleashed his shadows. They spilled from him like ink and coiled around my waist. Their touch was soft and cool, like the stroke of a finger. Then he wrapped them around Urdith's spikes until I was anchored to the dragon's frame.

I expected Urdith to protest but he flew on, unbothered.

"What about you?" I whispered.

Exekiel glanced at his powerful, dark wings. "I think I'll be fine."

His knuckles brushed along my jaw. My entire world shrank to that touch; to this moment and the feel of his body beneath mine. This time my kiss was just as hungry as his. I demanded his tongue—the taste of his skin. My fingers immediately went to the zip of his leathers. I pulled it down.

"Eager for my cock, little bud?"

I couldn't even deny it. I pushed my hand inside his trousers and wrapped my fingers around his hard, throbbing length. Exekiel bucked. I relished his reaction. The way this powerful being shook at my touch. He grunted and his head fell to one side. His hair slanted across his brow.

Exekiel watched me with hooded eyes as I dragged my hand down the smooth velvet length of his cock then back up. My thumb stroked over the tip.

He hissed through his teeth. "You do that so well. Mmmm…That's it."

My mate groaned. The sound was primal. I stroked him harder. My knuckles stung as they grazed the studs of his trousers that restricted my movements.

Fuck. This wasn't enough. I needed more of him. Sensing my frustration, Exekiel lifted his hips. I took hold of his trousers and pulled, just low enough to free his cock.

My mouth watered. There was nothing more beautiful than this Fae and his proud, thick erection. The sheer size of him still stunned me. The swollen purpling head was so hot. Its rigid stance, dared me to taste it. I took him in my hand again but Exekiel held my wrist.

"As much as I love the feel of your hand wrapped around me," he breathed. "Right now, I want the feel of your cunt."

Exekiel flipped a dagger in his hand.

My heart lurched. "What are you—?"

"Shhhh." He pressed the blade to my lips. His own slanted into a crooked grin. "Hold still."

Exekiel brought the dagger to the crotch of my trousers and cut at the fabric. I jerked but he gripped my hip and held me still.

"Don't move." His deadly pink gaze shot to mine then returned to his task of cutting what was essentially a flap into my leathers.

Once the material fell away, Exekiel hooked his fingers around the sides of the fabric at my inner thighs and pulled. He stretched until it had enough give for me to widen my legs, which he immediately did, then he yanked me against him.

Despite the fact that he'd just destroyed my outfit, the second our centers met, my pussy leaked and I unleashed a guttural moan. The feel of him made it difficult to concentrate or care about anything else.

With my hands braced on his shoulders, I rose up on my knees so I hovered over him.

Exekiel's eyes darkened. The hunger inside them made my pulse race. He slid a finger between my legs. His gaze devoured my response. My knees trembled.

"Look at you." He slipped beneath my underwear and dipped a finger inside me, then slid my wetness along my slit. I squeaked. My nails bit into his shoulders.

"Take a deep breath."

I did as I was told. The Shadow Saint fisted my underwear and ripped it off. I jumped at the snap of elastic that struck my backside. Exekiel pulled me down onto the swollen head of his cock.

"Fuck," I cried out.

My walls rippled and spasmed around him. He was so big.

"Come on, beautiful," he coaxed. "You can do it. Just a little wider for me."

My breaths were shallow, aching pants. "Fuck. Exekiel."

I rolled my hips which let me take in more of him. "That's it. Just like that."

Inch after perfect solid inch, my mate filled me; stretched me. My nerve-endings crackled. I scraped my nails down his hard-packed abs leaving light scratch marks in my wake. Sweat trickled between the grooves. I leaned in and licked it. I tasted the salt of his skin and flicked my tongue over his nipple.

Exekiel pushed deeper. "Do you like what you taste, little bud?"

He grabbed my ass and rocked me into him. My lungs seized. He was too much. Too perfect. Too flawed. He was everything one person had no right to be. The Fates had unfairly favored him; a god among mortals. And he was mine.

I sat straighter and rolled my hips. His jaw clenched as he pumped into me. His grip tight on my ass. My eyes rolled. No one could fuck me like him. No one ever felt like he did.

His fingers glided over my hips and up my back until they molded around my breasts. I gasped when he pulled down the neck of my off the shoulder blouse. My breasts bounced free. Exekiel cupped them in his hands and squeezed.

"Beautiful."

He brought his mouth to my nipple and sucked. His shadows seemed to instinctively tighten around me. My breath hitched. I undulated my hips. Every time I rocked back, his shadows yanked me forward, harder; forcing me to take every rigid inch of his iron cock. Pleasure spiraled through me. My vision spotted. Exekiel worshiped my breast. He licked and sucked like they were his last meal.

"You are my favorite flavor," he growled. "My fucking addiction."

He pinched one nipple between his index finger and thumb whilst his tongue flicked the other. My body hummed. I teetered on the edge of lustful oblivion.

Exekiel's shadows continued to guide me over his cock; to knead my ass and force my thrusts. I forgot everything. I forgot about where we were headed and where we'd come from. About the biting cold and our dangerous position. I was aware of nothing but him and how thoroughly he used me.

"Fuck!" Heat pooled between my thighs. The world spun.

"Are you close, little bud?"

Exekiel's hand curled around the back of my neck. The other dug into my hip as he worked me over his cock. His own hips reared up and struck new depths.

My cry caught in my throat. Power spiraled through my system and sparked in my blood. The burn of a melody danced across my tongue, but words scrambled in my mind.

"I'm coming."

My breaths sawed out of me. My release welled up inside.

Urdith roared—as if he felt the quake of my orgasm as much as I did. My thighs clamped around Exekiel as I rode him harder. My inner walls squeezed his cock. Ecstasy claimed my soul.

He groaned then unwove his shadows from around me and flipped me onto my back.

Panic and pleasure seized my chest. I was hung precariously over Urdith's back, caught between two dangerous spikes and death below.

Exekiel fell between my thighs. I blinked up at him and gripped a painful edge of Urdith's spike.

"What are you doing?"

"How many times can you come for me?"

Exekiel drove his hips into mine as shadows burst from his skin in a torrent of inky black. They spilled over us then fanned outwards and coiled around Urdith. Exekiel strapped me to my dragons hide. First my arms above my head. Then his shadows roped around my waist.

My eyes widened. Exekiel's grin was sharp, cruel and immorally attractive. His hips continued to pound. My heart continued to race—with anxiety, desire, shock.

Fuck. Exekiel's eyes were a blazing red as he impaled me over and over again. My back scraped on the rough dragon scales. I welcomed the pain. The brutal power of his thrusts. The way darkness almost swallowed him.

His hands speared through my hair and he brought his mouth to mine. I kissed him. Hard and reckless. Exekiel's shadows lassoed down my ankles next, then wove between my breasts.

The sensation was intoxicating. Like the stroke of salted smoke. My body tremored. Another orgasm vied to break free.

Exekiel grazed his teeth across my jaw then his mouth claimed mine again. His shadows grew taut and pulled. My pussy spasmed.

Shit. Deadly power and creeping shadows shouldn't be sexy but Exekiel made it R-Rated. His thick, stiff cock drove in and out of me until I was screaming. Shaking. Until I felt like I was surging out of my skin.

"That's it," he grunted. "Give me one more, beautiful."

His wings flexed. His fingers tangled with mine. I lost fucking control.

His own shout of pleasure rose as he pumped his hips harder. My walls jerked around him. Then, I erupted. A gush of liquid heat that spilled over his throbbing cock.

Eventually his thrusts slowed. My eyelids fluttered open in time to see his shadows recede. Tendrils of black curled around the edge of his skin.

"We have company."

Another roar split the night. This one was twice as loud and equally as ferocious as Urdith. My stomach lurched. I didn't have to look to know who or rather what had arrived. My mouth dropped open. I craned my neck to peer over Urdith's side.

A large hulking dragon swooped below us. Its giant wings outstretched. Revynath.

What was she doing here? I'd told her to stay put due to her enormous size and the fact that it would be hard enough to hide one dragon. Yet here she was.

I shook my head.

"Fucking dragon."

Although I couldn't help the smile that curved my lips.

41

EXEKIEL:
Negotiations with a Witch

It was close to sunset when we finally descended. According to the coordinates this small island packed with trees was where Councilwoman Nyla had chosen to hideout for the past few months.

Revynath landed first. Her shrewd gaze surveyed the area like she was seeking a threat. I imagined it would be hard to find anything here more threatening than her. The Crowned Sapphire towered above the trees from shoulder to head. Definitely not inconspicuous, but I doubted the dragon cared.

When we were close enough to the ground, I lunged from Urdith's back and flew the rest of the way. I'd ridden a dragon once before when I was younger. I'd disliked it then as much as I had now. There was no denying that dragons were powerful and majestic beasts. Sitting astride one was an experience like nothing else. However, I preferred my own wings. I'd never been one to freely relinquish control.

Varialla rode down on her dragon. In the setting sunlight, her skin was a deep brown highlighted with gold. Her hazel eyes were bright and beautiful when they met mine. It amazed me how stunning I found her; how drawn to her I was. Her nose scrunched and she let out a loud yawn. It was easily one of the cutest things I'd ever seen. She slid down Urdith's side and used her wings to slow her drop to the muddy ground.

"Before we go anywhere, I need to change." Varialla wriggled out of the leathers I'd torn during the flight, and exposed her supple legs. Despite having thoroughly fucked her, my cock twitched.

"Why change?"

She scowled at my grin. "Because I'm not going to ask this woman for help whilst standing in crotchless trousers."

She slid into a pair of shorts that I'd shoved into my pack. They were practically trousers on her. She tied her weapons belt tight to keep them from falling down.

I turned and took in our surroundings. We were in a jungle. The air smelt of herbs, spices and damp earth. Vines crept across the leafy ground and swung down overhead. Wildlife scurried up tree trunks and birds flittered from treetops. I took note of every sound; every creature, every change in the wind.

Varialla came up beside me and handed me a small leather-bound tome that had belonged to Nyla. The councilwoman had burned her belongings to prevent the Court from tracking her. However, she'd given two books on the history of the Conduit to Vladimir, claiming they were too valuable to destroy.

I took hold of the tome and summoned the power of *Fadea.* The three interconnected squares symbol of the Huntress fate glowed silver on the back of my hand. The celestial power latched on to scents and fibers of Nyla, I wouldn't have otherwise detected.

"Let's go."

I took her hand in mine and we began our trek. Sleep would have been preferable. We'd each only managed a couple of hours astride Urdith, but the journey had already taken close to a day. We didn't have long before it would be time to turn back.

We followed the pull of the Fate's guidance which tightened when I turned one way and waned when I turned another. Varialla kept her hand in mine. Her eyes as alert as her dragons at our back.

By some miracle she'd convinced them to stay put. I suspected it was because they could see over the trees. One glance in their direction and I made out Revynath's yellow gaze in the distance. She marked our every step.

"How happy do you think Nyla's going to be to see us, on a scale of one to ten?"

"A solid eight."

Varialla snickered. "That would be nice. Although considering she stole those files as a bargaining chip for her life, I'm not sure she'll love the idea of us taking them away."

"She doesn't have to love it." I turned as *Fadea* led me down a different path. "She just has to accept it."

Sunset eventually turned to night. Fireflies lit up the space between the trees. The force of *Fadea* urged us on, but I had no way of knowing how much further we had to go.

"My feet hurt," Varialla grumbled as she trudged behind me.

Her hand was no longer in mine. About an hour ago, she'd complained her palm was too sweaty. The reality was she'd wanted me to take the lead whilst she trailed behind.

"And your back is sore. And you're tired and you're hungry. And thirsty." I listed off her complaints since we'd started the trek and shot her a look over my shoulder. "Did I forget anything?"

Her brows pulled together. "You forgot being eaten alive." She swatted at her arm and the air around her. "These fucking bugs! They're worse than mosquitoes."

I grinned. I knew of mosquitoes and had to agree that what we had in the Isles were worse. Paralets didn't just feed on blood, they devoured the flesh and laid eggs in the wound.

"Don't scratch. That'll just spread the larvae." I ducked beneath a branch.

Varialla stopped in her tracks. "The what?"

"Larvae." I waited for her to follow but she didn't move. "The insect in its infancy before it matures. A maggot," I clarified.

She shrieked. "Get it out." Varialla rushed to me like I'd personally put the bites there and yanked on her sleeves. "Get it out. Get it out." She gripped my tunic in her small fists. "I can't have maggots growing in my arms."

"Fierce dragon shifter, last of her kind, commander of the sea…squeals at a bug bite."

"This isn't a bite." She pulled away with a sound of pure disgust. "This is an infestation!"

I shook my head. "You're hilarious."

"And you're a pain in the ass!"

"We still haven't tested that theory."

"Well, we won't anytime soon." Varialla rubbed furiously at her arm. White spots bloomed where the paralets had fed. "Unless of course, you'd like to bed some egg-infested siren."

I raised a brow. "Aren't all females egg-infested?"

She hurled an ardven at my head. I hadn't seen her pluck the fruit from the tree but the bright pink crop whistled past my ear as I stepped aside.

"Stop scratching."

Varialla flung up her middle finger and trampled ahead.

*

335

It was twilight when I sent my shadows out and finally felt something. I brushed Varialla's fingers with the backs of mine.

"There's someone in the trees." My shadows passed over the figure; curvy with a large bust and a bow and arrow aimed at us. I raised my voice. "I wouldn't do that, if I was you."

The figure tensed.

"By the time you freed that arrow, I would have hung you from the tree branch you're perched on." I turned slowly and looked directly at where I knew the witch crouched. "Come out, Nyla."

The councilwoman drew back her bowstring and fired.

Shadows shot from the edge of my folded wings. They knocked the arrow aside and yanked the witch from her perch. She hit the ground and struggled in their hold. Her sandy brown skin was smeared with dirt. Her plump lips were cracked, and her upturned eyes lacked their usual line of kohl.

I strode towards her. "That wasn't very nice, Nyla."

"Get these things off me."

"How can I be sure you won't try to kill me again?

The witch sneered. "Technically, you're already dead."

I released her from my shadows. She sprang to her feet with a glare. Her feet were bare and her outfit was fashioned from leaves.

"Nyla Foxhaven."

"Shadow Saint." She snarled, "How was the River?"

I chased away the encroaching memories.

"Cold."

Nyla folded her arms across her chest and looked to Varialla. "You're alive too."

"Sorry to disappoint."

"Someone has to take the throne. Might as well be someone who's genuinely fighting for the people."

"And you?" Varialla cocked her head. "What are you fighting for?"

"Myself." Nyla flicked dirt from her fingernails.

At a glance, she appeared bored, but I noted the tightness in her posture and the way her feet shifted; ready to run.

The witch shrugged. "Those in power only care about themselves. I'm looking out for me."

"And damn the rest of us?"

"You're already damned. It's only a matter of time before they claim the realm and your minds with it."

I wove my shadows behind her back; a wall in case she fled. "Not if you help us."

Her steely eyes turned to me. "What exactly is it that brings the infamous Shadow Saint and his queen to my tree stump?"

"We need the formula for the antidote, poison and anything else you have that might help us win this war."

Nyla stiffened.

"Before you think of refusing." I trailed my shadows up her arm. For the first time, her gaze darted around her and noticed the web they'd forged. "Don't."

42

VARIALLA:
The Toll of Church Bells

We weren't going to make it. Despite Exekiel's threats, Nyla had put up one hell of a fight when it came to giving us the files. At first, she'd claimed she'd destroyed them. Then she'd flat out refused to hand them over. As far as she was concerned, the Royal Court had already condemned the realm and its people to Zorsch. Those records were her safety net; leverage she could use in case any of them survived.

Ezekiel had seemed ready to torture the information out of her. I tried another approach. Nyla could have stolen the documents and run. Instead, she'd destroyed the Court's research facility because, deep down, a part of her had wanted to help. She'd wanted to do something to stop them and save the people. Though it pained her to admit it, a part of her cared. That was the part I preyed on until in the end, she'd relented.

Now, balanced on Revynath's back, Exekiel and I hurtled through the sky at breakneck speed and tried to race the dawn. We had until then before Godric would be waiting on the steps of the cathedral to film me coming out.

An echo of sun already glimmered on the horizon. My heart beat wildly in my chest. I'd hoped to get some sleep on this flight but I was too wired to close my eyes.

Exekiel and I poured over the information we'd taken from Nyla. There was a list of ingredients for the antidote with its exact measurements. Beside them were notes on how, in some cases, one milligram could alter the whole result.

I couldn't tell which ingredient reacted with the toxin but I was pretty sure Ilbryen would be able to figure it out. He was one of the realm's greatest alchemists, and poisons were his specialty.

"We're not going to make it," I said to myself beneath the wind's howl.

Revynath's wings sliced through the air. She moved like a missile; swift, focused and unstoppable. But the Isle's didn't seem to be getting any closer.

Revynath banked left. I gripped tighter with my thighs. My fingers curled into her smooth blue scales. My eyes started to water. I was part dragon. I was made to fly but not at this speed. I hunkered low. My hips anchored by Exekiel's shadows. He sat behind me. His hands on my hips and his breath on my neck.

Pinpricks of heat sparked through my rising panic when his lips brushed across my skin in an almost kiss.

"We're going to make it."

I wanted to believe him but every second that ticked by brought us closer to being discovered—to everyone who'd helped us being caught in the lie.

I swallowed my rising dread.

Another kiss had my pulse skipping for an entirely different reason. This one was at the hollow between my neck and collarbone.

My eyes drifted closed. "Are you trying to distract me?"

Exekiel stroked his hands over my hips. "Is it working?"

I opened my mouth to say no. His teeth grazed the lobe of my ear. My words faltered.

"Well?"

"Maybe."

Exekiel cupped my jaw and turned my face towards him. He lowered his head and kissed me. For one blissful moment, I was at peace. My panic was replaced with the very pressing demand of his kiss; the glide of his tongue across my own. I leaned in. His kisses were a paradox that left me reeling. They made me weightless and yet, I'd never felt so grounded— so sure.

Exekiel made an involuntary sound that had my heart pumping. The soft graze of his fingers crept up my shirt. I trembled.

Revynath's giant serpentine head swung to face us. Her yellow eyes narrowed. A puff of steam struck the top of my head.

I gulped—a full audible gulp. Knowing she wouldn't hurt me didn't make her death stare any less terrifying. Right now, the force of it was directed at Exekiel.

He sighed before he pulled back. "Message received."

Revynath's wings beat slowly. She gave a very pointed look at Exekiel's arms that were wrapped around my waist.

"He has to hold on," I argued.

Her yellow eyes barely flicked in my direction before she gave Exekiel a final warning glare. Its message was clear: *Hands to yourself, shadow boy.*

Urdith may have let us turn his back into a humping ground. Revynath was having none of it.

I'd been mildly surprised that she'd let Exekiel ride her without a fight. Either she really liked the Shadow Saint or we'd both silently agreed, that Urdith had earned a rest. I liked to think it was a bit of both.

"She has the same glare as you," Exekiel murmured.

My eyes narrowed.

"That's the one." He'd barely pecked my nose before Revynath swung her head back around to face us.

"Alright." Exekiel held up a hand. "You win."

My Crowned Sapphire emitted a series of growls that sounded like she was cursing him under her breath as she turned back to face the front.

"She has your temperament too."

I grinned and leaned back against his chest.

*

We didn't take the same route we'd used to leave the Isles. One glance from a distance had confirmed that almost every guard was stationed at the border. Instead, we plunged beneath the ocean. Revynath rolled us from her back then shot towards the surface. This was as far as she could go without being seen.

Like before, I brought Exekiel's lips to mine. He folded his arms around my waist like he was about to kiss me, then I breathed. I breathed air into and around him until a bubble morphed over his nose and mouth. We swam.

Instinctively, gills formed on my neck. My skin tingled and my legs snapped together, until a glimmering gold tail was in their place. Exekiel paused to take it in but there wasn't time. I yanked on his hand and we cut beneath the water. Low and out of sight.

We didn't resurface until we reached the depths of the lagoon where Loch had often met me. It was fitting that the routes he'd shown me in secret, as a way to manipulate my loyalty, were now the ones I used to destroy him.

My muscles protested as I heaved myself up onto the pebbled shore. My legs returned but ached like I'd run a mile. My breaths sawed out of me and I pushed to my feet.

There was the distant peal of cathedral bells. My stomach dropped. Sunrise was here. The morning prayers had ended.

"As soon as you get to the palace, have Lucinda remove the larvae from inside your skin using telapa tonic and tweezers," Exekiel ordered. Water dripped from his now wavy hair and off the end of his nose. "There aren't any paralets in the Inlands which means you shouldn't have that."

He gestured to the sickening star of white pustuled flesh on my arm from where I'd been feasted on in that fucking jungle.

I folded my arms across my chest as if that could help me forget it was there. Like the maddening itch wasn't a constant reminder.

Exekiel pulled me close. I'd barely caught my breath before he stole it with a kiss. "Whatever you do, don't get caught."

I hated that it would be another week, at least, before I saw him again.

I nodded once. "Right back at you."

Then, I ran.

43

VARIALLA:
AROUND EVERY CORNER

I arrived at the cathedral long after the sermon had ended. Puddles pooled in my wake as I charged in from the gardens and down the marble corridors to Satrialla's rooms. I pulled on one of her outfits—a short blue corset dress with puffy sleeves and a ruffled hem—then hurtled back downstairs. The cloak I'd worn when I entered two days ago was hung in the closet by the door.

I swerved around a corner and slammed straight into a wall of hard muscle. Familiar hands grasped my waist. My back was pressed against the wall. The scent of sea-salt and coconut assaulted my senses.

"Princess."

That word. That voice. My body seized. Ice slick in my veins. I blinked up at punishing blue eyes, a chiseled jaw, smooth hazel-brown skin and full lips.

"Where are you going to in such a hurry?"

The Rebel King pushed closer until his body was a hairsbreadth from mine. His dark gaze drifted over my hair. I'd done my best to dry it but water droplets sat on the top of my curls. He inhaled. It didn't take a genius to know he smelt the sea.

"Or a better question is where are you coming from?"

I shoved him back but he grabbed my arms and pinned them at the side of my head. I winced as his thumb pressed down on the paralet bites. I rushed to mask my expression but not fast enough. He'd noticed it, like he noticed everything about me.

Loch wrenched up the sleeve of my blouse before I could react. Triumph glimmered in his blue depths. His head cocked to one side in a predatory way.

"Interesting." His grip tightened. "Does it hurt?"

I hissed out a breath of pain. The harder he pressed, the more the bitemark burned like acid-soaked needles plunged into my flesh.

"That's one thing I love about the Inlands—no paralets."

I didn't hear what he said next over the pounding in my ears. He knew. He knew I'd left the Five Isles. If the seawater in my hair hadn't been enough, this had confirmed it. Paralet bites when there were no paralets in the area.

Power gathered at the base of my spine. I could kill him. No one was around and I had fire at my fingertips. I could turn his bones to ash and sweep him beneath a rug. To murder a man in a church; the thought should have been sickening but the temptation was sweet. I couldn't openly attack the bastard and risk the sirens turning against me, or have the people of the Court thinking I'd gone mad with power. But there was no one here.

Loch's jagged teeth flashed when he grinned. It was in a way that said he knew the direction of my thoughts.

He leaned in close. "If you think I'm the only one who knows I'm here or what you've done, you're a fool." His hips pinned mine to the wall. His breath was cold on my neck.

I choked down a breath of longing and revulsion.

"I don't know why you left the Isles, Varialla." His hand trailed down my neck. His thumb stopped at my pulse that beat an erratic rhythm. "But I will find out."

My throat bobbed against the pad of his thumb.

"Varialla?" Mother Margareet's voice sailed towards us. The red-robed beauty with kind grey eyes and soft pink lips had rounded the corner. She barely acknowledged Loch before she said, "Are you feeling better?"

"Yes." My voice came out breathless. I cleared my throat. "Yes."

Loch finally stepped back. I pushed off the wall and rubbed my hands down my thighs. Not to stop their shaking but to stop them from reaching out and pulling Loch against me. I hated the way he affected me; the bewitched instinct that overrode all logic and undermined my will.

"It's a shame you had to run out during the sermon." The Mother must have spotted my damp hair or slick boots because she added, "I hope the cold shower helped."

The lies slid easily off her tongue. It was impressive especially for someone who'd devoted their life to faith. I'd never been so grateful. The Mother approached and folded her arm around my shoulders. She spoke about remedies and dizzy spells as she walked me towards the exit and away from Loch. His stare burned a hole in my back. This wasn't over. The bastard knew I'd left the Isles. What would he do with that information?

I met Godric at the foot of the stairs. Mother Margareet gave the same excuses for the benefit of the orb he directed. The centaur glanced my way. Relief and something like pride shone in his eyes.

"Sorry, I kept you waiting," I said as we strolled towards the town square.

"You were worth the wait. I don't just mean today."

My steps faltered. I glanced at the centaur; the earnest expression on his face.

"It's about time we have someone who truly cares on the throne."

My chest tightened.

"As my orbs-director, I think you're supposed to remain impartial."

"As an oppressed Outlier, I think I'm entitled to want someone who sees me as me and not an object for their personal use."

The vehemence in his words swirled through me and settled in my soul.

I nodded. "Here's to being seen."

Above me, smoky letters formed the words: **Core value identified: 30 Points**

Godric dipped his head. "To being seen as we truly are."

*

My hair was the only thing that wasn't a mess. Thanks to the literal enchanted stylings of Lucinda Ironclaw, the top of my hair was slicked back in a bun, and the curls down the side of my face were perfectly in place. The rest of me, on the other hand, was in shambles. Mother Margareet had done her best to make me look presentable before I left the Cathedral but nothing could hide the bags under my eyes, my chapped lips and wind-stung cheeks. With every step I took my boots squelched with water that had soaked into the soles. I didn't even want to think about how bad I stank.

As soon as we reached my rooms in the palace, Godric announced that he needed the toilet. When the door clicked shut behind him, I raced into the bathing chamber. As planned my team of stylists were there waiting for me.

"We've got five minutes."

I kicked off my boots and shucked off my dress.

"We managed to search Victus manor," Lucinda started. "The contraption under the tarp was definitely a decoy and rigged to alert anyone when we came close."

Maximus snorted. "We almost got ourselves killed but at least we can safely cross that location off the list."

Which meant we were down to two possible places that the weapon could be being kept. There wasn't much time left for us to find it.

"Eudora? Odus?"

"Still breathing but barely." Colette's voice was soft.

Her words stung. I shook them off. We had the formulas now. Aquarius was working on a new antidote as we spoke.

I plunged into the pool and savored the warmth that seeped into my bones. "Count Mari?"

"Delicious," Cyrus waggled her brows.

Lucinda rolled her eyes. "He's secured us an ally in Fae Crest. Those in Soaring Summit would like to meet you this afternoon to discuss your vision and exactly what you'd need from them." She sauntered over and sat cross-legged at the edge of the pool. "But it seems promising."

Cyrus climbed into the pool. It didn't bother me like it used to. I welcomed her assistance as she massaged shampoo into my hair and I soaped up my soiled skin. Maximus sat on a wooden stool with his feet kicked up on the sink. He filed his nails and barely glanced my way. If we had more time, I might have pretended to be insulted.

"The public?"

Lucinda smirked. "Coming around. Almost half the realm is getting their fresh goods directly from Giant's Keep now."

I grinned. "Excellent."

"Primary Intendent," Godric addressed me by my formal title as he trotted into the chamber. It was the first sign that something was off. "There's someone here to see you."

Colette stiffened. Lucinda and Maximus shared a look that said they knew exactly who it was.

With the softest toweled robe known to man, wrapped around me, I headed into my sitting room.

My mother, the once savage queen of the Coral Court, sat in a purple velvet armchair. One slender leg was crossed over the other. She looked well. Her skin had more color than when I last saw her. Her hair was combed into an afro and she wore a gold headband that matched the shimmering shade of her dress. It fell to her ankles and was dotted with silver pearls.

She looked…regal.

Her eyes lit up when she saw me. She got to her feet and pulled me into a hug. I didn't know why it felt awkward; wrong. She was my mother; a woman I'd dreamt about meeting since I'd realized I didn't have one. In some ways she'd turned out to be everything I'd wanted. In other ways, where it truly mattered, she'd let me down. Maximus and the others said that maybe she needed time outside of Blacktomb Bay to see how much things had changed and that there was an alternative to taking over the realm. I wasn't sure there was enough time in existence to temper her rage.

Although I hoped they were right. Since my mother been the one to perform the Ceremonial Bind, there was maybe a way for her to undo it. All she needed was time.

"You're a hard one to find." She pulled back but kept her bony hands on my shoulders.

"I've been busy."

"Yes. Reading up on the Isles history and taking walks in the park?" She arched a knowing brow.

Of course, she knew. Loch had probably told her. However, I was still alive and in the Games. For whatever reason, Loch hadn't used the information against me yet. A sudden thought niggled at the back of my mind.

"Exactly," I said with a tight-lipped smile and took a step back.

Zenera glanced at Godric and the camera-orb over our heads, then back to me. "I wondered if you'd given any more thought to what we spoke about the other day."

I struggled to hide my disappointment. Since we'd met, my mother had barely asked about my life in England. She knew nothing about me and didn't seem interested in finding out. Every conversation was centered around explaining the past and trying to convince me to join her in the future. I squeezed my hair into the smaller towel I carried.

"There's nothing to think about."

Her fingers curled into her skirt and her shoulders stiffened. "Your birth is an opportunity for true change around here." She chose her words carefully. "Redemption for the Outer Isles. Freedom for your people."

"Freedom." I curled my tongue around the word.

It wasn't freedom to be controlled. To find out that the peace was dependent on a weapon. That my people and their power would unknowingly be its ammunition.

Zenera's jaw ticked. Her nostrils slightly flared. She wasn't just irritated. She was furious. It was clear in the flash of anger in her eyes. I suddenly wondered which one wanted revenge more. Her or Loch?

That niggling thought grew louder in my mind.

I turned to Lucinda. "I ordered breakfast. Has it arrived?"

We both knew I hadn't but she dutifully went to check the hallway.

"Not yet," she called.

My skin prickled. I kept my face a mask of calm. I couldn't give anything away.

"Alright, thanks." I returned my attention to my mother. "I need to get dressed. Is that all?"

Her eyes narrowed but she pulled her lips into a strained smile. "Don't let me keep you."

Her bony fingers dug into my shoulders once more as she pulled me into another embrace.

"You were born to rule and avenge your people," she whispered.

"Funny," I murmured. "The dragon shifters were my people too."

When my mother pulled back, her stare wasn't one of a mother to a daughter but of an enemy sizing up a threat they hadn't realized they had.

I swallowed the dejected feeling in my gut and my own rising rage. The ex-queen of the Coral Court nodded her head and left the room.

"About that breakfast," I said once the door had closed. I glanced at Godric.

The centaur faked a sneeze and flicked a switch that sent the orb crashing into the wall. It bounced across the tiles.

"Shit," he hissed and rushed to retrieve it.

It wasn't damaged. Those things were solid. But it brought us a handful of seconds whilst he scooped it off the floor and inspected it.

"Was anyone in the corridor?" I whispered.

"No."

"My mother told me she couldn't be more than a few feet away from Loch."

Glances passed between us. She'd lied. Time and proximity strengthened the bind between Loch and I. I hadn't spent any considerable time with him recently other than that night. Was that why she'd done it? They wanted to strengthen the bind by forcing me to be around him. They wanted to make it easier for him to manipulate and control me. Maybe that was why my body had responded so viscerally to his touch earlier.

Before anyone could respond, Godric returned and our masks slid back into place.

44

VARIALLA:
THE WEEKLY REVIEW

Applause rang through the auditorium. The sound jolted me from thoughts of impending war and damning secrets. I half expected someone in the audience to jump up and indicate the faded mark of the paralet bite that was hidden beneath the flowy sleeves of my peach-colored dress. I expected Loch to come out and demand my head. It had been a few days since I'd returned from beyond the Isles, but I'd only seen the Rebel King in passing. My mother even less.

The ruffled hem of my dress rose when I crossed one leg over the other. The gown Cyrus had chosen for me tonight, was considerably shorter in the front than at the back and exposed a hell of a lot of thigh. The top half was a fitted lace bodice dusted in golden glitter. I did my best not to fidget with the plumes of tulle and forced myself to focus on the audience gathered in the Gamers Dome. On my right and left were the other contestants; Vivienne, Kraxus, Bennet and Camal. We each sat in familiar red seats that were set up on stage.

Goather stood before us. The Conduit gleamed beside him. In its shimmering blue streaks of light, the contestant's names appeared. Numbers and tally marks swirled through the haze.

"It's the moment of truth," Goather bellowed. "The Conduit has been keeping score. Has anything changed since the week before?" He waggled his brows and tipped his feathered hat.

The people cheered. It was time for our Weekly Review to see who was in the lead. Goather pretended to tally up the points though the Conduit was doing the real work. All we could do was wait. The first time we'd done this, I'd been at number five. After discovering my dragons, I'd moved to number three. That was where I'd stayed last week. In the middle. Good but not good enough.

"Number five is Bennet Ridgely," Goather announced as the shimmering name appeared above the Conduit. "In fourth place, Kraxus V'alin. Followed by Vivienne Foraglade."

My heart leapt. It was now between me and Camal Silverhound. Apparently, the Games were being rigged in his favor but I couldn't figure out how. During Adir's reign, Evangeline had been coerced by sirens implanted on her team to throw the Game but that wasn't what was happening here. I'd handpicked my team besides Godric and I trusted every one of them.

Goather hollered some things to excite the audience but I was barely listening. My eyes remained fixed on the Conduit and the letters and numbers that swirled in its depths. Finally, my name appeared in second place, followed by Camal in the lead. The bastard threw me a smug look.

If he won the Games, he could dictate where the winner's ceremony was held. He could choose exactly where the Court wanted so the weapon could do the most damage. Despite us putting a dent in the amount of people we reached with their tainted produce, thousands of beings had already been infected and cured by the Courts antidote. They were still at risk if the weapon was used.

After the scores, we moved on to the Q & A portion of the evening. Each of us explained our plans for our reign and how our recent movements had lent themselves to that future.

Vivienne announced that she'd sourced affordable material to build the border wall and prevent the rise in crime and hate acts between the Isles. The material would come from Wolf's Waters—the Isle of werewolves—which she seemed to think would lessen people's prejudice towards them and was the start of a great alliance. Camal babbled about how he'd already started to return long lost relatives to their families in the Outer Isles, like he was some kind of hero.

Finally, Goather turned to me. "During the debate of Phase Two, you mentioned creating a day where Outliers would be invited to the Inlands. Where they could benefit from a fragment of the Conduit's power to repair their lands."

"That's right." The microphone hooked to my corset amplified my voice.

Goather gestured to the audience. "I believe we have a few questions regarding that tonight?"

A reporter in the front row with narrow pink wings that matched the shade of her hair and pointed ears, held up her hand.

Goather nodded at her.

"This day seems to be entirely for the benefit of the Outliers. What do you intend on doing for the Inlands?"

My jaw tightened. As if the Inlanders who had had everything handed to them for the last six centuries needed more. It was such an entitled Fae question but thankfully one I could answer.

"The Outer Isles weren't the only ones restricted during the Brutal War. Inlanders were imprisoned behind the shield the Shadow Saint built to protect them. Many of whom had friends or lovers in the Outer Isles."

Some of the reporters exchanged glances. They weren't on board with relationships between the supposed blessed and unblessed but they'd have to get used to it.

"There were those who wished to travel beyond our borders. To explore the Outlands and maybe more. That is what I offer the Inlanders. Freedom to come and go as they please. Agreements and treaty's will be signed so that they can travel into the Outer Isles without fear of harm or persecution. When the lands are fully reformed, we will alternate the locations for solstice celebrations and more."

"How do you intend to tackle the issue of sea monsters?" Asked an elf with porcelain skin and bright silver eyes. "The barrier also shielded us from them."

"As many of you know, Exekiel V'alin was the Protector of the Realm. He has assured me that if I win the Games, he would be happy to take up that role again, this time with a team he trusts."

I couldn't help the dig at the current Court. For so long, Exekiel had been lied to; his grief and rage preyed on. The Royal Court and Council had had him searching for threats to the Five Isle's borders and taking out monsters they'd lured in, whilst they met in private and planned to take over the Isles.

"There's one important issue you haven't addressed," barked a large man nearer the back. He wore a tweed suit and round spectacles over narrowed eyes. If I had to guess, I'd say he was a bear shifter based on his broad frame and the growl in his voice.

"As Ms. Vivienne Foraglade pointed out, since the barrier fell, crime has risen. How do you intend to keep the peace? Just because you will it, doesn't make it so."

"It does not," I agreed. "Which is why, like Ms. Foraglade, I will double security, not only at the border but in patrols throughout the isles. I also intend to restructure our military forces. The new army will be made up of both Inlanders and Outliers with equal rank."

This piqued their interest. The reporters straightened and some applauded.

The beefy man opened his mouth to say something else but I held up a finger to cut him off.

"I also find that dragons can be very persuasive."

Almost everyone in the crowd went wild. I relished their applause and smirked at the shifter whose cheeks had gone ruddy. That was something I could offer that nobody else could. The protection and might of dragons.

*

My steps were sluggish as I trudged down the palace corridors towards my room. Exhausted didn't begin to describe how knackered I was. I'd spent the morning in Evermore. I met the people and listened to their grievances. The afternoon had led me to lunch with my potential allies. Now I felt like I needed to sleep for at least a week.

Smothering a yawn, I rounded a corner and felt the presence of someone else. My spine stiffened. I wasn't alone. I couldn't make anyone out in the torchlight but I felt the prickle of their magic in the air.

A look over my shoulder indicated that nothing was there. I peered ahead into the shadows, particularly near the suits of armor. Still nothing. My heartrate quickened. Godric had stayed behind at the Gamers Dome. He'd been requested by Gwendoline to help with some malfunctioning orbs.

Still, I said, "Godric?"

No one answered. Everything remained eerily still but I felt eyes on me. Unease sank in my gut. After a final glance behind me, I moved faster. It was too quiet. Too dark. The perfect setting for—

I retched when a bag was flung over my head and pulled tight around my neck. Rough burlap scraped my face as I was dragged backwards.

My fingers hooked beneath the edge of the sack. I tried to pry it off; to take in air. My legs kicked and I slipped on the tiles. I tried to speak—to sing—but my mouth was pressed shut by the coarse fabric. I couldn't breathe, couldn't see.

Pain shot through the back of my skull.

Everything went dark.

45

LOCH:
Test of Endurance

It took Varialla a heartbeat to realize I had her. That everything she'd done to try and escape me had been for nothing. We were always going to end up here. With her at my mercy. Crippled by my control.

When her hazel eyes flickered open, they flared with a fury so potent I could taste it.

"It's time to test your endurance, princess. How long can you keep going?" I paced towards where she knelt in the center of the stone chamber. There was something delicious about seeing her there, on her knees. "How much can you take?"

"Fuck you."

Varialla tried to lash out only to discover her wrists were chained to the stone bench behind her that was nailed to the ground. It was the only piece of furniture in the room. Wide enough for me to lay her down on top of it.

"I'd rather be fucking you."

I delved into my power and caressed the bind between us. In my mind, it was a pale filament of magic. It blazed a burning silver when I reached for it. Her back arched and pushed out those delicious tits of hers.

I pulled again. Varialla gasped. Her head tipped back. I drew out the hunger I knew she felt for me. It was the same I felt for her; ingrained into the both of us centuries ago and left to intensify.

She gritted her teeth and hunched forwards. The scent of her reluctant arousal perfumed the air. My dick hardened.

Tonight, I would have her. We were in the catacombs of the palace. The very chambers where the Conduit had recently been moved to and where traces of it lingered in the air. Those remnants worked in my favor now to strengthen the Mate-Sworn bind it had been used to create. Not even she could resist it for long.

Varialla blinked. I kept a tight grip on the threads of power that bound us and stroked out her need. She whimpered. It was a fucking delicious sound.

I crouched in front of her. "Fates, I love seeing you on your knees."

I fisted her hair and tipped back her head. Her burning gaze struck mine. I grinned and lowered my mouth to her neck. I breathed her in. Sea salt and sugar.

"Time's up, Princess."

"This won't work," she hissed. "To consummate the bind, both of us have to be willing and I would never willingly fuck you."

I pulled back until my nose brushed hers. "Never say never."

I stood and flicked the switch on the wall by the steel door. The stone parted to reveal thick glass and five figures beyond it. Three had bags over their heads and hung from the ceiling by their wrists. Knox stood at one end and Adir at the other. Beside them were trays stacked with sharp objects—anything that would inflict pain.

I nodded to Knox who ripped away the first bag.

Varialla's skin paled and her eyes widened. "Colette."

"Colette," I confirmed.

Knox glanced at me. When I said nothing, he punched Colette hard across the face. Blood spewed from the sirens mouth and her body swung in the chains. I'd had fun dealing with the siren a bit myself before this. She'd been the one who opened the gates at Dragon Spire. The one who'd turned her back on her people to help the traitor.

Varialla sprang to her feet. The chains around her own wrists clanked behind her. She rushed closer to the glass until they jerked her back.

"Stop!" she shouted as Knox delivered hit after hit.

Colette pressed her lips together and held back her cries, but her face creased with every blow, and spit and blood dribbled down her chin.

"Stop!"

"This is the least she deserves after what she's done." I strode towards her. "We should and could put all of your heads on the chopping block." I circled her but Varialla's wide-eyed gaze remained fixed on the glass where her friend was being beaten. "However, I have told them how they can end this. They can tell me why you left the Isles and I'll set them free. Or you can stop this."

I came up behind her and rested my hands on her shoulders. She tried to pull away but I yanked her back. Her plump backside stroked my cock. *Fuck.*

"Give yourself to me and this stops."

Varialla tensed.

"This is your Test of Endurance. How much can you endure, princess?"

The second figure was obvious; a centaur. When the bag was pulled free, Varialla let out a strangled gasp. Her orbs-director, Godric Tor, hung from the thickest chains. Half his coat had been shaved. The word: Traitor, was carved into the flesh beneath. And his thick tail had been hacked off. Varialla shook her head as if that would somehow make the scene go away.

I grasped her hips and held her against me. I relished the way her firm backside moved against my dick when she tried to get away.

"Be mine and this ends."

"I will never be yours!" Varialla spun and shoved her hands into my chest.

Fire blazed from her palms. A rush of raging teal and scarlet flames swept towards me and filled the room. I wrenched on the bind between us and shielded myself in her power. She'd caught me off guard once before. I wasn't going to let it happen again.

When her flames finally receded, Varialla stood with her fists clenched and chest heaving, in a plume of thick smoke. I grinned from the other side. Everything, other than her smoldering chains, was intact. Stone didn't burn. Thanks to the bind between us, neither did I.

"Feel better?"

Varialla stepped back. "How—?"

"Because I own you."

I was invincible but her affection for these pathetic beings made her weak.

"This is just the beginning. Everyone who helped you defy the rules of the Games will suffer a slow excruciating death unless you give yourself to me."

The Gaming Council believed I'd captured Varialla to torture her for information then kill her. Adir assumed me fucking her was my brand of punishment. He didn't realize that once she submitted to my demand, I would seize control of her power and this realm.

"I will make you watch as they bleed."

The sounds of torture had stopped. When I nodded to Knox and Adir, they started up again. This time they didn't hold back. There was the distinct snap of bone. Colette finally broke and her blood curdling screams shattered the silence.

Knox strode over to our third captive next and ripped the bag away. It was a few seconds before recognition dawned since their face was so badly beaten. Varialla stumbled then rushed forwards. She'd melted her chains. They easily snapped and swung from her wrists when she raised her fists and pounded on the glass.

"Lucinda!"

Knox didn't wait for my cue. He tore into the bloodwitch. His knuckles cracked across her already swollen jaw.

"I'll do it," Varialla swiveled from them to me. "I'll do it! Fuck you!"

Her voice was shredded—shrill and deadly. The reverberations rocked through the room. For a heartbeat, I thought her fucking power might shatter the glass but it remained whole.

"I'll do it!"

"Willingly?"

Colette howled when Adir yanked on her finger and snapped it back. Varialla thumped on the glass like she thought she could break through it.

"Yes!" Varialla choked out. "Just. Stop."

"Turn around," I ordered.

She did. Her breaths were ragged. She couldn't hide the tears that dripped down her cheeks. She flinched at every blow and muffled cry her friends tried to hold back.

"Open your legs."

Her eyes flared. Hatred and horror filled their depths.

I nodded to Knox and Adir. They immediately stopped. Varialla's shoulders sagged with some measure of relief.

I stepped closer; crowding her. "Open your legs."

Her lips pursed but she obeyed. Her smooth thighs parted and I slid my hand between them. My other hand gripped her hip, holding her still when she tried to pull back.

"Behave." I stroked my finger along her dripping pussy. Varialla shuddered. My dick stiffened. "Wider."

Again, my little princess did exactly what I asked. She held my stare; her fists curled at her sides, as I worked my finger inside her underwear.

"This won't work." She sucked in a breath as she tried to fight the effect I was having on her.

"Ye of little faith."

Her mouth parted when I quoted the humans' religious texts and pushed a finger inside her. Her sweet pussy sucked me in with a need that made my dick throb. The chains around her wrists clanked as she shook and tried to fight the urge to move.

"I'm not forcing myself on you or vice versa. You can stop this anytime you like. But you're choosing—willing—to continue." I grinned and pushed another finger inside her.

Varialla let out a moan before she bit her bottom lip to stop it. Her legs quaked. I was so fucking hard I was going to tear through my slacks.

"I think we both know that as much as you wish you didn't, you want this, Princess. You want me." I pumped my fingers faster.

Varialla's nostrils flared with each shallow breath.

"Give in to me," I encouraged and guided her hips to move with my fingers.

Frustration and need shone in her eyes. I held her stare and pushed my fingers deeper, faster. She squeaked. Her face scrunched. I didn't stop—didn't slow.

I felt the exact moment I had her. She hiccupped over her breath. Her fingers flexed on my forearm and her hips involuntarily moved.

"That's it." I leaned in and caught the lobe of her ear between my teeth. "Be mine."

My thumb stroked over her clit. Varialla lurched and shoved me off of her.

"No!" She seethed. "No!"

I lunged for her. "You don't have a choice."

Gripping her arms, I spun her around and slammed her against the glass. I forced her to meet the broken and bloodied bodies of her friends. Adir lifted a small blade and slashed it across Godric's hide. The centaur bawled and kicked his hooves.

Varialla struggled to break free.

"You're a fucking monster!"

I pressed closer. "You're finally getting it."

I grasped her hips from behind. Her plump ass was fucking perfect. I pushed my dick against it and groaned. The need to have her; devour her, was intoxicating.

"Now," I snarled into her ear; loving the way her breath hitched. The way disgusted desire flickered in the reflection of her eyes. "Fuck me like a good little princess or watch your friends die."

46

EXEKIEL:
SHADOWS & DRAGONS

Vivienne drummed her fingers on the wooden table in Parker's dining room. Built for a goblin, it only came up to her knees as she poured over the illustrations of the old Conduit mine near the shore of Fae Reef. It was one of the last two possible locations for the weapon. It hadn't been used in centuries yet guards had recently been seen patrolling the area.

"We could enter through the east tunnel," she suggested. "The ground is uneven there and prone to collapse, so most guards skip it on patrol."

Parker shook his head and took a swig from his cup of ale. The goblin's nose drooped into his mug and came out covered in froth. "Being buried alive won't get us anywhere."

He pushed out his tongue and licked his nostrils clean.

Vivienne sighed. "Do you have a better idea?"

Maximus leaned over her. "What about that excavation shaft?" He indicated the area on the plans. "It's the most guarded entrance which would suggest there's something valuable there."

I clicked my tongue against my teeth. "There's no cover. They'd see us coming a mile off."

"We could separate." Kraxus leaned back in his seat and propped his feet up on the table. "Vivienne and I will go one way and the little shadow can take his chances on his own."

"Why don't we let Vivienne decide who'd she rather be with?"

"We stick together," she snapped before Kraxus could retort. Her eyes settled on me. "It's almost over. All of it."

She always had a knack for sensing what I didn't say. I nodded. Whatever happened wouldn't erase what the Royal Court had done or replace what had been lost, but it would be some form of justice. Of knowing that the Fate-stained fuckers responsible hadn't gotten away with it.

After centuries of suffering and separation, we would return the realm to what it had been before the land shift. Before barriers and tolls and prejudice shits rose to power. Varialla and I would remake the world on the backs of shadows and dragons.

Parker's laughter pulled me from my thoughts. It was surprisingly robust for a goblin of his size. It was like he laughed with the entirety of his bloated green stomach.

"Your big dream is to have a nymph sit on your face until you suffocate?" He cried at Shack; a goblin with pointed ears and wings the size of my hands. The anomaly suggested that one of Shack's parents had been Fae.

Parker shook his head. "The first thing I'm going to do is find myself a crafters job in the Eternal City. Then I'm going to settle down with a pretty goat shifter."

"Admirable goal, my friend."

The goblin narrowed his beady eyes and waved his bony finger at me. "I told you not to call me that."

It was true. He had. The day he'd gone behind his people's back to let me know my source and friend, Reek, had been killed whilst working on removing the wards around the weapon plans. It wasn't long after, that Parker became my source instead. My eyes and ears in the Outer Isles.

"It doesn't matter what you call us. In the end, it is just a word. It only has the power we give it." I raised my pint mug. "What matters is what we feel."

I brought the mug to my lips and took a deep swallow.

"Smug bastard," Kraxus grumbled before he turned to Parker. "Isn't he fucking infuriating?" He glared at where Vivienne stood beside me. "Him and his little shadows."

"Careful." Shadows wove between my fingers and around my wrists. Some slithered across the table towards him. "Sometimes they have a mind of their own."

The rabbit shifter leapt back. His large beefy frame snapped the wooden chair beneath him. I was surprised it hadn't broken sooner considering it had been fashioned for a goblin. Although their craftmanship was the stuff of legends.

Those around the table laughed. Another goblin with bright blonde curls and large red lips sauntered in with a fresh tray of pitchers and handed them out to the table.

"If we survive to see the end of this, you can call me whatever you like," Parker hollered.

"To the end and new beginnings," bellowed Shack as he raised his cup.

We all followed.

"To the end and new beginnings."

There was a sharp prickle of power in the air. I was already turning towards the small door of Parker's stone cottage when it almost flew off its hinges.

Two breathless goblins dressed in guards' uniforms charged in. They hunched over; their hands rested on knobbed knees.

"Dragons," the female panted. She yanked off her hat and dabbed away the sweat. "Dragons are headed this way."

I was outside before she finished the sentence. My stare went to where two massive creatures cut across the late evening sky. Their eyes rivaled the glare of the stars. Their wings caused an updraft that almost knocked the goblins off their feet.

It took me all of a second to notice that Varialla wasn't riding one of them. They were here…without her.

I stalked forwards. My steps bounced when Revynath hit the ground meters away, joined by Urdith.

"Where is she?"

The dragon's ignored me as their stares swept over the crowd that had gathered. Their eyes were cold. Their movements sharp and fierce. They were searching for someone they didn't see.

Urdith crouched low and bared his teeth in a snarl. Everyone except Maximus and I took a step back. Revynath turned her enormous head to look at me. There was a question in her fiery yellow gaze.

They'd thought Varialla was with me.

"She's not here." My muscles bunched.

Dragons always knew where their bonded was. It was how they found them when they matured into the necessary power rank. If Urdith and Revynath couldn't sense Varialla, it was intentional. It meant that she was somewhere warded and possibly underground; so deep they couldn't trace it.

"Where is she?" My tone was harsher than any should take with a dragon.

They didn't bother to respond. Urdith splayed his wings and took a running leap off the dock as he surged back into the sky. A bevvy of arrows and shouts went up from the border between the Isles. He sent out a blast of fire that had the guards running for their lives.

I unleashed my own wings and followed in his wake. I barely noticed the rush of the wind or the massive dragon that charged behind me as Revynath rose. My gut was hollow. My every thought consumed by one sick truth: Varialla was missing.

"We're right behind you." Maximus called.

He, Kraxus and Aquarius charged towards the longboats. The siren traded his legs for tails and dove into the sea, prepared to push the boat along faster. Vivienne took to the sky.

I didn't respond. I only delved deeper into my power and soared towards the city.

47

VARIALLA:
FREE ME

This wasn't me. This wasn't what I wanted, but at the same time, it was. It was everything I craved in this twisted toxic moment. Loch kept a tight hold of our bind like a noose around my neck. I choked on it. I lost myself to the dread and lust that swirled like a sick cocktail in my gut.

Somehow, I was on top of him. We were on the stone bench in the center of the chamber. My knees bracketed his hips as he moved between my legs and I responded. I *responded*. The strokes of Loch's hard cock made me so wet. My hips rocked into his of their own volition. I couldn't help it. Couldn't stop it.

Loch groaned. "Look how hard you make me."

His words and pulsing rhythm almost stopped my heart. I clung to my sanity as magic and need threatened to override my very being.

How did I get here? I had all the power in the fucking realm and it couldn't help me. Not here. Not against him. Loch had been playing this game long before I knew it existed and he'd made me his pawn and his prize.

"I hate you," I panted even as my toes curled and I blinked through a fog of lust that almost consumed me.

I'd stopped fighting him to protect Lucinda, Colette and Godric. I'd pretended to give in to buy myself some time to find a way out of this. Now my grip on my control was slipping. Loch was erasing me; who I was and the things I wanted. It was like a drug; a hold, I couldn't fight. The bind felt more potent here. Heightened and erotic.

"Oh god," I whimpered, and trembled on top of him as he rolled his hips harder and his nails dug into my ass.

My own nails bit into his shoulders. I gritted my teeth. We were only dry-humping but I was so close to coming.

Loch gripped my hand and placed it on his cock.

"Take it out." He sounded as desperate as I felt.

A part of me wanted to obey. My fingers itched to reach for his zipper. I bit the inside of my cheek and fought the urge.

"Do it."

Caged in his arms, I met his cruel blue stare. His cock stroked my clit. The decadent sensation burrowed into me. The bind pulled tighter. My heart raced. Still, I didn't move.

The sound Loch made was feral when his hand clamped around my neck and my back slammed into the cold, rough stone. He shoved me down and knelt over me. Pure venom in his gaze.

"Careful, princess."

Loch's other hand closed around my breast. My back arched. A loathsome moan made its way out of my throat but I wouldn't give in. I could never give in.

"Maybe you've forgotten about our deal." He tweaked my nipple between his forefinger and thumb. "Disappoint me and I will kill them and everyone else you turned into a traitor like Mother Margareet."

Blood drained from my face. Loch jerked his head at Knox. Despite his fierce grip on my neck, I managed to turn my head and peered at the glass. Knox donned a sharp silver knuckle-duster and kissed it. Then he delivered a punch to Lucinda that split her cheek.

I screamed, "No!"

Lucinda hissed through her teeth. Before she could use the blood that whelped up to cast a spell, Knox wiped it clean with a filthy rag. Then he struck again.

"I'm fine," she gasped out on a pained cry.

She wasn't fine. She was slowly being beaten to death, because of me; because I refused to fuck the enemy. But I couldn't. I couldn't give him that control over me, my power and my dragons. Control over the realm.

Knox struck again. Lucinda shouted. I flinched with every brutal blow. The harsh slap of flesh on flesh and the sickening thud of her body as she slammed into the glass.

My blood ran cold when Adir ripped off Colette's cream dress that was torn and stained with splashes of blood. She was naked underneath and exposed to his hungry gaze.

I had to stop this. Now. Loch grasped my chin and forced my stare back to his.

"Let me fuck you, Princess."

Acute pleasure shot through my system when Loch settled himself between my thighs and rowed his hips. At some point he'd removed my underwear. There was nothing but the soft fabric of his trousers between us.

"I can make this go away."

My chest heaved. My throat clogged. How did I make this stop? If I gave in, the realm was damned. If I didn't, Colette, Lucinda, Godric…

Oh god.

Loch took my legs in his hands and hoisted my knees up.

"You feel so good," he groaned. "Let me fuck you."

The urge to say yes stuck in my throat.

It's not real.

Every pleasure I thought I felt in this moment was fabricated, a manipulation by a bind I never wanted.

I scrunched my eyes closed and racked my mind as sounds of torture and Loch's hungry moans echoed around me. A symphony of seduction and sorrow.

I had to stop this.

Adir's harsh laugh made my head snap in his direction. The psychotic asshole had pulled a torch from the sconce nearest him and was running it over a steel rod. *No. No. No.*

He brought that heated rod over to Colette and slashed it across her naked back.

She screamed. The stench of burning flesh struck the air. I shoved at Loch's chest, frantic to get to her. Not that I could. We were separated by rock and thick panes of glass.

"Don't look!" Colette shouted as Adir struck her again. The metal came away red with her blood and bits of flesh. "Don't let this break you."

Her words had already shattered me.

Loch was a mad man; a monster. He had to be stopped. This had to stop. Power crackled through me. Adrenaline scored through my system. I couldn't give in, couldn't damn the isles, but I could kill us all in this fucking place. I could end my friends suffering and take these deranged, sadistic shits with me. I could cut off the head of the siren army and leave the

Council to suffocate in the ashes. I may not get the throne, but I would keep him from it.

Fire consumed everything at the right temperature. It could shatter glass, crack stone and incinerate flesh. Dragon's fire was the strongest heat source ever known. With it, I would bring this entire building crashing down on top of us. In a blast too quick for Loch to dodge or for my friends to feel the pain. Whatever might survive would be crushed beneath the wreckage.

Exekiel would lead our people to victory. The Isles would be free. I always knew I would kill Loch. If I had to go with him then so be it. One way or another, this dickhead had to die.

My stare swung to Colette. When her swollen eyes met mine, I hoped she read the apology in them. I hoped she'd forgive me for what I was about to do.

My hands curled around Loch's ass and I pressed him harder into me. For a heartbeat, he tensed. I rolled my hips. He groaned and brought his lips to my neck. I fought the urge to recoil. He was a fool to trust me in this type of situation but his arrogance had always been his undoing.

"Fuck, princess." He pushed his hand between us. Within seconds, he pulled out his cock. "I'm going to make you feel so good."

"I know."

His rigid length met my entrance. Fire erupted from my being. Vibrant swirls of teal and red filled my vision and seized my lungs. I poured every ounce of my power into incinerating the world. Flames shot from my hands and my throat.

Glass shattered. Jagged shards slashed my skin. The building groaned. The ground shook. It was just like I imagined. Everything would come crashing down. Whatever didn't burn would bury us beneath it.

The outside wall of the torture chamber erupted. Shadows swept in. My gut lurched. I pulled back my flames as Revynath shoved her giant head through the gaping hole she'd made in the side of the building and roared.

Exekiel was beside her. His eyes were blood red and his shadows as thick as acrid smoke. They spilled into the room and shot straight for Adir who raced for the exit. They coiled around the Primary and climbed up from his ankles to his neck. The entire time the bastard screamed. His skin blackened. His body convulsed.

The shadows pulled tighter as Exekiel stalked further into the room. Debris and glass crunched beneath his boots. He was the epitome of death, of power and damnation. He was the end and the beginning.

My gaze snapped to where Loch had been. He was gone. In the few seconds I'd looked away, he'd made his escape. I pushed to my feet and took a steadying breath. My head spun. I braced my hands out to the side for balance. Loch would not escape death today.

Adir's cries became erratic. His eyes bugged out of his head. The shadows squeezed tighter. His cheeks purpled. His head swelled. *Shit.* His brains were about to explode from his skull. Exekiel was a statue of destruction. His gaze focused and unflinching.

"I'm going after Loch," I shouted.

I didn't check to see if he'd heard me. I hurtled through the door and out into the passage.

48

VARIALLA:
To Kill a King

The building violently swayed. I braced my hand on the wall as I hurtled down the corridor after Loch. My heart ratcheted in my chest. Blood roared in my ears. I took the stairs two at a time. Power danced on the tip of my tongue and was poised at my fingertips. Loch wouldn't get away. Not again.

My thoughts drifted to Exekiel. I'd left him down there in the catacombs with my friends. I hadn't checked to see if they were dead or alive. If I'd killed them, because of Loch. Because of what he'd done to me at birth and what he still wanted to do to me. I hadn't looked because I wouldn't have been able to keep going if what I feared was true.

The ground shook. A chandelier crashed down behind me. Tiles ruptured as rock bounced across the floor. My fire had damaged the structure of the building. As I'd hoped, it was coming down. But the person I'd wanted buried beneath the rubble, had gotten away.

I ran faster. My lungs burned but I refused to slow, to stop to catch my breath or consider what had just happened. Rage was a familiar comfort. I leaned into its brutal embrace.

I screeched down marble corridors and came to the palace doors. There were no guards. Commotion sounded on the other side. I kicked them open and reeled to a stop.

The streets heaved with partygoers. There were belly dancing nymphs and tap-dancing centaurs. Goblins juggled amidst acrobatic elves. Shifters placed bets on brawls between their beast forms. Vendors foisted their wares on passersby. Everywhere I looked, someone walked with a lit-up balloon that changed shape when asked, or glowsticks that coiled around their arms and legs. There were games and rides and banquet tables laden with food and drink.

What the fuck?

It was like waking from a nightmare and tumbling into an unhinged dream. It was hard to believe that all of this had been going on whilst I'd been down in the crypts being twisted by magic; my friends tortured. It didn't make sense but I didn't have time to make sense of it.

My eyes scanned the crowd. Loch had to be here somewhere. He couldn't get away. Not now. Not ever.

I pushed through the throng and shouted, "Where are you?"

Heads swiveled in my direction. I didn't care. I had to find him. Every way I turned; my path was blocked by one socialite or another.

Frustration crawled up my throat. "What the fuck is going on?"

The words were hissed under my breath but a nymph with bright green pigtails and the Five Isles flag painted across her bare chest, waved her drink in my face.

"It's Solstice eve. The Season finale of the Games."

Those around her cheered.

I blinked at them. Solstice wasn't for another two weeks. I was about to point that out when a male centaur scoffed.

"The season finale is a fortnight away."

The nymph wrinkled her brow. "What are you talking about? It's Solstice eve. The Season finale of the Games."

Once again, those around her cheered in the exact same way they had before. They swayed to the music and sipped from their chalices oblivious to the looks they were getting.

The centaur beside me shook his head and continued on his way. The hairs on the back of my neck stood on end. Something was wrong here. A large crowd gathered in one space and they believed it was a date that it wasn't. A sick sense of foreboding turned my stomach. I darted through the crowd and tapped on the shoulder of a duck shifter in mid-transformation.

"What day is it?"

He looked at me like I'd lost my mind. His beak transformed back into a mouth. "It's Solstice eve. The Season finale of the Games."

Those around him whooped and cheered, just like those with the nymph. It was like they'd been programmed.

I continued through the people. Almost everyone I asked said the same thing. There were only a handful who seemed as confused as I was. Some caught on to the wrongness of it all. Others assumed the crowd had simply drunk too much of whatever was in their cups.

"Why in Fate's name do they all think it's Spring Equinox?" asked an elf with porcelain white skin and strawberry blonde hair.

I was about to tell her it was because the rumors were true. This was the weapon Exekiel had warned them about but the elf threw her hands in the air and started dancing. Her drink spilled across the ground and over those beside her. She didn't seem to notice.

"I can't believe we finally made it," she hollered. Her smile was bright and unnatural. "It's Solstice eve. The Season finale of the Games."

Those around us cheered. I staggered back. My ears were ringing. Alarm bells that screamed in the back of my mind. My gaze drifted to her spilled drink, to the one thing they all had in common. The silver chalices in their hands.

"They've poisoned the drinks."

No one heard me over the raucous music and din of the crowd. Those who did hear, chose not to listen. They were too lost in their cups and under the influence of more than a drink. There were sirens here manipulating the minds of those who drank the poison.

I strained to hear a whisper of their song but there was nothing. That shouldn't have surprised me. According to the plans, the weapon altered the pitch of a siren song to one that none, not even a Fae could detect. My stomach hollowed. The absence of the song was confirmation that *Sonu di Carghel* was being used. The Court weren't waiting for the season finale. They'd started the attack now.

"Varialla!"

I spun at the sound of that familiar voice. Maximus charged towards me with a horde of people around him. Probably the rebel recruits. Aquarius, Kraxus and Vivienne were beside him. I never thought I'd be so happy to see her.

"Are you alright?" he asked at the same time Vivienne snapped, "What do you need?"

Her question was easier to answer.

"The drinks are poisoned," I told them. "Destroy what you can; round up those who've been infected. Be careful. Anyone in this crowd could become an enemy. The weapon is on."

"Where are you going?" Vivienne barked as I took off.

I glanced back at her. "I'm going to kill a king."

49

EXEKIEL:
THE BAD DO BLEED

The palace was coming down. I didn't have time to heal all their injuries, just enough so they could stand. Lucinda, whose body had been covered in multiple gashes that would have bled out slowly, staggered to her feet. Her face was a mess of swollen bruises. The right side of her arm and neck were burned. The skin was cracked and blistered from Varialla's flames.

Colette struggled to cover her naked body with the remains of her tattered dress. She'd been whipped by a metal rod. Unlike the witch only her hair was singed from the fire. The centaur had been in the worst shape. His bones were broken and flesh hacked into. I'd fixed what I could. Now we had to move.

"Come on."

The building groaned. We moved fast; dodging debris that came down as we raced for the hole Revynath had blown through the wall. My shadows billowed behind me. Each one demanded death; needed to sate the hunger in my soul.

It had taken me all of a second to make sense of the scene in that chamber. Varialla sprawled on that bench. The blaze of her flames that had receded when I entered. The broken bodies of her friends. She'd been about to end it. End everything and everyone including herself.

Whatever tether I'd had on my shadows had snapped in that moment.

I glanced back at the remains of Primary Adir. My shadows had torn through the chamber and fed on the bastard's flesh. They'd squeezed the life out of him; shattered his bones to dust until his eyes had ruptured from his skull and his head exploded. Pre-Primary Knox had suffered the same. As far as I was concerned, they got off easy. Nothing would compare to the hell I was about to unleash on the rebel fucking king.

We stole into the streets where the alleged Solstice Eve celebrations were taking place. The weapon was already at work.

With the gleaming silver symbol of Fate *Fadea* alight on my hand, I stalked through the people. I ignored their shouts and the way some bowed or whispered prayers. My eyes cut through the crowd. My shadows writhed, searched.

"Where did they go?" Colette rasped.

I hadn't expected to find the three former captives on my heel. They were as close as they could get without being swept up in my shadows' rage. Their bodies were broken but based on the fire in their eyes and the harsh set of their jaw, their spirits were unbreakable.

"I intend to find out."

I pushed a hand into my trench coat and pulled out a vial of the latest antidote. I tossed it to Lucinda who caught it in one steady hand. She uncorked it and took a swig before she passed it on.

"Stay alert," I told them. "I won't wait for you if you fall behind."

As much as their safety mattered to Varialla, nothing mattered more to me than her.

"We won't," Lucinda croaked. "Now move."

The centaur finished the last of the vial and tossed it over his shoulder.

I ran. *Fadea* pulled on Varialla's essence that lingered on my skin. The taste of her on my lips. The memory of her body in my arms. She was close; somewhere in this sea of a thousand faces.

Almost every cast was out tonight. Only giants and werewolves seemed to have been excluded. I imagined it was because werewolves were too unpredictable to control, and giants were too large to be corrupted that quickly. Infecting them would take more than a few poisoned drinks.

My shadows rose when a small figure darted from the crowd and veered towards me. Her eyes were bright, her pale cheeks rosy with cold. Satrialla. She still wore her red Mothers robe, but it was thrown open and exposed the large bunny t-shirt she wore underneath. The hood was down and her brown hair unbound.

"Brother!" She lunged into my arms.

I gripped her shoulders and pushed her back so I could check that it was really her. What was she doing here? How had they found her? I'd left Satrialla in the safety of the Mothers in the cathedral; disguised as one of them. In the centuries she'd hidden there no one had discovered her identity. The nondescript robes and quiet nature of the Mothers had helped.

"The air is cold but burns with fire." She giggled; a high-pitched sound.

"What night do you think it is?"

Her gaze held mine; suddenly sharp and clear. "It is the end of the end."

Satrialla waved her arms and cackled.

"The end and the beginning." She pointed through the crowd. "The Council crumbles."

If I wasn't holding onto her, she would have spun out of my hands. I resisted the urge to shake her.

"Satrialla. Look at me."

Her eyes were more unfocused than usual. When I inhaled, there was the unmistakable stench of poison.

"Fuck."

"Do not worry, worry brother not." She tapped me on the nose with her finger then wriggled out of my grip. "The king runs."

"Satrialla, wait!"

I shoved a hand into my pocket, searching for the second vial of antidote but she was already twirling away.

"Satrialla!"

"It ends, brother. The bad do bleed."

She wasn't making sense. The toxin was already affecting her mind. I pushed through the crowd after her. She was all I had left from a life before now.

"Satrialla!"

She threw me the brightest smile over her shoulder. "Tears are salty. Their blood is sweet. Fire comes."

She flung a hand up towards the sky just as fire cleaved through the night. In its wake, Revynath roared. My head whipped from the swooping dragon back to Satrialla. These weren't the ramblings of a woman who'd lost her mind. She'd drunk the toxin and yet she spoke the truth in the same addled way she always did. Maybe it had something to do with the fact that her mind didn't work like everyone else's. Maybe a siren song couldn't twist what was already twisted.

I ran through all she'd said about the king on the run and how the bad do bleed.

"Have you seen them?" I rushed towards her. "Do you know where they are?"

Satrialla giggled. "I know many things!" She flung her arms wide and danced on the spot. "I know I survived for this."

I rocked back. Her eyes struck mine with such clarity it was daunting. Before I could capture the moment in my memory it was gone. Her face stretched into a vacant smile then she spun and drove her fist into the face of a siren guard.

The Fate-stained fucker stumbled. He had his pants down and a coerced nymph on her knees before him. His song faded as he blinked at Satrialla. The nymph's eyes widened in horror when she realized what she'd been doing.

Satrialla punched the guard again and again. With each blow blood spewed from his ruptured nose and bloodied mouth. He reached for the blade at his hip. My foot came down on his wrist. The bones snapped. He screamed and gurgled on his blood.

"No more singing for you!" Satrialla continued to bludgeon the guard. She tore at him with nails and teeth until his body was motionless beneath her. "Always fucking singing."

I didn't pull her off or soothe the startled cries of the people who reeled back in terror. This was retribution. It wasn't pretty or kind. It was fists bathed in blood. It was two hundred years of rage and pain. It was the anguish my sister had held in her splintered soul since the night her mate and child were murdered. Since the night the Siren Army had destroyed our home and upended our world. Not all of them were bad, but judging by the way the nymph now folded her arms around herself and spat on the ground, this guard hadn't been one of the good ones.

I welcomed Satrialla's wrath.

"When you're done, go back to the Cathedral."

She blinked up at me. She still sat astride the dead siren with his pants down. "I fight, brother. This time. This time I fight."

My fingers flexed. I wanted to drag her out of here. Satrialla was powerful but she'd suffered enough at these bastard's hands. I couldn't stomach the thought of something happening to her. I couldn't worry about her and Varialla too.

"You've done enough." I gestured to the corpse of the guard. He would never abuse his power again. "Go home."

She wiped her blooded hands on her robes and stood. Her smile was soft when she leaned in and kissed me on the cheek. "Do not fear."

"Satrialla—"

She pressed a finger to my lips; cutting me off.

"Love lives forever brother even if I am gone. I am ready. Ready. I will not run."

My throat tightened. Before I could respond, she ducked into the crowd. I considered going after her but something greater held me back. It compelled me to follow *Fadea's* guidance.

I let Satrialla go and turned. It felt like tearing away from a piece of my soul, the only piece of my past I had left, but I turned and ran towards my future; my mate.

50

VARIALLA:
FACE ME

My dragons soared through the night and rained fire down on our enemy. From Revynath's back, I watched them burn. I didn't stop to consider that these people may be under the influence of the weapon. Any guard that shot a flame-tipped arrow or launched a deadly spear, every Fae and winged shifter that hurtled after us through the clouds; my dragons incinerated.

I kept my gaze on the ground; on the people who danced amidst the chaos. The city was under attack and they didn't even know. Eventually they would. A siren song made one lose themselves but eventually that person realized they were lost.

I steered my dragons clear of them. We only attacked those who attacked us.

A figure in a familiar black and purple tunic raced through the crowd. I recognized his gait. Using my dragon sight, I made out his tight curls and hazel brown skin. *Loch.*

My thighs clamped around Revynath and I braced myself as we descended. Seeing our approach, the guards assembled. Flame-tipped spears were launched in our direction. Revynath swung out and swatted the weapons from the sky. Urdith took on those who attacked us from behind. In a single breath he incinerated the Fae that had been following us with a blast of red fire.

The guards rolled out the catapults and fired. Large boulders emblazoned with an aura of magic hurtled towards us. I didn't know what the magic would do if it struck its mark but from this distance my dragons were an easy target.

Hands out for balance, I pushed to my feet and said a silent prayer. Then I leapt from Revynath's back and grew my wings on the way down. Vibrant scarlet flames that solidified as they tore from my spine. Horns crowned my head. The wind howled and swirled icy tendrils through the fabric of my dress.

I kept my gaze on Loch. On the bastard who had manipulated, betrayed, beaten and caged me. My aim wasn't exact. The muscles in my spine knotted but through sheer determination, I headed in the relatively right direction.

When my feet struck the ground, it felt like the earth shook. I skidded to an ungraceful stop and searched the crowd that screeched and staggered away from me.

"Loch!"

He looked over his shoulder then sneered and continued on. The crowd parted as I pursued. Flames gathered around my fingers. I hadn't expected him to run but I was prepared to hunt him down. I would make him regret every second he underestimated me and thought I would never come for him.

The bastard was fast but I was faster. I tunneled into my power and pushed it into propelling myself forwards. My magic responded like a candle to a flame. Heat sparked through me and I careened through the air until I knocked into him. The bastard went down. His head struck the concrete.

He hissed and flipped onto his back. I pounced and gripped the sides of his head. I prepared to drive blades of fire into his brain. To shatter every cell the way his men had shattered my friend's bones.

Loch grinned. I should have paid attention. I should have realized the bastard would never run. He wasn't the type to back down or flee. He didn't have it in him. I should have realized but I was blinded by rage. I didn't pay attention to the people that closed in around me. I didn't care when footsteps approached from behind. But I felt the blow of a blunt object as it was struck across my head.

My vision temporarily faded as pain sliced through my skull. Before I could make sense of it, a bruising force slammed into my side. I went flying. My skin was scraped raw as I skidded across the concrete. With a snarl, I managed to swivel to my feet and glared at the one who'd hit me. Who now helped Loch to his feet. Queen Zenera; my mother.

I dimly registered the trickle of blood down my cheek from a gash that throbbed at my temple. The Rebel King sneered. His nose was swollen—probably broken, blood smeared down his face, and his lip was split. Somehow these things only enhanced his air of lethal charm.

His arm curled around my mother's waist. "I always knew you'd choose me in the end."

"If you'd done your job, I wouldn't have had to choose."

Despite her tone, my mother shoved Loch behind her. She protected him from me. He stayed close, his arm still around her waist. His fingers splayed possessively across her stomach. My own stomach roiled.

The need in Loch's eyes when he looked at her was different than when he looked at me. He wanted to own me. He craved my power and desired my body. He was as controlled by the bind as I was. But when he looked at my mother, his need was pure. Not forced or fabricated.

All I could do was stand there whilst the shards of my fractured mind pieced scattered fragments together. Whilst the people brawled around me and those who weren't infected ran for their lives; for freedom. I simply stood there.

My gaze swung from Loch to Zenera.

"Don't look so surprised, princess." Loch brushed his lips across the back of her neck. My mother shivered. "Don't you remember the first thing I said to you?"

I was about to retort that he hadn't said anything. That he'd appeared in my room and shoved his tongue down my throat, but that wasn't true. Right before he'd kissed me, he'd said, *"You're as gorgeous as your mother. Fucking beautiful."*

My insides turned. I was going to be sick. Just when I thought he couldn't sink any lower, Loch proved he was more depraved than I could imagine. They both were.

My mother had bonded me to this bastard. She'd wanted me to rule beside him and have his heirs. She'd wanted me to fall in love with this man—this monster—who was also her lover.

She shrugged when she saw the question in my eyes. "You didn't expect me not to sample the goods, did you?"

Her tone was so flippant; almost mocking.

"You're sick."

Not solely because of the things she'd done or still wanted me to do. But she was truly ill—she was sick in the head—if she thought I would ever go along with this. No wonder I'd first seen Loch as my father.

That had probably been their plan. To raise me together as my parents and shag each other behind my back whilst they groomed me to mate my fucking dad.

I rocked back. The truth of everything slammed into me. Neither of them had ever cared about me. I was a means to an end; a backup plan. I was a way in to the Five Isles but the bind gave Loch the control. If I'd remained in the Coral Court, I would have been designed to service his needs; my dragons at his command. My mother never saw me as her daughter. Loch never saw me as his mate. They both saw me as a weapon; a tool to be used and discarded.

"You're sick!" This time it was louder. My voice haunted and harsh to my own ears.

"Yes," my mother hissed and prowled towards me.

Again, she shoved Loch back, urging him to get away.

"I was sick of being shunned and abused for simply existing. I was sick of my people being forced out of jobs and left to starve." Power simmered around her. A hum that I felt in my bones. "I was sick to believe that I could trust you with the fate of our kingdom. Sick that I didn't know you would turn out to be just as weak as your father, sacrificing greatness for love."

"What?"

She took another menacing step closer. "Your grandfather; the King of Shifter Springs, had threatened to disown your father and cast him out when he learnt about his relationship with me and that I was pregnant with you." She tutted. "He had already arranged a political alliance and he insisted that Thraxen wed the bride he'd chosen."

I frowned. I already knew this.

"Of course, your father refused. He wanted to be with me but I wanted his title."

She glanced behind her at Loch. Perhaps checking if he'd run or more if he'd stayed—her anchor and support.

"Your father wanted to run away with me and live in exile." She almost smiled. "But I'd spent too long trying to claw my way out. Everything I'd been working on would've been undone. So, on the night he was supposed to announce his union with me, I coerced him to announce his betrothal to the shifter his father had chosen."

My heart kicked. "You did that?"

"So naïve." She chuckled. "Yes, I did that."

Her eyes turned cold. Water trickled from her fingertips.

"During the celebrations, when everyone was gathered, the siren army attacked to defend my honor. They were furious at the prince's betrayal.

"My plan had been to take out the king and a few others who would never agree to our union. Then after an appropriate length of mourning, your father would have announced his betrothal to me." She sighed. "Unfortunately, Prince Thraxen was a powerful shifter. During the attack, he broke through my song and tried to have me locked up. He vowed that he would let me live until I had you, then he would see me hung." She shrugged. "Naturally I killed him and everyone else."

White noise filled my head. Rage, grief and agony seized my lungs. My father had never betrayed her. He'd wanted me. He'd wanted us; a family. He'd been willing to sacrifice his title to get it. She was the one who chose glory over love. She was everything that was wrong in this realm.

Fire bloomed in my hands and I stalked towards her.

Zenera scoffed. "Are you going to kill your mother, Varialla?"

I hated the way her words cut. Despite everything, she was my mother. Thanks to the mark on my skin, I had some memory of that. She had only protected me because of what I could do for her, but she had still protected me and my sister. She'd been capable of love before the world had shown her nothing but hate. I didn't want to kill her. But if I had to, to protect the kingdom from her reign and Loch's bloodlust then I would.

I levelled her with a glare.

"Move." It was one command—one note with all the force of my power; imbued with the might of the ocean and the roar of dragons.

Zenera's eyes widened as she was flung sideways. Somehow, she spun in midair and doubled back.

Swift and cruel, she charged me. As she ran, she pulled water from the fountain and twisted it into deadly blades of ice. They shot forwards—straight at my head.

I raised my hands. Fire at my palms. The ice struck and splashed into a puddle on the ground. My mother didn't slow. She tackled me to the paved stones and pulled a dagger from her bodice.

In my periphery, I spied Loch making his escape. *No.*

My mother slammed the dagger towards my chest. I caught it. The blade sliced into my fingers. Blood spilled down my wrists and dripped onto my chest. Pain lanced through my entire being. My palm split open. She pressed harder. My eyes watered.

"You are a disappointment, Varialla." Her eyes flashed. Her teeth were bared and lethal. "I should have let you drown."

Her words were sharper than the knife. It inched closer as pain and the pool of blood that filled my hands, made it harder to hold on; to fend it off.

I gritted my teeth. "I don't want to kill you." I didn't want to but I would if I had to.

"Allow me."

A sword plunged through my mother's side. Her blood struck my cheeks. I flinched back. Her face contorted with an expression that seemed stunned someone had had the audacity to wound her. Her eyes widened and she staggered to her feet. With a snarl, she ripped the weapon out and flung it to the ground.

It hadn't been a killing blow. Something told me that was intentional. Her attacker—Vivienne Foraglade—wanted to draw this out.

I shoved to my own feet and blinked at the dark-haired beauty who now stood with her palms raised and her legs set in a fighting stance. Vivienne's hair was tussled, her clothes torn and exposed skin covered in gashes and dark welts. But her eyes were alight with magic and her white wings beat menacingly at her back.

"You have no idea what this woman has taken from me, from this realm." Vivienne was talking to me but her stare never left my mother who pressed a hand to her wound and tried to stop the bleeding. "You don't want to do this but we both know it needs to be done." She spared me a glance. "Allow me the honors."

I didn't know what to say. How did I give someone permission to slaughter my mother because if they didn't, she would kill us all?

A wall of ice shot towards Vivienne. Power crackled around the Fae. She leapt up and kicked straight through the structure. Ice erupted. Shards cut into her skin but Vivienne let out a warrior's cry and lunged for Queen Zenera.

I didn't watch what happened next. I heard Vivienne's murderous roar and my mother's harrowed scream as I hurtled after Loch.

51

EXEKIEL:
CHARIOTS & CHARRED REMAINS

It was carnage. Amidst infected partygoers that danced and sang like nothing was amiss, there were others who turned on the crowd. With poison-filled syringes in hand, they attacked those who weren't infected. Some screamed at their friends and family to snap out of it. Others fought back with fists and power. Most of them ran. They finally saw the plague for what it was. A lie. A rehashing of the Brutal War. Only now the target wasn't the dragon shifters. It was everyone.

I pushed through the crowd in search of Varialla. I didn't know how long I'd been looking. Minutes? Hours? Lucinda, Colette and Godric hadn't been able to keep up. They'd joined forces with Ilbryen and the others who'd gone after the weapon and handed out vials of the antidote to the uninfected.

Someone screamed. Every head in the crowd turned up. I followed their gaze. A familiar figure in a red robe plummeted through the air and struck the ground. The people tripped over themselves in their haste to get away. I moved closer.

My steps gained speed until I broke through the shrieking mob and staggered to a stop. Blood roared in my ears when I saw who lay at my feet. As if I'd been granted the gift of Sight from my father, I saw golden threads of life blink out on her lifeless body that was dusted with pale flecks of silver.

I dropped to my knees. Satrialla lay awkwardly on the concrete that had split from the impact of her fall. Blood pooled around her. Her eyes were open but unseeing.

My body shook. Not with pain or power, but rage. One that bled into my shadows. They rolled over my shoulders in the shape of wings and stretched from one side of the square to the other.

Sensing the imminent threat, civilians ran whilst soldiers closed in. My gaze went to the chariot overhead where Satrialla must have been thrown from. I got to my feet and surged into the air. A tornado of shadows swirled after me. They blew through buildings; pulverised the stone.

Someone shouted, "Stop him!"

Vines reached up from the ground and strapped around my ankles. The work of spring elves. More soldiers came. They pushed against my power with theirs. They tried to take me down, as if anything could touch me now.

I reached a hand to the sky. My shadows climbed higher and shot from the ends of my fingers. They wrapped around the fleeing chariot and I wrenched it down. Soldiers screamed and scattered when the vehicle struck the earth.

The vines around my ankles fell away. I landed amidst a whorl of shadows and moved towards the chariot. There amongst prone bodies and decimated buildings, Alexov hid beneath the wreckage of his ride. The threads of life that surrounded him were a shimmering silver. Remnants of it lingered on Satrialla's broken body. He was the one who'd flung her from that chariot.

His eyes widened when he saw me. The fate-stained fucker stumbled to his feet and ran.

I chuckled. "Do you really think you can outrun me?"

I tapped into my Fae speed and raced ahead. The senior councilman screeched to a stop when I materialised in front of him. He staggered back. His eyes anxiously scanned the deserted streets like he was looking for someone who could save him. I cricked my neck. Nothing could save him now

Alexov bared his teeth. An animal backed into a corner. "Here."

He tossed a pearl bracelet at my feet.

My gaze zeroed in on the familiar piece of jewellery that was now smattered with blood. Based on its scent it was his blood. Satrialla had injured him before he'd thrown her to her death.

"She didn't even put up much of a fight." His laugh was callous and grated on my nerves.

"It's over, Bravinore."

He stood taller, confident his words would break me. That they'd give him the second he needed to get away.

"As we speak your little friends that went after the weapon are being consumed by it and your precious little mate is riding the rebel kings c—"

Shadows leapt from the palm of my outstretched hand and plunged down the fucker's throat. They filled his lungs until black seeped from the corners of his eyes and dribbled down his chin. Alexov convulsed. His eyes bulged as he gripped his neck and tried to breathe. His petrified gaze swung to me. He tried to speak, to curse or beg. I didn't care. I poured more of my power into him. He drowned in shadows, screaming my name.

52

VARIALLA:
The Monster Within the Man

I left the brawling crowd behind as I tore down the smoldering wreckage of Infinity Strip. Loch was fast. Rage made me faster. He swerved around a corner; out of sight. I pictured the street in my mind then sang three notes. The ground caved under him.

I careened around the corner just as Loch leapt back from the chasm I'd created.

He spun; his serrated teeth bared and skin coated in sweat. "You can't destroy me."

His hand formed a fist and magic was yanked from inside me and pulled into him. I stumbled forwards. A headache split my skull. I gritted my teeth against the pain.

"You're kidding yourself if you think you can." Loch held nothing back as he siphoned more of my power into him. My vision swayed and nausea churned in my gut.

His grin sharpened. "We're connected; you and I."

I took deep measured breaths. "You're right." I nodded and inhaled through the pain and pull of his power. "We are connected."

I wrenched on our bind and the bastard's knees buckled. Terror slashed across his usually stoic face as I siphoned power from inside him and into me.

"The bind works both ways, asshole."

He paled. His body twitched. His face creased with obvious pain.

"What's the matter, your Highness?" Fire danced in the palm of my hand. "Afraid?"

Loch roared. As I shot out with my flames, he countered with water that he pulled from the air. Inside, he wrenched on the bind. I wrenched right back. Our power tangled between us in a deadly tug of war.

His cold blue eyes were like chips of ice. "Nothing beats water." Droplets of the moisture he'd taken from the air trickled from his fingers. "Give me land. I will erode it. Give me air. I will consume it. Give me fire. I will devour it."

He held me in his stare; his meaning clear. He was under the illusion, even now, that I would succumb to him. That I would throw myself at his feet and beg him to fuck me.

"Tell me, Lochness," I bit out the name I knew he despised. "How does water hold up against shadows?"

A grin split my face as Exekiel descended from the rooftops. I'd felt him up there. I'd recognized the thrum of his punishing power as it had crept towards us.

Anticipation coursed through me as my mate struck the ground and landed in a crouch. Concrete caved beneath his feet. The symbol of *Ulius* was ablaze on his knuckles. His head was bowed. His hulking wings rimmed in silver beat rhythmically at his back.

Exekiel rose. There was power in his stride as he stalked towards me. His hair was disheveled. His lip was split. His shirt torn open to reveal hard, sculpted abs glazed in sweat. Shadows wreathed his wrists and neck, and slid across his wings. It was hard to look away. Exekiel was a god; a thing of legends, a harbinger of death.

The heat of his body washed over me when he stopped at my side.

"You made it."

He grinned. "I couldn't let you have all the fun."

In the corner of my eye, Loch edged back.

I didn't look at him when I said, "Kneel."

There was power in my command. His knees bent but he didn't go down. I stalked towards him. The bind firmly fisted in my grip. I pulled and twisted

Loch's magic against him like he'd done to me so many times.

"Kneel."

The bastard's legs went out from under him. He hit the ground with a grunt. I pulled on the puddles of water around him and forged an ice dagger in my hands.

"You tried to take everything from me. My mind, my body, my friends." I glanced at Exekiel. "My home."

Loch's chest heaved when I placed the sharp edge of ice to his skin.

"You tried to break me."

I swiped the blade across his chest. The cut was shallow. Blood whelped from the gash. Loch hissed through his teeth.

"And now you think you can break me." He chuckled darkly. "I will end you, princess. I will destroy everything you love then I'll cut out your heart and fuck your cold, bleeding corpse."

Exekiel made a sound that was more monster than man. As if a beast lurked inside his skin.

I lifted the ice dagger higher and slashed again; carving open Loch's cheek. He let out a shout of pain. I shouldn't have enjoyed it as much as I did. I should have ended this quickly but I wanted him to suffer. I wanted him to know just an ounce of the agony he had inflicted on me and my friends in that chamber.

I sank into my power and pulled on the water inside his body. There was so much of it. My own body hummed. Magic crackled beneath my fingers. I wrapped it around his insides and sucked the moisture out. It was a slow torturous agony lacking the swift deaths I'd given the guards.

Loch's eyes widened. He gritted his teeth and tried to pull his magic back but the tendrils were locked firmly around my mental fist. The bind had been his method to control me all this time. Now it was mine to use against him.

"You can't kill me!" he shouted, despite the fact that the corners of his mouth had turned white and water began to seep from his pores.

"I can," I snarled in the bastard's face; anger thick in my throat. "But I won't. Not alone."

Loch would die but this death wasn't only mine to claim. He had tried to take everything from me and failed but he had taken everything from Exekiel. He'd been the very siren who had walked into Exekiel's home and led to the death of his family. His brother, his adoptive parents, his nephew who'd barely been two years old. It was Loch who had sent Satrialla mad. Perhaps more than me, Exekiel was owed this death.

I looked at him over my shoulder and nodded. "Together."

Exekiel's nostrils flared. Something like relief shone in his eyes.

He stepped closer. "Together."

His shadows whipped out and strapped around the Rebel King's wrists and ankles. They wrenched him off the ground and stretched him like a fucking star.

My heart skipped. The sight was terrifying and glorious. I didn't know what it said about me that I liked —no, *loved*— seeing this bastard strung up.

Exekiel's shadows tightened as they climbed higher. Loch's stare darted between us. At last, I saw the fear I craved.

"I made you," he snarled. "I own you."

He thrashed against the shadows hold and desperately tried to seize control of my power—control of me. But I'd built a shield of pain and hope around myself that he would never penetrate.

"You can't kill me!"

Black shadows rung around his neck and drew taut.

"And yet, here we are," Exekiel breathed.

Loch tensed.

"You're making a mistake!" Finally, it dawned on him that there was no way out of this. We would kill him and we would savor every second of his agony.

My magic tightened. The whites around his icy pupils began to crack. His skin wrinkled and his cheeks sunk. Water dribbled down his face.

Exekiel's shadows pulled and Loch howled at the sky as his limbs were stretched. As the muscles tore and his tendons popped.

I slowed down the pull of water from his system. I wanted him to feel his skin tear and his bones snap.

I wanted him to know the terror of being helpless and bound, like he'd done to me so many times.

Exekiel growled behind me. His shadows darkened. His power crackled and the earth shook. This was the end.

"You will never break me," I hissed, then drained the last of Loch's moisture from his skin as Exekiel roared and his shadows ripped Loch's limbs from his body. His arms and legs went in several directions. His head spun in the air before it landed with a wet thump and rolled across the ground. Loch Orqanz was dead.

53

VARIALLA:
GAME OVER

With each step away from Loch's mutilated body, I felt lighter. The bond burned in my gut. It sizzled and seared through my flesh. The Five Isles mark on my skin glowed a shocking gold. I staggered and gripped my side.

"Are you alright?" Exekiel asked.

When I could finally breathe enough to respond, I smiled. "I will be."

I knew without looking that the mark was gone. Loch's hold on me was gone. He was gone.

The feel of Exekiel's hand in mine anchored me to the moment. It held me together as the weight of everything that had happened threatened to shatter me beneath it. Was it really over?

We made our way through the ruin of the city and picked our way through the dead. So many lives lost—another brutal war. How many of these beings had been under the influence of the weapon? How many had been fighting to defend themselves because they weren't?

I stumbled into Exekiel when the ground tremored. He wrapped his arms around me and struggled to keep his own balance.

A familiar voice shouted, "Where the gorge have you been?"

My stomach flipped. In the distance, I made out two hulking giants thundering towards us. They crossed the space in seconds. One was definitely from the Hokuraz clan. He looked like a humungous ogre with a bulbous nose and pimpled skin the shade of rust. He was almost as tall as Revynath and nearly as wide. The second giant was more human in appearance but at least five times an average human's height. She was female with sandy-brown skin, dark eyes and thick, almost doll-like limbs. If I remembered correctly, her kind were of the Devrona clan.

Perched on the girl's shoulder was Lucinda.

My friend looked down at me with the brightest smile I'd ever seen. The right side of her face, neck and arm were charred black and wrinkled from my flames. Her battered body was hunched and bandaged, but she was here. She was alive. On the giant's opposite shoulder was Evangeline, and on the shoulders of the second giant sat Colette and Maximus.

Lucinda jerked her head then winced as if the movement hurt. "Follow us."

Her voice came out louder than it was; amplified by her magic. But I heard the truth—the low, hoarse rasp beneath her power. Suddenly I was right back in that chamber surrounded by her screams. The thud of her body striking the glass.

Exekiel's grip tightened on my hand. I blinked at him. The vibrancy of his eyes pulled me back to the present.

"Stay with me, little bud."

I nodded and refocused my mind. The war wasn't over yet. Together Exekiel and I followed the giants back towards the city center. I ignored the carnage around me and the throbbing in my ankle as we raced over broken buildings, shattered statues and through puddles of blood.

"We managed to round up most of them," Maximus shouted down.

Before I could ask what he meant, I spotted a large horde of giants and civilians gathered around a mass of people. Revynath and Urdith circled overhead. They emitted the occasional blast of fire and low, warning growls.

My chest tightened at the sight of them. They were okay, as fierce and beautiful as before. Dragons. *My* dragons.

"Ilbryen's administering the antidote to those who will take it, although it may be too late," Maximus added.

My gaze returned to the crowd who I guessed were the infected they'd managed to round up. As much as the weapon preyed on their mind and free-will, it looked like self-preservation had ultimately won out. The people didn't fight or try to take their chances against a horde of giants and two terrifying dragons. Instead, they stood together and glared at their captors.

"Those we couldn't control we trapped in there."

Lucinda pointed to a nearby building, where people pounded on the doors and slammed themselves against the windows. Blood splattered across the glass. Their minds were so far gone. They were so consumed by *Sonu di Carghel*, there was no way to pull them back.

"We think the weapon is still active." Maximus slid down the arm of the Hokuraz giant.

He leapt to the ground then turned to help Colette. Her steps were slow. One foot dragged behind her and half of her hair was singed. However, she looked better than she had in the catacombs. Exekiel's power of *Thesona* was slowly doing its job.

"Only we don't know where the weapon is."

The female giant set Lucinda and Evangeline on the ground. Evangeline hooked an arm around Lucinda's waist to hold her up.

"Gwendoline was last spotted fleeing the city. There's no one left to track. No inkling of where it might be."

"I have an inkling." It was a thought that had pressed on me since earlier tonight.

Vivienne, Ilbryen and Kraxus raced over to us. Vivienne moved with a limp but it didn't stop her from flinging herself into Exekiel's arms. For the first time, I didn't care. Not only did I know for certain, that Exekiel was mine and he would always choose me, but Vivienne, in some twisted way, had become a friend—or at least, an ally. I trusted her.

"Loch wasn't the type to run from a fight." I said to the others. "He did nothing without a plan. But tonight, he'd run. When I caught up with him, my mother had intervened so he could get away. Loch had led me to that square and I'm willing to bet it was for a reason."

My gaze collided with Exekiel's.

"The weapon."

We each turned heel and ran back in the direction Loch had led me.

I did my best not to look at where his remains lay strewn across the blood drenched streets. With the haze of my anger cleared, there was a bitter taste in the back of my throat. A cocktail of sorrow and bleak acceptance. Despite everything he'd done, the loss of the man I'd thought he was, stung.

We skidded to a stop and spun in slow circles. Each one of us scoured the area for a likely location.

"It would need a tall building with an unobstructed view of the town square," I pointed out.

"And a relatively large, flat roof," Maximus added when he caught up.

By my count, there were three.

Exekiel pointed to the rooftop of The Occult; a creative arts center for the musically gifted. "It's there."

Colette's brow lifted. "How can you know?"

"We forgot about one person." The three interconnected squares symbol of *Fadea* glowed silver on his forearm. "Camal Silverhound."

The intended winner of the Games and the shifter who was firmly in the Royal Court's pocket had been missing in the square tonight. This meant he was probably overseeing the weapon. Did he know that his allies were dead? That he'd already lost the war?

"You brilliant male," Vivienne gushed and planted a kiss on Exekiel's cheek.

I levelled her with a glare. Just because I trusted her didn't mean I appreciated her pawing at my man.

We took off. Exekiel was in the lead with me right beside him.

We didn't bother with the front door. Maximus and the others were lifted onto the roof by giants. Exekiel, Vivienne and I soared into the air. Exekiel held my hand to help guide me. We landed on the ledge in front of a startled Camal and at least fifteen sirens. They sat in rows of seats that were attached to a cylindrical, glass case and what looked like a giant brass gramophone.

Inside the case was Aya. Her eyes glowed and her hair billowed as she sang. Through the tubes that linked the sirens to the device, colored tendrils of their magic flowed from them and into her. Each one amplified the force of her song.

I wasn't surprised it was Aya. No one had wanted revenge more than she had after I'd killed her brother to save Exekiel.

Her cold eyes widened a fraction when they settled on me, but she didn't stop singing. If anything, she threw more force into it. With each note, a tangible mist sprayed from inside the gramophone.

I glanced at the others. They seemed fine. Either because, like me, they'd never been infected or because they'd taken the true antidote.

Aya's song faltered slightly when the thud of dragon's feet approached. A heavy presence settled behind me. Revynath's gleaming yellow eyes peered over the roof. Steam huffed from her snout.

The sirens pressed back in their seats.

"Keep singing," Camal shouted from where he sat on a single elevated chair in the back row. Like them, a tube led from the back of his hand to the device. He wore headphones which I guessed were an added precaution against the effects of the song.

I met his cruel stare and shouted, "It's over."

Aquarius, Lucinda and the others leapt down from the ledge and surrounded the sirens. Power pulsed from their raised hands. Blood dripped down

Lucinda's chin. She'd bitten her lip. Now a spell was on the tip of her tongue.

Camal sneered. He yanked the tube from his hand and stalked towards us. He didn't seem at all put off that he was being stared down by dragons and giants. He carried that same haughty arrogance as Loch; the kind that would get him killed.

The shifter flashed his canine teeth. "I don't answer to you."

He gestured for Aya to keep singing when she paused to look at us.

"No, but maybe you will listen to Loch."

On cue, Urdith dumped Loch's severed head on the rooftop. Camal jumped away from the splatter of blood then immediately threw up. The sirens screamed. Aya burst into tears of grief and rage. Her palms slammed against the case. Other sirens leapt up and pulled out the tubes like they couldn't get away from the weapon fast enough. I blinked when they fell to their knees at my feet.

"Thank you," they whispered. "We knew you'd come."

I looked from them to Camal who lifted a whip I hadn't realized he held. He was going to strike them. A gust of searing fire incinerated the shifter mid-swing.

My heart lurched. I gaped up at Urdith. Smoke curled from his nostrils. I didn't know what I expected him to do. Maybe growl or find a way to express some kind of apology but my dragon simply yawned. He *yawned* after he'd turned Camal Silverhound into nothing more than a scorch mark and a pile of ash.

More sirens unhooked themselves and staggered from the seat. Relief was evident in most of their expressions. I was right. Not everyone had known how Loch had intended to keep the peace in the Isles. They hadn't known the plague was a lie and that our acceptance in the Inlands was contingent on us being used as a weapon. If I doubted them at all, the lacerations across their backs were evidence enough.

Others glared at me and spat at my feet. They'd known the truth and had remained loyal to Loch and his vision. Some eyed his severed head with blatant grief. Their clothes weren't wet with blood. Tears didn't stain their cheeks.

"It worked," Colette gasped.

I followed her line of sight to the building where the infected were being kept. The giants had pulled away the chains and opened the doors. The people filed out. They moved slow and uncertain and gazed around them as if coming out of a trance.

I turned back to the sirens. "It's over." I gestured to the weapon. "This is over. The choice is now yours. Are you with me or not?"

54

VARIALLA:
AND THE WINNER IS

Somehow, the throne room had survived. Despite my fire that had destroyed half the east wing, this room with its rose gold floors and dark wood pillars remained. There was some smoke damage in the corners of the concave ceiling but nothing a few coats of magic couldn't fix.

Floor-to-ceiling windows framed in gold spanned across two walls. They let in the morning light and gave a clear view to the stunning palace grounds beyond. However, the true beauty was the Eternal Throne. The reason all these battles had begun.

It sat on a dais that had four large steps leading up to it. On either side of each step was a marble statue that depicted a cast of the Isles. A goblin for Goblin's Gorge knelt on the bottom step, opposite a satyr who represented those in Creature's Copse. On the next step a werewolf knelt opposite a siren whose tail was curled around her and her head bowed. The next was for the Fae. His wings were splayed; one knee bent and a sword pressed into the ground. Opposite the Fae was an elf. His smile was soft as he knelt and gazed up at the throne. On the final step was a statue of a giant. The large being sat cross-legged. Her head was bowed like the others. Opposite her was a witch with blood trickling from her lip.

As stunning as they each were, my gaze was drawn to the final statue behind the throne that represented Shifter Springs. A black dragon roaring fire hunched over the stone throne. Its wings were splayed and its eyes that gleamed like cut sapphires were narrowed. A keeper of the Kingdom.

The Eternal Throne itself was just as captivating. It was carved from black stone, warm gold and knotted tree branches, that made it look both elegant and fierce. The gold forked upwards from the stone back of the throne. It looked like a crown of daggers. Encircling it was a stunning design of twisted branches that curved to a point in the middle. Black leather studded with bronze padded the seat. The black stone arms were etched with the symbols of the nine Isles and dotted with flecks of gold that shimmered when they caught the light.

My attention was temporarily turned from the throne when the people gathered behind me gasped. I rolled my eyes. I didn't have to look to know my dragons were up to something.

Revynath's large footsteps shook the glass whenever she came too close to the building. I'd tried to order her to stay back, today of all days, but she never listened to me. Neither of them did. Now, both Revynath and Urdith occasionally peered through the windows and swatted at the glass which pulled startled yelps from the people inside.

Those who couldn't fit into the throne room spilled out into the corridor. An even larger crowd made themselves comfortable in the gardens and outside the gates. They'd set up picnic blankets and benches. Some beings danced or did little skits to entertain the people whilst they waited for the season finale ceremony to begin. It would be broadcasted to the entire realm on large holo-screens but some liked to be a part of the action. For most of the Outliers, this was the first time in centuries they'd been allowed to attend.

With the eyes of the Nine Isles on us, I stood to the right of the dais with my remaining competitors, Vivienne and Kraxus. We each wore the purple robes of the Royal Court; their hems edged in gold filigree. Our hoods were down. To mark the occasion, magic had been used to style our hair into a replica of our cast's emblem.

Vivienne had the crossing swords with wings in place of their blades for the Fae. I had the dragon within a clamshell for both the Coral Court and Dragon Spire. Kraxus's luscious locks had been styled into the horned tribal eye for the shifters. Attached to the eye were three interconnected squares. This was the symbol of his mother, the Huntress Fate *Fadea*, and marked him as Bravinore.

Above our head in smoky grey letters were our current ranks. Vivienne sat at number one. I imagined it had something to do with her incredible skills during the battle. As much as she infuriated me, she had been magnificent. When it mattered, Vivienne had set aside her prejudice and done the right thing. She'd fought for her kingdom like a true queen and even fought alongside some sirens. Kraxus was in third. Bennet hadn't racked up enough points to even qualify and was no longer in the running. I sat at number two.

Though I hated to think what the realm would be like under Vivienne's rule, it didn't bother me as much as I'd expected. After everything we'd been through and everything we'd lost, I was just grateful to be here, alive, with my loved ones in the audience. I'd done what I came to do. I'd freed the Outer Isles and rid the realm of the true poison that had plagued it; the monsters who'd been in power.

This wasn't the final tally. The people's votes counted for forty percent of each player's rank which meant things could still change. There was still a chance I could bring the realm into a new era. However, if I lost, I would gladly bow to Vivienne, so long as she kept her hands off my mate.

Vladimir and Evangeline, the two remaining members of the former Council, climbed the steps of the dais and stood before the throne. Orbs swiveled into place. It was time to announce the winner of the Games.

Adrenaline pulsed inside me. Hope sparked in my chest. After everything, I couldn't pretend I didn't want the Throne. The love I'd fostered defending this place and the need I felt to have the oppressed finally freed, and both halves of me united, was bone deep. But I steadied my breath and focused on the most important people to me, who stood in the front row.

A devastatingly handsome Fae in a black tailcoat embroidered with silver smirked at me. His pink eyes shimmered. His dark hair fell across his brow. My heart flipped. My cheeks heated. I didn't think my reaction to seeing him would ever change. Beside Exekiel, were Colette, Lucinda, Maximus, and the others. All of them were here, for me. All of them were alive. When I looked at them, I remembered that, in my own way, I'd already won.

"It has been a humbling time," Evangeline's voice echoed throughout the hall.

Camera-orbs panned over her and her sleek purple gown. Two weeks had passed since we took down Loch and the Royal Court. Since then, so much had happened and at the same time not much at all. The numbers of the dead were still rising and the wounded continued to convalesce despite tonics and healer elves. Exekiel had done what he could with the power of *Thesona* but not even he had been able to handle the sheer volume of injured beings.

The decimated buildings in the town square needed to be rebuilt, but the blood had been washed from the streets and the bodies collected for burial. Enemy or friend, we'd decided that each would receive a proper send off to Fatevale.

Then there were the enemies who still lived. Those who had supported the Court and fled. Our primary target was Gwendoline. Trusted members of the Royal Guard were on the lookout for her and the others but hadn't found any leads yet. The best development however, was that Ilbryen's antidote had been rolled out to the masses and the goblins had managed to dismantle the weapon. Now we needed to decide what to do with its parts.

"Before we tally the final votes, we will let each player make a final plea and allow those who wish to change their vote, time t—"

"This isn't necessary." Vivienne stepped forward.

Every head turned in her direction. Camera-orbs approached. She immediately smiled and adjusted her stance so they caught her good side. A true politician.

"We all know that there are only two people who are fit to run this realm." Apparently done with the camera-orbs, Vivienne spoke directly to the audience. "Two beings who have stood strong and stood for their people in the face of adversity most of us couldn't imagine. One of them stands on this dais."

Her eyes flicked to me. My jaw dropped.

"The other is out there in the audience." Her gaze lingered longer than I liked on Exekiel. Not that I could blame her. He had his own vortex. One look and he reeled you in.

Vivienne finally tore her stare away. "Those two people are Varialla von Hastings and Exekiel V'alin."

The audience erupted in raucous cheers. Some stamped their feet and chanted our names.

I almost fell off the dais when Vivienne bowed on one knee. "I vote for you, Varialla. Queen of Shifter Springs and the Coral Court. Born of both realms and the uniter of the Nine Isles."

Kraxus pulled his sword from its sheath and crossed it over his heart. "I stand with you, my Queen." He fell to his knee followed by countless others in the throne room who echoed the chant.

Countess Lynn; one of my earliest supporters, rushed forward. "I stand by you my Queen and your King." She turned to look at Exekiel and bowed along with everyone else.

I rocked back. The vote was unanimous. Evangeline dropped to both knees and bowed her head. She went lower than anyone else. Yet the true shock to my system was when Vladimir crossed his fist over his heart and bowed at the waist.

Goather who had been waiting at the foot of the dais, now climbed the steps. He couldn't hide the shimmer of joyful tears in eyes.

"Then it is settled," he shouted into his microphone. "The winner of the Games is our foreign temptress from beyond the veil; Varialla von Hastings."

"Zairenyth," I called over the howls of the people.

I stepped forward. The satyr handed me the microphone.

"Von Hastings was a name I created when I'd felt alone and unloved. When I'd needed to draw strength from something. But I'm not alone anymore." My people whooped and applauded. "Now I know that my strength comes from within me not from what people call me. I know love through all of you." My voice cracked. I sucked in a breath to steady my raging heart. "From now on, to honor the memory of my people—the dragon shifters of Shifter Springs, and my father who fought valiantly to defend them, I will go by his name. Varialla Zairenyth."

The applause was deafening; like a clash of thunder. A band of goblins began to play. My people sent up sparks of magic like confetti. My people. My kingdom. My home.

55

EXEKIEL:
FLEETING FAREWELLS

I'd never been good at goodbyes. No matter how many times I endured them, they didn't get any easier. Knowing that a light had gone out and could never be reignited. Knowing that new memories would never be shared. It was a bitter taste that never quite left my tongue.

With my toes buried in the sand, I shoved my hands in my pockets and looked out at sea. The number of ships that sailed carrying bodies of the dead was haunting, but they didn't compare to the number of civilians gathered on the beach to honor them and send their souls to Fatevale.

For the first time in centuries, giants stood with Fae, sirens with witches. The Nine Isles were united and we mourned as one.

There was an ache in my chest when the ship I knew carried Satrialla sailed to the head of the fleet. Her body, like the others, had been wrapped in leaves and twine. Yet the floating lanterns that would normally be attached to her arms and legs by golden thread were instead fastened to the ship itself. There were hundreds of them. Each lantern was lit. Their glow was enhanced by the dimness of the setting sun.

Since Varialla and I hadn't appointed our new Council yet, we stood at the front of the crowd, beside Vladimir and Evangeline. As was custom, we, and everyone in the crowd, each wore some form of chainmail. It was a symbol of us being the guardians to protect the souls as they passed.

Varialla squeezed my hand before she stepped forward to give the final farewell. Her light chainmail cape clinked against her scalemail dress.

"We are here today, to honor those who lost their lives in the recent war on our kingdom. Family, friends and lovers, who were taken too soon." Her voice seemed to rise and fall with the crash of the waves. "It is natural for us to mourn all the things they never got to do and I'm sure that we will. But tonight, let's celebrate all that they did; the lives that they touched, the differences they made and the time that we had with them."

I straightened and remembered Satrialla before the Brutal War. Before her mind had been taken along with my brother and her son. I remembered her laughing, playing games and forcing us to change

Drax Junior's soiled hide. I also remembered her closer to her final moments. How she'd wanted to fight. How, like a warrior, she'd charged into battle.

"Our enemies meant to tear us apart but their actions have brought us together."

Murmurs of agreement rippled through the crowd.

"They did not win. As long as we remember that, honor that, then our loved ones did not die in vain." Varialla tipped her chin higher. Hands clasped before her. "Now we send these souls to rest!" she bellowed. "May they go with the brave and the blessed."

A line of witches and warlocks moved to the shoreline. They enchanted the lanterns to rise, carrying the ships with them. They were helped by winter elves who pushed wind beneath the hull and sails, and a group of sirens who, together, managed to manipulate an ocean's wave. It bucked and helped nudge the ships into the air.

"Let them drift towards the Fates and burn among the stars."

With the final lament Varialla's dragons swept forward. Their mouths yawned wide and they breathed out fire. Blue and scarlet flames encased the ships. Sirens sang a song of passing. The living lifted their hands in farewell.

Varialla returned to my side and interlaced her fingers with mine. This time, I squeezed.

"She was brave until the end," she whispered.

I couldn't find words to speak. My eyes were locked on the ships of the dead; on the last family member I had.

Varialla brushed her arm against mine. "We're your family now."

It was like she'd read my mind. I looked down at her but my head turned the other way when a hand rested on my shoulder.

Aquarius stood beside me. "We all are."

Ilbryen stood beside him. Ryul after that. Followed by Parker. The goblin scowled but nodded his head in my direction. My throat bobbed and I nodded back.

*

Rebuilding a realm was no easy feat. Cloistered in the strategy room of the palace, Varialla and I poured over parchments that were sprawled across the oval stone table. Mostly maps, Game laws and requests of the people. We'd been in here for hours. Neither of us showed signs of slowing down. However, our newly appointed Council had slowly made their exits.

Lucinda, Colette and Aquarius had left for today's big event. Parker and the giant girl, Maliha, had left to check on the progress in the town square. Vivienne had been the last to leave. She'd claimed she was being choked by the sexual tension between Varialla and I.

At the time we'd both laughed but Vivienne hadn't been wrong. With everything that was going on, it'd been a few days since I'd tasted my mate's cunt. Since I'd sucked on her flesh or felt her walls clench around me. Now every time she brushed past, my cock saluted.

Oblivious to the havoc she was wreaking, Varialla bent over the rules of the Games and gave me a view of her full breasts trussed up inside her leather corset. A low growl rumbled in my chest.

She arched a brow. "Are you listening?"

I adjusted my trousers and cricked my neck. "Of course."

My stare slid to the map of the new realm in the middle of the table. Would it be wrong to fuck her on it? The ink wasn't dry yet. The cartographer would be pissed, but seeing as that was Calder, I didn't care too much. That wolf shifter had a lot of bark but no real bite.

Varialla's smirk was knowing but she returned to the laws.

"It says here that the Royal Court and Council decide the Trials."

"Do you want to change them?"

"To be honest, no. Those Trials helped shape me into who I am. They showed me sides of myself that I wouldn't have known otherwise."

I felt some relief at those words. I felt the same about the Trials.

Varialla gave a decisive shake of her head. "No. I don't want to change the Trials but maybe we can amend the penalty."

She flipped to the next parchment. "We can't change the fact that anyone who loses is stripped of their title and forced into service to the Crown, however, we can modify what that service is. It also doesn't say they can't receive a wage."

My interest piqued. Under the current ruling of the Games, anyone who lost was forced to become a servant in the palace. This was limited to menial tasks; cleaner, cook, gardener or errand boy, without compensation. Considering all competitors in the Games were some of the best and most powerfully trained beings in the realm, it had always seemed ridiculous that their skills weren't put to better use. In light of this information, it seemed that had been intentional. A way to keep the powerful suppressed.

"They can be anything?"

Varialla nodded. "Anything that serves the Crown."

"They could become members of the Royal Guard or spies for the Court."

"Those who are cooks can work their way up to head chef, planning menus and fostering a love for food." Varialla's eyes lit up.

"They could help battle the sea monsters in the Outer Isles." The beasts that continued to encroach on our territory.

"They can become landscape artists or work in the infirmary."

The list was endless.

Varialla tapped a gold-plated pen against her bottom lip. The rare instrument was a sign of wealth and used over quills in the palace. I watched as she sucked the end into her mouth. Whatever she said next was lost to me as my mind turned that pen into something else I could slide between her lips.

I swallowed a groan and imagined sucking that lip between mine. Of tasting the strawberry of her lip balm and the sea-salted caramel of her skin. *Fuck.* I didn't know how much longer I could pretend I wasn't fantasizing about her riding my cock.

We'd had a productive morning. We'd run through our plans on how best to start rebuilding the Eternal City. We'd documented our allies and appointed Aquarius and Vivienne as our liaisons between the Isles. We'd organized patrols and put systems in place to protect our people whilst we weeded out the remaining threats.

There was a lot left to do but we couldn't do it all in a day. However, I could think of several things that we could do with our time.

"This says names can be pulled from the Conduit until we reach one hundred contestants." Varialla's hazel eyes met mine. They were fucking beautiful. "That means players don't have to be forced into the Games. They can refuse and we can draw another name."

Her smile lit up the room. Although nothing compared to the way she smiled when I made her come. When I imprisoned her on my cock or tongue and had her dripping all over my face.

Varialla leaned over to retrieve notes on the ranking system. I tapped into my Fae speed and was behind her so fast, I almost stumbled. I grasped her hips and pulled her against me. Her ass pressed into my cock. I moaned deep in the base of my throat.

"Fuck."

Varialla's body tensed. "That wasn't an invitation Fae-boy."

I palmed her breasts and held her against me. "Everything about you is so damn inviting."

I pressed into her; made her feel the effect she had on me. Varialla gasped and her head fell forwards. My own tipped back as she rolled her hips.

"Fuck." I gripped the hem of her red pleated skirt and lifted it over her ass. A pink lacy thong sat snug between her cheeks. I groaned. I was so fucking hard. "Get these off."

My little bud obeyed. She wasted no time in shimmying out of her underwear. I let them get half way down her thighs before I drove two fingers inside her. Varialla moaned and her back arched.

I fisted her hair and yanked her back even further. I forced her to stare up at me as I played with her clit and soaked my fingers in her tight wet cunt. Fates, she was perfect.

Her lips parted as she struggled to breathe and emitted soft, little strangled sounds. Her brow was creased and she gripped the edge of the table hard enough to leech the color from her knuckles. She was so fucking hot.

"Look how wet you get for me. Look how your pretty little cunt soaks my hand."

My thumb rubbed in tight circles over her sweet bundle of nerves whilst I pumped my fingers, deeper and faster.

"You like that, don't you? Like the feel of me stretching you; preparing your pussy for the pounding I'm about to give it?"

Varialla bobbed her head. "Y-yes."

"Yeah?"

I pulled my fingers out and smacked her clit. She jumped. A sound of pain and pleasure tangled in her throat. I plunged back in. Her body sighed.

"Show me how much you like it."

I relished the squelch between her thighs. The way my fingers were drenched from her juices. Her scent struck the back of my throat and my eyes rolled. My mouth fucking watered.

"I'm going to fuck you on this table."

Varialla's hips bucked in response. She fell forwards; her hands braced on the stone. It was almost like she needed to put some distance between us; needed to catch her breath, as I brought her to the brink. I grasped her hip, holding her still, and hunched over her. I forced her to feel the pulse of my cock and continued to unravel her on the thrust of my fingers.

"I'm going to suck on your clit and lick your sweet little cunt until I'm drowning in the taste of you."

I twisted my fingers. Varialla moaned so deep, I felt it vibrate through my cock. Braced on her elbows now, my little bud pushed back into me and fucked my hand.

"That's it, beautiful. Show me what you're going to do to me. Show me how you're going to ride my cock like a good fucking girl." I brought my lips to her ear and pulled the lobe between my teeth.

"Fuck," she panted. Her body tremored. She was close. I was about to take her over the fucking edge. "Exekiel! O—ahh—"

My little beauty exploded. Her body jerked and twitched. Her inner walls spasmed around my fingers and hot liquid drizzled over my hand.

"Fucking beautiful." I dropped to my knees, spread her ass and licked her all the way down to her dripping cunt.

She gasped and juddered on my tongue. I slurped up every drop she had to give. My index finger continued to assault her clit. It coaxed out more of her desire that made my head spin. The taste of her was my personal brand of opiates. I growled into her hot cunt and plunged my tongue inside her.

"Shit." Varialla's hand slammed down on the table.

Her legs shook. I gripped the backs of her thighs and held her steady. I made her feel every lash of my tongue.

She was so perfect. So sexy.

"How did I get so blessed?" I growled against her before I plunged back in; deeper than before.

"Holy shit! Exekiel…I'm…I'm…"

Varialla scrabbled at the table. Her nails had turned to claws and I heard the unmistakable scrape of them as they carved grooves into the stone.

"I'm coming!" It was a cross between a scream and a whimper.

I burrowed deeper, lapping on her hot cunt more greedily as the taste of her spilled over my tongue and slid down my throat. I could have died down here and not known the difference between life and the promised nirvana of Fatevale.

There was a knock on the door. Varialla's extended cry of pleasure was their response. If there was any doubt of what we were doing in here, they knew now.

Another knock sounded. I pushed to my feet and spun Varialla around to face me. I pulled my ankle-cuff breeches down just low enough to unsheathe my cock. Her eyes flashed with the same hunger that throbbed in my veins. She leapt up on the table and spread her legs.

"Good girl." I palmed my cock and angled it at her entrance.

"Put your dick away, little shadow," Kraxus bellowed through the door.

"Fuck off." I nudged Varialla with the head of my cock.

Her eyelids fluttered. I groaned between clenched teeth and rocked my hips. Her arm curled around my shoulders, pulling me closer.

"You can't miss your first official duty as King and Queen." Kraxus jiggled the doorknob but my shadows held it closed.

King and Queen, not Primaries. We'd reverted to the old titles. Those before the land-shift. Before the divide. Those from a time when a Bravinore Fae like me, could bed a half shifter, half siren.

"Don't make me get Lucinda."

Varialla tensed like she meant to pull away but I stretched her over the head of my cock and watched her eyes roll. If she thought I could stop now she was out of her fucking mind. I pushed deeper; filled her with another inch. Her body went rigid and her walls rippled around me. Her mouth fell open. Her fingers bit into my shoulder. Her claws pierced my skin. I savored the fucking pain.

"Get out here!" Kraxus yanked on the door.

"We have to go," Varialla whispered even as she widened her legs and moved into me.

"Then I'll fuck you fast."

I grasped her ass and yanked her onto my stiff cock. She cried out. Her head thrown back. I pumped into her so rigorously my back burned. Her tits jumped. It was a vicious slap of flesh on flesh as I plowed into her; taking what I needed; giving what she craved.

I gripped the back of Varialla's neck and brought her lips to mine. I fucked her fast and hard and my tongue fucked her mouth.

The door swung open and slammed into the wall.

Fuck. I'd been so lost in my mate I'd released my shadows hold on the door.

Varialla scrambled to pull down her skirt, but I pumped my hips harder and faster. She wasn't getting away until I was finished with her.

"E-Ex-Exekiel," she stammered my name.

The way she tapped on my shoulder indicated she was trying to tell me to stop but her ankles were still crossed behind my back, her hips still slammed into mine and I was still balls-deep inside her.

Pleasure gathered at the base of my spine. I felt wild. Drunk on the feel of her; the tight clench of her cunt. The pillowed softness of her breasts. My cock throbbed. My heart hammered in my chest. I gripped her ass tighter and roared. Varialla cried out. Hot spurts of come pulsed from the deliciously painful head of my cock and spilled into her. Varialla quivered. My body trembled. My head bowed forward. Her own rested on my chest.

We stayed that way for several breathless heartbeats until Kraxus clapped his hands.

"Quite a show."

I blew sweat-slicked hair from my brow and finally turned my head to glare at the bastard over my shoulder. He wore his new Captain of the Guard's uniform. There was no symbol of the Nine Isles embossed on the breastplate but Kylin was working on a design. The elf had a knack for designing armor. In light of the new information, perhaps her service to the crown could be as a blacksmith, forging weapons and shields.

Kraxus stepped further into the room. My shadows rose. He merely eyed the mess of papers we'd sent flying and knocked to the floor.

"Tsk, tsk, little shadow." He shook his meaty finger at me. "Calder is going to be pissed when he finds out you messed up his map."

56

VARIALLA:
THE UNION CEREMONY

We were late. Judging by Lucinda's narrowed eyes and pursed lips, she knew exactly why. I rushed to close the dressing room door behind me. Thankfully, it hadn't taken me long to change and I'd specifically asked Kraxus to get us early. But I was still late.

"I'm sorry," I gasped. When she said nothing, I awkwardly tucked a curl behind my ear. "Better late than never, right?"

Lucinda's brow arched. "Is it?"

I hung my head and shifted from one foot to the other. She was right. There was no excuse for being late today of all days.

"What's ten minutes late when you're preparing for eternity?" Cyrus cried but instantly shut her mouth when Lucinda turned her death glare on her.

I may have only been ten minutes late. However, we all knew that it would have been longer if Kraxus hadn't come to get us. I didn't know what it was about Exekiel. After all this time I still struggled to pry myself away from him when he got his hands on me.

My toes curled at the memory of the way he'd bent me over that table; of how he'd knelt beneath me and sucked on my—

"Don't scowl," Maximus's shout cut off my thoughts. He set down his bottle of sparkling wine and rushed to retouch Lucinda's makeup. "What matters is that we're all here now and you are about to be unified with the woman of your dreams."

His words softened Lucinda's features. My heart warmed. Her smile was so bright I couldn't help but match it.

"I really am sorry. I can't believe I lost track of the time like that." I wrung my hands together. "There's nowhere else I want to be, Lucinda. Nowhere."

She met my gaze in the mirror then grumbled, "Get over here."

I ran to where she sat in the makeup chair and threw my arms around her shoulders.

"Careful," Maximus cried.

I looked at our reflections in the mirror. Tears filled my eyes. The burnt side of her face was still visible beneath the makeup, but the dry cracked skin looked more like faint lines now and the golden eyeshadow and rosy cheeks helped detract from what I'd done to her.

I doubted I would ever look at Lucinda without regretting my decision, even though she'd told me that in that moment, she'd wanted to die and not at his hand. She'd said that when she'd felt the flames, she'd been relieved. I clung to that and hoped it was true.

"You look beautiful." I hiccupped over the words.

Lucinda rolled her eyes. Sometimes I swore Revynath was her in dragon form.

"Don't start blubbering." But she smiled and patted my arm before she rested her head on my cheek.

"I am sorry I'm late."

"It's fine. On the day you and Exekiel have your Union Ceremony, you'll find me fucking Evangeline whilst wearing your dress."

Laughter burst out of me. Maximus whooped and Cyrus clapped her hands, far too delighted by the idea.

"Come on." Lucinda got to her feet.

My eyes drank in her dress. It was a deep shade of red and black with tight lace sleeves that came to her elbows. It had a square neckline that enhanced her bust and was decorated with red and black beads that continued in a pattern down her bodice. At her hips, the dress plumed out in rivulets of black and red lace and tulle. The entire look was finished off with a black and red ruby choker around her neck.

I shook my head. "Stunning."

My arm looped around hers. Maximus took the other side and Cyrus scooped up the dress's long train.

"Let the Union commence."

*

Uncontrollable tears slipped down my cheeks as Lucinda and Evangeline stood before the congregation and recited their union vows.

The Union Ceremony was similar to a wedding with a few differences. The partners walked down the aisle together. People didn't sit in pews but on the red-carpeted floor in a circle around the couple. White petals littered the floor at their feet and the pair stood beneath an archway of loping ice. However, the inside remained liquid and swirled with blue streaks.

Supposedly the structure symbolized the strength and fluidity of their love. How it would move and evolve over time but remain solid and unbroken. If the archway was broken during the ceremony, it was taken as a sign that their union was not blessed by the Fates and therefore would not last. I put as much distance as I could between the arch and myself as I stood behind my friend and dabbed at my eyes.

Evangeline looked equally as stunning as Lucinda. Her dress was almost an exact replica only it was blue with amber lace and tulle. It had no sleeves and was more ruffled at the hem. But they each had the same beaded design on the bodice and wore almost identical chokers. Where Lucinda had a ruby pendant as a bloodwitch, Evangeline had citrine as an Autmn elf.

They stood opposite each other with their hands up and pressed palm to palm as High Priestess Azalea Frost carried out the ceremony. I'd never seen Lucinda look so happy. Never seen her blink back tears of joy.

"For every grain of sand on a beach, I will love you. For every speck of salt in the ocean, I will treasure you." Lucinda recited as the High Priestess read the vows.

Evangeline repeated the sentiment, then the two of them turned and traded places. Now they stood with their fingers intertwined.

My gaze swept over the congregation. I couldn't help but smile when I spotted Colette beside Odus. He looked healthier than when I'd last seen him. His hide was soft and had regained some of its old shine. Colette's hand lightly rested on his. It had been about six months since Jia had sacrificed herself during Phase Two of the Games. It was clear the centaur wasn't over her or ready to start something new, but he spent a lot of his time with Colette. They laughed easily and got along well. She'd had a crush on him since they'd met. I hoped one day, when the scars healed, their friendship might become something more.

"For every star in the sky, I will adore you."

Over Evangline's shoulder, Exekiel's intense, pink gaze collided with mine. My pulse quickened. Was he, like me, imagining the day we were up here, beneath the archway of ice? The day our friends and chosen family gathered around to bless our union and witness the start of our forever?

I swallowed. My throat thick.

Both females stepped back. A group of goblins and satyrs near the dais began to play a soft melody. They used instruments that mildly resembled and mimicked the sounds of harps and violins.

Being an autumn elf, Evangeline twirled her fingers and wove a crown of leaves, white flowers and thorns around both of their heads. Lucinda inhaled sharply. Then she raised her hand and pricked her finger on one of the thorns.

She whispered an incantation I couldn't hear. Evangeline stiffened as the crown rotated and the thorns pierced her skin. Blood now trickled down both of their brows.

Azalea lifted her hands and the congregation did the same. I followed their lead.

"United as one. It is done," the High Priestess called over the music.

Evangeline beamed and Lucinda laughed as the Pre-Primary of the Isles, pulled her close and pressed her lips to hers.

57

VARIALLA:
THE TIMES FOREVER CHANGE

The simple beauty of the ceremony was in direct contrast to the extravagant bedlam of the after party. Every song the band played had the people on their feet. I learnt a few dances I hadn't seen before. They were traditional stomping and jumping routines that were generally performed at Unions.

Sparkling wine and other liquors flowed freely from fountains. Floating tables zipped through the crowd with platters of pastries, stuffed dumplings and other finger foods. The fancy updo hairstyles promptly came down. Tunic sleeves were rolled up and lace-up ties were undone. Shoes kicked off.

The joyful applause that had followed Evangeline and Lucinda's kiss beneath the arch were now wild wolf whistles as people cajoled the couple into a full-on make out session on top of the cake. I didn't care what anyone said, I was going to have a slice when they were done.

The ballroom had been transformed into an enchanted forest. Vines grew up the walls. A large tree stood proud and center; its leaves a canopy overhead with twinkling lights that draped down. Wildflowers were sprinkled across the hardwood floor and created a field to dance on. It was breathtaking. The atmosphere alight.

Supposedly when an elf had their union, it was their family's job to design the reception hall with their season. Evangeline's family hadn't let her down.

Cocooned in Exekiel's arms, with my head rested on his chest, I took it all in. My stare went to where Maximus danced with his sister; Laverna. My chest constricted. It had taken us weeks to find her but here she was. Her frame was painfully thin and her steps were labored after what she'd endured all those years they were apart. But she stood tall and her eyes were bright. It was the same ferocity I often saw in Maximus' eyes cloaked behind a smile.

Turning my head, the other way, I saw Evangeline's mother at the edge of the dancefloor. She seemed thrilled that her daughter had moved on from Adir. It couldn't have been easy for any of them when they'd realized Evangeline was mated to a monster. Although, apparently Adir hadn't always been like that.

According to Lucinda, Evangeline had cried when she'd learnt of his death. Adir had been her mate after all. However, she'd assured Lucinda that there was no one else she'd rather be with. That even if it hurt, she was glad Adir was gone. That he could never put her down or make her feel small again. She was glad she had a friend and partner in Lucinda. Not the dictator and tool of sexual satisfaction she'd had in the Primary.

In some ways I felt the same way about Loch and my mother. I couldn't say I mourned their deaths or forgave the things they'd done, but I mourned who I thought they were. Who they might have been if things had been different.

The happy couple glided across the dance floor. Lucinda said something and Evangeline laughed with her whole heart. I smiled. There was a lot of healing to be done for everyone but this moment confirmed we were going to be fine.

"I'm afraid I have to get going."

I tensed at the sound of Vladimir's voice. He always snuck up behind me like he couldn't help being a creep.

I plastered a smile across my lips as Exekiel and I turned to face the elf. His silver white hair was unbound and he wore a white silk tunic with blue embroidery, and matching trousers.

"I have an early start in the morning." He puffed out his chest. "Elf Bay isn't going to rebuild itself, after all."

To humor him, I said, "It certainly won't Lord Vladimir."

He unleashed a true smile at this. I couldn't help returning it. Exekiel and I had appointed Vladimir Lord of Elf Bay. It was the highest-ranking title of the Isle. Now, his duty was to help repair the damage that had been done.

After looking into things, we'd realized Count Victus had run the Isle into the ground. He'd almost drained their resources supporting the manufacturing of the weapon, poison and whatever else the Court had asked him to do. I couldn't say that I would ever truly like Vladimir but he seemed to know what he was doing. He cared about his people and at some point, we'd entered an unspoken truce.

He shook Exekiel's hand and kissed the back of mine. His lips lingered on my skin a little too long.

As he walked past, he whispered, "Did I ever tell you, you look spectacular when you come?"

I wheeled around, ready to punch him in the face, but he was gone.

Exekiel rested his hands on my hips and turned me around to face him. "When can we leave?"

His gaze stopped the world on its axis. His intense stare seared with a promise that struck between my thighs and spread heat through my entire body.

"We were interrupted earlier." He dragged his thumb down my neck causing me to shiver. "I wasn't finished with you."

His thumb moved to my lower lip. I couldn't help flicking out my tongue and tasting the salty tip.

Exekiel stiffened. "When?"

"Soon."

He pressed closer and pushed his thumb into my mouth. My breath hitched. We were the new rulers of the realm. This behavior was completely inappropriate. Still, I gripped his tunic and pulled him closer. I let him grab my ass and hike up my leg as he replaced his thumb with his tongue.

My heart ratcheted in my chest. His scent of warm apples and woodsmoke washed over me. I inhaled and trailed hungry fingers down the hard plains of his abdomen. I recalled exactly how these muscles tensed when he came. Heat shot straight to my core and I barely stifled a moan.

Exekiel brushed his lips across mine and almost stole what little breath I had left.

"And to think we once had a bet going on whether or not you two would kill each other." A familiar giggle sounded behind me.

I spun and found Eudora and Cyrus grinning at me. I pulled away from Exekiel and flung my arms around them. I sank into their familiar scents and tinkling laughter. Eudora's color had returned and there was a sparkle in her eye that had been missing the last time I'd seen her. According to Ilbryen she would need to have weekly doses of the antidote until he was sure the toxin was out of her system but he believed she would make a full recovery. Most of the infected would. Most but not all. Some we had lost and would continue to lose.

When we drew back, Eudora grasped my hand in hers. Her other rested on her Pegasus-headed cane with strength she didn't have until recently.

"I told you you'd be our queen." She stood tall. Her half-broken antlers caught the light. "I like to believe that had something to do with us."

"Without a doubt."

Eudora glanced over my shoulder to where Exekiel was now locked in conversation with Aquarius. He laughed at something the siren said; a deep rumbling sound that warmed me from the inside. There was an ease about him with Aquarius that he didn't have with anyone else but me. He was himself; unguarded and unashamed. He was with his brother.

"Based on the way that Fae was looking at you, I'd say you don't have much time before he flings you over his shoulder and carries you out of here."

I snickered.

"Before he does, I wanted to come over and say thank you."

"For?

"Despite the obvious saving the kingdom and saving my life," Eudora gave me a pointed look. "I wanted to thank you for the chance at a real life. A real career."

I squeezed her hand. Until now, nymphs had been forced to live in hovels in Creatures Copse but they had to earn the right to do so by carrying out menial tasks. A few were fortunate enough to rise to stylist but that was temporary and only lasted as long as the Games.

When Eudora had been removed from service at Residence Manor, she'd been forced to sweep the streets of Eternal City, groom the Pegasus and wash the carriages. Anything to survive.

Like all Outliers, she'd been paid with basic meals or nicer bedding. They were never given anything they could use to try and build a better life for themselves. Even those who chose to become street performers were capped at a certain level of earnings and were often taxed by the Court which left them with barely anything.

Exekiel and I had recently changed that among other things.

I shrugged. "I knew how badly you wanted to visit the library."

"Visit, yes." Eudora's eyes shone with tears and she spluttered a laugh. "But I never dared to dream I would work in it."

I blinked back my own tears and silently wondered when I'd gotten so comfortable in showing emotion in front of others. Showing that I cared.

"Always dream," I told her. "Even when it seems impossible."

"And who would have thought that I would turn down the opportunity to work at the library to become a Royal Guard instead?" Cyrus cackled and performed a series of fighting techniques.

"You're leaning too far to the left," Kraxus shouted as he sauntered over with his arm around Vivienne's waist. The smile on her face said she didn't hate the shifters touch. She even leaned into it.

If she ever got over her stubborn obsession with Exekiel which I was starting to think was pride, more than anything else, those two could be very happy together.

Cyrus rolled her eyes. "Yes, Captain."

We all laughed then broke into conversations regarding the new lay of the land, and how things would be run from now on.

I didn't know how much time passed before Exekiel was behind me. He slid his arm around my waist and drew me back against him. The unmistakable ridge of his hardening cock pressed against my ass and the base of my spine. My eyes closed. My body piqued.

Exekiel swayed us to the music. His warm breath shuddered on my neck.

"Say goodnight, Varialla." The low rumble of his voice sent shivers through me.

"Goodnight Varialla."

His fingers flexed where they splayed across my stomach. He bowed his head and his stubble grazed my cheek. I almost squirmed into him.

"Good girl."

Before I could say a proper goodnight to anyone, Exekiel gripped my arm and dragged me towards the double doors.

"What did I tell you?" Eudora cackled.

I glanced back at her. "At least he hasn't flung me over his shoulder."

A laugh bubbled out of me. As my mate pulled me from the hall and out into the sprawling gardens, I marveled at how much my life had changed. I was an ordinary girl from an ordinary town in England, yet here I stood with a crown on my head and the world at my feet.

My life had been fundamentally altered the day Exekiel whisked me away from that bar. Although it hadn't truly changed until I'd made the decision to change it and had decided to stay. I'd chosen to face the unknown and confront what terrified me most. That was when the real adventure had begun and I'd come into the power I hadn't known I'd had all along.

We'd barely taken ten steps before Exekiel pulled me to him and seared my lips with a kiss. It rocked the foundation beneath my feet and made my knees tremble. I leaned into him and savored his taste of warm apples and sweet wine. I indulged in the softness of his lips against his harsh grip on my waist.

My arms coiled around him. My fingers lightly brushed his wings. Exekiel groaned into my mouth. The sound ignited a furnace inside me.

Fuck. Would I ever stop wanting him, needing him like this?

His fingers raked down my spine and curled around my ass. He squeezed a handful as he hoisted me up and I wrapped my legs around him.

"Forever." He breathed the single word against my lips. "You are mine. Forever."

My heart slammed into my ribcage and my stomach flipped when he fastened his arms around my waist and surged into the sky. The world shrank behind us. In seconds, we were surrounded by stars.

"Where are you taking me?" I called on a laugh, over the cry of the wind.

Exekiel unleashed a slanted grin that made my breath catch. His piercing pink eyes were darkened to vermilion red. His black hair was tussled by the breeze. Shadows curled around the apex of his wings.

"I'll take you wherever you want to go so long as we go together."

My skin flushed. I kissed him, hard.

The roar of dragons behind us made me turn my head. Urdith and Revynath had launched into the sky after us. My grip tightened on Exekiel as he pulled me closer.

"Your dragons are perverts," he drawled with a smirk.

I couldn't contain my burst of laughter as we banked towards the ocean. Towards our future and the glorious unknown. I knew then that whether we were on land, in the sea or the sky, with Exekiel, I would forever feel like I was flying. Every day a rare experience. Every moment, a new adventure.

Did You Enjoy

The Season Finale?

If you enjoyed this book, please leave an honest review on Amazon, Bookbub and/or Goodreads.

Reviews and ratings are extremely valuable for indie authors like myself. It helps new readers decide if this book is something they would enjoy, and it gives me some invaluable feedback to keep writing the books you love.

I cannot wait to hear what you think and I truly thank you for taking the time to read this series.

To join my newsletter, stay up to date on my upcoming releases, & more, scan here:

9 781916 302679